Fannie
Good Girls Book Nine

Christine Young

Published by Rogue Phoenix Press, LLP
Copyright © 2025

ISBN: 978-1-62420-890-4

Editor: Amanda Armstrong
Cover Art: Designs by Ms G

Chapter One

Glasgow 1833

Fannie MacRae stared at the march of vehicles parading down the length of High Street. The steady clop of horse's hooves became a constant. From the harbor the sound of orders filtered into the other noises. If she wasn't so sick, she wouldn't be so angry with her sister. Nellie disappeared with her beau. Left her by herself…to find her way alone.

The River Clyde flowed to her left and the Cathedral of St. Mungo was to her right. Cold winds blew off the river. She coughed, wheezing as she tried to guzzle air from the busy street. Her throat was sore, raw. Tears filled her eyes as she battled the cold wind. She didn't want to be here. Should have stood firm against her sister's imploring way. Wished she was home in her nice warm bed sipping on a cup of warm mulled cider. Didn't understand how Nellie managed to talk her into this scavenger hunt. She'd been the third wheel as her sister was paired with her new beau.

As soon as she was able to sweet talk some man out of a monogrammed handkerchief, she could go home. *A damn monogramed handkerchief!* How the sweet devil was she to do that, especially when she disliked speaking to strangers? Could never figure out the necessary words. A blast of cold air swept her hat from her head.

"Oh no!" Too late to stop the event, her hand flew to the top of her head to catch air. "Stop!" What utter nonsense, as if her hat could understand what she was yelling. Fannie ran after the tumbling hat as the object of her dismay danced along the sidewalk then careened into the street. She bent to retrieve the wretched thing. At the last second, she pulled back. "No!" A passing carriage ran over it, crushing the hat flat. Her arms whirled, holding her back from falling into the path of another vehicle. With her hand pressed tight against her chest, she sucked in a gasp of city scented air. "Never liked the blasted hat anyway," Fannie muttered to no one in particular. She pressed her hands against her chest attempting to fill her lungs.

Letting out a slow breath of air, she was relieved she'd not dashed into the path of the vehicle. Thankful her spinning arms stopped her. Her hand once again hovering over her chest, she felt the pounding of her heart along with wheezing as air attempted to pass through her lungs. Without clear thought about what she was doing, Fannie walked, turning down one street then another. She didn't know where she was headed. In a daze of pain, Fannie stopped a few people to ask if they would mind handing over their monogramed handkerchief for a good cause.

Each time a crack of laughter would follow her question then the one word "No. You have got to be joking." One man even called her a little bitch after her inquiry. Exhausted from the evening, Fannie leaned against the brick wall of a building watching traffic on the street pass by. Closing her eyes for a moment, she listened to the rumbling of the wheels. Heard the chatter of people as they rushed to get home from a long day of work. Realizing she wasn't certain where she was, she fought the rise of panic. With slow deep breaths in then out, repeat then repeat again, she tried to stay calm. The people she now saw were mostly men. The women strolling the street were dressed to show off their bodies. In this weather, they were scantily clad. She thought the women must be ladies of the evening. The thought brought her mind to attention.

What did she know about ladies of the evening? Nothing. Did she wish to learn about them? No. Still, she was a bit fascinated as she watched the different ladies approach various men. They would posture. Push their breasts out. Sometimes money would exchange hands then the lady would go with the gentleman.

She was shocked to watch a man pull down the bodice of a woman's gown then fondle her. The lady pushed her bare breast forward. With his other hand the man pulled her skirt up. The woman wiggled seeming to enjoy the intimate contact. A deep flush of emotion crept up to settle on Fannie's hot cheeks. Pressing her cold hands on her skin didn't eliminate her heat flushed face.

This place is not somewhere I should be. No kidding, I should be somewhere safe. At home in my bed reading a good book.

2

Nellie would be at the house where all this started. The various couples would set out all the objects they gathered in order to figure out who won the game. Her sister would be drinking punch, chatting with her new beau.

Hah! Here I am still out in the cold. I should stop this nonsense and go home. I don't know where I am. Just keep moving. In time, you will figure everything out. Put one foot in front of the other. You are bound to see a landmark you will recognize.

She turned in an attempt to retrace her route. Dear Lord, she was tired. Her cold wore her down. Her throat ached. With dazed eyes, the buildings along her route swayed, swirled with terrifying speed. Fannie placed her hand on the wall to steady herself. Looking up then down the street, she searched for a cab. There was a row of them down the street. They were lined up in front of a large three-story home. If she could make it there, she would be on her way home to her warm bed. All she needed to do was give the address. The driver would do the rest.

Where was her sister? Fannie couldn't recall where the house was where she was supposed to meet Nellie and the other couples on this hunt. Was it where they began this ridiculous game? She didn't understand the why of the game. The purpose eluded her. There didn't seem to be any reasoning behind asking people to hand over their belongings. Told her sister several times she didn't wish to participate in the scavenger hunt. Nellie begged. She needed a third person so she could be with the young man who captured her heart this week. Nellie never stayed with any man for long. Nellie would explain to her she was looking for another Jasper or Jason. Their eldest sister married Jasper Kenworthy, the youngest was wed to Jason, his twin. They were both madly in love with their husbands. The two middle sisters were still single. They made a pact not to settle for anything less than true love.

For a few beats of her heart, Fannie closed her eyes, hoping when she opened them the world would no longer be spinning out of control. To her dismay, upon opening her eyes, the desired results were not in play. The road seemed to undulate. The hacks carrying people were hazy. She didn't know if she could put one foot in front of the other. The line of cabs seemed farther away than the first time she saw them.

Which way to go? She pushed away from the wall holding her up. Swayed on her feet for a second before she pulled herself together. Just take one step then another one. You can do this. Get to those cabs and you will be home in a jiffy.

Wetting her lips she looked up then down the street where she stood. Had no earthly clue as to which way to walk. She was lost, acknowledged the fact standing in this spot would never get her home. She could ask if anyone knew how to get back to the cathedral. Everyone in Glasgow would know where the church was located. She could try to walk the long blocks to the home where the hacks were lined up. Seemed going in that direction was her only rational option. Wished one of those vehicles would see her then come pick her up. Why would they? The drivers would believe she was a lady of the evening.

At the very least, she could hope one of the cabs would take her home. How did she get into this mess? What she wouldn't give to see someone she knew.

The horrible smell caught her attention before the words. "Lookee…! Look what I found. Just standing here all pretty like waiting for the two of us to come along. What do you think? Will she do us for a *wee* bit of fun? Do you think she's as pretty with all her clothes off? Would like to have a taste of her pretties. Those bubbies of hers…in my mouth…I'm salivating." A burly looking man spoke with his friend. They stood in front of her, blocking any hope of escape.

The voice was too close. The rancid scent of year-old sweat filled the air. She caught the odor of liquor on his breath. She couldn't seem to swallow a lungful of air. Fannie cringed against the brick wall, wishing for a way to melt into the stone. Her hands shook. She balled her fingers into fists to steady herself.

"A pretty lady…too pretty for the likes of us. *Tha i cho blasta*. She is so tasty," the man mumbled then smacked his tongue around his mouth, his voice gruff with emotion. Again, he licked his lips as if he tasted her on them.

Fannie wished she understood what they were saying. No one talked that way anymore, at least not in the city.

"Tasty morsal if I do be sayin' so meself. *Tha blasta*," the other offered, touching her cheek with the back of his hand then down her neck. Quivering with fear, she pushed against the brick wall. "You be comin with us, little misee. We'll be showin' you *feasgar math*. That would be a good evening for you. For us too. A little sportin' fun."

"Don't want a good evening with the likes of you," she muttered as one of the men in front of her blocked her path. His beefy hands were placed on either side of her head while his stomach pressed against her, holding her to the wall behind her.

"We want you for the night…all night long. Not giving you a choice. You're going to come along with us. We got a room just down the street. The bed is ready and waiting. We'll share you. You can have both of us. I'll do you first. Me partner can have you next. The two of us will take turns giving you pleasure."

Fannie shook her head. She did understand a bit of Scottish Gaelic but not much. These men were raw, hard looking, too strong for her to fight. Their clothing was ragged. Both wore beards. Must be straight off the docks. In that case, she might not be too far from the river. If she found the river, she might be able to find the cathedral. "No!" Panic glued her to the wall. *No, must get to that line of carriages. Those cabs are my only hope.*

"Ah, *tha blasta eun bheag*," the second man said as his grin widened. His hands were still on the wall on either side of her head. She felt the heat of his body pushing against her. Fannie tried to swallow the lump of dread caught in her throat.

A tasty little bird? Is that what these men thought about her? Had no idea what they meant. Knew their thoughts weren't good for her.

Deep in her chest, Fannie's heart thundered. Seemed she couldn't catch a breath of air. She tried to slip beneath his arms. He caught her by her shoulders. Shook her, her head banging against the bricks.

"You dinna be sayin' much. I do like a woman who doesn't talk a lot. Now come along with us. We'll be showin' you a good time."

"No," her voice held a calmness she didn't feel. Understanding the importance of this moment, she needed to get away from these two men before she became their evening's entertainment. "No!" she reiterated as loud as her raw throat would allow her. "No…don't want… I'm not what you believe."

Fannie closed her eyes for a moment, thinking of ways to remove herself from these men. Nothing tangible came to mind. Then… Breathing in the tainted air surrounding these two, she steeled herself to move fast. With a quick jerk of her knee, she brought it up as hard as she could between the man's legs. The shriek of pain coupled with the loosening of his fingers on her shoulder gave her the chance she needed. The man cursed. She lunged away. Raced down the street. Didn't bother to look over her shoulder to see if the two men followed. Headed straight for the line of carriages in front of her.

"Bitch!" one of the men called out as he gave chase. "Stop right there! You're going to pay for what you did to my friend."

No, she wasn't going to pay. She wasn't going to stop. Getting caught by these men was not her plan. Running, she headed for the well-lit house where she could hire a cab. She ran for about five minutes. Raced around two people who were chatting in the middle of the sidewalk to plow into another man. She hit him with such force, she fell back to land on her rump. She sat, her hands at her hips keeping her upright. Breathing hard she looked into a handsome face…a too handsome face…a pretty face. His eyes were pale blue…ice blue. The smile he sent her curled her stomach. She shivered. The man was dressed in black evening attire. The white shirt beneath the frock coat heightened his prettiness. He twirled a cane then leaned on it as he looked at her, examining her from head to toe. Her stomach twisted into a knot of revulsion.

The man was…handsome, slender for his height. His blue eyes twinkled as if he just found a present. Fannie shuddered. Didn't wish to be this man's gift. The smirk he flashed her was wicked, his teeth white. He looked as if he wanted to devour her or feed her to the wolves. Well, the wolves were after her. At least with the men chasing her, she understood the danger. With this man she did not. What did he want with her? Whatever it was she didn't plan to have anything to do with him. Fannie didn't have one doubt he had something in mind. The look the man graced her with reminded her of Lord Abernathy when he stared at Maggie.

"This *Caileag bheag* is ours," her first attacker said with a low growl.

The handsome man looked at her, a sly expression on his too pretty face. He pointed to the men. "What do you say, little girl? Are you theirs' for the night? If not, you will come with me. I've a cab waiting. I'll protect you. Keep you safe from these thugs."

"No! No to both of you." Fannie felt as if she must be jumping from the pan into the fire. There was no other recourse. She scooted back, distancing herself. Her gaze shifted from pretty face to the burly seamen. "I'm not anyone's plaything. Not for sale. Not going with any of you." With those words she realized what both men thought of her. They believed she was here to sell herself to them.

"You're one against two!" The man she kneed in the groin shouted from a short distance while he shook his fist in pretty face's direction. "You can't stop us from having what we found first."

"Seems this little girl packs a wallop. Besides, you lost the little girl. Didn't you? She says she doesn't wish to have anything to do with the likes of you," the man told her pursuers as the man she kneed in the groin limped up to them still holding himself.

"She's got to pay for hurting me." He shook his fist, punctuating his words. "I will make sure she pays."

"No, I'm not leaving her with the two of you. You lost. I won. I've got the little girl with me. She doesn't wish to go with you." He turned to her. "My name is Craig, Craig Halsey. Do you wish for me to save you from these two ruffians? Speak up. I don't have all night."

"Yes." She did wish to find herself safe from these two men who wanted her for themselves. Fannie also needed to keep herself safe from Craig. She didn't trust him. This man was smooth which made him a dangerous agent. She wasn't a whore. They believed she was. What else could she do? Accepting this man's help went against the grain. This man, who she didn't know, could mean her harm. She needed to deal with one hazard at a time.

"Come along then." Craig took her by her hand then helped her stand. "I'll get you somewhere out of the cold. Give you something nice and warm to drink along with a nice place to sleep. You will enjoy the experience. After you're more comfortable we can see what will happen. Got some plans for you. Something I believe you will appreciate." He looked to the carriage as if seeking advice.

His hand held her elbow tight as if she might run. The row of carriages was still in front of her. Perhaps she should try to get away. Where would she run to? At least this man didn't have a horrible stench around him. No, but he did smell of too much cologne, a sweet scent, cloying in the extreme. Her instincts told her she needed to flee. This man didn't mean her well. Instincts should be heeded.

When Fannie looked in front of her, she realized why the two men allowed her to go with Craig. A carriage waited for him with a driver, along with a second man standing by the door to help them inside. His hand on her elbow, he was taking her away. She couldn't go with Pretty Face. Where did he intend to take her? What the devil was going on here?

Mother? Anice? No, she was seeing things. Her mind was fogged over. She was sick. Hallucinating. Her mother wasn't sitting in the vehicle. *No!*

Fannie dug in her heels. Pulling back, she said with as much strength as she could summon. "No! I will not get in that carriage with you." She would fight until her power left her. Prying at his fingers, she tried to free herself.

Craig looked to her then back to the two men who accosted her. "I see. You wish to go back with these men? You would like to become their evening's entertainment? I can tell you they won't pay you as well as I can," he told her, one eyebrow arching as if he knew the answer ahead of time.

So, Craig wanted her for the same thing as these two. She wasn't a whore. Wasn't selling her body to any man. Was her mother sitting in the carriage? Her mind was playing tricks with her. Swallowing her fear, "No, just tell me in which direction the river is then I will be on my way. There is no need for you to bother with me. I can find my way home." By the look in his eyes, Fannie acknowledged the fact Craig wasn't going to allow her to leave him. She needed to think of something else.

"I'll take you to the river in the carriage. No need for you to walk." One more time he held her elbow. Pushed her in the direction of the waiting transport. "It will be much more comfortable for you in my vehicle. We will be able to talk about your future. You are lovely. Will command top dollar I've no doubt."

She was both annoyed with the man as well as terrified. Her options were limited to one. "No…" Fannie wrenched away. Surprised by her sudden move, the man lunged for her. Caught nothing but air.

"Little bitch!" He swore as he started after her.

In the split second before she jerked her arm loose, Fannie realized Craig held no good intentions toward her. If she stepped inside his carriage, she would be his for whatever purpose he decided. She didn't know why he wanted her. Nonetheless, she felt as if his purpose was not one she would like. If that woman was her mother, she would find herself in Lord Abernathy's bed before she could count to ten. Gasping for oxygen, Fannie ran as hard as she could. Stumbled once then a second time. Heard the pounding of Craig's feet behind her. He had to be gaining on her. Would catch her. She pushed herself harder, demanding the last bit of strength she possessed.

The light in the house she first saw what seemed like hours ago, beckoned to her. She had to find safety there before Pretty Face could catch up to her. Fannie didn't know what would happen at the house. Had to be better than what was going to happen to her here. Well, it couldn't be any worse. She needed to take the chance there would be a welcoming committee who would give her the necessary aid…a nonthreatening welcome…a safe shelter away from the elements acting against her. Tearing down the street then through the gate into the backyard, she flung herself up the steps.

"Help!" Her fists pounded on the door. Craig was close behind her. The only reason he hadn't caught her yet was because she surprised him. "Help! Please!"

"Bitch! Come back here! I'm not letting you get away from me." Craig passed through the gate just as the door opened.

"Help me," Fannie bent over at her waist gasping for air, almost fell into the room. "Please…please don't let him get me. I..."

A huge man, his skin as black as midnight stood in the opening. Muscles in his arms bulged. When he stared at her, she saw a light of compassion in his dark brown eyes. "Halsey, what brings you here? Suppose it's this little lady you're panting after. She doesn't look as if she wishes to become part of your stable."

A petite, redheaded lady stood behind the huge man, a broom in her hand. Her eyes blazed blue fire while her ample bosom heaved with indignation. She stepped forward. Swung the broom down on Craig's head.

"Get the hell out of my yard and off my steps, Halsey! You're not welcome here! Be gone! Pimping little girls who say no to you is not honest work. She looks to be too sweet for the likes of your clients." She hit the man again then again as Craig staggered down the steps to land hindside down on the gravel walkway.

"She's mine!" Craig yelled, shaking his fist at the woman who defended her. "You'll see. I'll get her back. Just you wait. She will be mine." He stood, dusted off his pants then walked from the yard.

During the altercation the huge man ushered her into the home. He seemed to be a gentle giant. She stood in the kitchen not knowing what to do with herself, shifting from one foot to the other. Delicious scents of food wafted around her. To Fannie's mortification, her stomach rumbled.

"You hungry? We've got lots of food," the woman asked with a charming smile lighting up her features. She was probably in her late thirties. Seemed to have a motherly streak in her. "I can feed you then we'll see what else I can do for you. Sit down. You can tell me why that horrible man was chasing you." Kindness was written in her expression, in her eyes, the way she looked at her.

A monogramed handkerchief. Who would believe?

As if magically, a bowl of soup appeared in front of her. She sipped the broth letting the warmth soothe her raw throat. Found pieces of tender beef along with vegetables within to help satisfy the hunger rumbling in her stomach. She didn't even realize she was hungry. Fannie ate until she could hold no more. Her throat still felt raw, though the warm soup soothed. She rested her hand on her throat. The proprietress of this house was patient. While she ate no one spoke.

The woman sat down across from her. "Now, I'm Hannah. In case you didn't realize, this house is a brothel. You don't look like a woman who would be seeking a job here. Halsey, the man who was chasing you, is a pimp. So, what can I do for you besides keep you from his filthy hands?"

Fannie had a few ideas about what a pimp was. She wasn't certain she could ask Hannah. Made no difference. Her throat was now so scratchy she couldn't speak except in a painful whimper. She tried to tell Hannah she was lost. The words came out in a croak. If she could speak, Hannah might put her on one of those carriages outside her home.

"You need a doctor, I see." The woman strode to the hall. "Angus, send for Saint. The lady needs some doctoring. Seems she can't speak a word without sounding like a frog. I'll give her a good dose of laudanum so she can rest. Sometimes on a Friday night, Saint is busy until the *wee* hours of dawn. He might not return my summons right away. We need to put her in a bed where she can rest."

The big man nodded. "Aye…I'll send Jacko for Saint. He'll make good speed. I'll help you get the little sparrow to a room. We've an empty one at the end of the hall last door on the right. Will the room do? Too bad she's not in the business. This one is very pretty. No wonder Halsey was after her. She'd make him a mint. What do you suppose she was doing in our neck of the city."

"Thank you, you are right about this girl. We could use someone like this one. She's as pretty as a peach. Would guess all the gents would want her," Hannah murmured then turned her attention back to her. "Come with me." She held out her hand. "Angus and I are going to put you to bed. Perhaps in the morning after seeing the doctor, you'll be able to tell me who you are. You *dinna* have a thing to fear. I'll take care of you. Can send you home as soon as the doc gives you a clean bill of health. As soon as you can tell us where you live."

"Here is the laudanum," Angus appeared with a glass of water. "She needs to drink the entire glass."

Fannie didn't understand why she trusted this woman. She did though. She drank the glass of water. The panic she'd been feeling ebbed as the woman was taking care of her. Angus picked her up in his arms then carried her up a long staircase to the second floor. Trusting this man, she set her head against his shoulder. Angus set her on her feet by the big bed in the room. Except for a chair by the fire and a huge armoire the only other furniture was a copper tub.

"I'll send up a hot bath for you. Might help you relax. Your shoulders are tense. Of course, after what you've been through tonight, there is a good reason for you to be anxious. Suppose I only know half of what happened to you this evening. Don't understand why you were in this part of town. You're lucky you picked this place to seek refuge. Believe all the other establishments around here would have put you to work on your back. Ah, don't suppose a fine born lady such as yourself *kens* much about working in the bedroom. Glad you're not going to learn. Do you have a name?"

She tried to croak out her name. What she said was far from sounding like Fannie.

Waving her petite hand in the air, Hannah said, "Never you mind. Maybe in the morning we can figure out how to get you home. If you can talk, it will make the chore much easier. Speech or not, you're in no condition to be anywhere except in a bed."

Hannah rummaged through a large armoire. Brought out a scarlet dressing gown. "You can wear this. It's clean. Make yourself comfortable. The bath will be here in about ten minutes. Don't know how long until the doctor can get here."

Nodding, Fannie tried to tell her thank you. Mouthed the words.

Hannah held up her hands to stop her. "You're very welcome. Don't try to speak. Doing so will only serve to make your throat hurt more. Now you just relax. I'll put a rush on the bath. By the look in your eyes, you're going to be asleep before the bath water heats."

Fannie watched the madam stride from the room, her skirts swishing around her feet. Hannah seemed to be a nice lady. The sound of a hot bath sounded divine. The thought of a doctor even better than heavenly. She eyed the scarlet dressing gown thinking about disrobing. She was in a brothel. She shouldn't take off her clothing. Didn't seem as if anything good would come of disrobing in a whorehouse. If she was going to take that bath, she would need to be naked.

With her hands folded prayer style beneath her cheek, she laid down on the bed. Closed her eyes wishing she dared try for comfort. Squirming, she changed positions. Her skirts bunched around her hips. All her clothing felt tight and damp from the misty fog of the evening. Hannah would never allow anyone to bother her in this room. Told her she was safe. Trying not to think too hard, she slipped out of her gown and underthings to don the scarlet dressing gown. It was made of silk, soft…comfortable. She tied the belt around her waist.

She lay back down on the bed, closed her eyes waiting for either the doctor or the hot bath. She must have dozed. Her mind seemed to be a muddled mess. When she opened her eyes, a man was standing, framed in the doorway. He strode into the room. Smiled at her. He must be the doctor. His shoulders were broad. Didn't look like any doctor she'd seen before. He was by far too handsome. Doctors were old. He was Saint. Or…was he a saint?

Beside her he sat on the bed. His golden fox eyes shimmered in the candlelight. He cleared his throat a couple of times before he spoke. With the back of his knuckles, he touched her cheek then her forehead. "Downstairs, Hannah told me you don't talk much. I can appreciate silence. A chatterbox can be annoying."

When Fannie nodded, she set her hand on her throat in an effort to tell him where she hurt. "C…c…ant ta…" He set his finger on her lips, shaking his head.

"Soft. You look flushed. Is it too hot in here? I can open a window. Angus must have built the fire too high." The man set his hand on her forehead again. "Not too hot. Were you going to take a bath? I'll wait for you. Go on. Take your bath while the water is hot. I'm not going anywhere." He smiled, flashing even white teeth. "I'll just watch." He slipped off his jacket then undid his cravat, so his neckcloth hung loose down his chest.

Fannie didn't understand what he told her. Swinging her legs over the bed, she eyed the hot bath water with eager anticipation. She could imagine the heated water closing around her. The scent of lavender rose with the steam. She liked the scent. Looking over her shoulder she saw the doctor sitting on a large chair, his long legs stretched out in front of him. He'd poured himself a glass of something golden…just like his eyes.

When she thought of a doctor, Fannie envisioned an older man with silver hair coupled with bushy eyebrows of the same tone. His eyes would crinkle with tiny age lines when he looked at her. This man's hair held no hint of silver. He was dressed in evening wear. The cut of his black suit fit his broad shoulders to perfection. His white shirt contrasted along with the dangling cravat he untied. The cut of his britches molded to his muscular legs. She blinked several times wondering if she was imagining this man. Her heart skipped a beat then another. She must be dreaming.

"Don't hurry on my account." The doctor motioned toward the tub. "I've nowhere to go tonight. I'll wait for you to finish. I'm certain the hot water will feel good as will I enjoy the show."

As she turned her back on the doctor, Fannie let the dressing gown slide down her body to pool at her feet on the floor. Disrobing while the doctor looked on seemed a bit strange…different from the norm. Tonight was far from normal. Must not be real. Because of the laudanum her mind must be playing tricks on her. Once before she'd had a dose of the drug. Her imagination toyed with her mind that time also. She stepped into the steaming bath, sinking down to her neck. The water curled around her, rippling around the coldness. The tips of her breasts hardened when they bobbed out of the water to meet the cool air. She soaped a sponge with lavender scented soap.

Fannie ran the sponge along one arm then started on the other. The doctor kneeled by the tub, one finger swirling in the water. His eyes focused on hers. Anxious with him so close, she swept her mouth with her tongue then heaved in the doctor scented air. Her stomach was doing flip-flops. "Let me help with the sponge. The washing will go much faster if I give you aide. After you're done here, we can get on with the business at hand." A strange ache blossomed deep within, a sensation she didn't understand.

The doctor took the sponge from her shaking hands. This didn't seem quite right. He did wash her. Didn't appear interested in anything except finishing the bath for her. When she watched him, he gave her an encouraging smile then nodded toward the bath towel.

"Stand up." He held the huge bath towel for her. "This will also feel nice. It's been warming by the fire. Hannah thinks of everything. Do you need help drying yourself?" His soft chuckle seemed strange in the light of his efficiency in washing her. She pressed her hands on his shoulders to help her stand.

First, she shook her head then nodded. She didn't comprehend what she wanted. Her limbs felt weak. Her mind in crazy disorder. Fannie thought this might be what people talked about when they spoke of new discoveries in medicine…a personal touch. Before she could give a more definitive answer, he rubbed the towel across her shoulders then the rest of her. For a few ticks of the clock on the mantel, he cupped one breasts, ran his thumb across the hardened tip. In response to the intimate caress, she shuddered. Pressure pulsed within her then seemed to ache. He held her hand then led her to the bed.

"I'll get you a drink. The brandy will sooth your nerves. You are shaking. Don't be afraid. I won't hurt you. There is no reason for you to be nervous." He walked away from her, found a second glass, then splashed brandy into the crystal glass. Strolling toward her, he held a glass of brandy in each hand. His small grin reassured. She nodded to him thinking the drink would be nice.

No, Fannie didn't think he would harm her in any way. Didn't he take the Hippocratic oath? She stared at the dressing gown on the floor. The small piece of fabric seemed a mile away from her then she looked back into his golden fox eyes. She could drown in those gorgeous eyes. She lifted a hand to touch his cheek then let her fingers fall back.

He chuckled again. His smile caused her heart to weep. She'd never seen any man so beautiful. "I can't work my magic if you've clothing on, even a dressing gown. You, my fine lady, need to be naked. Slip under the covers just the way you are. Drink some of the brandy. After you've finished the first glass, we will see what transpires." He tossed his loosened cravat on the chair near the fireplace.

She did what he told her. He handed her the glass of brandy. With special care, Fannie sipped a small portion. The liquid warmed her aching throat along with her stomach. The potent drink also diminished her stretched nerves. When she finished, she held the glass up for more. He obliged, tossing more of the amber liquid into the crystal she held out.

After she finished the second glass, he set it aside. Touched her cheeks with the back of his hand then smoothed his hand down her neck. Lingered where her blood rushed in a thunder of fast hard beats. Good, he understood her throat was raw. Bent closer until she felt his warm breath against her lips then the sweep of his tongue. She shivered, strange new sensations coursing through her body. He caressed her mouth with his, taking tender concern. With his potent touch to her lips, she jerked, startled by the contact that was unexpected though quite nice.

"Easy now…open your mouth to let me inside. I need to feel your warmth, the heat of you," he told her without blinking an eye.

Fannie did what he asked then said, "Ah…" understanding he would want to look at her throat. Hannah must have told him about her inability to talk. Pleased she wouldn't need to explain what was bothering her.

The doctor cracked a chuckle as he leaned back to look at her. He held her chin with one hand. The other rested on her shoulder. His fingers were warm. He squeezed as if to encourage her. "Not so wide, sweetheart. Just enough so I've access to your warmth." His lips closed over hers. The taste of brandy coupled with warm man filled her senses. Fannie wasn't at all certain what was happening. One of his large hands skimmed down her arm then back to her shoulder. The other held her head in place while he explored her mouth with his. She felt his tongue rub against hers, testing. Yes, he was discovering how hot she was. Treated this foray with hungry exploration. She heated from the tips of her toes to the top of her head. Felt each breath of air as it entered her lungs. Pressed against his white shirt, her nipples hardened.

She felt his tongue slide over hers, once then twice. Rubbed. Increased the pressure. He repeated the process while he changed his position. She moaned as his hand once more caressed her shoulder then her arm. He stopped his exploration to speak. "Give me your tongue, sweet one. Put yours in my mouth. Need to feel you inside me."

Understanding was beyond Fannie's imagination. She'd never had a doctor ask such strange things. She wondered if he could tell what was wrong with her throat when their tongues clashed. In her life, she'd had few doctors. None of them asked her to... Well, they always wanted her to open her mouth then say ah. When his mouth framed hers again, she did as he asked. Felt the soft, silken texture inside his mouth along with the raw heat emanating from him. A small whimper rose from the back of her throat. The penetrating sound rippled into his mouth.

His large hand rested beneath her breast right where her heart bellowed with the frantic tempest he created. Fannie wasn't certain that was something he was supposed to do. He must need to listen to her heart. *With his hand?* She closed her eyes, reveling in the feelings encompassing her. The brandy joined with the laudanum in her system to relax her to the point of no return. She was sleepy as well as disoriented. Unable to hold a clear thought in her spinning head. With each touch of his big hands, she burned from the inside out. He scorched her. Her body arched as his lips moved lower, touched upon her belly. She felt wet in the dark secret parts of her. His hands examined places she never thought a doctor would touch. His fingers slipped between her thighs, separated her. Touched upon a sensitive part of her, lingered there as her hips bucked in opposition to his fingers. She needed something she didn't understand. Spiraling higher then even higher, she arched against his body, his touch.

Fannie cried out as her body catapulted into hundreds of different directions. He rose above her. Set his mouth upon hers again. "Just a second." She watched as his clothes vanished, to land on the floor beside the bed. Her doctor came over her, entered inside her. She jerked with the sudden pain. He told her he wouldn't hurt her. Moisture filled her eyes, tears slipping down her cheeks.

"A virgin whore…?" He brushed the tears away with his thumbs. "I won't move for a few seconds. The pain will fade. After the sting of my entry vanishes, I'll give you more of what you want. You're new to this profession. I understand."

How the hell did he know what he said?

With no more warning, her doctor was on top of her, deep inside her. He filled her. She tried to register the words he spoke. Attempted to make sense of something that didn't make any sense at all. Her brain was too befuddled by the brandy coupled with the laudanum to sort through what was happening to her. Without notice she'd felt the heat of him. He was right. The pain did vanish. Within her, he began to move, slow at first, then hard and fast. His fingers touched upon her with intimacy. She spiraled with the renewed contact. Her body convulsed as he filled her, pushing into her, deeper each time. She was outside herself. Beyond her mortal body. The ripples of pleasure consumed. When she shattered, his mouth crashed against hers while he rocked her. Warmth filled her.

He was above her now, smoothing her hair away from her face. "I'm sorry. I didn't know you'd never been with a man before. All Hannah told me was that you weren't a chatterbox. She never said anything about virgin territory. I'm pleased I was your first." He set his forehead against hers.

Still not comprehending what happened, she nodded. Her lashes drifted closed. She fell asleep feeling the weight of his body on top of hers, blanketing her with life giving warmth. Felt the heat of the man penetrate through him into her. As Fannie drifted into oblivion, she realized she liked the way his big body fit with hers. Enjoyed the way he covered her. Wished this dream had been real.

When she woke, she slept on top of him. Her breasts pushed against his chest. Her legs sprawled across his. Entwined. Fannie didn't understand why her doctor was still here. While she felt better, she still couldn't speak. Her mouth was dry. She ran her hand across his chest. Stopped to feel his nipples then run her fingers through the spattering of dark hair on his chest. Curious, she followed the line of hair to his waist. She was fascinated by the differences. Wanted to feel what made him so distinctive from her. He stopped her with his large hand on top of hers.

"If you aren't too sore, we can do this a second time. Otherwise, your questing fingers will need to stop. I can only take so much foreplay before I lose control."

Foreplay? Sore? Lose control? Fannie questioned as she stared at him. While she wasn't certain what he meant she did feel an ache between her legs. A sensation different from anything she'd known before. She shook her head, her long hair spilling around him, curling around his shoulders. Words still didn't form. She didn't wish to croak out the one word. *Please.*

"Good…" Her doctor filled her again. She clung to his shoulders, her nails biting into his flesh. "I find I need to feel your warmth surround me again. You are soft. So very wet. I like that…" He kissed her. Set his lips against hers. Swept his tongue inside her.

She experienced him deep inside while she felt the same amazing feelings erupt within the secret place, before this man, she never knew existed. The same as happened last night completed her. Arching her hips she brought him deeper into her. He pulled her legs around his flanks. He thrust deep. Hard. Cried out when she erupted so completely she felt certain she flew to the sun. Her nails scarred his flesh. He collapsed beside her, rolled to his side bringing her with him.

Next time she woke, she realized she needed to leave this place. Her doctor was asleep. He was beautiful. She swept a strand of hair from his eyes. Ran a fingertip along the bridge of his nose. Wished she could see his eyes, his fox eyes. She would never forget those eyes. The effects of the brandy along with the laudanum was gone. Fannie's mind was no longer befuddled.

With sudden despair, she understood what had happened to her. What she didn't understand was why. She didn't intend to stick around to discover the truth. Didn't wish to see this …doctor…ever again. She must have put her trust in a woman who was untrustworthy. This man couldn't be a doctor. She'd just lost her virginity to a man she didn't know and hoped she would never see in her lifetime. Fannie didn't even know his name. Didn't know the name of the man who took her innocence. She inhaled a deep, ragged breath of air.

Fannie had to find her way home. Couldn't stay in this brothel a moment longer. Didn't wish to face the consequences of last night. Rising from the bed with quiet stealth, she stared at the man who claimed her virginity. Recalled the scavenger hunt that eventually brought her here. The men who attacked her. Halsey who wanted to take her to his home or someplace. The woman she saw in the carriage who she thought might have been her mother. All this because she was looking for a monogramed handkerchief. She remembered the carriages lined up in front of this home. Maybe they were still there. She did have money. Kept a small reticule in the pocket of her coat. She could hire a hack to take her home. She would be safe soon.

Looking at the man on the bed, she groaned, a soft sound vibrating in the back of her throat. She would never see him again, thank God. Didn't know how she would ever face this person if she did come across him. Knowing what he did to her, how he played her body, mortification would set in.

God, she didn't even know his name. Didn't want to recall what she'd done with her doctor. He couldn't be a doctor. Who was he? It was true. She was no longer a virgin. What she wasn't was a whore. What if she got pregnant from this encounter? What would she do? She would need to tell Jasper, her guardian. Dear Lord, was she just like her mother? Anice slept with countless men.

Shaking off her thoughts, the potent need to flee this place rushed into her in waves of mortification. She didn't belong here. With fluid fast movements, Fannie dressed then grabbed the dark brown bag sitting by the door. The bag Nellie must have given her to keep the items from the scavenger hunt safe. In the next second, she was out the door, racing down the steps. To her relief there were two hacks in front of the home. She rushed forward. Gave her address to the driver then paid him. She was on her way home.

~ * ~

For Fox Taggart the evening could not have gotten any better. He started out with five thousand pounds then managed to increase the sum to fifty thousand in a few hours of gambling. He supposed a bit of luck went his way. Sitting at the table, gazing over the room, he sipped his brandy, felt the heat slither down his throat.

More than pleased with the outcome of the evening, he decided to celebrate his good fortune with a no strings attached dalliance. Thought about going to the widow he'd seen last night. Decided against that idea. Release was on his mind. Needed to ease his taut nerves. He'd been to Hannah's before. The brothel as well as the girls were clean, even sweet. The establishment was an honest one unlike some of the others in that part of town.

After tonight, he now had enough money to make improvements on his logging adventure then buy more land. Last winter's storms were hard on the ranch. He tried to be self-sufficient. He owned several head of cattle and would like to increase the herd. Had hens as well as a rooster. In the lakes the fishing was exceptional. Maintained a vegetable garden. Several fruit trees had been planted. The plans he made would now come to fruition. His ensuing grin reached deep into his heart. Jake Taggert, his father, had nothing to hold over his head. He could no longer induce him to remain in Scotland. Jake wanted him to play a role in his business adventures. Wanted him close. As Jake told him, Michigan Territory was too far away.

Jake encouraged him to give up on the land. Fox couldn't. The land along with the mountains was in his blood, logging was all he ever wished to do. His logging camp would always be a part of his heart as well as his soul. He could have sold the twenty-four thousand acres spread of timber for a huge profit. He didn't want to sell. What he wanted was to live on his land, to bring up a family on the acreage. He needed a wife along with children who would appreciate the world he loved as much as he loved the place. Clean open mountain air with none of the problems of the city. His children would be able to roam the land without fear. They would inherit the empire he planned to build.

"Well, you got what you wanted." His father slapped him on the back, grinning. Fox felt certain his father wasn't pleased with tonight's events even though he smiled. "Got everything you need to hide out in Michigan for the rest of your life. No telling what you'll find there besides hard work from sunrise to sunset. You could have sold the land then come to work for me. You'd be a rich man."

"Got exactly what I want, Dad. No thanks to you. Don't wish to work for you or live in the city. Want to build an empire my children can inherit." He did love his father, the ultimate manipulator that he was. Fox respected him too. He'd earned his money from the ground up. Their problems stemmed from the fact they didn't want the same things.

"You do understand I would have lent you the money. Told you the fact a couple of times." His father chuckled as he patted his back again. "Though I would rather see you stay here in Glasgow instead of hightailing it back to the states. I do understand that's what you want. What you don't know is the truth. I do respect your decision."

"With interest." Fox understood what the interest would be. He'd find a woman for him to wed. By doing so, he would owe no interest on the loan. No, his father's notion of interest was also something he had no wish in doing. He didn't want a wife who was handpicked by his father. He was looking for love. If he couldn't find that elusive factor by the time he was forty, he'd marry the first attractive eighteen-year-old who came his way. Forty was young enough to start a family as well as a dynasty.

"I'm a businessman," Jake reminded him as he nodded to a passing friend. "What else would I do besides charge you interest?"

Fox also nodded to a few people as he walked through the gaming hall. He'd lived in Glasgow half his life. The other half was spent in the wilds of Michigan. He knew his preference for the land. "I won't be home tonight. Don't wait up for me. Plan on doing a little celebrating before I head back to my home. Once I'm back on the land, there will be work…hard work until all is as I want it to be." He thought of the journey. The devil, he despised sailing. Hated the sea. The overland trip would be difficult but more enjoyable than rolling waves.

"Ah, seeing to your needs," Jake said, grinning. "Wouldn't need to pay for a whore if you had a wife. When are you going to settle down? A good girl would be just what you need. I do know of a couple of sisters. Either one would make a fine wife. They've been brought up well. Travel in all the right circles. Do business with their guardian."

Fox pinched the bridge of his nose hard, reeling from his father's interference in his life. "I'll marry when I find a woman who will love me more than she loves herself or my father. Don't wish to meet anyone you might pick out for me. If they were bred in Glasgow, they might not wish to live on a homestead in Michigan. Need a woman who won't dissolve at the sight of a warrior." He meant the words. He'd been in love before, even had a fiancée. Strange how his fiancée, the woman he believed loved him, married his father. She still flirted with him each and every time they were in the same room. Offered up her mouth for kisses as if he would oblige. God, he felt bad for his father. The woman chased everyone who wore pants.

"You should pay more attention to your bride," Fox tossed out with growing agitation. "She might set her claws into some other man. Turn the tables…" Seeing the look on his father's face, he let that statement die a lingering death. While he felt certain Jake loved Beryl, he didn't believe for a beat his father's wife loved him. Perhaps his feelings were sour grapes. The woman betrayed him with an older man. Jake was old enough to be her father. What the hell did she see in him?

"Discussion of Beryl is off limit to you, son. My wife…our relationship is between us." His voice was ragged. Fox heard the pain in Jake's voice. Knew he shouldn't bring up the past. What was done couldn't be undone. Jake understood exactly who his wife was.

Fox acknowledged the fact his casual words hurt his father. Didn't like himself much for doing so. After what the man did, he shouldn't give a damn about either. He raked his fingers through his hair. "You're right. What is between the two of you is not my business." That was all the acknowledgment he was going to give his father. "Don't wait up."

"I wouldn't. Not when I've a wife as beautiful as Beryl waiting for me in my bed." Jake chuckled, his voice soft.

The words made Fox flinch. Hell, he didn't understand why. Knew he was better off without the lying, little bitch. Still, the thought hurt. A man didn't appreciate the fact he lost his fiancée to an older man. Once Jake thought she was happy with him. Later, she told him she couldn't bear to live in Michigan. Didn't like the isolation. Needed what a city could provide for her. Wanted to go to balls, dance the night away. Hold dinner parties as well as flirt. Except for flirting, she could do none of those things in Michigan. There would be times during the year when the winter snow would keep them isolated in his home.

Outside, Fox hailed a cab, gave directions to Hannah's place, then he sat back to reflect on the conversation he had with his father. After he decided there was nothing else he could have told the man who sired him, he set his mind to making lists of the improvements for his property. He let his head lean back on the seat. Listened to the sounds of the night. The carriage slowed then stopped. He drank in the scent of the chilled air. Caught the aroma of fresh cooked food. Hannah's place was well-known for its cuisine. He wasn't hungry for food. What he needed was a woman who would place no demands on him. Someone who wouldn't talk his head off. A lady he could have sex with tonight then leave whenever he pleased.

Taking a few seconds for thinking, he stood in front of the three-story brothel. The lawn surrounding the building was manicured with precision, the paint fresh. During the ride some of his ardor cooled. Fox wasn't certain this was what he wanted. Maybe his father had a point. A wife would have been nice to come home to. He didn't have a wife nor were there any possibilities on the horizon.

"What the hell…" he muttered to himself. "I'm here. Might as well take advantage of the opportunity." He pinched the bridge of his nose. Maybe some of the tension he felt during the long hours at the gaming table would lessen. Who was he kidding? Most if not all the tension in the back of his neck resulted in his conversation with his father. The man tried to manipulate. His ploy wasn't going to work.

With a drawn-out sigh, he stepped up to the front door. Music blared all around him. Scantily clad ladies entertained gentlemen in the parlor. A few seconds later, he was greeted by the big bodyguard Hannah employed. "Angus," he said as he stepped into the foyer. "Nice to see you. I'm here for a bit of pleasure. Do you have a girl who isn't going to talk my head off? Don't want a chatterbox tonight. Not in the mood for conversation. Just need to…" He broke off with the rest of his thoughts. Why else would he be here if it wasn't to relive his needs?

Angus tossed his head back then after a bark of laughter, he said, "Follow me. Got just the right gal for you. Doesn't say much unless asked a question. Then only to be polite. Has untold secrets. Come on in. She is new here. I'll let Hannah know who you want. She'll send you to the right place. You'll have a nice enjoyable evening with the little lady. She is fresh down from the highlands. Fairly new to the profession."

"Thanks…" Fox followed the huge protector of the house to the office where Hannah worked. He stopped at the door. The lady must be in her early forties or late thirties. She was still pretty. Her smile welcomed him.

"You're back, Fox. Missed your handsome company. Where the hell have you been all these months? Not across the ocean in that heathen place they call the United States? Ah, see the truth in your eyes. You like the wild land better than this fair city. Can't say as I blame you. Doubt if you've got pimps in those mountains of yours." Her laughter trilled around her. "What can we do for you tonight? Got lots of beautiful girls. A new lady, young, might be perfect for you."

"Angus says you've got a lady who won't talk my ear off. Don't want a chatterbox. Will most likely stay the night. What do you say? Can you put me in the loving hands of a lady who will keep her mouth shut?" He did have his preferences. Women who spent the entire time talking were not to his liking.

"Got the perfect lass for you. Go on up the stairs, her room is the at the end of the hall, last door on the right. Just give a little knock then go inside. She will be expecting a guest so you won't frighten or startle her. Guarantee, she will be ready for you. I won 't even ask for you to pay more for the silent treatment." Hannah laughed again before sending him on his way. "Don't be a stranger. You're a true gentleman. We like having you here. All the ladies appreciate your talent."

After he opened the door, Fox took in the ambiance of the room. Two candles burned on a counter flooding the area with a warm tone. If this wasn't a whore's bedroom, the sight might have been romantic. The whore was pretty, perched on the bed, her feet tucked beneath her. Long blond hair curled around her shoulders before falling to her waist. She wore a scarlet dressing gown that molded to all her delicious curves. Flickering shadows from the candles played along her body, giving her face a golden quality. He imagined her naked. Thought to taste her breasts, sip on each pretty pink nipple, savor until the sound of her pleasure rippled into him. He could see the imprint of her nipples on the dressing gown. With that poignant thought, he swelled against his britches. Jesus, he had sex last night with the widow. At this beat, he was primed as well as ready to plunge into secret depths. He didn't want to explode before he could give her pleasure. He ran his hand along the back of his neck, hoping for control.

Hours later, lying in bed, he recalled the first time with her. Thought of the moment he crashed through her maidenhead. Her cry of startled pain reverberated in his head. She'd not expected pain. At least it didn't seem to him she did. Hannah should have told him the girl was a virgin. He might have treated the moment different. Maybe Hannah didn't know. The virgin factor might not be something a lady new to this profession would tell the madam of a brothel. Hell, he didn't know her name. His arm lay across his face, shielding his eyes from the light of the candle.

A virgin whore.

The second time with her was better than the first. She was responsive. He didn't imagine the raw passion she poured into her lovemaking. The way she whimpered then cried out when she reached the sweet, coveted pinnacle. Fox knew women. Understood what they liked as well as how to caress their feminine parts to make them wet as hell. He enjoyed the ride with her. What he found with her was something that might last him until he reached his home. He planned on leaving within the week. Jake wouldn't be too pleased when he discovered his intentions. His father mentioned a dinner with the two sisters he hoped to introduce to him. Wished for him to marry one of them. Hoped for an engagement. His father could dream. The dream wasn't going to come true.

Fox wondered where his little virgin whore got herself off to. If she'd been in the bed, he would have considered another round of early morning sex, something he enjoyed with the right woman. The lass wasn't in the room. Supposed she could be just about anywhere in the building. He could use a hot cup of bitter coffee, American coffee, the stronger the better.

Ah…he was in Scotland. They drank tea. He needed coffee to spark early morning energy. Didn't enjoy beginning his day without the bitter brew.

The knock on the door startled him to a sitting position. The whore wouldn't knock on her door. Who the hell was it? His sheets fell around his waist. Another knock followed the first one. What…?

He didn't intend to answer. Whoever was outside would let him know what they wanted.

"The doctor is here. He's ready to see…" There was a long pause then she continued. "Says he is sorry for taking so long to get here. Seems he had a busy night," Hannah called out. "You decent?" She stepped inside the room. Eyes widening with surprise, her gaze stuck on him.

"What the hell?" Fox muttered deep under his breath. A quick search of the room found his pants on the floor near the tub. "A doctor." Who needs a doctor? I don't. You must have the wrong room."

Hannah's face paled when she recognized him. He still didn't understand. Fox saw her swallow a lump in her throat. She cleared her throat before beginning. "The more prevalent question is what are you doing in this room? I sent you to the…" she stopped talking for a few seconds. Passed the palms of her hands along her gown. "This could be bad, very bad. Always do get my right and left mixed up. This was not the room I sent you to. Couldn't be. This was the little lady's room. She was sick."

"You sent me to the last door on the right. Tell me what's going on." Fox didn't enjoy feeling as if the world was not turning the right direction. He was angry about the intrusion, angrier about the fact the lady went missing. What did she need a damn doctor for? "Are you telling me I was not with the girl I requested. You know, the non-chatterbox? The whore who wasn't going to talk my ear off."

Clearing her throat again, Hannah began, her bosom heaving with each drawn breath, "Did you have sex with her?"

"The lady is a whore. Of course we had sex. Sex is what I paid for. It's what I came here to have. What? Did you think I would pay for sex then not take the woman?" Fox didn't think he was going to appreciate what was coming next. The look on the madam's face was not the expression of a pleased woman.

"The lady might be a whore. That is true. I doubt it. She was sick. I gave her this room because she couldn't talk. Needed a safe place to rest. In her condition, I couldn't send her back on the street. Called for Saint but he wasn't able to make it here until now. Where is she? What did you do with her?"

"How would I know? The bed was empty when I woke." Fox pushed the sheets off, intending to dress. Wasn't surprised to see the blood on the sheet. Neither was Hannah. The madam made a face at him. Looked from the bloody sheet to his member. He twisted with the unwelcome urge to cover himself. He didn't like the way this inquisition was proceeding.

"The lady was no whore. She was a virgin…" Hannah turned to head for the door before spinning back to face him. "You had no right…" Once more she broke off as if she understood she was wrong to berate him for something that was not of his making.

"Christ, madam," he pushed his hands through his hair. "What did you expect? I'm not a saint," Fox looked to the doctor. "This is a whorehouse, a very nice one. Nonetheless, the ladies who work here are expected to be whores. Expect to be paid for sex. Didn't know she was a virgin until I broke through."

Fox had his pants pulled on and fastened. He realized then his bag was missing. "The lady might not be a whore but she is a thief!" He pointed to the spot by the door where he left his bag. "She stole my satchel. Best you know where to find this virgin whore." His voice was harsh, his feelings crueler. If he ever found his virgin whore he'd strangle her thin white neck. "I want my satchel back."

"Was the bag so important?" Hannah asked, but the expression on her face told him the question wasn't necessary. "I don't know her name. If you recall, last night she couldn't speak. Of course, I don't know where to find the lady. She is a lady. I'm certain of the fact. What she was doing in this part of the city is beyond me. Though she was running from a pimp."

"Contained fifty thousand pounds…" he gritted out between gnashing teeth. "I want the money back. You need to do all in your power to discover who this lady is as well as where I can find her."

Hannah threw up her hands, shooting him a look of disgust. "Can't give you something I don't have. How do I know you're telling the truth? This could be a ruse on your part. No…" Hannah paused; one finger pressed against her chin. "You would never make something like this up. Fifty thousand pounds should not be much of anything to a man of your standing."

"Don't doubt me. Thought this place was honest. The money was meant for my business in Michigan. If you haven't guessed, it's my father who has the considerable bank account, not me." Inside he was sweating. All his dreams of rebuilding his home along with his business had just gone up in flames. "I'll call the constables. They can rake over this house with a fine-tooth comb. Search every square inch of the place. Maybe we'll find the girl. When we do, I've questions."

Hanna swiveled to confront the burly bodyguard. "Angus, search the house. His satchel of money has got to be here. Don't believe our little lady is a thief. She couldn't have taken it with her. Did you set the bag down somewhere then forget about it?"

"See that you do search every inch. I would not set the bag down out of my sight. The money inside the satchel was my future." Fox was tucking his shirt into his pants. His anger was overflowing. His hopes along with his dreams dying. This was not what he expected upon waking up this morning. With his money safely in the bank, he intended to leave town within the week. Hell, that was most of the money he had in the world. He no longer had the five thousand pounds he began gambling with. He didn't have another five thousand pounds for another night of gaming. Should have forgone the brothel. Hindsight was always the very devil.

Hindsight.

Two hours later, bathed and with a change of clothing, Fox sat in the breakfast room of his father's townhouse, sipping strong black coffee. His dreams vanished because he needed a whore. A virgin whore no less. He despised himself.

"My, my, you don't look as if you got up on the right side of the bed," Beryl waltzed into the room, poured herself a cup of tea before adding cream and sugar. She bent over to kiss his cheek giving him a bird's eye view of the valley between her breasts. He jerked away but not in time to miss the dampness of her lips on his face.

"Stuff it, Beryl. Don't want anything to do with conversation or you." Fox was not in the mood to speak with anyone, especially not this woman who he despised.

She made a face at him then smiled while she tossed her hair over her shoulder. "Now, is that anyway to speak to your stepmother. Should show me respect."

"Suppose you earned whatever you get flat on your back while spreading your legs for my father. No baby yet? How is Father taking the news? Jake wants an heir. Since I don't wish to have anything to do with living in the city, the old man wants a second heir. You're going to need to do better or Jake might find another woman half his age to bed then marry." One dark eyebrow arched toward the ceiling. He shouldn't speak to her in this manner. Couldn't help himself. This morning his entire world crashed down around his shoulders. He would start over. Would work for his father until spring. Win the money back. He needed to be in Michigan.

Beryl stood behind him, her hand resting on his shoulder. Fox shrugged the offending hand off. She set her fingers back. He didn't intend to play any of her games. "Try being nice once in a while," she said, her voice sweet with stinging venom.

Fox pushed her hand from his shoulder.

She bent close to whisper in his ear. Touched the tip of her tongue to the lobe. "I'm always nice to you. Feels so good to be nice. If you would allow me, I could be even nicer."

He stood, knocking his chair to the floor with the force of his movement. He picked up his coffee. Fox needed to speak with his father. Jake would be in his office now. That was where he was this time of day, every day. So predictable it hurt. Fox hated predictable. Loved the spontaneity of his life. One never knew what would happen from one day to the next. He thrived in that atmosphere.

The door to the office was open. Fox strode inside. Shut the door behind him. Brought up a chair in front of the big desk where his father sat. His father didn't show his age. Except for a few gray hairs around his temples, he could be thirty instead of almost fifty.

Jake tapped his finger on the cherrywood. His eyes narrowed as if he knew this would be bad news. "To what do I owe this visit? Thought you'd be upstairs packing since you are so eager to get away from me as well as the city." He leaned forward, his forearms resting on the desk. The pads of his fingers tapped on the surface. "You have a change of heart? Are you staying longer? If so, you'd make an old man happy."

Fox lifted one shoulder in a shrug meant to be carefree. He didn't want Jake to realize how devastated he was. "Lost the money. So…one might say I'm staying a *wee* bit longer."

The tapping stopped. Jake's brows drew together in a frown. His lips thinned. Silence heaved around the room, stretching Fox's nerves to a snapping point. His stomach lurched. Jake sat back, his hand forming a steeple beneath his chin. The pose was thoughtful.

"How? Don't like to hear bad news. You were smug last night after your win. What changed in less than twelve hours?"

"Stolen by the little whore I bedded. Guess what I intended to pay her for the night wasn't enough. She wanted everything I owned." The bitterness in his tone was still there. Wouldn't go away for a long time, if ever. He didn't like confessing to his father the reality; he was done in by a virgin whore.

"What are your intentions? I gather you are not planning on leaving the city until you've managed to get the money back. Don't understand how the lady could get away. Doesn't Hannah just hire regulars?"

"One way or the other I'll find a means."

"I see. When you can, you will find the gaming tables again. You could lose."

"True. Will work for you until I've enough money for another game of chance. Mean to win the money back. Start over. You know I'm skilled at games of chance. Lots of luck at the card tables; seems the opposite at whorehouses. Counting cards is easy for me. Need to be in Michigan by summer." Fox lifted his shoulders, trying to shrug off his disappointment. Didn't work.

"You will understand if I'm not disappointed by the news. You're better off here in civilization than pursuing this ridiculousness…" Jake cleared his throat seeming to think better of spouting his opinion.

Dreams…I'm pursuing my dreams… They are not ridiculous.

"As well you know, to me…Michigan coupled with my dreams are far from preposterous. I belong out there just as you belong in the city. I love the clean air along with the open spaces, the spontaneity of each day. There are never two the same. One can look for miles and see only the mountains along with the trees. Timber is my livelihood." Fox didn't wish to get into an argument with his father. The two of them had been over this topic too many times to count. They didn't need another go around. Nothing would change.

Jake's fist landed hard on top of the table. Papers jumped. "Hell! You could die in a snow drift. No one would know for days…months…" Jake waved his hand in the air, clearly frustrated by his desire to live in the untamed land.

"My men would find me." He leaned forward, his forearms resting on the desk. Met his father's gaze with hard determination in his eyes, understanding there was no compromise between the two of them. "I'm not stupid. Not going to die in a snow drift. Would never take chances that would have me in a situation I could not climb out of."

"You could be shot by outlaws," Jake pointed out. "There are any number of ways to die out there."

"Could be run over by a carriage on High Street," Fox, in turn, pointed out, his tone bland. "Don't get your hopes up that I might stay in Glasgow to help with your business. That's not going to happen. One way or the other, I'll find the money I need to leave in fine style. If I'm unable to raise the funds on my own, I plan on looking for someone willing to invest in my company. Don't mind another partner if he is honest. Though I would plan on a buyout clause."

"Very well, if you plan on working for me, I'll need you to accompany me to a dinner meeting I've arranged. Are you going to stay here?" Jake studied him. "Work for me? You will be my right-hand man."

"Yes. What kind of dinner meeting?"

"With a wealthy friend of mine. Jasper Kenworthy is his name. He's a marquis. Has a twin brother name of Jason."

"What's the business?"

"The man wishes to branch out, to invest in my shipping line. You do recall we've a lucrative trade between Virginia and here. We supply Scotland with good Virginia tobacco. Believe the man might be interested in your plan. Probably won't appreciate a buyout clause."

Fox wondered how much of this shipping line would be part of his inheritance. His father told him he would lend him fifty thousand. He didn't want his father's groats. Needed to make this deal by himself. Didn't wish to be under Jake's thumb.

"He wants to invest…" Fox pondered those thoughts for a few ticks of the clock sitting in the hall. He didn't care one way or the other. His father would pay him a salary. He would do whatever it took. "A dinner meeting in two nights, you say?"

"From tonight."

"I'll be there." He sipped from the cup of coffee he brought with him from the breakfast room. "Anything important I should know?"

"Jasper is the guardian of two young ladies. Very inappropriate…the females live in the townhouse with him. Though there are a few extenuating circumstances to take under consideration."

"How did something so contrary to the moral values of his city's fine upstanding people come about? What are these extenuating circumstance? Something I should learn about?" Something about what he said made him sit up with interest. He found himself curious "Not the best thing. Though doesn't seem as if the house is a bachelor's residence."

"The ladies are his wife's sisters. Maggie is his wife's name. She is the oldest of four. His twin, Jason, is wed to the youngest, Tessa. Maggie will be there with her. Beryl will also attend. Don't know who else will be in attendance."

"If you are planning a bit of matchmaking, I'm not looking for a wife. Nothing to hold me here in this part of Scotland if that's what you had in mind. Besides, a Scottish wife would never keep me here. I'm going back to Michigan. If I wed, which I'm not going to do for the foreseeable future, my wife would go where I go. I need a woman strong enough to live in the backcountry, one who will love the mountains as much as I do."

"Beryl burned you that bad." Jake held up his hands in surrender. His old man understood Beryl was not a good topic of conversation between the two men. "Should not go there. I've no regrets where it comes to my wife. I love her. Loved her from the first moment I set eyes on her. It has never failed to amaze me that she wanted me."

"The woman wanted your money," he said with a snigger. "Beryl is a gold digger. You were the better catch. Better than a dirt-poor timber baron. Besides, when I met her, she pretended to love the ranch while all the while she begged me to move to the city…any city."

"You weren't poor until you lost a sizeable amount of timber in a flood," Jake pointed out. "You're not poor now. At least you wouldn't be if you sold the land."

No, he wasn't. Nonetheless, Jake had more money than he could spend in a lifetime. Even if he lost a ship, his financial status wouldn't be fazed. Lots of money was what Beryl wanted. Fox understood he shouldn't belittle his father's relationship with his ex-fiancée. He should be happy for him.

"What is my salary?"

"Let's negotiate this later. The money will be substantial. While I don't wish for you to leave, I'm not going to try to keep you here with a meager amount of money. I'm no scrooge. I appreciate a man's worth. You are worth far more than rotting on land away from people who love as well as appreciate you. Even though you don't wish to be part of my business, you know it well."

Fox hands fisted. He bellowed. "Leaving is what I want! My land is what I want!"

~ * ~

"Fox sent a constable to oversee the search of the brothel. We left nothing unturned. The brown satchel he claims to have come here with has vanished. The money disappeared with the bag. The girl had to be the thief. As he explained, there was no one else in the room." Hannah ran her hand along the back of her neck while Angus looked on, a sad expression in his deep brown eyes. Hannah stiffened her shoulders, determined to make the best of this situation. "Don't believe for a moment the lass stole the money. I'm a good judge of character as you've always told me. Her life had been threatened. She sought refuge here. What did I do for her? I failed to protect her interests. Sent a man to her to take her virginity."

"She is a lady. The way she was dressed…her speech. Wouldn't have need of the groats. She comes from wealth. That much was apparent," Angus acknowledged her sentiments. "The rawness of her throat was also not a pretense. The lass was sick."

Hannah felt desperation down to the tips of her toes. She wished she could find the money so she could return it to Fox. "This little incident could ruin our reputation. Devastate us. What are we going to do? Can't have people believing our place of business would employ girls who were thieves. Don't know how to find her. The little gal never gave us a name. Poor *wee* lass couldn't speak."

"That's Halsey's business. Cutthroats along with whores. He pimps everything out. His girls seldom last more than a few years. He rides them hard, uses them up real fast. When you dared to talk with the man, thought he might have some clue as to the name of the girl. When the lass was mentioned, he got this gleam in his eyes. Thought then and there he was lying through his teeth." Angus stood at the back door staring out at the waning light of the day. "Remember when I heard her pounding on the door begging for help. The little gal was frantic to get away from that man. Of course, at the time she didn't know what lay in store for her with Halsey."

"Halsey didn't know the girl's name either. Hoped when you lugged him over here, he could give us some type of clue about the lass. Nothing. Think he's lying. I'd wager the man knows more than he's telling us. He had a flicker in his eyes." Hannah repeated her earlier sentiments about the encounter. She set the tip of her finger on her chin. "Yes, Halsey had that look in his eyes when he's after something or someone. He was after the girl for a specific reason. The question is why. Other than he needed a fresh new face in his stable. I'll wager there is something else behind his infatuation with this particular young lady."

"Told us he rescued her from the hands of two seamen. Rough sort…she ran right into him. Landed on her little butt right at his feet. Seems pretty convenient to me. Mumbled something about a monogramed handkerchief. What could that be about?" Angus asked as he turned back to Hannah.

"She didn't leave anything behind as a clue. Who the hell is she? The rich sometimes go on scavenger hunts. A way of playing with each other. A monogramed handkerchief might be what she was after when she strayed into the wrong part of the city. She must have been lost." Hannah was pacing the tight confines of her little office. There are only a few blocks between the better part of town and this district. Might have been possible for her to wander here without knowing where she was.

Hannah couldn't afford anything to happen to her business. She fought to keep her girls safe from men like Halsey. Struggled to make certain all the ladies in this house were taken care of. Saint was on a retainer. He doctored the ladies if they were abused. Delivered their babies when their precautions didn't play out. She tried never to allow a man to abuse the women she employed. Angus helped her see to that. Oh, abuse happened once in a while. The abusers were never allowed back in her front door. She always made certain Saint saw to the injured gals.

"Why would the girl steal Fox's money? To me that's the bigger question. A brown satchel could not have been on the list for her game. Fox told us he gave her brandy. The drink mixed with the laudanum she gave her would have left her mind muddled. She might not have known what she was doing. Do you think that's possible?"

"Anything is possible. The lass wasn't feeling up to snuff. Could it be conceivable she didn't know what was in the bag? Maybe thought the satchel was hers?" Hannah asked, feeling more than puzzled by the missing bag, rehashing all she recalled from the night before. She felt as if she grasped at straws.

"When she opens it, she will return it here or send it with a messenger. Would hope the girl has enough common sense not to bring it herself."

The girl was a mystery. One she'd love to solve.

Chapter Two

Six weeks later, Fannie felt much better. She could speak now without a rasp in her voice, though she was still a bit hoarse. She didn't recall all the details from the night she lost her innocence. Some of what she did remember was horrible. She did something she could never forgive herself doing. Waiting until marriage to be with a man in that way, was what she planned. There were also bits and pieces of the night that were missing. She recalled everything that happened before she reached Hannah's establishment. It was after Hannah brought her to her room where she had memory lapses.

Yes, six weeks passed. Seemed Jasper had guests for dinner several times over that period. She never went down to dinner on those evenings. She didn't wish to meet anyone new, though Maggie told her there were hopes either Nellie or herself would find the son a fitting companion. A companion…a fancy word for beau. Behind closed doors, she heard talk of an engagement. How could she ever explain her loss of virginity to a man who might want her?

When she looked at the oversized chair Nellie was sitting in next to her, she wished she could find some place to hide. Wished she could erase the nightmare. She knew she'd been intimate with a man…more than once. The devil, too many holes in her brain existed from the evening in question. Empty spots she couldn't account for. When she woke early the next morning cuddled next to a man she'd never seen before that night, she didn't know what to do. Her mind was still hazy, though clearer than the last time…

He told me to say 'ah'… Like a fool I opened my mouth for him. As if I was being…he chuckled. He thought what I did was funny. Maybe he didn't ask me…he did wish for me to open my mouth. He put his tongue inside me…among other…things.

Doctors did the same. Needed to look at their patient's throats. They

36

asked them to say ah so they could see the throat better.

He touched his tongue to mine. Sucked mine into his mouth.

When he did suck on her, Fannie liked the warm vibrant sensations filling all of her, smothering her with an urgency she didn't understand.

He put his head on my chest…my naked chest. Rubbed his palm as well as his face across the tips of my breasts. He kissed me there on my nipples.

Doctors did the same too. They needed to listen to the heart along with the lungs. They didn't kiss their patient's breasts. When he did, her body seemed to hum to life, ached in the most delicious places. She wanted him to kiss her again then another time. Didn't want him to stop.

No, doctors didn't kiss the tips of their patients' breasts or touch them in the most intimate place imaginable.

This man put his sex inside me. Twice. I let him. He made me feel the most incredible sensations imaginable. I was so hot. I thought I would go up in flames. Hotter than the sun. Hotter than anything imaginable. Was there anything hotter than the sun? Maybe the center of the earth?

She was a befuddled mess. Been the same way going on six weeks. When she looked at her sister, she saw her lips moving. Nellie was chattering on and on, no doubt about something inconsequential. Didn't she sense her distress? No, Fannie didn't want Nellie asking questions she didn't want to answer. Didn't wish to recount the scene from Hannah's bordello. Couldn't tell her about her doctor who had the strangest bedside manner imaginable. She understood she needed to dismiss her thoughts about this man. She didn't know his name. Never asked.

Couldn't.

Not after what they'd done together.

The devil he was handsome.

The madam told me I'd be safe with her. She lied to me. I wasn't safe from the doctor. No, he isn't a doctor. I don't even know his name, this man who took my innocence. He called me a virgin whore. He expected me to do his bidding. Laughed when I didn't understand what he wanted.

Fannie thought she might have brought something with her from the whorehouse. Couldn't remember if the notion was her imagination or not. The entire evening was a nightmare. First, the seamen who attacked her, then the other man who wanted her to get in the carriage with him. He was pure evil. If she did bring something with her, she didn't know where it was. Whatever it was, it would need to be in her room. She looked every day. There was nothing different or out of place. That was part of the problem. She didn't remember what this object was. If she remembered, she might be able to find it. She would return whatever it was to the brothel.

When she woke after the first time, he… dear lord. She found herself sprawled on top of him. His legs were hairy as was his chest. She recalled the way his golden fox eyes grew darker after he kissed her. The second time he put her hand on him…on his. She touched him. He was hard and very hot. She felt as if she caressed satin.

Her fake doctor put his tongue inside her mouth. Yes, then pulled hers inside his. The vivid scene would never leave her mind. That wasn't all he did with his tongue. He licked her belly then lower. Her stomach quivered when he nipped there, she shuddered then arched against him.

Fannie groaned. Looked up to see if her sister heard the small noise. Nellie still chattered on and on about the scavenger hunt. The game she'd not wished to play. The folly that got her into a wealth of trouble. She talked about her new beau, Dillon. During the game, they had been so involved with each other, the two forgot about her. They left her on her own. Nellie had been with this young man longer than usual. She held tender feelings for him.

That wasn't the worst part of the night. Again, her mind went back to the beginning of her troubles. With thoughts of the two burly seamen, she shuddered. One touched her breast. Didn't feel the same as when her doctor touched her there. Halsey was worse though. He was a pretty faced snake. She never found out what his plans for her were. Recalled thinking she saw her mother inside his carriage. The idea was ridiculous. The cold must have been messing with her head.

Hannah told her she would keep her safe. She didn't. No one kept her safe.

How did she end up wandering into that dangerous part of the city? Oh, she remembered. It was the damn monogramed handkerchief. Fannie tried to bring her focus back to Nellie and the words she was spouting. She fixated on her sister's mouth. Found herself reminded about her doctor's lips.

They were soft…firm. She enjoyed the way they felt on hers…on other parts of her.

He gave me brandy. The drink was warm…very soothing. I'm not ever going to drink brandy again. Never. Never ever!

As was their usual habits, the sisters spent time before dinner talking over the day's events. Most of the evenings, Tessa along with Maggie joined them. Tonight was different. Jasper invited guests to dine with the family. The two men had been here several times before. Jasper ate with them at their home. Fannie didn't feel up to dining with guests, with men she didn't know. With a deep breath of air settling inside her lungs, she vowed to make her apologies again, then ask for dinner in her room. She would have Nellie tell Jasper she didn't feel like meeting anyone new. As usual when she declined to meet these guests, Maggie would wonder what was wrong. Would come to speak with her.

"Maggie told us these men were most likely to become business partners to the Kenworthy's," Nellie said as she sipped her tea. "That's why they have been dining with us so many times. The son is handsome as sin." Nellie didn't need to find another beau. She had Dillon. "Dillon is coming to dinner also."

"Too old," Fannie muttered while thinking of the man who took her innocence. He was so very handsome he stole her breath. His large body blanketed hers when he came inside. The weight of him warmed her soul. He filled her with himself. She didn't know if she could call what they did making love. He was sweet. Told her the pain she felt this time would never happen again. He must have guessed they would do it a second time. If she stayed, would they have done it a third time?

She remembered the coupling. A soft moaning sound rippled from the back of her throat. She cried out when her body fragmented into tiny shards of pleasure. At the time, she'd felt swollen and wet. Before that evening, she never knew anything like those sensations existed. Tessa told her lovemaking with her husband was nice. This was more than nice. What she felt went beyond description. Remembering, her body shuddered.

Nellie looked at her with a strange expression marring her features. She touched the tip of her finger to her chin then tapped. "Fannie? Whatever is wrong with you? Are you sick again? It's not like you to be sick." Nellie reached over to place her hand on her forehead. "Cool to the touch." She sat back, her arms crossed beneath her breasts, pushing them upward. "No fever. Why were you moaning? The sounds you were making…? They sounded quite remarkable…as if you were enjoying something decadent."

Fannie waved her hand in the air in an attempt to dismiss Nellie's thoughts. With her outrageous words, heat rushed to her face slithering downward to reach her toes. "Nothing is wrong with me that a good night of sleep won't cure. I haven't been sleeping well. Not engrossed in the business interests of Jasper or Jason or these other fellows. Don't wish to eat dinner tonight with three people I've never met. I'm going to stay in my room or…," Fannie mumbled, while her thoughts were still centered on the night she spent in the brothel coupled with the man who stole her innocence. While she didn't wish to think about the evening, she couldn't help herself. There was so much at stake. If she wasn't pregnant, she would never need to mention the unfortunate incident to anyone. "Believe I'll catch up on some of my reading. A good gothic romance will fill the bill. One of those where the heroine faints in just about every scene. I'll have cook send my dinner to the library. Need to be alone tonight with my thoughts."

"You should meet these people. Would do you a world of good. Since Tessa and Jason married, you've been too reserved. Maggie thinks the younger gentleman is handsome also. Would make a fine catch for some lucky girl. They are father and son. His name is Fox. Quite the unusual name. Don't you think?" Nellie seemed to be waiting with heightened expectations for a response.

"Can't trust a fox. They are wily devils. Can't trust men. They are cut from the same cloth," Fannie shot the statement toward her sister. Nellie could decide for herself what to make of her words. After her debacle that night, trust was not something she would ease into with any man. She never quite understood why the unknown man came to her room, expecting to make love to her. She didn't work for Hannah. Didn't the man understand?

"That way of thinking is jaded. You're too young to distrust all men," Nellie returned, a frown creasing her forehead her lips thinned. "I'm not planning on giving the man my innocence, not even Dillon, unless there is a proposal along with a wedding. Would never trust a man in that sense. As you mentioned, they are all wily. Even Jasper along with Jason, found ways to bring our sisters to partake in their wishes. We both learned Maggie succumbed before the wedding. No one knows about Tessa. Suppose it's none of our business."

Yes, she was drowning in her mind. She was way over her head in deep water…deep, deep water. There were consequences to what she did. There were no precautions taken. Maggie told them about precautions. She was afraid of the results of that night. Had to wait a little longer to make certain of the truth. She crossed her fingers. Would cross her toes if doing so was possible. If she were…how would she explain her condition to her family? How could she face them?

Oh, it's nothing. I spent a night in a brothel with a man I don't know. Thought the man was a doctor, visiting to take a look at my throat. Turns out he was one of Hannah's customers. He believed I was his whore for the evening…bought as well as paid for. Her sisters would send her to Bedlam. Maybe that night was just her wild imagination playing havoc with her befuddled senses doped on laudanum. Perhaps this was her worst nightmare playing out and nothing she remembered was true. Maybe everything was true. She didn't want to play this reality game.

While Maggie along with Tessa had been truly innocent, both sisters made certain she and Nellie understood how a girl became enceinte. Taught them the time of the month when conception was most likely to happen. Fannie groaned again. The time couldn't have been more perfect. A profound sixth sense told her she didn't stand a chance of winning this waiting game. She was carrying this unknown man's child. The babe would be a bastard…just like her. Wincing with unforgivable shame, she didn't want her baby to be fatherless. Not only would the child not know his father's name, neither would she. Her stomach twisted in knots. It was a condition her stomach had been in for weeks, six weeks to be precise. Her life foreshadowed her child's. Moisture filled her eyes. She needed to be strong…strong for both of them.

What to do?

The night in question, she rushed home, her heart pounding so fast she couldn't breathe. The hack she hired brought her straight to the front porch. When she undressed, she saw the blood on the inside of her thighs along with his seed. Her chemise as well as her pantalets were stained. She threw her undergarments into the fire. Watched them go up in flames then scrubbed herself clean. Understood she could not wash anything away from her head. Could never make the night vanish. The nightmare remained to haunt her waking thoughts as well as ghost her dreams each night, even into the daytime.

She vowed she would never take laudanum coupled with brandy again in her life. She'd been so muddle-headed she thought the man was a physician. Had done everything he suggested. Thought he was in her room to help her. The doctor's name was Saint. Fannie thought that was a strange name for a man to have. Hannah told her he would come to see her. Instead of the doctor, she must have been given a client.

Why?

Hannah told me the doctor would visit. What was I to think? When a man appeared in my room…? Believed he was there to check out my sore throat. Didn't imagine he had nefarious purposes. He didn't because he believed she was a working girl. The man paid for her virginity.

Your fake doctor watched you take a bath. You were naked. Didn't protest that invasion of privacy. He kissed you. Don't deny the fact, you liked what he did. Touched you where you could never have imagined. No doctor you have ever seen has kissed you. He brushed his lips across hers. Set his hand on her naked belly. Did other things too. All of which she enjoyed. Thinking about those pleasures sent more heat rushing to her face. Blood pounded in her ears just as it had when he was kissing her. Could she never stop blushing?

"Fannie?" Nellie's voice floated around her. Sucked her down farther into her morbid depression of thoughts. She looked up to see concern written all over her sister's face. "Fannie, where are you? What have you been thinking that has made you blush with what must be embarrassment. Something happened you're not telling me about. We share everything." She was waving her hands in the air. "Come back to earth before…well I don't know what I mean. Your mind seems to be flying among the stars."

This wasn't something she would share with anyone. All she wished for now was to melt into the woodwork. Sink so far away she wouldn't need to come up for air. Mortified that her sister recognized her embarrassment. "What? Oh?" Fannie was disillusioned by all that happened. She looked at her sister with an accusing glare. Shook her finger at her, meaning to throw the blame in Nellie's direction. "It was all your fault. You know that, right? All this is your fault!"

Nellie blinked a few times clearly confused by her statements. "Me? Fault?" Nellie placed her hands on her chest. "My fault? I don't understand. Don't know what you are talking about. You haven't been in this conversation from the very beginning. You've had this dazed expression on your face. Where are you? What are you thinking?"

"You went off with your friend…what's his name…Dillon. Paid no attention to me. Sent me to find a monogramed handkerchief. I didn't want to be there with either of you." Fannie closed her eyes, inhaling the perfumed scents in the room. This was not well done of her. Neither was what Nellie did to her in order to pursue her new beau. She, along with her admirer, left her alone to fend for herself. "Didn't want to play that stupid game of yours. I was by myself. A monogramed handkerchief…no one would give me theirs. If they had, it probably would have been used and nasty. A piece of cloth I would never wish to touch." Fannie understood she was being petty. She could have told Nellie a resounding no to participating in the ridiculous child's game. Nellie always had this way of sucking her into her plans, even when she'd rather be home sipping hot chocolate and reading one of her romance novels.

"Dillon, my friends name is Dillon Montrose. Yes, we wished to be alone. You knew that. You're just being obtuse. He's charming as well as sweet. Didn't know you were so…" Nellie threw up her hands in what appeared to be frustration. "Didn't know you were so miserable that evening. You should have said something. We would have figured out some way to be by ourselves. I need to get to know that man better. Believe I'm in love with him."

"You think you're in love with every new man who looks your way. I was sick and I did tell you countless times how I felt about everything." Fannie let out a long breath of air, wishing to be left alone. Even her sister's usual cherished companionship was unwanted.

"Yes, I understand now that you've made your accusations obvious. You don' have to take your misery out on me. You're in a grand pique. If I understood the why of it, I could help out. As it is you are keeping secrets and expect everyone to do your bidding." Nellie rose as if she meant to leave. She smoothed her hands down her skirts Then pointed at her. "I didn't know you were sick. No one did."

"I told you too many times to bother counting that I wished to be home. I didn't feel well. My throat hurt like the very devil," Fannie shot out again, trying to put emphasis on the fact she'd been sick. She wasn't going to feel guilty when her sisters mouth turned down in a pout. One she'd no doubt practiced in front of a mirror. What happened to her would put anyone off their game.

"Are you going down to dinner?" Nellie asked as she stepped toward the door. "It is time. Heard the bell ring to announce our guests. Jasper will expect us. They will be sipping pre-dinner drinks in the parlor. From the way you are acting, you could use a drink. Maggie won't be pleased if you refuse another time."

"No. Don't wish to be with anyone this evening. I'm not in the mood to carry on chatter that means nothing. Not in the mood to meet people I'll never wish to see again. Just not in the mood," Fannie finished on a sour note. "This is a prime example of how you never listen. I told you earlier I would have my dinner sent to the library."

"Very well, suit yourself. I'll tell Maggie you want to be alone with your thoughts. Again. Won't tell her the other part." Nellie gave a little hrmpf of annoyance before she left the room. The door closed with a soft snick.

Fannie wished she could close her mind the same way, shut everything out. Ah, well…this doctor who wasn't a doctor could go to the devil. What would she do if she ever saw the man again? She wouldn't. There was no way they would ever run into each other a second time. He was in her past. Forging ahead was all she could do now. If she was pregnant from that night, she would deal with the consequences. When Anice, her mother, discovered her truth, she would laugh, cast aspersion to her character. Might even suggest her as a mistress to Lord Abernathy. No, she wouldn't dare bring that man up again. Her mother had attempted to wed both Maggie and Tessa to the horrible male. Failed in both attempts. Jasper along with Jason would protect her. Maybe she could move to another country. She heard the United States was huge. She might be able to lose herself there. Could say the father died a tragic death.

If you did that, moved, you wouldn't have anyone to help you. Your sisters would still be here in Glasgow.

No, moving was not the solution to her problems. Fannie needed her family around her. She set her hands on the flatness of her belly. Prayed there was no baby. Unless there was something wrong with her and she couldn't conceive, her prayers would go unanswered. She'd missed her time.

Still in a stupor, misery surrounding her, Fannie walked to the library. The room was her favorite place in the Kenworthy home. She thought there must be more books here than one could read in a lifetime. Climbing the ladder she perused the readable material. Found a gothic romance she'd not read that looked interesting. The story line would be titillating. Maybe she didn't need anything stimulating. No, she'd rather find herself lost in someone else's romance than in her nightmares.

Her dinner arrived, along with Maggie, who sent her a look that clearly stated she should tell her what was bothering her. Wasn't going to do what she silently pleaded until she was certain about the baby. Maggie placed the tray on the table next to the big wing chair she decided would be most comfortable. After kicking off her shoes, Fannie pulled a blanket over her then tucked her feet beneath her. Fannie sent Maggie a look that said leave me alone. Don't ask me questions. I'm not in the right frame of mind to talk.

Maggie ignored her. "Are you feeling better? Nellie says you were acting strange. Told me you moaned. You're not sick again. Do you want to tell me what's bothering you?" Maggie asked, stepping back to study her. "Your face is still pale. Looks as if you've seen a ghost. Remember we sisters have always shared everything. We stick together, through thick and thin. No one can help if we don't understand the difficulty. Did mother do something?"

Nellie reminded her of her mother too. "No, there is nothing to talk about. To my knowledge mother hasn't done anything, at least not in the recent past." There might be a little something to talk about in another eight months or so. She would need to figure out her life before that time happened. Would need to make plans. She felt terrified at the thought of becoming a mother without a husband. Anice would laugh in her face. She would point her shaking finger at her then call her a whore.

A virgin whore. Did those exist? In her case, yes.

Maggie sat down in the opposite chair. Fiddled with a curling strand of hair that framed her face. Looked from the tray to her. She was obviously trying to think of something to say. "Since that evening six weeks ago when you were so sick, you haven't been yourself. You never come to dinner when we have guests." She held up her hands. "I understand you were not feeling well. But now…now you are no longer sick. Though you are still pale. You've not left the house in those weeks either. Fresh air would do you wonders."

"I'm just…" Fannie lifted her shoulders in a gesture that would tell her sister to not be concerned. "Tired. Don't know what to do with myself. You along with Tessa are married ladies. Nellie has a beau who she will no doubt marry. I haven't met anyone I'm interested in getting to know better." If she looked inside herself, her comment was a lie. She thought she might like to get to know her no-name man better. Good God, how much better did she wish to know him? Maybe she'd like to learn his name. What would she do if she learned his name? He had sex with a whore not a potential wife.

Maggie leaned over to pat her hand on top of hers. She sat back, a frown on her face. "That isn't what is bothering you. When you want to talk, let me know. I will be here as will your other sisters. You forget all four of us have been each other's sounding board for years. We've talked about you and we've come to the decision you are not yourself. Something happened that you are keeping from us. Believe whatever it was occurred the night of the scavenger hunt. Am I right?"

Fannie was tired of finding herself studied by her sisters. Scrutinized by them. Wished to be left alone with reliving her nightmare. Whatever hunger she felt earlier, vanished. She needed to reassure Maggie so the questions would cease. "I'm fine…truly I'm fine. Go enjoy your guests along with the delicious dinner cook prepared. The roast smells wonderful along with the baby potatoes in the butter sauce. Are those mushrooms in the wine sauce? One of my favorites. There is no need for you to be concerned about me. Just been feeling a bit of the doldrums lately. Feeling sorry for myself and all." Fannie asked about the food hoping to change the subject of her sister's scrutiny. Then she gave Maggie more things for her to analyze.

If Maggie kept questioning, she was more than likely to tell her all about what happened to her. About her doctor, the man who in one night changed her life forever. Maggie had this way about her that would draw out confessions. She forked a piece of the roast, chewed for a few seconds debating what she wanted to say. Nothing, was what came to her mind. This was all too new as well as private to her.

Maggie's fingers drummed on the arm of the chair making a soft sound. "Suppose I need to get back to Jasper along with our guests. The young man, Fox is his name, is a handsome devil. Not as handsome as Jasper. You should come speak with him. Perhaps you would be interested in him. You said you haven't met anyone. Fox might be the man for you. One never knows."

"Don't wish to speak with anyone right now." Heat rose to her face. With her pending pregnancy, getting to know another man was impossible. Didn't wish to explain to a man on her wedding night her virginity was lost in a whorehouse. "Except my sisters," she was quick to point out so as not to offend the oldest sibling. Fannie found she was holding her breath waiting for Maggie to get bored enough to leave.

"The men are wealthy. The father owns a few ships that sail to the States as well as other places. He has other investments. Wants a wealthy partner to invest in the shipping line. Seems Jasper is interested. His son owns a timber camp in Michigan Territory. While I knew Michigan was in the States, I had to ask where it was."

Alright, she would play into Maggie's hands. "Where is Michigan?" She flipped the pages of the romance novel she selected. Wished she could give better hints to her sister that she wished to be left alone in her unhappiness.

"In the Midwest…not that far, far west but it's situated in country where few people live. Fox said the land was rugged, freezing in the winters, hot during the summers. Sometimes snow fell so hard the drifts at times would cover the window, reaching the roofs of single floor dwellings. Told us how he loved the land."

"Sounds miserable…" almost as miserable as she felt. "Who would wish to live in a land that harsh? He must be either stupid or foolish." Wrapping her arms around herself, Fannie shivered. Felt cold wash through her all the way to the tips of her toes.

"Fox says when spring comes and all the snow is melted, beautiful wildflowers bloom in the fields. He makes his living cutting the timber, sending the trees downriver to sawmills." Nellie had this way of droning on about things no one cared about. Maggie didn't. So why was she being such a bore now? It was beyond the pale.

"Sounds nice." Fannie plucked at her skirt, watching the material rise then fall. Beneath her gown, she curled her toes. A long puff of desperate air shuffled from her lips. She couldn't stop thinking about her problems.

"You should meet him. Truly, he might be interested in you and you him." Maggie paused once more, her gaze traveling to her face. She let out what sounded to Fannie as a disgusted puff of air. For a beat she turned her attention away. Resigned, she began, "So, if you are not coming down for dinner, I'll leave you to your musings and the full bottle of wine. Seems you wish to wallow in something. Dillon is here tonight too. Do you think Nellie is truly interested in the young man?"

Fannie lifted her shoulders in what was meant to be an indifferent shrug. The two left her with no means to return home just so they could be alone together. At this point in time, she resented both of them. Blamed them for her troubles. "Seems to be. They left me alone and defenseless so they could be by themselves," her voice bitter, Fannie understood she needed to get over her pique. At the moment, she thought irritation at her sister was the exact right way to feel. She already established to her satisfaction; Nellie was the source of all her problems. She could put the blame for her pending pregnancy squarely on her sister's shoulders.

"If you change your mind, you could join us after we eat. I'm certain Fox would enjoy getting to know you. He's a pleasant young man…a gentleman. The two of you would make a dashing couple." It didn't seem Maggie wished to leave. She kept talking, spouting Fox's virtues. "Your blond hair and fair complexion next to his dark hair is a nice contrast. He's still sporting a summer tan even though he has been here for about two months. We've never kept secrets. Now…" Maggie paused, her lips thinning as she seemed to be trying to think of something more to say. "Believe you're keeping a big one…secret. Wouldn't hurt to tell me. This secret you are keeping…doesn't have anything to do with mother, does it? Has Anice dipped her hand into your life. We both comprehend what she did to Tessa. Don't trust the woman. Is she holding something over your head?"

Yes, I am keeping a secret, and as soon as this guest of the Kenworthy's discovers I'm carrying a baby in my womb, he will flee in the opposite direction. No man would want a relationship with a woman who lost her virginity in a whorehouse. He wouldn't have to know that part. Could pretend I was raped. Could have been, except I got lucky. Hah! There was no luck involved. I wrestled myself out of two scrapes to find myself enduring a third. "Nothing to do with mother," Fannie told her in all honesty. "Mother has no hold over me."

A virgin whore no longer.

If I'm pregnant, my child will be a bastard...just like me. Fannie cringed at the horrible thought. Nothing to do about the circumstance she found herself in now. She was positive she carried that unknown man's child. It had been six weeks since their encounter. She was never late.

Moisture blossomed in her eyes, stinging the back of her throat. She turned away from Maggie who hovered at the door to the library as if she could say something more that would help her realize she should meet this young man. There was nothing more to be said. Seemed they both understood that for a fact.

Fannie felt empty, void of emotions other than despair. She had no idea how to proceed with her life.

"If you are bent on this course, I'll leave you alone. Please remember you can come to me anytime. Whatever has happened, promise I won't judge."

Fannie nodded, staring at the fire, small flames burning with color against the blackened wood. She heard the door close as Maggie exited. Felt the silence in the room, the loneliness, fingers reaching out to suck her into a path she couldn't change.

There was a pain in her heart. Fannie rested her hand on her flat belly. Nothing except a few embers popping could be heard. She let her head fall back against the chair. Listened to the beating of her heart. The big grandfather clock in the hallway chimed eight times. She heard the chattering of two maids as they walked down the hall. Couldn't make out what they were saying. Didn't care.

She drank the glass of wine that her sister brought with the tray of food, eying the bottle while thinking it might not be prudent to drink all of it. No, she needed to drown her sorrows using the rest of the bottle. Fannie shut her eyes. She must have dozed. She woke to the sound of bootsteps. A shadow loomed above her for a few seconds. A sizzle of fear simmered along her spine. Who was this man? One of the guests?

This person must not know she was in the room. He was looking at the array of books on the vast shelves. He held his hands behind his back. His broad shoulder narrowed to trim hips. He selected one then sat down across the room from her. The big chair looked out on the gardens. All she could see now was his profile. As he thumbed through the pages, he looked up. She sucked a bite of air, certain he must have seen her. He went back to flipping through the pages. She let out a tiny sigh of relief, understanding this was not a good situation. Being alone with a man again didn't bode well for her.

While Fannie watched him, he didn't seem to be reading. For some reason she was curious about this male person. Felt somehow drawn to him. With the large chair facing the window, she couldn't make out his features. What she could see of him, reminded her of someone. A man she didn't wish to remember.

She couldn't possibly know this person. Must be the son. What the devil was he doing in the library? Fannie was told this was a business meeting. Wouldn't he be meeting with Jasper and Jason?

If he was from this faraway place, maybe he didn't care about business. Michigan, that's what Maggie told her. The place was somewhere in the United States.

As if he heard something, his head jerked up. His gaze bored into hers. With instant clarity, she recognized him. Fear wracked her body.

"You!" They cried in unison.

~ * ~

Fox lost interest in the dinner conversation before the second serving. The girl, Nellie, chatted nonstop with her beau. Dillon was his name. Jasper and his father were immersed in the conversation about the products they would ship. Maggie remained quiet as did Tessa as if they were content to watch the proceedings. He didn't have anything to add. Both women upon occasion contributed to Nellie's conversation with the young man she was entertaining. Fox was certain those two were in dire need of a chaperone. Dillon held the young lady's hand beneath the table. He wondered upon occasion what other shenanigans were going on where no one could see.

Maggie frowned at Nellie when she made a startled gasp. Nellie closed her eyes as if she was in the moment of an orgasm. Those two should not be carrying on at the dinner table. Both Jasper, along with Jason, seemed oblivious. One of the sisters should speak up.

Fox needed to get away. Since his horrible night at Hannah's, he'd not been with a woman. He'd been celibate for six damn weeks. For some reason Fox couldn't fathom, he couldn't get the little thief out of his head. His very own virgin whore. He saw her naked standing in the bathtub water slowly dripping down her body. Watched a drop form on the tip of her nipple. Saw her eyes when she climaxed her first time. There was so much more he recalled with vivid clarity. Felt his body swelling with the images.

He felt like a fish out of water. That's what he was, a fish out of water. Only now, he was a timber baron too far away from his spread to feel comfort in these surroundings. Loathed cities. He was out of his element. Unused to formal dinners with business partners. That wasn't true. He could talk business with the best men. Most of his business dealings were in a saloon or sitting around a campfire. Wanting to, then doing it, were two different things. He would rather talk about timber. Speak about the best places to sell as well as how to get the logs to market. New inventions that helped deliver the logs in a more timely fashion were also at the top of his list to discuss.

With his father scowling at him, he excused himself. If he needed to stay here any longer, he would find himself pulling out his hair with frustration. "With your permission, I would like to go to the library. Need to be alone with my thoughts. Father, you don't need me. The two of you seem to have everything well in hand. Have nothing legitimate to add to the conversation. Do you mind?" He looked around the table. "If all of you will excuse me, I'll take my leave. Let me know when you're ready to return home." He pushed out his chair as he stood then set his napkin on the table.

Maggie's hand started to rise as if she meant to stop him, then her fingers dropped to the table. Her lips pinched together in a face that might have made him laugh in another time. Her smile didn't go unnoticed but he didn't know what to make of her expression. For a few seconds, he thought she meant to say something to him.

"You should stay," Beryl put her voice into the mix. She set her hand on top of his, rubbing her palm against the top of his hand. "Don't go just yet. We will miss your company." She batted her dark lashes. Beryl was an attractive woman. He didn't care any longer. She made her choice for a husband. The man wasn't him. Now that the choice had been made, a heavy burden was lifted from his shoulders. Fox didn't think he ever loved her. Infatuation, lust, were both possible emotions. She had this way about her.

He felt the coldness of her hand. If the gesture was meant to keep him in the dining room, it was doing the exact opposite. The sooner he left, the better he would feel. Fox didn't like being in her company. He always felt trapped.

His father cleared his voice then addressed Beryl. There was a sultry twinkle in his eye, a smile parting his lips. "No, there is no need for my son to remain here. Fox and I can hash over any pertinent information tomorrow at work. Make decisions. Let the boy have some alone time if that's what he needs. The Lord knows I've kept him busy these last six weeks since he decided to go to work for me. Hasn't had a moment to himself. Yes, he was willing to work from dawn to dusk if that's what it took to get back to Michigan sooner. I've put him through his paces. By the time he leaves Glasgow, he will be ready for a vacation."

"I'll keep you company. The man doesn't truly wish to be alone." Appearing to ignore Jake's advice, Beryl set her napkin on the table then started to rise. "I'm certain the two of us can find a great deal to speak about in the library. We have unfinished business as you well know," she directed her words to Jake.

"No! Never!" His voice was harsher than expected. His breath caught in the back of his throat while his stomach twisted. The last person he needed with him was Beryl. If she accompanied him, she would rub herself all over him, push her voluminous breasts against his chest. Would try to get him to kiss her. She was a notorious flirt. He would have to fight her off if she behaved in the normal fashion around him. His father should keep his wife under lock and key. Beryl was a danger to all mankind.

Sensing his distress, Maggie rose then flashed a brilliant smile in

Beryl's direction. "Come." With a twinkle of mischief in her eyes, Maggie linked her arm through Beryl's. The command was clear. She grinned at him as if she knew some deep, dark secret. Perhaps she did. Maybe she sized up his stepmother within the short amount of time. "We must give the man some breathing space. Let's go have a cup of tea in the drawing room while we wait for our men folk to finish their brandy in the other room. Do you play the pianoforte? I wouldn't mind some music."

Fox almost hooted his laughter at the face Beryl made. She'd been done in by Jasper's sweet Maggie. Her cannons snuffed out before she could fire them in Fox's direction. If Maggie had not intervened, there was no doubt in his mind Beryl would have accompanied him to the library. If she did, Fox would have walked out the door then hailed a cab. He wasn't about to be cornered by that man-eating woman. He was in no fitting mood to be with anyone, especially Beryl. If those fifty thousand pounds had not been stolen, he would have boarded a ship to New York harbor six weeks ago. Instead, he was relegated to business duty, something he loathed along with Beryl's flirts. In truth, if he still had the money, he might have remained a few more days. Though he did need to get home.

Fox missed the serenity of his land coupled with the danger. No day was the same. Every time he closed his eyes, he saw the aspens moving with the wind as the breeze swept down the mountains to the valley below. He heard the pine trees whispering in the breeze. Embracing the scents coupled with the sounds exhilarated all his senses. By the time he returned, the snow would be melted from the valleys. All that would remain of the white stuff would be in the higher mountain passes. The streams would be rushing down the mountains filled with snow melt. Fox breathed in deep, wishing it was the cold Michigan air filling his nostrils.

He walked past two maids who were chattering on about something. When he reached the door to the library, he hesitated for a few seconds. His father would send for him when he was ready to leave. For now, he would entertain his thoughts, redirecting his energy to what was most important for him. Thought about his virgin whore. Who the hell was she? Why did she steal the money? Neither Hannah or Angus believed her a thief. If not, who then? The two insisted no one in the house would have stolen anything. To his knowledge, no person entered the room while he was there. He supposed she could have had an accomplice of some sort. Perhaps a man visiting the brothel. Neither would have known what he carried in the satchel. Nothing made sense.

Letting out a deep breath of air, he set his hand on the knob then turned. The door opened in silence. He stepped inside. He caught a thin whisp of lavender on the air. There was a play of light from the hallway into the library. His shadow was cast across the floor. A lamp burned on a table near one of the large wing chairs, manufacturing a warm glow throughout the library. A large window overlooked what must be the gardens. As per everything about this townhouse and the Kenworthy's the gardens would be meticulously maintained.

He smiled at the floor to ceiling shelves of books. This was a man's domain. He could relax here. Decided he needed to increase the size of his library. For a few seconds he directed his attention at the fire in the grate. It had been tended to recently, flames leaping in a colorful display of reds and golds. At the window overlooking the garden he paused to look outside. His hands behind his back, he rocked on his heels. He wondered what kind of romantic trysts went on in the gazebo he saw down the lighted path.

The pathway his gaze followed was lit with lanterns. The trail led to that same gazebo. The twins were enamored of their wives. He supposed the summerhouse would be a trysting place for them. This home was beautiful, well-tended inside as well as out. He wouldn't expect anything different from the Kenworthy twins. He'd been a bit surprised when both were in residence having heard the younger twin, Jason, spent most of his time with his young wife at the country estate. There was quite the age difference between husband and wife. What did age matter if the two were in love? His father was much older than his wife. The difference was even greater between them than Jason and Tessa.

There was another sister he'd not met yet. Fannie, he was told was her name. He liked the thought of her name. Fannie…he mused. Wondered if she was as lovely as her three sisters. Ah, he doubted if he'd discover that truth. She didn't seem to wish to have anything to do with the dinners. What difference would meeting her make?

One way or the other, he meant to be home by the beginning of summer even if he needed to borrow money from his father. His father insinuated he would give him the funds if he wed. His father wished for him to marry one of the sisters. Told him a marriage would cement their partnership. While he wished for a family, he wasn't about to marry some Scottish chit who would clamor to remain in Scotland. One who was not strong enough to survive the harsh climate of the land where he lived.

A wife.

Yes, Jake insisted he would give him the fifty thousand pounds if he wed a woman from this country. The old man believed he would have stronger reasons to return to Scotland. He didn't think a city bred girl would survive in Michigan. The mountains could be dangerous. She would never understand the hazards.

What his father didn't understand was that his timber company couldn't be left alone for long periods of time. His business would never survive or thrive if he made yearly trips to Glasgow. He did employ good men. The fact remained it was his home as well as his responsibility. His home was where he intended to live. The place where he would bring up his family. Jake could visit him any time he pleased. Could even bring Beryl with him. Beryl detested Michigan. When he left this time, it would be many more years before he returned to Scotland. If and when he sired children, Jake would wish to meet his grandchildren. Fox would never be disappointed with a visit from his father.

Instincts cut into his musing. Sensed he was not alone. Swiveling, searching the room for the small noise he heard, his gaze met a woman sitting in a chair that faced the fireplace. For several seconds, they stared at each other. Her eyes were huge blue pools, long blond hair tumbling around her shoulders. Recognition set in.

"You!"

Hell, it was his virgin whore! He found her. Now he wouldn't need to borrow money from his father. He would shake her until she told him what she'd done with his groats, all fifty thousand pounds of them. His gut tightened with the new prospective. He enjoyed this moment. Soaked in the frightened look on her face. She should be terrified.

His life was about to change for the better. Providence just stepped into his domain with a resounding bang. He was going to get his money back then he was travelling home on the first available ship. Nothing would stop him. He sucked in a deep breath of air before he spoke. "What are you doing here? In the library? If you're a servant, shouldn't you be working…earning your keep? Oh, I forgot, you supplement your wages by working in a brothel as well as stealing." He was pleased the little thief was sloughing off. He would now have the opportunity to question her. If she'd been at work, he might not have run into her.

She paled to the color of new fallen snow. Her chin went up at the accusations he made. The book she'd been reading slipped to the floor with a thud. "I…" The lady moistened her lips. Her soft lips. He recalled how they felt within his mouth. "…live here," she told him a blink. "I-I…" She seemed at a loss for words.

"One of the maids in the Kenworthy's employ? Shouldn't you be working? Doing something besides reading." Fox looked to the title of the book, "This drivel?" his query was made with a sneer to his voice.

Fox watched her bosom heaving. Saw terror take over her features. "No!" With wide frightened eyes, she rushed for the door. Her feet seemed to fly across the floor. She'd had a change of heart. Appeared she didn't relish the confrontation.

Fox wasn't about to let the little thief escape to the hall. Didn't intend to chase after her. He meant to end this fiasco now before his father summoned him to leave.

He was faster. With quick reflexes, he reached out then grabbed her around the waist. Hauled her against his chest. He caught her scent. The aroma left him spellbound as it had done that night six weeks ago. *Little witch. Enchantress.* She understood how to entice. How to gain a man's attention. This little harlot was not going to get away from him ever. He meant to have answers. "No you don't. You've got some explaining to do. I want answers before I let you go." Truth was he wanted to hold her. Felt the need to toss her skirts then experience her soft acceptance of his flesh within her sultry confines. Cursed himself then her. Should haul her down to the police headquarters.

Stiff as the poker by the fireplace, she sat on his lap. His hands on her hips held her to him. Forced her to remain where she didn't wish to be. He saw the terror in her eyes. She should be scared. When she closed her eyes, he thought she would faint. Her breath heaved in uneven gulps.

"D…d…don't t…touch me." She managed to stammer a few words. He meant to touch whenever he damn well pleased.

Couldn't help himself, he grinned at her discomfort. Fox meant to use her fear to work in his favor. Hell, she should be petrified of what he intended after what she'd done. "Seems I've the power here. I'll do what pleases me, not you. No, never you. We can begin where we left off six weeks ago. You left me. Would have enjoyed morning sex with you. We do have now…this moment." He passed his hand across the tip of her breast. Felt the hard nipple he'd tasted, savoring the tip inside his mouth. Remembered her little sighs of pleasure with the heated contact.

"Let…me," she gulped another breath of air. Squirmed against him in a futile attempt to stand. "Go. I don't want to be here. You've no right to keep me in this room." She pushed on his shoulders. They didn't give with the added pressure. "I'll…I will scream."

"…and bring unwanted attention to us? I don't think so." He cupped her breast in the palm of his hand. She wasn't wearing a chemise beneath her gown. With a few flicks of his fingers, he could see as well as feel her breasts again.

Deciding patience was the best route to follow in this endeavor, he refrained from causing her further stress. He settled his hand on her hip. Fox intended to remain calm. It would not be in his favor to show his anger as well as his desire for his little wanton thief. At this time, she was too frantic to give him the response he needed to hear. He saw the rapid beating of her pulse at the base of her neck. Was reminded of a humming bird's wings

"Shall we start at the beginning? That night you must remember when you lost your innocence. Given what transpired, I've a hard time believing you were ever naïve. So," he paused to give her time to catch her breath as well as cool her rattled nerves, "what were you doing at Hannah's?" She tossed him that wide blue-eyed stare that sucked him into her web the first time he saw her. He realized she was either going to lie or not answer.

This encounter she wasn't drugged beyond thought processes. Though he saw she'd been drinking. A half-full bottle of wine sat on the table. Her glass was empty. She would need more if he was going to retrieve information from her closed mind. He splashed more of the wine into the crystal. The siren in front of him was drinking with the best Kenworthy wine inside an expensive crystal glass. "You've got a great deal of nerve, acting as if you owned this place." He handed the full glass to her. "Drink."

"No…" the one word was a thin wail. She was shaking her head, pushing away from him.

Her refusal angered him. Didn't she understand she had no rights here? "If you don't consume this on your own, I'll pour this tasty liquid down your pretty white throat. You might not like that. Seems you didn't have an issue with drinking my brandy while you were seducing me in the damn brothel." Curse her beautiful hide. Fox was fast losing patience. "Drink!" Her eyes glazed over as he set the glass to her lips. Tipped.

Hell, he remembered how soft those lips were, the taste of them. Just like before, she opened her mouth for him. Sipped the wine from the glass. "Put your fingers around the stem. Down the wine. After the wine is gone, we will see if you are more amenable to talking. If not, we can move on to finishing off the bottle. Intend to get answers from you tonight." Fox wanted her to become more compliant. The wine would help. Perhaps another glass or two would aide him in his endeavor for the truth to be told. She drank this one then finished off the second glass he poured for her. He needed her tipsy. A loss of inhibitions would loosen her tongue.

"I don't…" She didn't stutter as much. The words seemed to end there. Finishing a sentence would be nice.

"What you do or don't want doesn't matter to me." This was about what he needed. "What is your name? If I'm going to hand you over to the constables, I would like to have a name for you. Virgin whore won't do, neither will little thief. They would look askance at me." He waited for several beats for her to come clean. "Your name, little thief…or virgin whore, whichever you prefer. I would favor a name. What do people call you besides, virgin whore and thief? I would know."

She was shaking her head. Tendrils of her blond hair were falling loose to tumble around her shoulders. She took a long haul of the third glass he handed her. The bottle was empty. Maybe he needed to move on to something more potent than wine. When she spoke, she wasn't looking at him. Seemed to be staring into the fire. "Fannie…" she whispered on a thin note. "My name is Fannie."

Fox couldn't help the grin or the bark of laughter he didn't hold back.

"Fannie…a fitting name for a whore and a little thief. Remember touching your delicious butt. The soft flesh quivered with need when I fondled you. Tasted your sweetness." He recalled all of her. The lady never complained or told him no. She did everything he asked. He whispered close to her ear. "I think you lie. Your name isn't Fannie. One of the sisters in this house…that's her name. Don't pretend for me. I of all people understand what you are."

Fannie was holding her hand on her chest. Her eyes crossed, beautiful bubbies heaving as she tried to draw air into her lungs. "I don't feel well," she murmured, her voice so thin he needed to lean over to hear the soft-spoken words. "I'm not a whore or a thief. Don't understand what you are talking about…accusing me of. Believed you to be my doctor. Hannah told me I'd be safe there. I wasn't. You took something from me. You sir are the thief. I would hear an apology."

His howl of laughter caused her to stiffen in his arms. "If you give what is mine back to me, I won't turn you over to the police nor will I tell Jasper about your nefarious dealings. Won't tell him how you acted the whore. Though, because you are living here, he should be apprised of your sticky fingers. You do appear to have an affection for the finer things life has to offer." He placed his hand beneath her chin, trailed his thumb across her lips, remembering the feel of her in his arms. "I would need a promise from you. If you can vow never to steal from the Kenworthy's, you will still have this job come tomorrow morning. Of course, I'm certain Hannah would employ you at her brothel. Your skill was impeccable even if it was your first then your second time. I will vouch for your talent as a whore. You might make a great deal of money. Won't need to steal. Heard you ran from Halsey. That was well done of you. The man is a pimp. He would never treat you as well as Hannah. Yes, before I leave Glasgow behind, I will make a point of visiting the brothel with my recommendations."

"You don't understand…" Again, her voice faded into oblivion while she was shaking her head. A lone tear slipped down her cheek. Moisture seemed to clog her throat. "Hannah told me she was sending for a doctor. I got you instead. You're not a doctor, are you?" she accused as if trying to put him on the defensive.

He wasn't going to feel sorry for her ploy even though what she spouted about the doctor was true. "You do realize the consequences of what you've done. I would think you'd be more than willing to hand over that brown satchel you stole from me. I'm positive you don't want to end up in jail. That would not be a good place for you, a woman. I hear women are forced many times by the guards who are employed to protect them. They are raped. Don't wish that for you."

"I'm…" She sent her tongue across her lips. "I'm pre…" The word didn't want to form. She turned her head away from him, rejecting his pleas for the truth.

Fox was afraid he might understand what she was about to say. "What you are is a thief as well as a liar. You won't divert me by telling untruths. I'm not a fool when it comes to women's ploys." The problem…what she thought to tell him could be true. She didn't take a whore's precautions when they had sex that night. A whore would have known how to prevent pregnancy. Being an innocent, this lady most likely didn't know anything about sponges. He didn't withdraw. Before Hannah sent him to her room, she should have educated the girl about prevention.

She was looking at him, her eyes dazed with confusion. "No, I don't have a brown bag. You can search my room. I've not stolen anything from you, sir. Nor would I." She spread her arms. "You can search me."

Mentally, he undressed her as he stared hard at her. He would like nothing better than to strip her to discover the proof of her words. Fox let out a whoosh of air. Stripping her wasn't necessary to see she carried nothing extra beneath her gown. "Good ploy, like the way you flirt with that sweet pink tongue of yours to divert my anger. If you undressed, I could take you here in the Kenworthy library. Would you cry out my name when I give you your pleasure. The temptation of your body is not worth what you stole from me." No, even though he'd enjoyed her passion, her lithe and very delectable little body was not worth fifty thousand pounds. He didn't understand how to pry the truth from her. She kept everything within her charming self.

"I'm not flirting. You are a despicable cad to make such loathsome accusations. I…I don't know your name." She tried to push away from him. He didn't intend to allow distance between them until he had what he wanted. "I hate you. Loathe what you took from me. You had no right to waltz into my room pretending to be a doctor. You pretended to be a saint.

Hah!" She was blasting him with all her cannons. Seemed she was gaining steam. Might be exiting through her tasty little ears.

For all her denials, Fox wanted to both strangle her as well as kiss her senseless. He wanted to feel her beneath him while he pumped into her. Her channel as he remembered it was sweet…tight…hot as hell.

She was delectable. "Little liar, what did you do with my money? Searching your room would prove pointless. I'm positive if the bag was there, you would never have offered me the chance. As for you, we can proceed." He ran his hands along her sides then down her legs. "Not much room for a satchel here." He cupped her little butt in his hands, remembering the feel…the exquisite pleasure. "Where is this bedroom located? Up on the third floor? We could go there for more carnal pleasures. A place where no one would interrupt us. The library is not private." Fox paused. Didn't wish to find himself so sidetracked he forgot his purpose. "So, where is the satchel? Do you have an accomplice? A man, this person must be a man…maybe a brother since you were a virgin…a virgin whore." She pushed away from him. He drew her back. "Not so fast."

He cupped her breast in his hand. Held the rounded globe weighing the jewel. Wished she was naked. Passed his palm across the tip. She wore nothing beneath the corsage. He could flick the buttons open. Taste her essence. Carrying her to her room had delicious ramifications. Fox realized he needed to stop thinking with his member instead of his brain.

Intimidation might work wonders. He watched the trembling of her chin. A good actress was his first impression. A damn good little performer. She probably practiced in front of a mirror. He knew Beryl practiced all types of faces while she watched herself. All women were cut from the same cloth. They would flirt to get what they wanted. This one offered more than flirtation. She offered her entire body.

She set her hands on his chest then pushed. Again, he held her tight. Continued to run his palm across the tips of her breasts. Shaking her head, a perplexed expression on her beautiful features she tried to speak. Nothing came out then, "Don't do this to me! Don't lie! I never stole anything from you!" she screeched. "I've no idea what you are talking about. I don't have a damn bag!"

"Perhaps with a bit more to drink, the alcohol will jog your memory.

Make you more talkative. Never wanted a damn chatterbox. This silence, though, is ridiculous." A bottle of brandy sat on a counter near the window where he'd been staring at the garden below. Setting her on the chair by herself he strode the distance then poured them both a glass. He pointed at her. "Don't try to run. I'll catch you. Fleeing will be a waste of energy. Make this situation worse." Now he stood over her. "Here…maybe this will jog your memory. Get your tongue working. Drink it. If it's necessary to get you tipsy in order to uncover the truth, I will."

"No," Fannie pushed the glass away, shaking her head. Her brows were drawn together. Crease lines marred her perfect features. "After…"

"Brandy won't hurt. It was the fact the liquor was taken with the laudanum that put you in the dazed stupor that was so endearing. Asked for a girl who wasn't a chatterbox," he reiterated. "Don't remember if you said more than a dozen words the entire night. Liked that fact. Except for the end of the evening when you stole the satchel, I got all I asked for then a little bit more. The second time was nicer than the first. You knew what you were doing. Opened up all your beautiful feminine parts for my avid attention without my asking."

She stared at him, a blank look on her face. She scrunched her nose as if she was disgusted with some fact she might have uncovered. "You're Fox? That's why you are here. You are one of the guests, you along with your father. I didn't want to meet either of you. You're a horrible man to make insinuations about me. Accusations that are far from true. Nothing you can prove. You should apologize for what you did to me that night. I'm not what you think. Not a whore or a thief."

Fox was exhausted, frustrated beyond endurance. Unable to get any information from her, he was at a loss. He needed to shoot her down before she directed the conversation in another way. "You have my money! Hand it over! I mean it. I'll call the constables. You'll end up in prison." Thought he should get to the most pressing point of the facts. "All fifty thousand pounds that you stole six weeks ago. I want the money before I leave tonight. You, my dear, walked right out of the whorehouse with my brown satchel. Hannah searched the entire damn house! Turned up nothing."

Her eyes widened as she stared at him. Her throat moved as she swallowed hard. Within her lap, her fists clenched tight. She moaned. The sound was not one of female pleasure. More like misery. "Money? Fifty thousand pounds? Brown satchel? I don't have any idea what you are talking about."

As if she remembered something, one more time her face turned white. The glass holding the brandy slipped from her fingers. Crashed onto the floor. Amber liquid spread, seeping into the blue carpet. Her head lolled to the side. Fannie was as limp as a rag doll.

"Well hell!"

She fainted.

Curse her beautiful white hide. She fainted. He needed help. Looked to her then the door. This was a ruse to send him from the room so she could run. How far could she go? Not very far. He touched his finger to the pulse at the base of her throat. The beat was steady though slow. She moaned; the sound soft in the fading light from the fireplace. He shook her. Her head flopped. She did faint. Hell, he had to do something. He'd wanted to solve this issue between the two of them before his father was ready to leave. Didn't want to bring the Kenworthy's into the conversation involving his stolen money.

Fox had no other recourse but to bring the rest of the household to the room. Transporting this incident to its proper conclusion would have been better left in private. He thought he might have been able to coerce the truth from her. As it was, now there was no choice. Disgusted with this turn of events, Fox stepped into the hall then headed toward the parlor where he was certain the rest of the family were chatting. He poked his head into the room. His father along with Jasper had been in deep discussion. Neither man noticed him for a full twenty seconds. He cleared his throat, not wishing to disturb the conversation between the men yet needing to get their attention.

Jasper saw him first. Looked up, a startled, surprised look on his face. "Fox, do come in. Your father and I have just been…"

Threading air through his lungs, Fox held up both hands interrupting his host. "One of your servants fainted. She is in the library. We were…a…having a discussion of sorts. One I'd rather keep between the two of us. It's private unless the issue between the two of us cannot be resolved." He never wanted all this to happen this way. It might be a while before the events of that infamous night six weeks ago were ironed out. He truly didn't wish for the gel to lose her job. As it stood now, he would need to be patient. Fox wasn't certain he wanted to divulge their prior relationship. A choice might not be available to him.

"One of my servants fainted?"

Jasper was on his feet dashing to the hall, Jake close behind. Seemed the rest of the assemblage followed. All would be apparent in less time than he could imagine. Fox rushed in behind Jasper and Jake. Jasper was in the midst of closing the large double doors to the library when she moaned.

The soft complaint brought everyone's attention to Fannie. After the sound, she lay still on the canape where Fox placed her. One arm was thrown over her eyes. Fox's attention was swept to the soft rise of her breasts. The way her legs seemed to stretch on forever. That night they'd been wrapped around his flanks.

Jasper cleared his throat before pinching the bridge of his nose. He brought his gaze to Fox. "Thought you said it was a servant who fainted. This woman is no servant. She is—" Jasper wasn't able to finish the words.

"She's not?" Fox asked, baffled now by Jasper's comment. "Who is she?" If not a servant, she was someone more important to the household. While he continued to shadow the woman's figure, he felt a slight twinge of unease. Wondered if this woman could be the missing sister. The one who always kept to herself. Fannie…she said her name was Fannie. Good God no!

"Maggie's younger sister. Why would you believe she is a servant?" Jason said as he looked just as concerned as Jasper.

Fox knelt beside her, his hand stroking her cheek. "Something she told me or more honestly everything she didn't say. Never denied being a servant when I assumed she was. Denied all else we spoke of."

"I'll get the smelling salts." Maggie dashed from the room.

Tessa stood framed by the door, her hands prayer fashion beneath her chin. She looked wide eyed, unhappy. "Oh dear… Oh dear. I knew there was something wrong with her. For six weeks she hasn't been herself. Oh dear… Nellie left her all alone to fend for herself that night. She was sick. Should not have been out of the house. Should have been in her bed. Something happened? She wouldn't tell me. We always confide in each other. There must be something terrible…" Tessa was rambling nonsense to him.

Fox was shocked by the new facts coming to light. He recalled when she aborted the word pre.. Bothered by the information, Fannie believed she might be pregnant. If that was so, he was positive he was the father. Nothing she did tonight was an act except for her lies about the satchel. If she didn't know anything about the bag, where was the money? Who did know? Could she have been robbed when she left Hannah's place. He learned Halsey had been after her. Maybe the pimp had the groats. At this point anything was possible.

Maggie arrived with the smelling salts. With a few whiffs Fannie groaned then blinked her eyes open. She let out a funny little snuff of air then tried to sit. Fox helped her to a chair, hovering over her. He didn't understand his potent concern. Well, if anything happened to her, he would never retrieve his fifty thousand pounds. If he was honest with himself, his concern for Fannie, went beyond the money. A strange wave of protectiveness washed through him. Right now, she appeared as a lost waif who hadn't eaten in days. This lady was in dire need of someone to look after her. Hell! He wasn't applying for the job. Was he?

"What happened?" she asked, brushing hair from her eyes. Fannie stared from one person to the next until her accusing gaze riveted on him. "I…everything went black. Then…" She didn't say anything more. One more time she looked around the room at the staring faces.

"You haven't been yourself these last weeks," Tessa accused, though her voice was soft with caring. "Why did you faint? Is there some reason we should understand? You've never fainted in your life."

Both he and Fannie understood she fainted because of his threats. Not because of some unforeseen illness or a possible pregnancy. Couldn't tell her family either of those reasons. In time, there might not be a choice except for a complete explanation. Maybe not complete, there were some details needing to be left out. A few facts that should remain private.

"I don't need a doctor," Fannie proclaimed out of the blue.

"Of course, you don't. I'm not going to send for one." Maggie picked up her hand, rubbing the back. "Maybe you should enlighten us as to what happened the night of the scavenger hunt. Something did happen. We all know your hidden reality for a fact. You insist it's nothing but I wonder."

"N…nothing happened!" The look she tossed over her shoulder to him spoke volumes. If he read the expression correctly, she was imploring him to keep his mouth shut. For now, he would tell no tales. The ball was in Fannie's corner. He would follow her lead.

"I'd like to speak with Fannie privately," Maggie said as she studied her sister. The oldest realized there were truths here that needed to be understood.

"But not tonight. I don't think she is up to withstanding an interrogation," Fox said, then regretted the words. It was not his place to dictate when the sisters spoke.

Fannie looked to her sister standing just inside the double doors. "He's right. I feel…drained. Just wish to go to bed."

"I understand."

A private talk at any time was not what Fox wanted but he had no choice. "Of course." Ah hell…he couldn't tell anyone in this room about the brothel. Would never jeopardize his father's business venture with the Kenworthy's.

Beryl stepped farther into the room, unknowing what happened earlier. Realizing only the fact the girl fainted. "Pregnant," Beryl announced. "The serving wench is enceinte. That's the reason she fainted. Nothing surprising about that. We all know their morals are beyond the pale."

Fox rubbed his hand behind the back of his neck. Everyone stared at him. He felt cornered, even though no one except Fannie comprehended his role in this evening's events. There was only one thing he could do.

"I will marry her!"

~ * ~

Lord Abernathy leaned back, stretching his legs out in front of him. Anice sat on the opposite wing chair sipping a full glass of wine. He preferred brandy. Halsey was expected any time now with his report on the girl. The two sisters plagued him for six weeks now. He'd almost gotten his hands on Fannie. He'd been so close. He could practically taste her sweetness. Anice assured him, they would nab her next time she left the home.

"Fannie should be in the upstairs room that awaits her. Bought a special house in the country just for the girls. No one will learn where we've stashed them. We should have had her six weeks ago. You would have been having a damn good time with her. Curse Hannah along with her bodyguard," Anice murmured between sips of wine. She closed her eyes for a few seconds as if she savored the rich red wine or was thinking of more ways to torment her daughters. "The girl hasn't been acting the same as usual. She never leaves the house. Not even to go with Nellie on the outings the two of them never missed. After her night at Hannah's, she changed. Do you think she is still a virgin?"

Abernathy tapped his fingers on the arm of the chair where he sat. Virgin? A virgin was only necessary in a wife. "One way or the other, it doesn't matter to me if she's still complete. Learned virgins are only good in a wife. Like my women experienced. In this case, I'll be able to teach her how I like sex…hard…fast…messy…with multiple partners. Love to hear the screams of pleasure or pain." Nelson lifted broad uncaring shoulders. "Can't tell the difference. Don't care. Fannie…ah, she is a lovely young woman. It was fortuitous that she was left alone by her sister. We failed to capitalize on our brief taste of luck. Now, getting either one of them alone will be more difficult."

"No, well, it doesn't matter. We don't have Fannie yet, or Nellie. I want to know what we're paying Halsey for when he doesn't deliver on the goods. He's been chasing after those two for more than six weeks with nothing to show for his efforts. Maybe, Nelson, we should take matters into our own hands. We could separate the two…I could call one of them home. That ploy worked with Tessa." Anice was trying to think of something that would draw Fannie from the Kenworthy townhouse. They had so many guards around the girls.

"Neither girl will be stupid enough to come with a summons from you. You will need some dire threat to hold over their heads. Don't know what that could be. Can't use the same ploy twice. The twins watch over them like hawks. Even the carriage driver makes certain the twins understand where the girls are going." Nelson leaned back on the chair. He studied her, following the line of her gown, seeming to trace the curves of her breasts then her hips. He stopped there. Heat crashed into her from Nelson's ardent perusal of her body. Anice loved sex with this man. Adored sex. She never knew what he would do. He always treated her to something outrageous. Sometimes he hurt her. Afterwards he would always soothe her. She liked sex exciting and rough around the edges, dirty, hot. For her, with pain there was always pleasure.

"When Halsey gets here, we can have a threesome. I know how much you enjoy having four hands along with two mouths titillating all your feminine attributes. I would wager your juices are flowing just thinking about sex with the two of us." Nelson patted his thighs. "We could start now. Why waste time. Come here, Anice. It's been too long since I've been inside you, filling you, feeling the excitement of your blistering heat."

Anice didn't want to give him what he asked on the first request. She understood if she denied him for even a second, anger would simmer. The man was dangerous when his temper flared then overruled his actions. She liked the practical application of his fury when sex was involved. Enjoyed controlling him, seeing him ferocious. Didn't mind a bit of pain for the amazing results of his endeavors. Her climax would be hard. Would endure for seconds on end.

She ran her tongue along her bottom lip then fiddled with the tiny pearl buttons running down the front of her gown. Nelson watched her fingers. She played with his emotions. Felt himself swelling as he watched her uncover parts of her. He tapped his nail on the brandy glass. She flicked open the top two then the third one. Leaned over to give him a better view of her huge endowments. Nelson loved to suckle her breasts, their taste exquisite.

"I want you now, Anice. Your flirting will get me into you hard and fast. Hope you didn't wear anything beneath your gown. Don't want to rip your clothing in my haste to feel your heat surround me. Will, if it's in the way."

"Don't you know? That's what I want too. Hard and messy. Fast and shattering. Don't care how you get me there. Hurt me. Spank me. Bite here or there. Tie my hands above my head then spread my legs wide. You know I relish everything you do. What haven't we tried?" She undid a few more buttons before playing with the ties to her chemise.

"Ma'am, Halsey is here. Should I show him in?" Her butler waited for her to speak.

She turned to give the prudish man an eyeful of her charms. She postured for the man who blushed. "Yes…this can wait. Send him in."

"No!" Abernathy said with a low growl. "Give us five minutes tops. That's all sex with your boss will take. Wait, let Halsey in now. He can be part of this fun. We were just speaking of a threesome. Anice, finish with the damn buttons."

"Ah…" Anice moaned as Nelson picked her up. Tossed her on her hands and knees. His fingers closed around her breasts. With his legs he pushed hers apart. Was inside her pumping before she could catch a bite of air. She screamed, shattering into hundreds of pieces just as Halsey walked through the door.

"Need a third party?" Halsey asked as he stepped inside the drawing room. "Or someone to watch the debauchery? I do enjoy watching nearly as much as participating. Will I get to enjoy the little darlings when we finally catch up to them?"

Anice turned, her breath panting. Nelson twisted her nipples. He was still hard and inside her. She gulped for air. Had not expected Nelson's sudden entry. While he didn't hurt her, she wasn't ready for a round with Halsey participating. "Not right now." Anice sat on the floor smoothing her skirt around her legs. He surprised her. Next time it would be her turn to shock the arrogant lord of the realm. She meant to turn the tables.

"Anice, you don't make the decisions here. We do what I say. I'm in command of this enterprise. I make all the decisions." Nelson tugged on her bodice, her breasts falling free. Turned to speak with the pimp. "Touch her anyway you like?"

"Don't mind if I do."

Halsey grinned as he sucked one of Anice's large breasts into his mouth then bit. He unfastened his pants, his rod standing tall with anticipation. He brought Anice up from her position on the floor. Tugged her skirts around her waist then shoved into her. Pumped hard and fast until she cried out again. Closing her eyes, Anice wilted on the man. Had not expected this attention either. Her head lolled on his shoulder. He removed her clothing except for her stockings and shoes then set her on a chair.

"Like my women naked, vulnerable, open to me. What do you say, she's quite pleasing. Are we ready for another round?"

"Yes…" Nelson said, watching the older woman who scowled at him. They took advantage of her. What did she expect? Anice always wanted sex. Anyway. Anywhere. Anytime. What did she have to frown about?

He rang for the butler who stepped into the room as if he'd been waiting at the door for the summons. "Bring the lady her dressing gown. Would you enjoy taking Anice? She is in need of a bit of punishment. She thinks she can command what transpires here. We punish women who overstep. You are welcome to her. You may put her over your knee. Spank her if you like."

"I didn't like that," she said, looking at Nelson, panting hard with the exertion. "I don't want to do this again right now."

The poor man backed from the room without answering.

"What you like makes no difference to either of us," was Nelson's smooth reply. "We were anticipating the first time with Fannie. She will have us both. Maybe two or three times before we allow her to rest." He turned to Halsey, enjoying the company of a third party. All that would have made this better was a bit of cocaine. He wondered how much stamina that would give Anice. He needed to remember to bring some with him next time he visited her. "Would you like something to drink?" he asked while he watched Anice curl her long white legs beneath her. "A brandy?"

"Fine…" Fastening his pants, Halsey sat on one of the chairs then accepted the drink. "I've no news worth telling. Nellie flits about the city with Dillon on her arm. Fannie still hasn't left the house. The Kenworthy's had dinner guests the other night…Fox Taggart and his father were there." Halsey relaxed in the chair sipping his brandy. "You will need to either separate Nellie from her beau or figure out how to get Fannie out of the house. I've a twenty-four-hour surveillance on the home. Don't know what else to do. Can't hardly barge into the home then abscond with the girl."

"Can't you figure out how to separate Nellie from Dillon? That seems an easy enough task. We don't care which girl you abscond with first though we do wish to have both women in our abode. Right now, Nellie is the easiest mark. Find a way to separate the two lovebirds," Nelson said, a bit of disgust in his tone.

"Not without someone figuring out who I am and that I'm after the girls. Don't want to end up in prison myself."

"I'll think of something. Now…" Anice must have realized the look in his eyes. Watching her with Halsey made him hard. Thinking about Fannie or Nellie in his power swelled him even more. For now, Anice would have to do. Settling for second best was not in his nature. Tonight second best would be his only choice.

Abernathy pulled her onto his thighs. Spread her legs across him. Anice tossed her head back. "No," Anice told him quite clear in her opinion. She didn't think he would concede to her wishes. Wasn't positive she wanted him to. Telling him no was always a thrill.

"What can you contribute to this scenario?" Nelson asked Halsey, his voice smooth as silk. Nelson bent to take her breast into his mouth. The hot suck on the globe caused her to cry out. Halsey kneeled behind her, paying ardent attention to her butt. She flinched when he bit. Anice didn't like this man.

The mating was over in seconds. Anice lay sprawled on top of him, panting, gulping air. She would be useless for a few more minutes. "You can have her next time," he stared at Halsey. "When we have the girls…" He shook his head as he lifted Anice then set her on another chair. "I won't share until I grow bored."

Chapter Three

Fannie was sitting in her bed, covers drawn beneath her arms, reading the gothic romance she'd gone to the library to find sometime in the evening. She couldn't seem to concentrate, all the words blending together. Realizing if she'd remained in her room last night, she would have never encountered Fox nor heard his ludicrous accusations. Nor would she have received that outlandish proposal. His words were not phrased as a proposal. What he spouted was more in the vein of a demand.

A chocolate pot and cup sat on her nightstand as did the croissant their housekeeper brought to her this morning. For the time being, hunger seemed elusive. She didn't wish to go downstairs for breakfast. Knew she wouldn't appreciate the confused stares she would receive from her sisters. Never thought to see the man who stole her innocence. Didn't know how to continue. He would try to see her again, making his wishes clear.

Since she didn't leave her room, Maggie would come to see her. As the oldest of the sisters, Maggie was taking on the role of surrogate mother with quiet intensity. She would pry into her life. Ask questions Fannie didn't wish to answer. Would want to know if she was pregnant. She was. At least she believed that to be true. Wasn't positive.

Fox's outrageous proposal last night left her flabbergasted. Why would he ask her to marry him? He didn't like her. Accused her of theft as well as called her a whore. If she'd fallen to the level of a harlot, her falling was due to his seduction that night in the brothel. While she couldn't say he took advantage of her, he did. Fox didn't know she was under Hannah's protection. Didn't understand she was ill. Since she could never take back that night, she would need to live with what happened. As to the money, Fannie had no idea what he spoke about.

When she heard the knock on the door, she wasn't surprised even though she flinched. Her heart jumped a beat before it steadied. She exhaled the lump of air that caught in her lungs. Needing something to hold onto, Fannie picked up the cup of hot chocolate that was no longer hot. Sipped. The beverage landed like a stone in her stomach.

The door creaked open. Maggie looked around the side, peering at her with a look of concern. "May I come in?" She didn't wait for an answer. Stepped right through into the room then let the door close behind her.

Fannie understood, Maggie would do whatever she thought best. "Suppose so. If I said no, would my wishes matter?" With a tiny lift to her shoulders, "Besides, you are in the bedroom. Who's to tell you no?"

"In this case you're right. We will have that talk I promised last night. Need to understand what is happening here. If you need protection, well, Jasper will give you whatever it is you might wish." Maggie stepped into the bedroom before gently closing the door. "You understand we need to talk. Why did Fox propose marriage to you? Seems extreme when the two of you don't know each other."

"Talk about what?" Playing innocent would never work with Mags. Her brows knitted together in an unavoidable scowl. She made a face at her sister, not intending to make this any easier for Maggie than it was for her. Talking was not necessary. There was nothing her sister could tell her that would change anything. At this time, she wasn't ready to confide.

"Don't be perverse," Maggie followed as if she lost whatever patience she might have had. "You've done little but mope around the house. Most of the time your sulking takes place in your room. You never bless us with your company. That's not like you. You've always enjoyed being with people along with your sisters. Frankly, I mean to get to the bottom of your real or imagined plight."

"I'm not stubborn." While she didn't wish to admit to the fact, Fannie knew she was the most stubborn of all the sisters. "Ask me what you want to know." Thought she should get down to the point. If she did, Maggie might leave her alone. If she didn't, the entire morning would be taken up with this silly interrogation.

"You would tell me, wouldn't you, if you were pregnant." This came as a statement not a question. When Maggie spoke the words, she looked away as if she was embarrassed by the question.

Still, the comment didn't surprise Fannie. She was expecting something to that effect. Didn't realize her sister would shoot straight to the point. The question must have been on everyone's mind since the woman, Beryl, she thought that was her name, stated the fact for everyone to hear. Something kept her from answering the question so she answered a different one hovering in Maggie's head. "I'm not pregnant."

"Could you be?"

"Immaculate Conception?"

"Don't be blasphemous."

"I'm sorry." The lie had to remain. Truth couldn't be part of this story until she understood what she intended. While she didn't have many choices, she did have a few. She could weather the storm and keep the child. It might be possible to marry Fox, the father of the babe. Then, she hesitated to even think the thought, she could get rid of the baby. She had three choices. None of them viable.

Maggie let out a slow breath of air. "I'm sorry too. Sorry I felt the need to ask the question. You did faint last night. Wish to get to the reason. It is not uncommon for a pregnant woman to faint."

"I'm tired all the time. Is that sufficient? Since my illness, I seem to need to sleep more than usual. That man last night shocked me. I..." She moistened her dry lips trying to come to terms with the facts she dared relate to her sister. Telling anyone how she knew him, wasn't possible. Sifting in a deep breath of air to help her think, she began, "I thought I would be alone in the library. When he wandered in..." Fannie let her words hang in the air for a couple of seconds. Telling Maggie anything more was beyond what she could do. She could never tell her Fox stole her maidenhead while she was in an upstairs room at Hannah's brothel. Could never tell her she was drugged but nonetheless a willing participant.

"You will come down for luncheon?" Maggie asked as she stood, concern still etched in the worried look she shot her way. She reached out then pulled her hand back. "You must join the land of the living sometime. Hiding up here in this room is not healthy. I speak for everyone in the family. We miss you."

"I know I've been reclusive," Fannie said, not wishing to disagree again. She didn't want to be around anyone just now. For peace in the family, she needed to do this her way. "I will bathe and dress. Visit with my sisters along with their husbands if you promise no one will inquire about a possible pregnancy. I've had enough accusations in the last twenty-four hours to last me a lifetime."

Her sister was shaking her head as she began to back from the room. She set the tip of a finger on her chin as she looked hard at her, "Can't make that promise. Wish I could. We both understand sometimes we think with our feet. What I can guarantee is that I will make certain all will know what you told me. Will not be able to stop the speculative looks that might come your way. Will that do?"

Fannie sucked in a huge drought of air. "Suppose it will have to be enough. I would also hope no one mentions the not so gentlemanly proposal." She hoped her sisters along with the twins would respect her wishes.

"Good, then I'll see you in another hour for lunch. We will take a carriage ride around the city. Perhaps the sunny day will brighten your spirits. Would you enjoy shopping? You haven't bought anything new for a while. I'll ask Jasper if he wouldn't mind paying for a few new things for the two of us. You might wish for a new gown for the party this evening."

At the notion of going to a party, Fannie sucked air. That was the last place she wished to be. Tried to ease the way with Maggie. None of her problems were Maggie's doing. "Shopping would be nice. Don't feel in a party mood. Would rather remain home where I can read." Fannie needed to figure out the next steps she should take. Through the grapevine of gossip, she learned of a madam who had ways to rid a woman of an unwanted pregnancy. She set her hands on her still flat stomach. Despite her fears, the thought repulsed her.

"I know you will make the best decision possible." Maggie kissed her on the forehead then left. Fannie rang for a bath. It was a little more than an hour later when she walked into the small area where the family ate when they were at the house. All eyes seemed to bore into her. She didn't think anyone believed she wasn't pregnant. They would need to take her word for that fact. What she longed for was to leave the city behind. Country air sounded wonderful. Maybe she could convince one of the twins they would be happier in the country home.

"How are you?" Nellie clapped her hands together. Her smile was broad, welcoming when she looked her way. "Was worried about you. Would you like to go with Dillon and me to the Weaver's party tonight. It will be great fun. You can dance. I know you love to dance. I think your…" She looked to Maggie as if for guidance. "Fox might be there. You can dance with him. He seems to be," here was where Nellie blushed. "He seems infatuated with you. Asked you to marry him. Do you know that man?" Nellie blurted out before she could curb her tongue. "Is he the one who…?"

Fox was the last person she wished to see or talk about. If he danced with her, he would spend the entire time accusing her of theft then calling her a virgin whore. He despised her. And…he didn't ask her to marry him, he made a statement that he would wed her. Never asked. That was something else she couldn't stop thinking about, the proposal that was so far from a proposal the statement was laughable.

"Maggie and I are going for a ride then shopping. I'll be too exhausted for dancing. If I'm not around, you'll have more fun with Dillon." She lifted her shoulders in a small shrug as if wishing to make the next point. "Three is a crowd. So, they say. At least it was six weeks ago when the two of you abandoned me to my own devices." Fannie understood she should have left the past where it was, in the past. She was sorry the moment the words left her mouth.

Nellie sucked in air, her eyes widening. She began to shake her head, a ferocious scowl forming between those wide green eyes of hers.

Maggie tossed a curious glare her way. "Nellie abandoned you? Why ever would she do such a thing? This is the first we've heard of the desertion. Because of the threat our mother holds, the two of you understand you are supposed to stay close. We still need to remember our mother doesn't mean you well. Lord Abernathy is a persistent danger. Neither will stop until they have what they wish or the two of you are married and well out of their reach." She sent her angry look to both of them.

Fannie felt the heat of embarrassment climb to her cheeks. She had not meant to toss those damning words out to the family. The fact was a sore point between the two of them. Until now, she'd kept the information private. The events of the last twenty-four hours had been trying, stretching her nerves. Seemed everything was public knowledge. Soon her pregnancy would also be known to the family as well as all her friends. She would no longer have friends. She would be labeled.

Nellie's napkin hit the table hard. She stood, knocking the chair to the floor. Her hands planted firmly palms down on the table, she yelled. "I didn't abandon Fannie! She was to search for a monogramed handkerchief. She could have followed us. Gone with us. When she turned down a different street, we weren't certain what to do. Told Dillon we should go after her. When we returned to find her, she'd vanished. In my mind, Fannie set off in her own direction all by herself at her whim. I'm not at fault here. Wish she would stop harping about that night." Nellie was in full out defensive mode.

As Jasper righted the chair, he spoke. His voice was soft. "Sit and calm yourself, Nellie. There is no reason to yell at Fannie. I'm certain your sister can tell us why she believes you deserted her."

Unable to say anything more, Fannie stared at her fingers that were in her lap. Supposed there were two sides to every story. She inhaled several deep breaths before returning her gaze to her family. "That is one interpretation of what happened, Nellie. Truth is, you, as well as Dillon, wished to be alone. It turned out to be at my expense." That was as far as she intended the explanation to go.

"What happened? Say no more unless you are willing to explain what happened the night in question. I for one know you came home in the wee hours of the morning," Nellie shot back, her face flushing with color seeming unable to give up on the argument. "What were you up to? What did you do? I'm not taking all the blame." That information was something else they kept private for the last six weeks. Now that part of the evening was out in the open.

"Girls! Stop!" Maggie clapped her hands together. She looked between the two sisters, pointing an accusing finger at both. "We have never been at odds before, not this way. Always, have we stood together, a united front. What has happened here?" Maggie turned to her; her anger very real. "Keep your accusations to yourself, Fannie, until you are ready to give a better explanation of all that transpired six weeks ago. The two of you are keeping secrets that will soon explode. I won't have it."

"Don't believe I want to go on that excursion or the party this evening. I'm better off keeping my own counsel. It's obvious there is a wide rift between Nellie and me." With that announcement, her hands trembling,

Fannie set her napkin on the table to depart. She was unfit for company. All Maggie said held merit. She wasn't ready to tell anyone anything. Still looked for a way out of her predicament. What she needed was time to figure out her course for the rest of her life.

Fannie disliked herself. There was a life growing inside her. She contemplated ridding herself of the baby. Possibly she was wrong and she was late. If she waited another couple of weeks maybe all would be well. She would be able to stop worrying. If she waited too long, one of her choices would vanish. She didn't know how Fox would feel if she ended his child's life. Since he didn't like her, he might not wish for the child or her. Fox could be relieved to learn the babe no longer existed.

Maggie caught up to her before she reached her door. Stopped her with a hand on her arm. "Come with me. I'm not going to allow you to languish in your room. I would ask Nellie to come with us, too, but I doubt if that's a good idea considering the argument we all witnessed. The two of you are going to need to find a way to makeup."

She was floored by the second invitation. Felt certain Maggie would backpedal. "You want my company? Truly wish to spend an afternoon with me?"

"Of course, you're my sister and I love you. You are going through a difficult time. Would love to help." Maggie hooked her arm through hers. "Jasper ordered a carriage. He insists on an extra man to accompany us. Doesn't believe Anice will try anything with a guard at attention. At the moment there are too many questions to leave anything to chance. Don't wish for you to remain in the house for another six weeks."

"You certain?" In twelve weeks, she might show the evidence of her evening in the brothel. She groaned.

With the sound of her groan, Maggie looked at her a puzzled expression in her eyes. "Yes, we will have a fun time, the two of us. And," Maggie paused for a beat, "believe it would do you good to go out this evening. Nellie tells me it's a small affair. Mostly the young people the two of you have been seeing. You'll have fun."

She doubted that but didn't wish to start another argument. Inside the carriage they chatted about the last year they'd all been together beneath the Kenworthy's roof. The times had been both fun as well as frightening. When

Tessa was kidnapped by Lord Abernathy, all tried to hold on to their hope she would remain unscathed by the despicable man. Were shocked when they found out the Duke of Southcliff rescued her. How long would Nelson Abernathy along with their mother haunt their lives?

Nelson Abernathy wanted Maggie for his wife. She thwarted his attempt to marry her by fleeing then hiding from him. The night she ran, she had the luck to run into Jasper. Both fell in love the moment they set eyes on each other. Tessa, on the other hand, fell in love with Jason when she first saw him too, only under different circumstances.

Fannie wanted to find love for herself. Fox ignited a fire within her that was still burning. She first saw him through drug glazed eyes. She'd thought, dear God, how could he be so handsome? So tall? The height of the man along with the breadth of his shoulders set flames burning her until they scorched. She didn't know if those feelings meant she loved him. If she was pregnant, he was the father of her child. There had been no other man in her life.

Would he acknowledge the child as his? At the mention of her possible pregnancy, perhaps that was why he said he would marry her.

She didn't want a bastard. Understood the devastating effect the label could have on a person. If she didn't marry Fox, her child would be known as a bastard. She'd half expected to see him today. Perhaps he was having second thoughts about his announcement. Overnight, he might have changed his mind.

"We're here," Maggie announced as the carriage rumbled to a halt in front of the modiste's shop. Their driver helped them out.

Maggie gave instructions to their driver. He was to remain here. Stand guard. If he wished he could wait inside the store. They were the same directives Jasper gave him. He nodded then resumed his post beside the carriage.

Fannie waited; her hands folded in front of her. She gazed down the street in both directions, remembering other times the sisters shopped together. Not looking for anything in particular, she gave a startled gasp at the sight of him. She didn't think she would ever see the man again. A dark shadow swept through her. A tremor of fear seized her. Seemed as soon as he realized she saw him, he darted into the blackness of an alley. Her breath caught in the back of her throat. She reached out to steady herself on the carriage door.

"What?" Maggie must have heard the surprised intake of air. "Fannie? You look as if you've seen a ghost. Did you see something? Mother?"

Her hand at her throat, she nodded. "Yes, I saw something. Not mother. Did see a man. Let's go inside. Don't feel safe out here. I will tell you once we are inside." She realized her words would do nothing to ease the curious and concerned expression on her sister's face. What she wanted was to forget she ever met that man. He called himself Craig. Hannah called him Halsey. Someone, she couldn't recall, told her he was a pimp. Ah…it had to be Fox. He intimated the man wanted her in his stable of females. He would sell her to any man who wanted to pay the price for her.

What did all this mean?

Was Halsey following her? Whatever for? Couldn't he find other women for his use? There had to be more to this than what met the eye.

Anice.

Her mother might have been inside Halsey's carriage the evening in question. She remembered thinking she saw her. The sickness left her feeling uneasy, dazed at times. After the first encounter she was terrified. For that matter, Lord Abernathy could have been with Anice. Was Halsey being paid by her mother to kidnap her? This was something else she needed to tell the twins. Didn't know how she could unless she divulged more. Could she swear them to secrecy? Fannie didn't wish for her sisters to learn anything about what happened to her the night at the brothel. Didn't wish for anyone to blame Fox for taking her innocence. Fox was as much a victim as she was. She lost her innocence. He lost fifty thousand pounds. Fox came to the brothel to buy a whore. What he got was a virgin.

Secrets never worked out in her benefit. What if Anice had someone following Nellie? Her sister should learn about the possibility. Since Tessa's marriage to Jason, they'd all become complacent. She realized now, they could not let down their guard. They must always expect the unexpected. Couldn't take reckless chances.

Shopping was far from the pleasant afternoon Maggie anticipated. Her sister spent most of the afternoon trying to make her smile. She finally thew up her hands in what appeared to be exasperation. They made few purchases. Nonetheless both were ready to leave. Fannie was pleased when Maggie called a halt to the shopping expedition. "We're going home," Maggie told her. "You're clearly not enjoying yourself. Don't fathom how I ever thought to shake you from your gloomy mood. You will go to the party tonight. That is a must. I insist." With that said, Fannie understood she pushed Maggie too far.

Fannie wasn't surprised by the ultimatum. With meekness she didn't feel, she nodded, giving into her sister's demand. Another argument was not something she would enjoy. She could make this concession. Made the decision she would speak with Jasper about Halsey before this evening. He needed to be apprised of her knowledge. If she found herself separated from her sister again, she didn't wish to end up in the pimp's hands. If either did, Jasper would need to know where to find her.

The silent ride home left Maggie frowning at her. The scowl deepened when she requested to speak with Jasper upon entering the foyer. Maggie slanted her a sideways glare. "What do you want to speak with my husband about?" Maggie sounded suspicious.

Fannie couldn't blame her. "It's private," Fannie told her as she tilted her chin to the stubborn angle she was known for assuming. With her heart racing, she felt the consequences of what she was about to unleash building within. "I will leave it up to Jasper to confide or not confide in you as to what we discuss." She did understand the promise she meant for him to give might not hold to his wife. The case she made for her privacy would need to be strong. Would need to tell him enough, but not everything.

With her hands clasped in front of her Fannie walked into Jasper's office. She focused her attention on the man sitting behind the huge desk. His brows were drawn together in what seemed to be puzzlement.

Fannie's heart pounded deep in her chest. Dread pushed in on her as she stopped in front of his desk. Her knees were about to give out. Thought a prudent idea would be to flee. Now, Jasper looked at her, an expectant expression on his face almost as if he realized she had something important to tell him. Waving a hand, he offered her a seat. Waited for Keir, the butler, to pour tea.

Once Keir left, closing the door behind him, Jasper asked, another frown marring his forehead. "What is it you wish to talk about?" His kind voice unnerved her. Fannie felt as if he saw through to her soul, could read her mind.

She suspected he wished to speak of the non-proposal of marriage or whether or not she was pregnant. One could jump to a wealth of conclusions about his curiosity. Seemed he was waiting for her to begin this conversation she initiated by her request to see him. "I will only speak of the night in question if you give me your word this won't go beyond these walls. My words are not to be common knowledge in this household. You may speak to Jason if you wish. My sisters should be told only what is necessary for their well-being." Fannie folded her hands in her lap. She felt as if her nerves were stretched taut. Felt as if she was reliving that night six weeks ago. Her blood pounded in her ears. He had to promise. Fannie didn't know what she would do if Jasper refused her one request.

"Don't know if I can make a promise such as the one you are asking. I'm not used to keeping secrets from my wife." His fingers were steepled beneath his chin, eyes narrowed in careful thought. "Suppose my silence depends on what you tell me."

What he told her wasn't good enough. Unable to stop, she was shaking her head. He needed to give his word. She exhaled, thinking. "Maggie can't know about the details of that night." The fact she could have been raped was not something she wanted her sisters to know. What happened was far too private to become common knowledge.

He tapped his fingers together a frown of puzzlement on his features. "Go on."

"If you wish to speak with generalities, I can offer no resistance. Part of what I'm about to tell you, everyone will need to learn if my assumptions are correct. Believe once you are apprised of the situation, you will agree more readily to the silence I'm asking for." Fannie needed to count on that fact. Nervous, she sat forward, resting her clasped hands on the edge of his desk. "My sisters can't know most of the specifics. I…" Again, she found herself shaking her head while she thought on the words, she could use to garner his compliance. "If there was another way for me, I wouldn't tell you."

"Why?"

"They don't need to know all about what happened to me when I was separated from Nellie and Dillon. Just you, and Jason if you believe he needs to know. If he were home now, I would have also asked him to hear me out. That's all I ask. The information would be mortifying for me. My sisters would try to do something to help. Oh, I don't know. Just wish I could forget that horrible night. If they hover, I'll never be able to put what happened behind me. I'll keep thinking. Oh…!" She'd been gesturing with her hands. Now, she dropped them onto her lap a sour sensation in the pit of her stomach. "Don't want their pity or their fear. Don't like them hovering over me as if I was an infant. What has happened, happened. Nothing will change if they know except their opinion of me as well as the way they will treat me. Don't wish for anything to be different between us." She hoped they wouldn't look on her as if she was a whore. She wasn't. She'd known only one man.

"I will promise. See that you need to get this off your chest. Why don't you start at the beginning." Jasper sat back in his chair appearing relaxed. He seemed at ease with the promise.

"What? Oh!" She looked straight into his golden flecked eyes, swallowed the sip of tea so fast the liquid burned her tongue then all the way down her throat to her stomach. "The beginning, yes. That would be when Nellie left me alone, to fend for myself. You remember that night. I was sick. My throat hurt so bad I couldn't talk. Every word I said came out in a harsh croak." She found herself playing with the material of her skirt, twining the muslin between her fingers. "Lost my favorite hat…"

He nodded. His hands were steepled beneath his chin, eyes focused as he digested her words. "Go on. How did Nellie leave you? Do you know why? You both spoke a bit of the circumstances at lunch. The two of you are not in agreement as to the manner in which the events transpired. I would think the truth lies somewhere in between."

"I don't know. When I looked up, she was gone. I was supposed to ask people for a monogramed handkerchief. Don't like approaching strangers, especially by myself. At the time, I should have just come home and asked you or Jason for the item. Proceeding in that direction would have been easier as well as more prudent. Instead, I wandered for a while. Don't have any idea how long I was stumbling on the streets. That part of the evening passed by me in a blur. Everyone I stopped either laughed at me or gave me a heated no. Didn't know where I was going."

"Yes, men do appreciate a monogramed handkerchief. Don't like to give theirs' up to a stranger," he said in what seemed to be tongue in cheek monologue. He reached over to pour her more tea. Plopped one sugar cube into the cup. "Go on."

"After that, it seemed I felt worse with each passing second. The road in front of me was blurred. Wandered for a few more minutes. Didn't feel as if I could take one more step. I was leaning against this brick building with my eyes closed feeling sorry for myself." She paused to sip her tea. The liquid warmed the cold settling in her bones, the cube of sugar an added bonus. Fannie didn't know how to say the next bit.

"You were attacked?" he asked, his guess surprising her. Fannie's eyes widened with disbelief. "You must have wandered into the wrong part of town. It's not difficult from High Street which is where you began this quest for a handkerchief. Am I right? Somehow you left the street you were supposed to be on behind you."

"Yes, two men held me against the wall. One man pressed his body on mine. They thought," she swallowed hard, looking at Jasper as if he could understand without her explanation. "I was a whore. Wanted to take me to their room. Not that I would have granted them their wish. I didn't know where I was." She gulped a good portion of air for courage. "Down the street, I saw a line of hacks in front of this three-story townhouse. It was painted yellow. The place looked…ah…friendly? Thought if I could reach those cabs, I could hire one and they would take me home."

"That didn't work out for you."

Surprised by his bland expression. Seemed he was trying to make the retelling of her story easier. "No, I did what you taught us. Hoping to get away from the horrid man who pinned me against the brick, I kneed the man who was holding me prisoner…in the groin. Shrieking with what must have been pain, he let me go. When I ran, my path was straight into another man. I was knocked down, landing hard on the ground. The stranger helped me stand. Defended me against the two other men who were claiming me as if they owned me. This one wasn't rough around the edges. He had a pretty face. Learned later his name is Halsey."

Jasper sucked air at the mention of the name. It was obvious Jasper recognized the moniker. Resting his elbows on his desk, he tapped his fingers together. "I take it this isn't the end of the story. If Craig Halsey was the man, I'm thinking you were in major trouble. How did you get away from Halsey or did you?"

"Yes, I got away. I was lucky. No, not the end of my story. I realized within a couple of seconds I didn't want this man's help. Didn't wish to be anywhere near him or his carriage. Picked up my skirts then ran as hard as I could. The house with the hacks in front of it was lit up, cheery. As I said, the townhouse appeared friendly. I prayed maybe the people who lived there would help me. Had to take the chance. The backdoor was closer to me than the front. That's where I headed."

"Did they help?"

"Yes, A huge dark-skinned man named Angus opened the backdoor. Halsey was right behind me. A lady named Hannah hit Halsey with her broom, ordering him from her premises. He complained. Said I was his. Hannah told him a resounding no to those words. As she kept swiping at him with her broom, he fell down the backsteps."

"Hannah's brothel?"

"You know about Hannah?" Her eyes widened in surprise.

"Every adult male in the city knows about Hannah's place. Most have been there a time or two," Jasper told her tongue in cheek, his voice dry. Seemed to realize what she was wondering. "Doesn't mean I go there," he was quick to add. "Would never humiliate Maggie that way. I love your sister."

She sipped the tea again watching him over the brim. "Hannah saved me from Halsey. She fed me because my stomach was growling. After I finished eating, she tried to figure out what to do with me. By then my throat hurt so bad I couldn't speak at all. Couldn't even tell her my name. She sent a messenger for some doctor named Saint then she showed me to a room where I could sleep."

That was about all the story she was going to relate to Jasper. Realized she left out an important part of her tale. She would need to backtrack a moment. The main reason she wished to speak with him. Needed to make certain he understood this terror extended into the present. "The funny thing was, I thought I saw Mother in Halsey's carriage. Dismissed the idea as being absurd. Something I might have imagined because I was so sick everything I saw was a blur. Now, after today, what I saw that night might have been real. What happened this afternoon is the main reason I needed to speak to you."

"What did you see?" Jasper was leaning forward, curiosity in the depth of his golden eyes. His hands clasped tight in front of him.

Fannie understood the concentration on his face, the apprehension in his eyes. Thoughts of Maggie's problems with their mother along with Tessa's would be simmering in his head. The need to protect herself along with her sister was prevalent.

"Halsey. When I looked his way, he ducked into an alley. I know the man I saw was him. Would recognize Halsey anywhere. His pretty face is stamped in my head."

"If not for this incident, you would not have spoken to me?" His voice was harsh. Fannie understood his reason.

"No."

"You weren't harmed at the brothel?" The harshness changed to a more soothing tone.

"No. Hannah told me I was safe there. I was. Nothing happened. She sent me hot water for a bath. After I bathed, I slept." She hated the lie she was telling Jasper. Comprehended the fact that soon she would have to tell him everything she left out today. Soon, he would realize she lied to him. Might never trust her again. "I was safe. That's all you need to know," she repeated, needing to convince herself keeping certain information from him was in her best interest. In the present, that was all he needed to learn about the night in question.

"How did you get home? Maggie told me she heard you come in early that morning."

"I did. I woke up before the doctor arrived. Decided I would hire a hack. When I looked out the window, there was still a couple of them waiting for customers. So, that's what I did." Relief elevated her. She managed to tell him what was necessary.

"I see. You do realize you could have been hurt that night. You girls are to never leave each other alone. Believe this was an accidental oversight on Nellie's part. Though it would be nice for peace in the family if you would forgive her. Believe I understand if you cannot. The night was horrific for you. Part of the fault can be put directly at Nellie's feet."

"Yes, I suppose I should make amends. The apology could go both ways. Don't you think?" After all that happened to her, Fannie stiffened at the thought of apologizing to Nellie. She didn't feel the least bit apologetic.

"Did you tell Maggie you saw Halsey this afternoon?"

"No, didn't believe she would know who he was. You should tell her about the man and the fact I thought I saw mother. That part of the story she should know along with Nellie. Can't take any chances. Don't wish for any of my sisters to learn I spent the night in a brothel. Nothing happened. Hannah was true to her word. She kept me from harm. No one bothered me." She looked to the heavens hoping for forgiveness. Was surprised Jasper didn't guess she lied.

"Suppose I should. Will be difficult without telling her how you knew Halsey or that you saw your mother in the carriage."

"What do you think I should say?"

"Don't know. Certain you can think of something believable."

Fox's conversation with his father was not something he was going to enjoy. The marriage statement, once said, could not be taken back. He'd not thought too far ahead when he blurted the words. Fox understood he would hold true to his declaration. If Fannie carried his child, that was the problem, the if part of his thought process was out of his control. Six weeks passed, Fannie might have a good idea whether or not she was pregnant. Speaking with honesty with her was necessary. He needed to sit down with her then ask pertinent questions. Ones that would give him the answers he needed. Should have gone to see her this afternoon. Didn't because he had some serious thinking to do on the matter.

He finally saw a way home to Michigan. Marriage to Fannie would be no hardship. She was beautiful as well as passionate. Innocent that she was, in his bed, she heated him to his soul. Looking at her sent vibrations of lust straight to his sex. His male parts swelled with anticipation while thinking about lying naked with her pressed tight. When he woke before their second time, she was sprawled on top of him. Even the night when he interrogated her in the Kenworthy library, he wanted her.

He didn't know how to find the money. She denied stealing the satchel so vehemently, the fierceness of her words gave him doubts. If he didn't know better, he might believe her sincerity. His blurting out words about the marriage pleased his father. Jake was ready to give him the fifty thousand pounds without the blink of an eye. After all, marriage to a Scottish lass was what his father wished for. He wanted him to marry a Scottish woman so he would maintain his ties to Scotland.

Marriage to a city lass might never workout for her or him. The land where he lived could be brutal. He understood the truth better than anyone. Fannie could despise the rugged country he loved. She'd probably never been into the highlands which might compare. His home was nestled in a rich valley near a huge lake.

His father didn't know much about the sisters. Knew they'd been in some trouble involving their mother and a man named Lord Nelson Abernathy. Jasper rescued Maggie and Jason did the same for Tessa.

Was Fannie in trouble also?

Is that why she was at the brothel? They never got around to speaking about her presence at Hannah's place. The question was at the top of his priorities to learn. Perhaps the only trouble she was in was his possession of her. If she was pregnant her life would change with dramatic impact.

Agreeing to go to this party could end up becoming a huge mistake. He only acquiesced because he needed some time to speak with Fannie. Was told she would attend along with her sister, Nellie. He needed to discover if she carried a child in her womb, his child. If there was a child, he didn't have one doubt the babe was his. Realized she might not be forthcoming with the information. In any case, by seeing her in a social setting it would be easier to set up a more private afternoon meeting on the next day. He would meet her at Daryl's bakery which was near the Kenworthy townhouse. After he sent a message as to his intentions, Jasper replied that he would make certain she arrived.

He certainly couldn't ignore the ever-developing situation. With the money in hand, he wanted to leave on the next ship to the states. Needed to marry the girl first. He dreaded her reaction when she realized how she would travel to Michigan. The journey would be difficult as well as long. With his original plans in mind, he'd thought they could take a train out of New York for part of the distance. After the tracks ended, they would take a wagon the rest of the way. Even if they took a boat for a portion of the distance, they would still need a wagon for the overland trip from the Mississippi to his home.

"I'm glad you're going to meet Fannie MacRae. Seems," Jake poured them both a brandy before addressing his son again. "Not that I'm not appreciative of the proposal you announced last night, but do you know this woman? Seems as if the two of you were in the midst of a heated argument when she fainted. Is she pregnant with your child? Ah, suppose whether she is or not is none of my business. Though we will all learn the truth in a matter of a few weeks. Why keep the secret? Where did you meet the young lady?" Jake asked, as his queries came perilously close to the truth.

Jake posed too many questions he either didn't wish to answer or wouldn't. "Can honestly tell you I've known her for six weeks give or take a day." His statement would set the wheels turning in his father's head. Jake could surmise all he wished. They both knew what happened six weeks ago.

"I would like to set up a time to discuss the marriage with Fannie before I divulge the particulars of our relationship. I realize in passing that I never asked her if she was pregnant. Was more concerned about another matter between the two of us. I'm certain most women would appreciate a proposal. Under the circumstances," Fox held up his hand to stop a reply or a comment, "I wish to speak with Fannie in private. If she agrees, we will wed as soon as possible then book passage to New York. The trip home will be exhausting for her. Mean to tell her as little as possible about the overland trip. Don't wish to scare her or give her reason to tell me no."

"You're right. Don't enlighten her as to what to expect. Knowledge will only serve to frighten the lass. Would guess she knows little about the United States. Might not have heard of Michigan. She looks strong to me. A good wife for a man who lives in the rugged land. Doesn't appear to be a delicate wilting flower. Are you going to take a wagon on the overland route to your home? Suppose you would not take a stagecoach."

"Before Fannie came into the mix, no. Now I'm considering a coach.

I could hire someone to transport the supplies I'll purchase in Wabasha. We can travel part of the distance on the river. Done that before. None of the choices are comfortable. Part of my decision will be determined by the weather." *As well as her state of pregnancy.* "You do understand you won't be seeing us for quite some time?"

Fox realized he expected her to accept his proposal. It would be just like a stubborn woman to refuse the father of her child. If she did, he would need to find the words that would change her mind. She might decide to deny her pregnancy. The devil, he might have to stay long enough to make certain. No child of his would be born a bastard.

"I should be going now. Don't wish to spend too much time at the party, no more than necessary. Also, don't want to miss Fannie if she decides to leave early. She seems to enjoy a more solitary existence than her sister. I'm certain if she is in attendance, she's been coerced in some way."

Fox found he liked the idea of seeing her again. Last night the confrontation was unsettling. He'd been angry with her when she denied taking the money. The fact she fainted scared him. When Beryl announced the reality she must be pregnant, he was dumfounded. Decided the child must be his. When he met Fannie, she was innocent of men. Ah, he'd kissed every inch of her precious, delicious body. Enjoyed the sweet feminine sound of her pleasure. Fannie possessed a passionate, giving nature.

The party was in full swing when he was announced. A waiter stopped with a tray of drinks. Fox picked up a glass of wine as he searched the room for Fannie. Noticing Nellie first, he strolled in her direction. If he didn't see Fannie, he would ask her sister her whereabouts. If she wasn't at the party, he didn't intend to spend any more time at the gala.

Nellie was in animated conversation with Dillon. Waving her hands in the air she said something that made Dillon bark with his laughter. Fox smiled at the pair. They looked good together. He cleared his throat to get the couples attention. "Is Fannie here this evening? I don't see her." Fox wouldn't be surprised if she declined to attend. She seemed a bit reclusive. Liked to read. Even if he didn't see her tonight, he had Jasper's agreement to send her to the bakery for tomorrows afternoon meeting.

Nellie slanted him a broad smile, the little flirt. "Fannie is here somewhere. She's most likely found an out of the way room where she can be by herself. Fannie didn't wish to attend. Maggie insisted. Suppose she came along to gain peace in the house. Seems the Kenworthy home has been in an uproar since last night. Well, that is not entirely true. It's been tense within the walls of the house going on six weeks. The mood revolves around the horrible mood Fannie has been in."

Nellie did enjoy talking, also placing blame. So, they were all in an uproar at the Kenworthy townhouse…for six weeks. How very interesting, Fox mused. There must have been a great deal of speculation about the possible pregnancy. Last night, though, the news seemed to take everyone present by surprise. "Believe I'll go look for her. Have a reasonable idea as to where she might be hiding herself."

Fox took a second glass of wine from a nearby server then made his way through the house. He found the hostess then inquired about the library. The woman gave him directions. Opening the door, he wasn't surprised to see Fannie curled up on an oversized chair staring into the fire. She held an unopened book on her lap. When he stepped inside, she glanced his way, a weary look in her eyes.

"Brought you a glass of wine," he said, his voice low, stepping forward. "Thought you might want some fortification." If she relaxed a bit, she might be easier to visit with. Though his intentions were not of the visiting nature.

"Oh!" She jerked, appearing startled by his intrusion into her private domain. "How did you find me?" Fannie accepted the offering of the wine. Sipped before she spoke again. "Thank you for the wine, not for your company. Need to be alone with my thoughts. Didn't expect to see you." She stiffened her back, "I don't wish to talk to you or anyone. Just waiting here until I've permission to go home."

He lifted his shoulders before smiling. "You don't have a choice in the matter. How did I find you?" Fox repeated for her benefit, "Your question is a good question. Fannie, I wish to talk to you. So, we will proceed my way. Talking to you is why I'm here. The single reason I am at this gala." He sipped from his glass. "As to how I found you, had a hunch. Asked our hostess if it was alright with her to stop by the library. She quite willingly gave me directions. I'm beginning to understand you very well. Give you a book," he peered at the title, his grin widening, "good or bad you will be content. At my home in Michigan, I've an extensive library. The number of books will please you. I'll make a note to purchase some gothic novels. If you tell me ones you would like to read, I will have them sent to my home." He wondered if that information would soften her toward him.

When she sipped the sweet Bordeaux, she closed her eyes. Seemed to be digesting all he said. Fox thought her expression interesting. Wondered what she was thinking about. From what she said a few moments ago, she would be attempting to figure how to get him to leave. He wasn't intending to leave until he possessed answers to some of his most pertinent questions.

"Why are you here at the party? Do you know anyone? Yes, well, I suppose you do or you would have never received an invitation." She looked over the rim of the crystal. Stared at him for a few seconds before she tasted the wine again. "I want you to leave me alone. You know I'm not comfortable with you." She looked straight into his eyes. "Don't you?"

For the time being, he intended to ignore her wishes. He wasn't going anywhere. If she did carry his child, he would never leave her alone. "To see you. Discussing something important with you is why I am here." Fox didn't intend to delve straight to the point. She could wait since she was being difficult. He had a myriad of questions for her. As it stood at the moment, if he pressed her, she would walk out on him. He didn't doubt that little thought. In time they would need to get to the most salient points. Fox didn't have a great deal of patience for games. He wanted to be home by the end of May. Sooner, if possible.

"I've a difficult time believing you are here to see me." Fannie lifted her lily-white shoulders in what appeared to be an indifferent shrug. "You don't like me. Believe I'm a thief as well as a whore. Oh, you must want to interrogate me again about your damn satchel! Last night I told you all I know, which is nothing. The night in question is a fog in my brain."

"Not all." He reminded himself he had another purpose now that he no longer needed the satchel full of groats. If she had the money, and she did, his little brown bag would be found. When the money was discovered, he would pay his father back the pounds he was loaning him on his marriage to the Scottish lass. The improvements would be made to his home along with his business ventures.

Tonight she looked lovely in her ballgown. Though he liked her better wearing nothing at all. From his point above her looking down, he was treated to the sight of the valley between her exquisite breasts. He remembered how each one felt cupped in his hands. The soft satin feel of the firm globes. Would never forget the taste of her aroused woman's endowments. Fox managed to stifle the groan threatening to leap from the back of his throat. What did she remember about the night they spent together, naked in each other's arms? She'd been drugged with the laudanum then he gave her brandy. Fannie might not recall much of anything.

He stepped back to get a better look at her. Rested his foot on the hearth. Firelight played across the fragile bones of her high cheekbones. Fannie caught her plump bottom lip between her teeth. He had a very distinct recollection of the taste of that part of her. Needed to taste again, not tonight. Not unless she begged. If she begged, he would find himself more than willing to sample whatever Fannie offered.

He fetched a deep breath of air into his lungs. Caught the scent of Fannie. Listened to the vague strains of music coming from the dance floor to filter muted into the library. Heard the embers in the fire pop. If she wanted to dance, he could hold her in his arms. Pull her close so she could feel how much he wanted her. Thinking about her caused him to swell with need.

"You are wrong about my true feelings for you. I like you a lot. Loved your body beneath mine along with the heat of your tight sheath when I was inside you seeing to your fulfillment. What I don't like is the lie between us." Fox watched the ever-changing emotions on her lovely face. Saw her eyes widen then darken with anger. The blue of her eyes reminded Fox of the clear blue lake on his property on a sunny day. In the summer swimming was divine. "Can you swim?" Playing with her in his lake, both of them naked, blasted through his all-male brain.

She looked at him as if he had a hole in his head. Maybe he did. Tilting her head a bit sideways, she asked, "Which lie?" After speaking, she frowned at him them wrinkled her nose as if she realized she might have just stumbled into uncharted territory. She did. Fox had not thought there was more than one untruth between. If she knew she carried his child, there was a lie of omission separating them.

"There is more than one untruth?" Fox questioned, lifting a brow, thinking about her unbridled honesty. She was honest. Lied about his missing pounds. It was possible in her dazed state she didn't remember taking them. "I thought the only falsehood between was the one about my hard-earned money."

"Hard-earned? Heard you won the fifty thousand playing cards. In my mind, the scenario doesn't constitute working hard."

"Yes." He didn't intend to prevaricate. "I won the money. Gambled and won. Doesn't matter now. You have the pounds, not I. When are you going to tell me what you did with my money? Did you spend it all? Is that why you can't lead me in the direction to find what is mine? Did you give the groats to the poor?" He tossed the question out to see the look in her eyes. "I'm certain you don't have a partner."

"I don't have your damn money or your satchel! Never have!" She yelled. Her fingers grasped the stem of her glass so tight he wouldn't be surprised if it snapped. Seems her calm vanished. Her breasts rose when she inhaled in order to continue her rant. "Don't have a clue as to what you are talking about." Her voice steadied.

To Fox, Fannie looked as if she meant to toss her wine in his face, maybe even the glass. If she did, he'd retaliate in kind. He wasn't the type of man to allow a woman to abuse his person. "What is the second lie?" he asked, his voice softening to a whisper. Wondered what she would come up with to tell him. He was damn sure she wouldn't wish to mention the possible pregnancy. Though they would speak about his babe growing in her womb. "I'd like you to tell me what you meant." He sat down in the chair next to hers. Stretched his legs out before crossing his feet. Set his glass on the side table nearby.

"I misspoke," Fannie said in a thin whisper, while lowering her dark lashes. They were long, enhancing her eyes. "There is no second lie or third or fourth. If you don't want to threaten me about the missing pounds, why are you here?" On that note her voice wavered. "I would know the truth."

"For answers that are important to me. I'm here to discover some unanswered truths that have my mind befuddled. Things you've started to say then stopped short of revealing what you were thinking. Tell me…" Fox broke off. It was too soon for him to confront her with the child. He watched her bosom rise then fall. Faster now that she was agitated. Appeared as if her mind was traveling in a myriad of directions.

"I won't marry you." She'd set her wine next to his. Her tiny hands were fisted in her lap where she was staring. He wished to see her eyes. Fannie had the most expressive eyes. The way they changed color as well as widened at certain times gave indication of her true feelings. He was beginning to understand when she lied, they turned vague. The girl wasn't used to telling lies. She didn't know how to deal with the consequences.

Fannie couldn't meet his gaze. What he witnessed right in front of him told a wealth of truths. She must understand how expressive her eyes were. He supposed it was better to go straight to the point, to the reason he was here speaking with her in isolated splendor. "You will. If you are carrying my child in your womb, we will wed as soon as possible."

"I can't possibly be pregnant. It happened just once." Fannie was quick to say while acknowledging the depth of their night together. Then she was shaking her head, staring at him. "I'm not carrying your child or any other person's. Before that night I'd never…" she caught her lip between her teeth. "You know my truth. Since then, I haven't been with a man."

He didn't think she'd been with anyone else. "Twice," he corrected her with a grin. "And it only takes one time if it's the right time of the month. You should understand the minor fact. Has no one ever taught you about conception?" He watched moisture form in her eyes. "Tell me why you fainted. There might be a plausible explanation. Something besides a pregnancy you deny. If I'm right, believe I heard you or someone say you've never fainted." Fox was searching her words as well as the expressions flitting across her face for answers. In the last few seconds Fannie's face turned red, a vibrant shade of red. So, she was embarrassed by his honesty. Left his question unanswered about how much she knew.

"You terrified me. Terror is the reason why I fainted. Was shocked to see a person I never thought to meet again." Fannie was quick with her answer. "Recalled what we did together. I was mortified."

"All you say might be true. Are you pregnant with my child?" Since she set herself up, he decided to pursue the topic further. If she didn't give him the information tonight, there was always tomorrow. At times he was a patient man. Realized this was one of those moments he needed to tap into all the tolerance he possessed.

The material of her gown was wound between her fingers. He

reached out. Placed one of her hands between both of his. Lightly massaged her wrist before trailing the tip of his finger higher until it met the tiny puffed sleeve of her gown then back down. Her flesh was soft and warm, resilient. When he caressed her, a passionate response shivered from her.

Fannie turned her head away from his gaze. He brought her hand to his lips. Pressed a kiss to the top then turned her fingers over to touch the palm with the tip of his tongue. Felt the slight vibration of her body. She tugged on her hand. Fox let her go for now. She was a prickly little piece. A vision to delight any man in her light blue ballgown. One more time, the thought he liked her better wearing nothing at all rumbled through his mind.

Her chin tilted into the air. "If I am enceinte, I won't stay that way." There was a wealth of determination in her voice, in her words. What she implied terrified him.

Fox jerked back. Anger flooded him at her statement. He wanted to shake her until she had a small measure of sense. "You would risk your life to rid yourself of an innocent baby? The process of aborting a child is not a simple one. You could bleed to death. Might injure yourself so severely you could never carry another babe." He felt outrage so deep he shook. Fox was incensed. "It isn't as if I haven't offered to protect both you and this unborn child of ours. I will marry you. Give the child a name. You will not rid yourself of my child!" His stomach turned sour at the notion. For a few seconds he couldn't breathe. His heart pounded for more beats than he could count. He felt helpless. The only way he could stop her was if he was with her night and day. She would do what she wished despite his words of warning as well as displeasure.

Fannie's eyes blazed blue fire. Her body tensed as she formed her next words. "You don't love me. I will not marry a man who doesn't love me!" She sounded both fierce as well as determined in her denial.

He thought certain smoke would sweep from her in a steady stream. What the hell did love have to do with this situation they were undergoing? Together they were pregnant. While the babe wasn't planned, Fox was pleased. He cared for her. Lusted after her beautiful body. When he looked at her, he was famished to know more of her. Fannie carried his child. With that said, there was nothing more to consider. After she intimated she would abort the child, he felt certain she held his baby in her womb. If she didn't realize the truth, she would not have thought that far ahead. Fannie as much as admitted to the fact. A young woman would not consider such an act if she wasn't desperate.

I don't want Fannie to feel desperation. I don't know how to change the feeling harboring inside.

Fox meant to repeat this until she believed what he said, one thousand times if necessary. "I will care for you and our child. Will protect you. Give our child my name. What more is there?" With frustration eating at him, he lifted his shoulders. He waited for an answer he could understand. "Tomorrow, sooner, if at all possible, I will speak with Jasper on this matter. We will set a date. I wish to leave for my home in the next week." Her face paled. Perhaps he said too much. Pushed too hard.

She turned from him but not before he saw tears in her eyes. Feeling a desperate need to console, Fox pulled her into his arms. Pressed Fannie against him. With all her wonderous curves, she fit him to perfection. She mumbled something he couldn't understand into his chest. Her hands clung to his shoulders.

He put a slight distance between them, tilting her chin up so he could hear what she had to say. As if she realized he didn't understand, she repeated herself. "I don't want to leave Scotland." The words were whispered on a thin wail. "Don't want to leave my sisters. We've always been together…almost always. When Maggie was in trouble we were separated for a couple of months. Other than the one time, we've never been apart."

With the tip of his finger, Fox caught a silver tear as the drop slid down her cheek. When he put the drop to his lips he tasted the salt. His heart went out to her. He never had siblings. Fox didn't understand the deep connection between them.

"I can't stay here. My life is across the Atlantic in a beautiful land filled with thousands of lakes. You will come to love the country there. Our children will love the land too." He wondered how much convincing he would need to do.

"I wanted to find a man who loves me. Just like Tessa and Maggie. Their husbands love them." Fannie pressed her wet cheek on his chest. Hoping to make her feel better, he smoothed his hands along the contour of her back down her sweet butt he recalled kissing the second time they made love in the brothel.

The dampness of her tears slid through the cloth. Fox didn't like the notion his words made her cry or his lack of words. "Love might come. I do love our child. Have admiration for the mother." He placed his hand on her belly. Thought for a moment she might flinch away from his touch. She didn't move.

Fox sucked in a deep breath of air, pleased with Fannie's reaction. Her soft belly was still flat. Would be so for another month at least. When they were on the ship taking them to New York she would begin to show. Swelled with his child, Fannie would still be a beautiful woman.

He lifted her chin. Watched her sweet pink tongue glide across her mouth, an invitation for a kiss. He was not immune to the request. With slow finesse Fox lowered his mouth to brush across hers. Once then twice while he waited for her response to his undemanding possession. When it came the sound was a delight to his ears.

Covering her mouth with his, he pressed against the opening of hers, encouraging her to allow him inside. She did his bidding, parting her lips. His tongue glanced along hers, rubbing against the soft warmth. She met the gentle pressure with equal force. He was immersed in Fannie. Caught by flames that had been left smoldering for the last six weeks. During those long days, he'd thought of two things. His money and how Fannie would feel to him when he possessed her again.

What did it matter if he loved her or vice versa? Between them they ignited an unquenchable fire. Flames licked him everywhere, sending him to the sun then back. Fannie would keep him warm in the cold winter nights in Michigan. He cupped her small butt in his hands. Pushed her against his throbbing member. Into his mouth she whimpered with a soft mewling sound that rippled ribbon-like from her divided lips. The ribbons seemed to wrap around them holding them united, surrounding them with their blistering heat.

He wished they were someplace private. Somewhere he could strip her of her clothing then kiss every part of her. Kiss her in the deepest most sensitive places on her beautiful body. Her fingers wound into his hair then along the back of his neck tugging him closer.

"What! Oh!"

"Damn," Fox muttered, understanding they were interrupted.

Not wishing to tear himself away from the lovely siren in his arms but understanding the need, Fox slowly lifted his head. Focused on the two people standing highlighted in the library door. Fannie moaned her disappointment at the loss of contact. He shuffled in a deep breath of Fannie scented air before he spoke. He gave a light caress to Fannie's cheek to apologize for the withdrawal of his attention.

"Nellie? Dillon?" he questioned. What were they doing here? Perhaps it was a good thing they arrived. Would have been better if they'd knocked first. They would not have caught him with his questing fingers on her delectable rump. Before their unwanted appearance, he'd been eyeing the sofa nestled against the wall. Thoughts of lying Fannie down on the couch had been rampantly bombarding his mind.

"Fannie?" Nellie asked as Fannie buried her face into his chest. Fox held her against him until she calmed. "What are you doing with Fox? How well do you know this man? He was touching your butt." The question was accusatory.

Fox continued to soothe Fannie. He whispered for her ears only, "You don't need to answer your sister. What we were doing isn't her business."

"Come along, Nellie," Dillon said, sensing the intrusion into their privacy and was tugging on Nellie's arm. "We need to leave these two lovebirds alone. Though I do appreciate your terminology. Never heard you use that word before. Butt…hmm, gives pause for thought. Could frighten a man."

"No!" Nellie tugged her arm free from Dillon's grasp. Fast and furious, her words came out of her mouth. "Fannie needs to explain herself!"

"No, Fannie doesn't need to explain anything to you. If she wishes to do so, the explanation is up to her," Fox said, his voice soft, deceivingly soft. He was furious as well as irritated with Nellie's intrusion into their privacy.

Dillon appeared to realize how angry he was. He spoke to Nellie. Placed her hand in the crook of his elbow. "We will see the two of you on the dance floor. Seeing what we interrupted, you probably should not remain in the library much longer."

As soon as Fannie realized what her sister walked in on, she was embarrassed to the tips of her pretty nipples. Red stained her breasts along with her cheeks. If they interrupted a few minutes later, her state of dishabille would not be questionable.

Dillon managed to lead a protesting girlfriend from the room then close the door. Next to him, Fannie was shaking. Her body was still pressed against his. With wide confused eyes, she stared at him.

"Come, you need to sit. All will be fine. We were kissing, that's all. I would wager Nellie has found herself in a similar situation with Dillon." Fox carried her to one of the large wing chairs then sat down with Fannie on his lap.

She looked at him with a hesitant and weary smile on her bee-stung mouth. "They saw us kissing," she murmured. "Your hand was not appropriate. It was placed on my bottom."

"Your sweet butt," he corrected with a soft chuckle. "I was shocked to hear Nellie use the word. Will never forget. Would you say butt for me?"

"No…she will tell Maggie. Maggie will inform Jasper. After all I told him this afternoon, he will begin to draw a conclusion I wish he wouldn't."

Those words of Fannie's had Fox backpedaling. He would ask more about what she inadvertently said later. Finding out what she told Jasper was imperative. He didn't appreciate going into a situation with half the information. What the devil did she tell Jasper? Fannie could never have told him they made love in Hannah's brothel. If she found herself confronted with unanswerable questions, she would skirt the truth.

"I'm certain Dillon has kissed Nellie. Touched her places in the heat of the moment that she should have objected to. We did nothing wrong. Nothing for you to be ashamed of doing." Fox knew if they interrupted them a few minutes later they would have seen more, much more. He kept his hands at her waist. "We will stay here until you feel ready to meet the two of them head on. I understand you are angry with Nellie. Don't let her accusations rile you more."

"Why? Why were you kissing me when you believe I'm a thief? For that matter, why was I letting you kiss me? Touch me?" She sounded perplexed and looked adorable.

Thank God she didn't mention the fact he didn't like her. Liked her too damn much for his randy man parts to remain in control. Fox tapped her on the nose, going for a lighter touch to this scenario. "I kissed your charming mouth because you taste heavenly. Your body pressed against mine causes me to lose all sense of responsibility. Pleased you didn't mention the fact you think I don't like you. I do. Don't kiss ladies I don't like. Never have. Never will."

"I'm not going to marry you."

They were back to marriage. She could protest all she liked. Protests or denials would never change their future. The two of them were meant to be together. "We will see. Believe your sisters will have something to say about a marriage when I tell them we've made love…twice. And…" He continued after a slight pause, "you are pregnant with my child. We need to leave before I'm unable to resist you." If left alone in this library much longer, the number would have risen to three times.

"Will you take me home? We can say goodnight to Nellie and Dillon then leave. I don't wish to stay," Fannie murmured on a weak note. She appeared distraught. "Don't wish to try to find my way home alone. I've done my duty for Maggie's sake."

He wished he could wrap her up in the protective shelter of his arms. At this moment, Fannie looked far too vulnerable. A slight breeze might blow her over. "You will promise to see me tomorrow afternoon at the bakery. We haven't finished talking about our future. Perhaps we should cement our relationship tonight. If they are available, conversation with Jasper and Maggie would be appropriate under the circumstances. We will tell them we've known each other for a while. Tried to keep our romance a secret."

"Why?"

"Well," he paused in thought, "damned if I know. We've a few minutes during the ride to think of a reason or two." He didn't believe he would be able to come up with something believable. every time he looked at her, he wanted her more. If they'd been seeing each other, he would have been an ever-present guest in the Kenworthy townhouse. The fact he hadn't seen her for six weeks seemed to make him want her more.

~ * ~

When they entered the Kenworthy townhouse later in the evening, Maggie and Jasper were sipping wine in the drawing room. Maggie was on Jasper's lap, giggling. Jasper, enjoying himself, was kissing Maggie's neck, murmuring how much he loved her. His large hand cupped one breast, roaming across the hardened tip. Jasper wanted to pull her bodice to her waist, fondle her beautiful breasts. Suckle. Didn't dare. Either Nellie or Fannie could walk in on them. Jason left for the country home about the same time as the girls left for the party. He harbored thoughts of carrying Maggie to the bedroom. The devil, they needed more privacy. There were too many people coming and going in his household. Maybe they should take an extended vacation to Ireland. Renew old acquaintances.

Maggie saw them first. She let out a little shriek. Jasper thought the sound was one of pleasure because of his questing fingers. She pushed at his hand. Struggled to right her skirts which were half way up her legs. She was straddling him. Her soft white thighs on either side of his legs.

"No...not moving my hands." He bit her on the tip of her ear. Realized he needed to redirect his motives. Needed to touch her darkest, sweetest secrets.

"Fannie and Fox," she murmured, continuing to push at his arm along with the hand that was traveling up her leg to more intimate territory. Squirming, Maggie, tried to get off him. With his hands on her hips, Jasper held her down. "Jasper, we're being watched by my sister. Fox too," there was the sound of panic in her voice. "You can't...I...please."

He heaved a frustrated sigh still not moving his hands away from her. Understood these two people needed to talk. Could have waited for a more opportune time. Maggie was perfect where she sat astride him except for the sudden unwanted appearance of company. "I see." He didn't' wish to see. Jasper let his hand drop away before he acknowledged the pair who looked as if they mended a few of the problems between them. Fannie was leaning into Fox. His arm was wrapped around her. "To what do we owe this visit, Fox?" Jasper asked as he tucked Maggie in next to him. He wasn't going to let her move. Her head fell against his shoulder.

She whispered, her voice distraught to his sensitive hearing. "Jasper, I don't like this. Let me sit on my own chair."

Jasper supposed he should let her up. Hoped this was a courtesy call and nothing more. They would say good evening then Fox would take his leave. When he took a second look at the expressions on the two faces in front of him, he understood this would take longer than he hoped. Taking his hands from her waist, he allowed her to remove herself from his thighs. Maggie sat on a chair next to him, fluffing her skirt.

She sent him a brilliant smile before mouthing the words. "Thank you. Later, I will make this up to you."

She gifted him with the same smile that always brought him to his knees. Her words had the same consequence. After this conversation he meant to carry her to their suite of rooms. Lay her down on their bed. Strip her. Would make love to her the entire night. For the next few minutes, hope that was all this meeting would be, he would curb his appetites.

His butler appeared in the room. Gave everyone a quick nod. "Wine? A few snacks for your guests?" he asked. "This appears to be a long conversation about to happen. The young ones have this look about them. Maybe two bottles of wine would be more appropriate. There are four of you."

"Are you staying?" Jasper looked to Fox for the answer before he ordered the food and drink.

With the nod and the serious expression in Fox's eyes, he said, "We've, Fannie and I have decided to marry. Wanted you and Maggie to be the first to learn about our plans. Thought to speak to you tonight before I take my leave."

Fannie hit him on the arm, saying, "You can't tell them that bit of nonsense. I've not said yes. There hasn't even been a proposal. Besides, the last time I remember, I said I wouldn't marry you."

He grinned then continued to speak as if she wasn't saying no to a marriage to him. Jasper thought it odd. "There is a ship going to New York, leaving in eight days. I hope seven days is enough time to make the arrangements for a wedding. Doesn't need to be anything fancy. Just need to make all this right."

"No arrangements necessary," Fannie blurted. "I'm not…" Fannie didn't finish the words. Fox's fingers tightened on her waist. She gasped.

Jasper realized there was more to Fannie's story than what she apprised him with this afternoon. He needed to understand what was happening between these two before he could condone a wedding. Though, neither needed his blessings. They were both of an age to make the decision on their own.

While he liked Fox Taggart, if Fannie didn't want him for a husband, he wouldn't allow Fox to run roughshod over her. By the way Fox looked at her, Jasper realized if he wasn't in love with her right now, he would be soon. Jasper also understood all the girls were holding out for love. Would be surprised if Fannie slept with him. Anything was possible. Could this have something to do with the night she spent at Hannah's brothel?

Not unless Fannie is pregnant with his child. Conceived six weeks ago when she was lost as well as relying on her wits to survive. With Halsey along with his pursuit of her she ended up at Hannah's.

If Anice had anything to do with Halsey, if she paid him to kidnap her daughters, Fannie was better off with Fox in the wilds of Michigan than here in Glasgow. There she would be untouchable. That left Nellie to be protected. He would have to give this more thought.

"Have a seat," Jasper motioned to them. "Why the hurry to marry? Could take some time. Get to know each other better. Find out if you are suited to each other," Jasper pointed out.

His slow grasp of their story was growing with both information along with assumptions. Decisions should never be made on assumptions. Fannie told him nothing happened at the brothel. Insisted she wasn't hurt. Based on untold facts, he would wager this pair slept together that night. Somehow Fox must have believed she was a whore. What a conundrum. Fox would have crashed through her shield proclaiming her innocence. He would feel responsible. In the next breath, he would ask for her hand. An honorable man wouldn't want a child of his to carry the name of bastard. Marriage was a permanent situation.

"Been away from home far too long. The business doesn't run itself. Need to be at my logging operation. My men are skilled but there is only one other leader among them. With the end of winter, they'll begin to cut timber again."

Jasper wasn't certain of a speedy wedding. He needed to learn more about Fox. The sisters would wish for her to have a real wedding. One with flowers, a dress, whatever else went into the chaos of wedding planning.

Anice would learn of the marriage. She would crash the ceremony. There would be pandemonium.

He needed to return to the basics before he got lost in a myriad of inconsequential ideas that were now plaguing his conscious thought. "The two of you have known...how long have you known each other?" He found himself tapping on the arm of the chair waiting for an answer.

"Six weeks give or take," Fox said, as he stood behind the chair where Fannie sat. He set his hands on her shoulders, squeezed. The gesture cried out his possession. Fox would never allow Fannie to gainsay his plans. They would indeed marry before eight days passed. What would happen next was up to Fox and how he handled this difficult situation with his wife to be.

"I don't understand how or why the two of you have been hiding your feelings from the rest of the family. Six weeks you say...give or take a day." Maggie paused as she appeared to be thinking over what she should say next. "Until last night, we didn't know the two of you knew each other. Whenever you, along with your father, came to dinner, Fannie declined," Maggie said as her gaze shifted from one to the other. Fannie looked down, hiding her eyes. Fox's brows knitted together as if he wasn't thrilled with the statement as well as looking for words to explain the state of their friendship.

Maggie's understanding of the situation was good. Jasper didn't comprehend either. There was so much here the couple were not saying. "As Maggie just said. You, along with your father, have been to the house numerous times. Fannie never gave any indication you knew each other. Always refused to come to dinner when you were here. I wonder why Fannie declined," Jasper pointed out. "You need to explain." Then he turned his attention to Fannie. "If the two of you were lovers, why wouldn't you come to dinner when they visited? Would seem you would appreciate seeing the man you were in love with. Why?"

"It's private just between the two of us," Fox spoke up, overriding the answer Fannie might have given. "Neither one of us knew where our fledgling relationship would end up. While Fannie didn't wish to leave Scotland, she also understood my need to return home. She was afraid. Hence the reason why she stayed in her room so much of the time. All of you believed she was sulking. That wasn't the case. Fannie's heart was with me but she was afraid to admit to the fact."

That was quite a bunch of blarney Fox dished out. He possessed an agile tongue along with a swift mind. Ah, well, after Fox left, he would get Fannie's side of the story. Last night they acted strange, not anywhere near loverlike. At one point, Jasper felt as if Fox loathed Fannie who was now his intended. He scowled at her more than he smiled. His expression never softened toward her.

"If the two of you are to receive our blessings, more will need to be said. I'm not convinced this courtship is agreeable to Maggie's sister. Fannie, did you tell Fox about Halsey? Seems that is something he should understand." Jasper's question brought an intense reaction to Fox's face. His eyes darkened with concern, coupled with anger.

"What?" Fox bent over to look at her face. He reacted as if he didn't like what he saw. "Halsey? What do you know about that pimp! The man is dangerous. You stay away from him!"

"As if I would go anywhere willingly with that man." Fannie placed her hand on top of Fox's. "Can we speak about Craig Halsey later? Maybe tomorrow at the bakery. I would be more than pleased to tell you what transpired between us. It wasn't pleasant. Hannah saved me. Gave me the room upstai…" She stopped, seeing Maggie's frown of concern or wariness.

"You know the man?" Fox's fingers tightened on Fannie's shoulders. "Don't wish to wait until tomorrow. Tell me now. Let's hash this over before…" he stuffed his finger through his hair before returning his hands to Fannie's shoulders.

Jasper relaxed back to watch the play between the two supposed lovers. While Fox was furious, Fannie was reticent. It was obvious to him Fannie didn't wish to tell the story in front of Maggie. She almost gave the whole game away by mentioning the upstairs room. Jasper knew Maggie must have heard. Would jump to a conclusion, perhaps more than one would flit through her mind. While he'd promised not to tell Maggie that Fannie spent the night six weeks ago in a whorehouse, he felt the information was going to be divulged tonight. Perhaps the cat was already out of the bag.

"Wouldn't say I know him," she muttered, appearing to wish herself anywhere but here. Caught her lip between her teeth. Appearing to have no other recourse but to explain to Fox, she began. "The man accosted me when I was looking for a monogramed handkerchief."

"Why the hell were you looking for a monogramed handkerchief? That's ridiculous!"

"It was a scavenger hunt, my part of the game."

"Good God, no!"

"Unfortunate for me, yes. I ran to a huge home down the street. Managed to get into the backyard then up the steps before Halsey could catch up to me. Hannah was there with a broom swatting at the man as well as swearing. Angus gave her moral support. He pulled me inside the house."

"That's how you came to be at the brothel for the night?" Fox asked on a hushed breath of air. "Hannah saved you from the little pimp."

"Fannie was at a brothel? She spent a night there!" Maggie screeched her outrage at the situation. "A whorehouse… Why didn't you tell us?"

"Believe your reaction to that bit of news should give you the answer," Fox pointed out with a bland tone to his voice Jasper was positive he didn't feel.

With calm that Jasper didn't think Maggie felt, she turned to Fox. "You thought our Fannie was a whore?" The accusation was strong enough to make Fox flinch. "You took her innocence. That's not right."

"Yes, you're correct on all counts. Though I cannot be faulted here. Hannah sent me to her room by accident. How the hell would I know she wasn't a whore?"

Jasper leaned toward his wife, "Hush, Fannie says nothing happened. We need to believe her." He saw the blossoming color on Fannie's cheeks and after that a slight tinge of red on Fox's face. Jasper thought if Fannie was indeed with child, the babe was Fox's, and it was planted in her womb the night she found herself alone and lost in a dangerous part of the city. Fox was stepping up. He wasn't about to leave Fannie alone in her condition. Fannie was fighting him on the principal that he didn't love her. The man must have some feelings or he wouldn't be insisting on marriage. There were other ways for a man of means to deal with a bastard child. Marriage was not a necessity.

Seemed Fannie was fading fast. She was leaning against the back of her chair, eyes closing spasmodically. Jasper understood everything she wished to remain a secret from Maggie was unveiling itself one horrible moment at a time.

Fox straightened. "Believe what happened that night is between Fannie and myself. While I could explain my part in the scenario, it is up to Fannie what she wants to reveal. I suggest the questions concerning the evening in question be terminated. Fannie is exhausted by the last twenty-four hours which have not been easy on her."

Jasper tapped his fingers together beneath his chin while pondering his next move. He began by saying to Maggie, "What is important here has not been spoken. I would have gotten to this later but we got sidetracked. The major fact is that your mother, Anice, has hired Halsey to kidnap the girls. Fannie told me she saw Anice in the carriage Halsey attempted to get her in the very same night when she escaped him. She also saw him at the dressmakers yesterday afternoon. Fannie will be much safer across the Atlantic Ocean than she is here in Glasgow."

"Fannie, go up to bed. You are exhausted. Jasper and I will decide on a date for our marriage. I'll apprise you of everything we talk about tomorrow when we meet at the bakery." Fox brought Fannie to her feet then walked with her to the base of the stairs.

Jasper watched Fox kiss Fannie with gentle ease on her forehead. Fox loved her. He might not know that small but important fact. In Jasper's mind there was no doubt about his feelings for Fannie.

A few beats of his heart later, Fox returned to the drawing room, nodded to both. "Do the two of you have any more questions? Will you approve of our marriage? Fannie is reluctant because she is afraid. Can't blame her. A lot has happened in the last twenty-four hours not to mention the shadows enveloping her from the past six weeks that haunt her."

"You took her innocence in a brothel," Maggie said, her chin tilted in the air. "How dare you? You are no gentleman."

"Yes. That is all I'm going to say on the matter. I wish to marry your sister. I will cherish her as well as protect her."

"You don't love her," Maggie protested.

"I care for Fannie a great deal. Want what is best for her along with the *wee bairn*. The two of you are welcome to visit us in Michigan any time you choose. The country is lovely, even in the winter, though I would advise you not to visit when the snow is six feet deep. Deep snow drifts make traveling difficult."

"I don't understand what just happened here," Maggie muttered as she looked to Jasper for some consoling words.

"I will take my leave. Believe I would like to escort Fannie to the bakery. In lieu of the information I received about Halsey coupled with Anice MacRae's interest in Fannie, I feel she would be safer in my company than with your driver. Will be here at one o'clock to escort her. After we have some private time to plan the next course of our lives, I will return her to your home. We can set the date on the 'morrow."

With a few more words between them, Fox took his leave. Jasper watched him walk out the front door.

"Well, that went well," Jasper turned to his wife. "What do you think will happen next?"

Chapter Four

At twelve thirty, Fannie found herself pacing in her upstairs bedroom. She waited for Maggie to come for her to tell her Fox arrived. Fannie didn't have the courage to come down for breakfast. In her room, she ate a croissant. Drank the hot chocolate the maid brought her. Having Maggie confront her about the time she spent in Hannah's brothel was not on her list of something pleasant. Maggie would chastise her as if what happened could be set directly at her doorstep.

The clock on her mantle ticked away each second. One chime announced she still had a half hour to wait for Fox. What should she do? Fox was insisting they marry. Fannie didn't know how she felt about that arrangement. She enjoyed his kisses. From what she recalled from her dazed state when they made love, she enjoyed the intimate contact too, more the second time when he didn't hurt her.

Fox accused her of stealing from him. Despite her denials, he didn't believe her. Fox didn't love her. It was obvious he wanted the *bairn*. Fannie sifted in a breath of air. Closed her eyes, wishing this wasn't all happening so fast. In eight days or less, they would be married. A man who didn't love her would own her. He did tell her he cared for her, would protect her as well. She would be hauled off to someplace she never heard of before yesterday. Michigan. Where the devil on that continent was that?

Fannie set her hand on her flat belly. There was a life growing inside her. Of that, she was positive. What if she did all this for the baby's sake and she wasn't pregnant? What if she was wrong? Only six weeks had passed since that night. She was late, more than a couple of weeks. There had been no other symptoms. She'd not had morning sickness. Other than ever present nausea both Maggie and Tess endured, she didn't know what she would feel. Asking either Tessa or Maggie about symptoms was out of the question.

I could ask Fox.

With that thought she felt heat rise from the tips of her toes to the roots of her hair. He might pose the question to her. Fox wouldn't want to marry her if he wasn't certain she carried his child. He didn't like her. No, she needed to remove that concept from her head. Fox told her the assumption wasn't true. He didn't like what she'd done. Except for the theft, he enjoyed her company he told her. Appreciating her companionship would have to be enough to last her a lifetime.

How would he know if he enjoyed spending time with her? They'd spent so little time in each other's company. He couldn't know. He must be grasping at some idea he could set in front of her to appease her. Fox told her he liked her soft, little body. Their shared kisses. Other things he liked too, more embarrassing words. Were those simple things enough to build a relationship on? Fannie didn't see how that could be. A person needed to like other characteristics of the person they wed.

What would she do in Michigan? He told her he owned a logging company. She didn't know much about cutting trees. Was the work dangerous? Fannie supposed it might be. He also owned a small herd of cattle. Told her he tried to be self-sufficient as much as possible.

What would she do? Fox mentioned they didn't have neighbors. The closest settlement was a full days ride from his home. His spread was almost autonomous. In the summer they grew vegetables. There was an apple orchard. She would can fruit along with the vegetables. She didn't know how to can anything.

Canning?

The knock on the door brought her swiveling to focus there…at the door knob. A quick glance to the clock told her it was too early to be Fox. "Who is it?" her voice quivered. She was afraid the knock was from Maggie. Her sister who she didn't wish to see.

"It's me, Maggie. May I come inside? You didn't come down for breakfast. I'd like to talk for a few minutes. Before Fox arrives," she said, her voice soft. "Please, I need to apologize for the way I acted last night. It wasn't well done of me."

Fannie opened the door. "We have fifteen minutes before Fox is supposed to arrive here." An apology would be nice. Fannie needed to feel the comradery they always knew before this happened to her.

"May…we should sit." Maggie smoothed her hands along her skirts. "I won't take long but there are a few things that need to be said." She paused. "I need to say. My conscious bothers me."

"By all means," Fannie's voice was tight with emotions. The air was stilted and tense. She wasn't about to begin the conversation. Maggie would need to figure this out all by herself. "Have a seat. Don't let me stop you."

Sitting on the edge of her chair, Maggie began. "I *ken* you are angry with me. Please hear me out. I'm sorry. I judged you last night. That wasn't well done of me. Spoke with Jasper for over an hour afterward. I realize now nothing that happened was your fault. You were sick. Left alone to fend for yourself, you did the best you could. You did survive. That fact is important. Since the brothel was mentioned, Jasper apprised me of your evening of terror. I'm sorry." Maggie pleated then unpleated her skirt.

"So, you understand why I became reserved? I felt terrified of my shadow. Didn't believe I would ever see Fox again so I never mentioned him. I could never tell anyone what happened that night. Hannah told me a doctor would be there to see to me. Until Fox discovered me in the library, I didn't know his name. He didn't know mine. He confronted me about some money he believed I stole. Now I'm expected to marry him. He believes I'm a thief and a whore. Why would he want to marry me?"

"Do you love him? A silly question, I guess since you barely know the man," Maggie mumbled. "Believe he is at least a little bit smitten with you."

"I like him except for the fact he believes I stole fifty thousand pounds that night. If I did, I don't know where the money could be."

"What? Does Jasper know about the stolen money?" Maggie was quick to ask. "You need to say something."

"No, didn't tell him. Shouldn't have mentioned the money to you either. The loss of Fox's groats is between the two of us as it should be." She lifted her shoulders as much to shrug off the missing pounds as to ease the ache in her neck muscles. "What does it matter, Maggie? Fox wants to marry me. I can't tell you I'm enthusiastic about the prospect."

"Jasper told me Fox has the look of a besotted man. His gaze follows you wherever you are. When he looks at you, my husband tells me there is love in his eyes. I don't understand how he sees that though I do believe

Jasper."

"You're crazy husband's notion is foolish," Fannie said, her voice soft, wishing the words were true. She couldn't say she loved Fox. Yet…yes, she cared for him. Didn't understand why. "I would like to believe him. I can't."

The clock chimed once. It was one o'clock. Fannie jerked when she heard the sound. Her breath hitched into her lungs. The palms of her hands were sweaty with nervous anxiety. Fox would be here to pick her up for the outing. They would chat about what? Seemed all that needed to be said had been said. What more was there? No matter what was said this afternoon, she would marry him in less than eight days.

Maggie reached out to touch her hand, to reassure. "Don't be worried, Fannie. What I do believe is that Fox will make you a good husband. He is responsible. I hope in time the two of you will come to love each other. Love is what makes the relationship so much more. I do understand couples wed for other reasons."

"Such as an unwanted pregnancy?" Fannie couldn't help the bitterness in her tone. It was there. Maggie heard.

"Fox is doing right by you. He is protecting you. Because you will be in another country, no one will know the child was conceived before the marriage."

"Jasper is right. I will be safe from Anice if I'm across the Atlantic. Now the two of you will need worry only about Nellie. Dillon will help protect her. Perhaps they should wed too. We could have a double wedding." Being safe from her mother was not a reason to marry a man, any man. Fannie was afraid she was about to make a horrible mistake. Perhaps the worst mistake of her life.

Maggie stood then held out her hand. "Come, let's go downstairs. When the two of you return, we will negotiate a wedding date. We will put the day off for as long as possible. My guess is your man has booked tickets on a ship leaving here. We will be bound by that time standard. Might not have eight days. Imagine he is in a hurry to return to his home."

Together they walked down the stairs. Fox stood in the foyer, smiling at her as she made her way to him. His grin was wide as his eyes appeared to darken. Seemed he watched each footstep as she walked toward him.

"You look lovely," Fox told her while he held out her cape to wrap around her shoulders. "Outside the storm will soak us to our skin. It is raining like the very devil," he told her as he adjusted the fasteners, the backs of his hands touched the tops of her veiled breasts. Her body gave a quick jolt of recognition while her breath hitched. With her lips parted, she blinked up at him, questioning. "We might need to make a mad dash to the carriage. What do you say? Are you up for a quick sprint?"

"No…no, I don't believe so. I can't run with these shoes." Stunned by his words, she wasn't certain what he meant. "I'll put my hood up. Won't get too wet. Fox…truly I don't need to make a mad dash."

Fox laughed. "I'll carry you."

"No." She put her hands in the air thinking to stop him. "You can't. I'm too heavy."

At the door he was true to his word. Fox swept her into his arms. Startled, Fannie grabbed hold of him. Her fingers wound around his neck. The soft texture of his hair surprised her. She sipped in Fox scented air. She liked the way he smelled.

"Fox!" she squealed. "Put me down."

"Not on your life," he murmured, his breath brushing against her cheek. "Like the way you feel in my arms."

Fannie liked the feelings too. He was strong, muscles bulging while he held her.

After the butler opened the door, he sprinted down the steps. Rain sluiced from the dark sky, the drops pounding around them. She clung tighter to him. Pressed her face against the breadth of his chest. He skipped over a puddle before reaching the carriage. The driver stood beside the open door.

He set her on a seat. Jumping in behind her, he pulled her into his arms. His lips brushed across hers, soft then hard. Deep then light. Fannie opened for him, realizing she loved the taste as well as the scent of Fox. Wanted him to never stop kissing her. The tips of their tongues collided, gamboled against each other.

Her wish wasn't granted.

He set her on the opposite side of the carriage, grinning at her. Reached out to touch her cheek. "That's enough of that for now. Don't think it would be in good taste for me to ravish you in the carriage on the way to our luncheon. If I did, you would look a mess, your hair in a wild tangle, lips swollen, bee-stung and adorable. One kiss can lead to another then more. Did you realize what one kiss can lead to?" Again, he reached across the distance, to caress the line of her jaw with a fingertip. Placed a quick kiss to the tip of her nose. She frowned at him. Pursed her lips.

He hooted his laughter. "You want more kisses. I will grant you those later. Whatever you wish. We will find a private place after we accomplish our business today. I could have my driver, tour the city while I give you all my attention."

"Of course not," Fannie denied as heat flushed her face with the acknowledgement that was exactly what she wanted. Needed to understand more about this kissing business along with what came after.

Fannie wondered if the grin on his face was a besotted grin. Unwilling to look at him this second, she fluffed her skirts again. Stared at the tips of her shoes to keep from looking at his mouth. Maggie mentioned the fact Jasper thought the man smiled at her in that manner, the love-struck way. Told her Fox's gaze followed her around the room. When his deep chuckle caught her attention, she looked up eyes wide. Reveled at his focused gaze. At the moment, he was looking at her breasts. Because of the rush of excitement, she was breathing deep. Much to her chagrin they were heaving. She crossed her arms to stop the frantic movement. Fannie didn't like the fact her breasts moved so much.

Sitting back, his arms stretching across the top of his seat, he crossed his legs. They were long, well-muscled. In order to stretch out, Fox had to sit sideways. He looked relaxed as well as indifferent to the situation. In opposition, she felt tense. Apprehensions strung taut. Was uncertain of how to act or what to say.

Nervous, she smoothed her skirts again. Folded her hands on her lap to keep them from shaking. She didn't want to look at him. Understood she couldn't resist. Tipping her head to one side, she sent him a hesitant smile. Somehow, she needed to change the silence which was unraveling her. Needed conversation.

Sipping in a drink of air for courage, "What do you want to talk about?" Fannie asked, wondering how she could carry on a conversation with this man when he appeared so smug. The rumbling of the carriage against the cobblestones, made some noise in the quiet place where they sat.

"You…us…but not right at the moment. There are other more pressing matters that need our consideration." Fox placed his hands behind his neck. Seemed to reflect for a few seconds. "I've done a great deal of thinking about Halsey along with your mother. Tell me about this man, Lord Nelson Abernathy. What do you know about him? This is important for me to know."

"Lord Abernathy is a horrible excuse for a man. He is beyond redemption. Mother has joined forces with him. My mother who despises her girls looks to him to hurt us. Did you know? We are all bastards, each and every one of us." Fannie was terrified of Nelson Abernathy. She didn't understand how to tell Fox all his deceits. "He is hateful. Will do anything for my mother as long as doing so degrades one of her daughters. He did wish to marry Maggie. After the aborted attempt he tried to turn Tessa into his mistress. You see, he wanted revenge."

"What part in this scheme of Anice's does Halsey play. He's a pimp. The girls he brings in to work for him are not ladies. They are down on their luck. Need money more than respectability. You, my dear, do not fit the profile. He wanted you for another reason. Jasper told me you thought you saw your mother in the carriage with Abernathy. Are those words true? Would your mother sink so low as to sell you to a pimp?"

"Yes." There was no doubt in Fannie's mind about all of Fox's questions. "My mother was seen on the balcony of one of Abernathy's homes having sex with him just after Tessa was able to escape." Fannie shuddered at the thoughts flashing at blinding speed through her mind. While she didn't know exactly what having sex with Nelson entailed, she understood what her mother did was deplorable. Was having sex different from what she did in the brothel with Fox?

"That puts the attempted kidnapping into a different light. I'm assuming the reason he hasn't succeeded in the last six weeks is because you have failed to leave the house. Since you saw him when you visited the dressmaker, he is watching for you to make a mistake. I'm here for you. Need to keep you from his little harem of women. Not going to allow you to mess up."

"Mother has wanted to give all of us to Lord Abernathy. Both Maggie and Tessa defied mother. Beat her at her games. Now she is after me and Nellie. I don't know what part Halsey plays in this drama my mother has concocted. Certain the only part would be disgusting as well as degrading."

"My sources imply that Lord Abernathy and your mother work together. That Anice is a mistress of his. She's available for sex whenever he crucks his little finger in her direction. Could my information be true? If Halsey catches up to you, would you be given to both men?"

"Where Anice is concerned, anything is possible. Mother is insatiable. She loves sex. Doesn't appear to make a difference who she has it with. What you learned is probably factual. As I said earlier, Jason and the Duke of Southcliff watched Anice and Abernathy have sex on the balcony of his townhouse. That's a long story. Probably fit for another time. I only know what little I overheard. What was said was probably not meant for my ears."

"Tell me all of it." The harsh demand startled Fannie. She blinked a few times as she digested the severe command. "In order to keep you safe until we leave for my home, I need to know all of the facts, revolting or not. At least all of what you know." He spread his hands. "Don't wish for you to fall victim to these people."

"Alright." Fannie recounted everything from the party on Christmas Eve when Lord Abernathy announced his engagement to Maggie then how she escaped the ball to end up at the homeless camp. Went on to tell him how Maggie ran away with Jasper to Ireland. They were married there. The man who she thought was her father tried to kill Jasper or Maggie. She was never certain who the target was only that Maggie caught the bullet. She jumped in front of Jasper at the last minute to save him.

"And…Tessa…" Fox encouraged. "Perhaps that story should wait. We are almost to the bakery. You piqued my curiosity when you mentioned the Duke of Southcliff. He is well known to my father. Seems he worked or works for the Scottish government," Fox paused for a few beats. "A spy of sorts."

"Yes, he and his wife are very nice. They took Tessa in when they had no idea who she was. Rescued her actually from the arms of the man who guarded her. Tessa refused to give Lacie her name. She thought Jason would annul the marriage. Mother led her to believe Jason's father was hers also. Anice believes she is above reproach. Thinks she can do anything she likes."

"We will need to take care. You are not to go anywhere alone. Must have someone to look after your safety."

"Don't wish to go anywhere unless it's with you."

The carriage rolled to a stop. His grin, Fannie thought, might be besotted. This time his smile spoke of some secret he planned. "Here we are." Fox helped her out. His hands on her waist lingered for a few seconds. Set her hood on her head before stepping back to study her profile. "You are a delight to my eyes, Fannie MacRae, soon to be Fannie Taggart. What do you say? Should we try out some of the wonderful pastries Daryl bakes. The sweeter the better, yet none could be as sweet as you, my dear."

Fannie touched her hand to her heated cheeks. His words scorched her. "You should not say things you don't mean. While the compliment is nice—"

Fox interrupted before she could finish. Set a finger to her lips. "Ah, but I mean every word I say. Would never speak anything that isn't true. If you recall, I've tasted you just about everywhere it is possible. Now, in this, don't gainsay me." He wrapped his arm around her, escorting her up the steps. When they stepped inside, the little bell at the door chimed. It was a merry sound. Made her smile.

"Alright."

He bent to whisper close to her ear. "We can speak more about your delicious charms later." Touched upon the lobe with his tongue. Another round of heat coursed through her.

Stuttering, trying to keep her mind from the enveloping fog, she spouted trivia. "Did you know this Daryl who owns the bakery is the sister to the Duke of Southcliff's wife? That Lacie still does all the bookkeeping for Daryl. Seems Daryl can bake but she's horrible with numbers. The business was thought to be failing simply because she couldn't keep track of her money."

"Fascinating," Fox murmured on a dry note.

Casting him a sideways glance, she said, frowning. "You don't need to be sarcastic." She fumed at his hoot of laughter. "Thought you wanted to learn everything."

"I do. I wasn't being sarcastic. What you recounted was interesting. Don't know anything about the sisters."

"So, you say." Her back stiffened. Fannie didn't think at this juncture Fox was telling her his true feelings.

"Yes. So, I say."

Fox pulled out a chair for her to sit. As he brought her hand to his lips, he bent his knee to the floor. Held up a small box as he flashed a huge grin. "Fannie, will you marry me?" For the first time that day, Fox appeared nervous, riddled with anxiety. His hand trembled while he waited for an answer. Sweat beaded on his forehead.

"What did you say?" Fannie asked, never expecting a proposal. For a few beats of her heart, she wasn't certain she heard right. "I…" She tried to swallow the lump in her throat. Didn't understand what to make of the words. He couldn't mean them. Fox would never tease her with a proposal in front of others.

"Will you marry me," Fox repeated for her benefit.

The few people sitting in the bakery stopped their chatter. All of them, each and every one looked at her. Turned their attention on them. Nervous energy stretched her nerves tight. She wiped her sweating hands along her skirt. Fannie's heart lurched to her throat, skipped a beat or two. Her eyes widened as the realization of what he asked set in.

The box was open. Held within the velvet blackness, a diamond surrounded by sapphires peaked at her, twinkling in the cheery room. He held her hand. His thumb passed across her wrist, once then twice. The gesture spoke to her, heated her from the inside out.

She couldn't swallow. Wasn't able to think. He shouldn't have done this here when saying no would create a scene. The nerves she thought she saw earlier vanished. His confidence shone in the light of his eyes. He nodded to her, attempting to encourage.

"Fannie?" he questioned his voice soft. "Say, yes, I promise I will make you happy. We are good together. You will be the mother of my child."

She understood he was speaking of being good in bed. Recalled the night of her deflowering. He was just as he said. He did please her. In the room a quiet hum of anticipations circled throughout. Everyone seemed to be waiting on tenterhooks for her answer. It was taking her so long to give a response, the patrons weren't certain she would accept the ring. Fannie didn't have a choice. With Halsey after her, coupled with her pregnancy there was only one answer she could give. He didn't love her. Was love so important?

"Yes," Fannie murmured, closing her eyes. "Yes." When she opened them, it was to see a broad smile on Fox's mesmerizing face. He was grinning as if he found that fifty thousand pounds he believed she stole from him.

The buzz around her grew to a crescendo as all remarked on her answer as well as the long delay. Her response should have been enough said. Seemed he wished for more. What did he want her to say? She was confused. His thumb passed across her wrist again. Fannie stared at him baffled. She parted her lips.

"Yes, what?" Fox persevered, intending to put her in a place she could not back away from. "Yes, to what?" he asked again. "I'd like to slip this ring on your finger. All these people are waiting for your full answer. Yes, is just not enough. You might tell me later you were saying yes to a second pastry."

She swallowed the lump in her throat. Disliked the fact he pushed her so hard. This was too new for her to wrap her head around the proposal. "Yes...yes, Fox, I will marry you." For them there was no other choice. He took her innocence. She was pregnant with his baby. What more was there to do?

He doesn't love me. I hoped for love. Didn't one of her sisters tell her to be patient? Love would come with time. So far, they'd not spent much of that precious commodity together. Time was such an elusive word.

The resounding applause startled her. She jerked her head to look up. She saw not only the patrons surrounding her but the employees as well. They were clapping, cheering for them. Talking as if this was the greatest experience of their lives. Everyone around her was smiling. Fannie didn't feel a smile. Just fear that she might be making a horrific mistake.

In that moment of disorder, Fox slipped the ring on her finger then kissed the back of her hand. "I promise you will never regret this. I know I won't. We will have a good marriage. I vow to you that you will love your new home." He paused for several beats of his heart. "At least I hope you will love my home, my heart. Now you are part of my heart."

"Kiss the girl," the cry reverberated in the small bakery. Then the three words became a chant. "Kiss the girl. Kiss the girl. Kiss…"

"Believe I will do just that." Fox pulled her into his arms. Pressed the length of her body against his. His hands held her at her waist.

Fannie found herself staring at his mouth. Her tongue danced across her lips as she waited for the post engagement kiss the patrons called for. She trembled thinking about the kiss, his taste, the sweet pleasure she knew his lips would bring to her. Recalled the one in the coach. His mouth touched upon hers. Her fingers wound into his hair at the nape of his neck as she needed to get closer to him. She rose to the tips of her toes. His hands at her waist tightened, brought her even closer against him. She felt the evidence of his arousal press on her belly. She whimpered as he deepened the kiss, touched inside. Felt the heat of him along with the urgency of the devoted pleasure singe her.

With gentleness he drew back. Ran his thumb across her bottom lip. To the deepest part of her soul, she felt her need for him rise to a fever pitch. Her desire for him ran rampant within her. Fannie understood how it felt for Fox to possess her. Fox could have tossed her skirts right here, taken her on the floor in the bakery. She would not have protested.

Somewhere in the back of the room, a cork popped, then another. Daryl tapped a spoon against a bottle. "Champagne for everyone. It's not often we're witness to a romantic proposal. I'm honored to have observed the proposal along with the agreement. This beautiful lady accepted this handsome man, right here in my bakery. What a delight they have honored my establishment. Appears as if the proposal came as something of a surprise to the young lady." The woman was busy pouring champagne as she continued to talk. "I'm Daryl by the way." She set two glasses on their table before filling them with the bubbling liquid. "Champagne for everyone," Daryl repeated. "Wish Donal was here to listen to the proposal. He will be green with jealousy when I tell him."

"I'm Fannie MacRae," she said smiling as she accepted the offered glass.

"Who is this lucky devil?" Daryl asked running the full extent of her gaze along his features. "She is a beautiful lady. Hold to your promises, young man. We all heard the spiel. You vowed to make her happy."

"Fox Taggart," he said, grinning at her. "You're right about my Fannie. She is a very lovely lady." He paused a few moments, ran his eager gaze along her features. "I intend to keep all the promises I've made. With me as her husband, Fannie will never want for anything."

Except love.

Once all the glasses were filled, Daryl held hers high. "To this lucky couple who are about to embark on the journey of matrimony. May Fox Taggart's pledge to Fannie always make her happy and hold true. My husband once told me the same things. I haven't regretted a moment of my marriage. Donal is a special man. He even puts up with me working. Has never complained about the early hours. Though there are days when he rolls over then mumbles about the untimely morning."

With that said, they sipped the drink, staring into each other eyes. For the first time, Fannie felt as if this strange relationship of theirs might have a chance of working. She realized she wanted to make him happy. Didn't want him to have regrets about the way this all came about. Didn't wish for Fox to feel forced into a marriage he might not have wanted.

They ordered pastries along with tea for her and coffee for Fox. The excitement in the bakery ebbed as the witnesses to his proposal left the premises. Soon the bakery was empty except for the two of them. The employees were clearing the tables. Making arrangements to close the shop for the day. On the door, the sign was switched from open to closed.

Daryl stood at the table still grinning at them. "You two lovebirds stay as long as you wish. We've a lot to do before leaving. Seems the two of you have your heads together in conversation. Take your time," Daryl repeated.

"Thank you," Fox told Daryl. "We won't be long. We've a meeting with Fannie's brother-in-law soon to iron out the details of the wedding day. When we're finished eating, we will be on our way."

"Ah, Jasper and Jason Kenworthy. Know the men quite well. They've helped out a few nights when we go to the homeless camp nearby with day old bread and whatever goodies are left over from the day." Daryl left, turning to walk back to the kitchen.

Fannie watched her go. Tugged off a piece of her doughnut. Chewed before she spoke to Fox. "Maggie apologized for what she said or didn't say last night."

His forearms rested on the table. He fiddled with his coffee cup before replying. "I'm glad. Maggie didn't understand the facts surrounding our night in the brothel. I'm certain Jasper explained them to her later. You were trying to survive. Neither of us could have done anything different. I'm happy that it was me who found his way into your room. Now, shall we speak of something more appealing?"

"Such as?" She looked at him with curiosity. Saw the smile in his eyes along with a touch of fear. Didn't understand what he would be afraid of.

"We will depart for my home in seven days. You must get your things in order. There will be room for you to bring anything you like. The wedding will take place in six days. We will have our wedding night in the hotel. It's a Saturday. Do you have anyone you'd like to invite? If you do, we should send messages out tonight."

"Six days?" she questioned, feeling a sensation of alarm sneak up her spine. In six days, she would be married. On the seventh she would leave her sisters behind to go to a land she never heard of before Fox. Montana or was it Michigan? A deep feeling of loneliness settled around her. She would have no one to confide in. "That's all the time I have? Six days?" She stirred the tea in her cup. "I don't know if I can do it. What if…" she stopped then, understanding nothing would stop him from departing, not even her wishes.

"Yes. You knew I was eager to return home. I've been away since October. That's a long time. Understood I would never be able to return until after the snow melted. My visit with father was long. Now I feel an urgency to return. It's February. By the time we reach the territory there should be very little of the white stuff left to get in our way. The roads will be more passable. The journey should be easy for you. If we were to wait, you would be farther along with your pregnancy. The trip would exhaust you. Not willing to take chances with you or the baby."

She nodded to him, keeping further protest from escaping from her thoughts. All he said was true. Though she had no idea about his travel plans. Realized she would not be sitting in a carriage. Had never been on board a sailing vessel. "What is your home like?" She asked while she gazed at her ring. The stone along with the setting was beautiful, sparkling when sunlight danced on the diamond. He must have spent a great deal of money on this piece of jewelry. He would have bought a wedding ring too. Fannie had no idea as to his finances. His father was wealthy. Didn't put her soon to be husband in the same category. "I…could you tell me a little about your home? I'm interested. You know. I'm also afraid. Are there Indians?" she blurted, wishing she'd not gone that route. If there were she didn't wish to learn about them.

"Well, first off there is no reason for your fear. As to Indians, there are a few who are living in a settlement nearby. These Native Americans are peaceful. They don't threaten us where we live. Might be different if we were farther west. If so, we would need to take great care." He stretched his legs out in front of him. "My home is two stories. Has five bedrooms on the top floor, two on the bottom tier. There is a large kitchen along with a parlor on the first. In the United States, the main room that we live in is called the parlor. It's the same as the drawing room. My office is on the first floor. If you like, you can use one of the downstairs rooms as a sewing room."

Fannie flinched at his words. Liked the fact he was giving her a room for herself. Sewing was something else for her to worry about. "I'm not very good with a needle. Can't sew a good seam. Will I need to sew?"

"Only if you want to. The town closest to us has a fine seamstress as I've been told. There are also wives of some of my employees who would be pleased to sew for you. I would assume you would like new gowns from time to time. What do you do well?"

A small spurt of relief filled her. After his next words she knew another moment of despair. "I don't know how to can or grow vegetables. Can probably pick apples. Plucking fruit from a tree shouldn't be too hard. I don't do anything well. I can't even play or sing. I am good with numbers. I could keep your books for you." She brightened.

His hoot of laughter echoed in the space where they were sitting. "You will learn whatever is needed. If you wish you can keep my accounts. What would you like to do with your free time? Can you ride?"

Looking at her hands in her lap, she shook her head. "Can't do much of anything. Don't have any skills most women have. Can't swim either. You once talked about swimming in the lake near your home." She lifted her shoulders in frustration. Then looked into his eyes. "I'd like to learn all those things. Would love to feel useful as well as needed. As I am now, I'm not any of those things."

"I will have a lot of things to teach you. Swimming, riding, canning. You will swim naked with me. Skinny dipping is pure bliss. The lakes are so clear a blue the sight makes a man's breath catch in the back of his throat. If you do have a way with numbers, I'd be glad to give over my books to you. Dislike keeping books. Would rather be outside in good weather as well as bad."

"That doesn't sound like a very good idea, skinny dipping. You would see me naked." Fannie fiddled with the fabric of her skirts. Seemed he was rushing her with his bold talk. In six days, she would be married to the man. He would see her without clothing if that was what he wished anytime he wished. For her there had only been the one time. That night she didn't make a conscious decision to rid herself of her clothing. She'd thought he was a doctor. Had also been surprised at his unusual way of doctoring. And…she was drugged out of her mind.

"Wouldn't be the first time." He caressed her cheek, his eyes alight with what seemed to be amusement. "Though the night you are thinking about, the light wasn't good. In full sunlight, all your curves will delight me. We could make love in the lake with nothing but a slip of water between us." His hand curved around her neck.

"In sunlight? In the lake? Do people do that?" Fannie questioned. She felt herself shaking. Didn't know if she was nervous or excited at the prospect. She would also… "I would see all of you. I don't recall very much about the way you looked. Except I remember thinking you were too handsome as well as too young to be a doctor," she blurted then immediately regretted the words.

He let out a short bark of laughter. "Yes. Yes, and yes, to the first three questions. You think I'm handsome?"

She wanted to get away from the talk about Fox seeing her wearing nothing at all. Fannie felt overwhelmed at the prospect. Didn't wish to answer his questions. She tossed him a shy glance, "I'm pretty much useless."

Fox shook his head at her comment. "You will be a wonderful mother to our children. How many would you like?"

The sudden question startled her. Felt her mouth gaping open. He diverged from the earlier conversation. "What! Oh, you keep surprising me. I don't know. Never thought about children before. How many do you want?" Fannie tossed the question back to him, bewildered. Could people decide on the number? She didn't understand how. Her hands resting on her belly, she knew she didn't decide to conceive this child.

He sat back again tapping his fingers beneath his chin. "Well," he shot her a wicked grin. "Suppose three or four would be nice. Two boys and two girls, though I do understand we won't have a choice as to the gender. Would that be acceptable?"

"What if we have all girls?" Most men wanted boys. "Would we try for a fifth time for you to have a male heir?"

"Hope they will look like you and not me, the girls," he stated, with a crooked half smile on his lips. "We would only try a fifth time if that was what you wished. Child bearing is hard on a woman's body. I want you with me for a very long time."

Fox stood, held out his hand for her to take. "We should return to the house for our meeting with Jasper. It's getting late. He and Maggie will be waiting for us. Yes," he looked at her puzzled expression. "The two did understand I meant to propose this afternoon. Are waiting now for your answer."

They stopped at the door for their coats. Rain still fell from the sky in torrents. Fox waited for the driver to see them then open the door before he lifted her in his arms again to race for the safe haven of the vehicle.

Once more, with tender care he set her inside the carriage. Again, when he followed her, he pulled her onto his thighs. She realized he wanted to kiss her. She wanted his lips on hers too. "This time I'm not going to stop with one kiss. Intend to kiss you until this vehicle stops. Want your lips to appear well loved. Everyone will know your answer the moment they see your bee stung mouth." Fox set his hand on the curve of her hip, smoothing his hand along the bend.

With slow finesse, his mouth claimed hers. Touched upon her, stroked the flesh, left moisture behind. She loved his kisses, the sweet taste of him. Their tongues slid across each other while she thought if he always made her feel this way, hot and excited, her heart racing, she might never regret the hasty marriage to a man she knew nothing about. She was crazy to accept, crazy not to agree to this marriage. For both of them there had been no choice in the matter. No, Fox had more choices than she. He could have ignored the fact he was the father. Could have left her on her own.

I'm learning about him. He's learning I have no skills. Like Lacie, I am good with numbers. I read and write very well. Perhaps I can help with his business. I can keep all of the accounts. That would make me feel useful.

"Where have you gone, sweet? You withdrew from me into some secret place which had no admittance for me. You've never withdrawn before." He touched her damp lips. "Shall we try again?"

"Yes, sorry…" Withdrawing from him was not her intention. "Please."

His hand roamed along her ribs. Stopped to cup a breast. He rubbed the palm of his hand against the hardening tip. A little whimper followed. Fannie remembered when he caressed the crest with his mouth, suckled her with tender care. A shudder of desire surged through her. Fox set her hand onto his swelled sex. She wanted to see him as she did the night in the brothel. Wanted to see if he was as superb a specimen of a man as she remembered. Six days then she would see him again.

She pressed her hand against him then looked up to see him gazing at her. His eyes dark with a wicked promise of pleasure. "Easy honey. You do know what you do to me. You experienced it firsthand. As much as I would like to, we don't have time to do this before we reach your home."

Nodding, she said. "You do know what your kisses do to me too." She moved against him. His hand touched her ankle before traveling higher.

"Aye," Fox replied looking content with her comment. "I know."

"I'm wet," Fannie blurted then felt heat flush her from her ears to the tips of her toes.

At her words Fox sipped air. Grinned. His hand moved higher then higher still. He touched the flat of her stomach. She felt her belly contract.

"Should I see just how damp you are? See if you are ready for me, dripping with your sweet nectar. Not tonight, sweet, but soon. Six days until our wedding night. Until then, I mean to keep you as aroused as possible. Damp all the time. Need to be inside you. Yes, for your best interest, it's fortunate we are in a carriage as well as way too close to the Kenworthy townhouse for me to break my vow of celibacy. Not going to make love to you until after we are married."

"Does it make a difference?" Fannie wasn't at all certain she cared. She was no longer a virgin. What did it matter if they found pleasure before the ceremony?

"Yes, Jasper apprised me of the fact your sisters along with you do not wish to make love until the vows are said. I will hold to the same fact about you. It's unfortunate…no," he stopped himself. "I'm pleased you were at Hannah's brothel. If not for the strange happenstance, for that unusual pattern of events bringing us together, we would never have met. We would not be getting married in six days. You would not find yourself traveling with me to Michigan."

"You're happy that you are forced to marry me?"

"Imagine I am."

The carriage stopped. Between the bakery and the house, the rain ceased also. With more dignity than when the two left, they walked up the steps hand in hand. Fannie thought it was better to be carried. Loved finding his arms around her. Enjoyed nestling her nose against the hardness of his chest.

The ensuing conversation would be about the days before the wedding. Fox made his plans. She never told him she didn't have any friends to invite. He wouldn't believe her. Nonetheless, all she hoped for was that her mother didn't get wind of the ceremony. She did not wish Anice to show her face there.

~ * ~

When the new couple entered the drawing room, Jasper and Maggie along with Nellie and Dillon waited for them. All held a predinner drink. They chatted until Jasper noticed he and Fannie framed in the doorway. All conversation stopped for a moment. In unison both couples smiled at them.

They didn't seem concerned that Fannie might not have agreed to his proposal. Fox felt pleased. He'd been worried about Fannie accepting this new way of life. When she mentioned he'd been forced to marry her, he realized at that point marrying her was what he wanted. Knew even with these strained circumstances, he would never propose unless wedding bells were what he wanted. What he needed was a wife. Fannie would do just fine. His father hoped he would choose a wife from Scotland. By an unusual circumstance, he'd done exactly what his father wished. To his ultimate surprise, the fact pleased him.

"Can I get the two of you a drink?" Jasper asked, looking from one to the other with a smile on his face seeming to realize Fannie said yes. "A sherry for you Fannie? Perhaps something a bit stronger for Fox."

"I'd like a sherry," Fannie said while she looked from Maggie to Nellie. "We had champagne at the bakery. Daryl was sweet. She, along with her customers, acknowledged us. Cheered our engagement."

He was surprised when Fannie volunteered that information. "I'll take brandy," Fox brought Fannie her drink then stood behind her with the snifter in his hand. One of his hands rested on her shoulder. He squeezed with a gentle touch telling her silently all would go well. He didn't know how she felt being the center of everyone's attention. He wished to encourage his soon to be wife.

For a few seconds in the bakery, when he brought out the ring, he'd been nervous. Afraid she would continue to refuse him. If she didn't agree to become his wife, she might try to rid herself of their baby. He could never allow her to pursue that path. Now all strained emotions evaporated. He felt eager to get on with his new life along with a determination to learn more about Fannie. While he was certain Fannie thought six days wasn't long enough, he wished he could find a small parish church to marry her tomorrow. The few kisses they shared served to remind him of just how much pleasure he received from their lovemaking.

"So, I see the engagement ring on Fannie's finger. Suppose the symbol means she said yes," Jasper said, beaming at the couple. He barked a crisp chuckle, "Breaking out the champagne must also be an indication."

Fox nodded, gave her shoulder another gentle squeeze. "Yes, Daryl toasted us. Brought out a couple of bottles of champagne to share with us along with her customers. I was pleased with the sweet reception." He settled his thumb on the pounding pulse on her neck. Smoothed a finger along the column.

Wondered if she was nervous or excited. In the carriage he vowed to himself to keep her sultry heat dripping. A few minutes ago, she proclaimed herself wet. Wasn't certain how he could keep her aroused with an audience of four. He could try. Before she retired for the night, he intended to see her alone in the library to seduce as well as charm her socks off.

"Oh! Can I see your ring?" Nellie asked as she rushed forward.

Fannie held up her hand for her sister to see the symbol of her engagement better. "Yes," Fannie murmured. "It's beautiful. At least I think so." She looked to him, appearing insecure at the incident. He did want her to approve of what he purchased. Perhaps he should have asked her to pick it out.

"It's lovely. Fox has good taste." Nellie pronounced then looked to Dillon who seemed to be ignoring her. In any case, he appeared immune to the look of longing Nellie shot in his direction.

Did Dillon plan on a proposal to Nellie soon? He might not intend to marry for a while. Fox wondered how old the man was. Didn't look more than twenty-four or five. Nellie was older than Fannie. At this tick of the clock, Dillion seemed to be ignoring Nellie and her pointed gaze. The observation didn't bode well for their future. Fox didn't wish to believe the lad was using Nellie. Hoped she was able to tell him no before she too became pregnant. At this juncture, Fox wasn't certain Dillion would step up to the challenge.

"Thank you," Fannie said, then gave a tiny gasp as he tripped his finger along her neck then back to the pounding of her blood at her pulse. He smoothed his hand along her shoulder then down her arm, enticing more tiny ripples of breathy air.

Jasper, along with Maggie, both noticed though they chose to disregard the gesture causing Fannie to blush a gorgeous shade of pink. He enjoyed teasing her, testing her sexuality in front of her sisters. He didn't intend to allow her to forget the blistering passion between them. Ah, yes tonight he would gift her with more possibilities.

"We need to hash over the wedding plans. You told me if Fannie agreed to marry you, the wedding would take place this coming Saturday," Maggie stated with a pitiful sigh following. "We've a great deal to accomplish before we can rest on our laurels. Five days is not much time to see to the details."

"Yes," Fox agreed with Maggie's statement, amused at her words. Seemed she was asking for more days. "I've passage for two to New York leaving Sunday, the day after the wedding. We don't have much time for detailed arrangements. The basics are all that is needed. I'm eager to return to my home. Start a life with Fannie." Fox paused to caress her cheek with his knuckles. Caught a tight drawn breath of air. "There is more than enough room for her to take anything she wishes."

"So soon," Maggie said with another wistful sigh, telling everyone she hoped they had more time. "Can't you stay tell the end of February? The crossing would be easier in March. The weather not so frigid. Will be fewer storms. Northeasters can be frightful or so I've heard." Maggie turned to look at her husband as if he could change the plans. Jasper shook his head as if warning his wife, pleading would get her nowhere.

"Yes, we must leave on the day I booked passage. As I've made my wishes clear, there is no other choice for me. The next passenger ship to New York won't depart until the end of March. I realize planning the wedding in such a short amount of time is far from ideal. Nonetheless, it must be done. Spare no expenses. I will pay for everything. Hire more people if the need arises."

Fox wanted the wedding to take place before she showed her pregnancy. Hoped her mother would not attend this affair. Understood she would never be sent an invitation. Nonetheless, from what he'd heard about Anice, if she got wind of the wedding she would show up without an invitation. He didn't know if anyone in the immediate family realized she was six weeks pregnant going on seven. Didn't know if she'd had any symptoms that would alert her sisters. He hoped this would remain between the two of them. Jasper and Maggie would have heard them mention her pregnancy. There hasty wedding had nothing to do with her pregnancy.

Jasper cut into his thoughts with the next statement. "While the two of you were at the bakery, I decided on the small church near the city. The setting is beautiful. Visited there with Maggie. Spent some time walking around the gardens. The site is perfect for the ceremony. The reverend didn't have an issue with the wedding taking place on Saturday. His wife volunteered to bake the wedding cake."

"Good, I wish Fannie to have a wedding gown for this occasion, a white one. Otherwise, she may choose whatever she wants." Fox turned to Maggie to make his wishes clear. "Tomorrow would it be possible for you to take Fannie to the dressmaker. I would have two men accompany you for yours as well as Fannie's protection. During the last few hours, Fannie has apprised me of the man, Halsey. I've heard of him, as has most of the men in the city. Won't take chances of the little pimp abducting my soon to be wife. If guards are not possible, I will oversee her protection." Speaking the last words his voice was harsher than he intended. He cleared his throat. "I don't wish for anything untoward to happen to Fannie."

He thought he might decide to go with them even if Jasper provided two guards. Intended to stand by the dressing room door to assure her safety. Thought of seeing the gown before the wedding. Knew doing so was bad luck. Gambling on his future wife's security was not something he was willing to do. Found it odd that he was becoming so shielding of Fannie.

"Of course, I'll take both Fannie and Nellie. We will all get new gowns for the event. I know what you are thinking, Fox Taggart." Maggie shook her finger at him. "You cannot go with us. It's bad luck for the groom to see the gown before the ceremony. No, we won't allow that to happen. No we won't. If anyone goes with us, it will be Jasper. We will need to send a message to Jason and Tessa. They will wish to come back in order to attend the ceremony."

Jasper spoke up with a tentative chuckle, "I will provide three men. One personally assigned to each of the sisters. Agree with you. We cannot be too careful. Fannie did tell us she saw Halsey in the shadows last time she visited there. Perhaps I will also go with the ladies."

Plans for the wedding continued. They ate dinner then Fox, after excusing himself along with Fannie, placed her hand in his then strode to the library. She'd been reticent for a few beats of his heart. Thought for a few seconds, she might refuse. He understood she must be overwhelmed by the turn of events. Everything was unfolding quite fast. For him they could never be married soon enough.

Fox brought a bottle of wine and two glasses with him as he escorted Fannie to the library, his free hand placed on the small of her back. She wouldn't comprehend his intentions as she sat in one of the large chairs by the fireplace. With vivid detail, Fox recalled the night she sat in the very same chair. When he saw her, for the first few beats of his heart, he found himself speechless. Believed he found the little virgin whore from the brothel who stole his fifty thousand pounds. He did. She wasn't a whore. Though she did steal the money. Where the devil was it?

After splashing wine into both glasses, he handed her one. Studied her as she placed the rim on her lips. Fox stepped back to lean against the second chair to continue to focus on her. She would be wondering about the next minutes. Would wonder about his intentions. That was good. He wanted her to question as well as wonder. Needed to feel her responses to his seduction. Fannie was a beautiful woman. Decided he would try to recall the weight along with the texture of her breasts. Wanted to discover if the twin globes were fuller now that she was with child. Was her belly beginning to round? Not yet, he surmised.

She positioned herself with her feet on the floor and her back stiff. "What are we doing here, Fox?" her words sounded as if she wasn't certain why they left the others to be alone. "I would spend time with my sisters. There are so few days left." She swallowed a bit of the wine. Closing her eyes, seeming to enjoy the drink. When she opened them again, she did manage a weak smile. "We will be together on the ship then the overland trip in close quarters. My sisters will remain here. How long will the voyage take?"

Ah, well, yes, she realized that soon he would be her soul companion as well as her eager bed mate. Was she having second thoughts? He paused a moment to consider his words before he blurted something that would set his plans back. "Jasper assured me they would all visit us next year during the summer months. By then there will be a little one waiting to greet them all. Our child will meet his or her cousins. Those moments will be nice. My father has also informed me he and Beryl will visit in the coming year. He's pleased I've decided to marry. Has implied he'd like grandchildren. What he hasn't learned is the small fact there is one on the way."

"A year? I've never been away from my sisters for any length of time. A few years ago, we were all so close we *kenned* each other's thoughts before we spoke them. Even when Maggie was in Ireland running from Abernathy, she was gone only a couple of months. I don't like the idea of being alone. It frightens me."

"You will have me. I will make certain you have everything you need," Fox felt a tiny flare of annoyance at her words. He wouldn't call the emotion anger. Still, he wondered about their life. What it would be like? He didn't wish for her to be terrified but didn't comprehend how to assuage her fears.

Fannie bent her head to stare at something on the floor, perhaps her feet. "Yes, I will have you. You're not the same as my sisters. There will be no silly girl-talk, giggling until I can't breathe for lack of air."

"I hope not. For one thing, I don't giggle," his tone was bland, thinking about all the obvious distinctions between them. "Glad you understand the differences between us. Your sisters cannot heat you from the inside out as I can. Cannot gift you with exquisite pleasure that has you panting with your need, crying out for your completion. Cannot give you children to warm your days." Fox pointed to her flaming cheeks. Good, she remembered the kisses they shared this afternoon and perhaps the more intimate moments at the brothel. Tonight, he would remind her how his fingers could create magic between them. He wanted to recreate the tiny sounds of desire that would bind them together with ribbons of longing as well as passion.

"We shouldn't be here, alone, unchaperoned." Never letting her gaze meet his she sipped her wine. Swallowed. Continued to stare at her feet. "We should return to the drawing room, you know. Don't want my reputation to be ruined."

His bark of laughter brought her head up to meet his gaze. Her wide blue pools questioning his laughter. He thought her comment adorable in light of the fact a chaperone would be wasted on the two of them considering her status. "Too late for a chaperone, my sweet, far too late." Unable to help the drift of his gaze, he focused on her small belly. Soon she would swell with his child. He found the fact a miracle of delight. His laughter changed to concern. "How do you feel? Have you felt any nausea?"

"No and my sisters, they don't know I'm with child. Why would Maggie let us be alone like this? Jasper too? There wasn't one word to stop us. Anything could happen in here. You could seduce me."

"You seem to forget Maggie knows."

Seducing his sweet Fannie was the exact nature of his tactics. This campaign would bind her closer to him. Slow steps took him to her side. Fox took the glass of wine from her hand, setting both on the nearby table. He continued with his scheme to charm her until she was unable to think straight. Until her blood raced and her breath quickened. He intended to taste the delicate flavor that was Fannie. The one he recalled from the night in the bordello. Quick deft moves brought Fannie into his arms. He settled on the seat with her straddling his thighs.

"Fox!" she yelped. "What are you doing?"

He couldn't describe the reaction in any other way. Fannie pleased him. "What? You know you wish for more shared kisses. Maybe even more than kisses in tender places I've yet to discover. Even at Hannah's place, I didn't sample all your delectable charms. Can you recall all the places I touched that night? I would grant your every wish. Shall we see what I can uncover then kiss? Would you enjoy my kisses here, sweet?" He placed his lips on the long white column of her neck. Sipped on succulent tender flesh. She wriggled against him, legs pressing against his.

His hands settled on the tender curve of her hip. While he didn't intend to make love to her tonight, he did intend for Fannie to need him with the same compulsion he felt for her. Primed as well as ready for the wedding night was the way he sought. He didn't know how she truly felt about him. She didn't love him. Neither did he love her though he cared about her, lusted after her. Must have felt cornered when she saw him that night in this room. If either of them was forced to wed, it was Fannie. A pregnant woman had few choices in this world, a man's world by design.

"I'm…" Fannie looked down. Saw where her legs were spread wide. Must know she was sitting on the confirmation of his need for her. She was open for him, for any part of her he wished to seduce as well as charm. He couldn't hide his arousal. His lips fancied the area above her corsage. With his teeth, he toyed with the top button until it popped free of its confinement. Wished she wore a ballgown. One that was low cut. One he could tug down her arms to reveal the rounded globes he intended to cherish tonight.

"I like the way you look sitting on me." His voice was a soft throaty sound that seemed to catch in the back of his throat. Thoughts of her beautiful body were burning him alive. "You wanted me to teach you how to ride. Believe you were thinking of riding a horse. There is more than one way to ride. You could ride this man. One day, perhaps our wedding night, I'll teach you how to ride me. As for now, my fingers wish to see if you're indeed wet as you told me while we were in the carriage on our way to the townhouse. Are you damp for me, Fannie? Is your sweet nectar flowing nonstop as I hope?" He slipped his hand beneath the fabric of her gown. Felt her open her legs wider for his quest, handing him an open invitation to explore her soft skin.

"Fox? Are we talking about the same thing?" she queried as her hands settled on his shoulders, gripped him as if she was holding onto a lifeline. "I don't understand. Oh! What are you doing to me?"

"Don't suppose you do comprehend all of my manly intentions. In time you will. Promise you will enjoy all we do here this evening. If there is something you don't like, you must tell me. A man should never be left in the dark about what his woman likes or doesn't appreciate." His lips brushed hers, soft, light as a feather. Smoothed his thumb along her jaw then lower to wander down her neck. He intended to distract her so he could discover tender intimate places beneath her gown. He swept his tongue across her lips requesting her to part them for his entrance just as her thighs were separated for him. While he wasn't going to enter into her with his sex, if all went the way he planned, his fingers would find entrance. He would bring her to that point of no return where she would shatter into millions of pieces. Yes, he wanted to see the way her eyes would look as she reached for the sun to find the flames.

Her fingers gripped his shoulders. Even through the fabric of his shirt, he felt her nails press. Fannie's head was tossed back. His kisses skidded along the long white column of her neck. Paid careful devotion to the rapid pace of her heart. Suckled at the point where her excitement could not be hidden then bit with light finesse. Just enough of a bite to elicit a sharp, startled gasp of unexpected pleasure. Fox moved back to her mouth. Pulled with his teeth on her bottom lip until she opened for him to discover more heat, more dark sultry mysteries. One hand slipped two more buttons free of their confinement. Her gown opened, one piece by tiny piece at a time. After that two more buttons popped free as their tongues played a sweltering dance of penetrate then retreat. Beneath her dress he undid the ties holding her pantalettes together. Tugged on the band until her stomach was his to stroke. Placed his hand on her soft belly, spreading his fingers from hip bone to hip bone.

Fox groaned. He was torturing himself. Waiting for her was going to be the death of him. "Tonight, I'm going to teach you how to ride my fingers. Won't be as exquisite a pleasure of riding my sex which we will do Saturday night. However, the ecstasy will be all yours. This will give you something to look forward to."

"What if someone comes in here? I don't want to be naked." Fannie questioned even while ribbon like whimpers encircled them, held them together as new lovers should be entwined. "Fox?"

"No one would dare enter into our realm of privacy. Jasper understands we need time alone. He's realized we have not seen much of each other and wonders." Fox understood Nellie might search for Fannie. There were so many unanswered questions between the sisters. Jasper and Maggie would never intrude on this dalliance of theirs. Would understand how much they needed these alone moments.

When the last of the buttons were set free, he pushed the fabric aside then down her arms. Felt her shiver as the material floated free of her body. Beneath her chemise, Fox saw the subtle rose color of her nipples that were hardening as he watched. The soft roundness of her breasts beckoned to his searching fingers. He longed to suck them deep, taste the delicate flavor of each hard bud until they were elongated beyond anything she'd seen before. Playing with each until the mercuric magic was over the top. Until tiny feminine sounds of her urgency consumed her. Fox needed to hear his name echo from her.

"Are you certain?" Fannie asked, even while her fingers dallied with the buttons of his shirt. With deft speed she was undoing them, pushing his shirt away, pulling the tails from his trousers. The inquisitive little minx. The palms of her hands traipsed across his chest brushing the tips of his hardened nipples. He groaned his pleasure. Delighted she was not frightened by what was transpiring here.

"Positive. Should we up the stakes?" Fox loved to gamble. He would bet on the fact they would be left alone for at least another hour if not a little longer. There was too much fabric between him and his questing fingers. Wanted her breasts freed from the confines of her chemise. Yearned to fondle all her sensitive white flesh.

"How so? What do you mean up the stakes. I *dinna ken*." her question wobbled from her lips in a thin, whispered stream of words. "I would not wish for anyone to see me like this. Only you, even then I'm uncertain. You have seen me before." She looked down then witnessed what had him enthralled. He could see her all the way to her navel. Fannie was open to his roving gaze. If he pushed the fabric farther apart, he might be able to see the wheat blond hair of her mound.

"Undo your chemise, sweet. Give me free access to those beautiful full globes that intrigue me. Want to cherish your jewels with my mouth as well as my hands. Wish to suckle you deep inside my mouth. I recall the flavor of you. Want to relive your taste. See if your flavor is the same as I remember."

To Fox's amazement, she responded to his request. Nonetheless, before he could taste her breasts, she brushed her cheek against his chest then set her mouth on his small male nipples, sucking hard as he would do to her. Her tongue swirled around one tip then moved on to the other. Well, if she was going to linger on his chest, he would discover more intimate territory below her skirts. With her enquiring seduction, his breath caught in the back of his throat and a low moan of exquisite pleasure followed.

With the ties of her undergarment released, he slipped his hand beneath the fabric. Once again, spanned her soft belly with his fingers from hip bone to hip bone. Felt the flesh beneath his hands constrict with the sizzling contact. She gasped, her breath fluttering across his chest, touching upon his damp nipples. Fox slipped his fingers lower, through the soft curls of her woman's mound to feel the secret petals between her thighs. His Fannie was soft everywhere, her nectar flowing flaunting her gratification. She was ready for anything they might decide. No, he needed to wait.

The sultry honey poured, dripping between her thighs. He wanted to push them farther apart, taste her petals. He would when he was assured of absolute privacy. Fox sent one finger then two into the softest most velvet part of her. At the gentle but surprising intrusion, she bucked, arching her back so the jewels he'd wished to taste a few ticks of the mantel clock before, passed across his lips. With his teeth he caught one hard bud. Suckled the tip until she gifted him with her fascinating feminine whimpers. Discovered

Fannie was riding his fingers. Without his help she moved up then down creating a rhythm of need.

Hell, he tortured himself. He should free his sex then sink into her honeyed depth. Filling her with his member, stretching her to take all of him within her tight channel would be magnificent. Why wait for the wedding night?

Hell and blazes, she was so damn responsive. Fannie surprised him, startled every male part of him. Fox understood he needed to bring this to the proper conclusion before someone did intrude. Jasper would only give them so much time alone. The man would bank on his using caution.

"You're killing me," Fox moaned as he sipped on each sensitive tip. Fannie was going to be the death of him. He'd forgotten how fast she was to respond. How sweet her cries of pleasure were to his ears. No, if he didn't wish to experience this for the rest of his life, he would have never asked her to marry him. He would have set up a trust for the baby along with her. He would have never wedded. This pending marriage was right for both of them. Together, with her fiery passion, they would burn down the nights and maybe a few days. The mornings would be his too.

Peering over her shoulder, Fox saw they'd been here a little over an hour. It was time to bring this to an end. While he loved a good game of cards, liked to test his luck with other things too, he wasn't going to test the waters of Maggie's restraint much longer. Fannie's sister would be at the door soon. The time had come for Fannie to reach the sun to burn higher and brighter than she ever thought possible. He would orchestrate the mercuric magic. Before, when she reached for the sun, she wasn't at her full potential. She'd been drugged with laudanum coupled with brandy. This time would be so much sweeter than the last.

Finding the tiny pearl that would send her body into a cataclysmic release, Fox massaged the small jewel. Tempted with all the expertise he knew. He brought her mouth to his. Slid his tongue deep inside where heat flamed at his touch. Just as his fingers were sliding in then out of her his tongue was doing the same within the scorching heat of her mouth.

He felt her body milk his fingers, pulsing along the length until she cried his name into his mouth. She bucked on him, arched against him until the shattering of her body stilled. Fannie's head fell against his chest. Her forehead was dampened with sweat, from the flames he created within her small, perfect body. Her full breasts pushed against his chest. He was pleased.

His Fannie was breathing hard. Each tiny gasp of air delighted him. Caused her breasts to dance across his chest in a vibrant display. When she finally calmed, Fannie pushed away with her hands. Looked at him with wonder in her eyes. Again, her sumptuous breasts did a tiny jog on his chest. Glazed over eyes, met his. A small smile creased her lips. He set a finger on her mouth to keep her from speaking. Felt the remaining dampness put there by their shared kisses. The wedding night would not come soon enough. His patience was ebbing. After tonight there were four more to get through.

"Oh…" Fannie sighed after several seconds passed. "I… I forgot what it was like. I…don't know what to say."

"Next time you will ride my sex. Next time, we will both reach that rapturous high you came down from just now. Did you like that, sweet? We would do it again if I wasn't afraid we might have some company soon."

Fox didn't wish to move his fingers from inside her. If he dared, he would bring her to another delicious climax. For his almost wife, the stakes in this game they played in her sister's home were too high. He needed to cover her before someone entered into this private domain of theirs. Didn't want anyone seeing her with so little covering her.

With a heavy exhale of air, Fox slid his fingers from the warmth of her passage. He didn't want to do so. If there had been more time, he could have brought her to another bliss filled release. Didn't want to cover her lovely breasts. With shaking fingers, he tied the strings to her pantalettes then pulled the ribbons of her chemise together. Fox fastened the row of buttons that danced up the front of her gown. Before he secured the last one, he placed a soft kiss on the reddened spot on her neck. He supposed he spent too much time giving that place his ardent attention. The telltale evidence would remain for a few days.

"I, well yes, I did. Is that all there is? There was no pleasure for you. I don't care if we wait until after the marriage. The deed has already been done. There is no reason for restraint. After all, I do carry your child."

"Watching you was pleasure enough for me. Now, while I guaranteed you that no one would enter into our private sanctuary, I don't wish to tempt fate with my arrogance. One of your sisters is bound to wonder what we are doing in here for over an hour. They will leap to the right conclusions. Jasper will hold them both back but only for so long. We should expect company." Fox finished dressing her. "Ah, there is nothing I can do about your hair. It's a tangled mess. Suppose they will believe we were kissing. Kissing is alright for an engaged couple. Couldn't keep my fingers from winding into your beautiful hair."

Fannie reached up as if to see what he'd done. "It's a mess, yes? Is this how it will always be when we are doing this?"

"I suppose so. Love to run my fingers through your hair. Love the feel as well as the silken texture of the strands." When they finished making love, she would always appear a beautiful mess.

"May I?" Her hands were on the buttons of his shirt. Before he could answer, her fingers were moving, fastening each button, "Can I tuck your shirt into your…britches?" Her small pink tongue flitted across the fulness of her bottom lip.

Fox was positive he knew what she was thinking. "Minx. What do you think to find down there?" Inside his chuckle threatened to leave his mouth. If he wasn't careful, they would erupt from behind his teeth. The look she tossed him was delightful. While she lowered her lashes, her smile was playful. She was delectable. He blessed his luck that Hannah never remembered her left from her right. Was pleased he stumbled into her room in the brothel. Satisfied, she'd given herself to him.

"You, that male part of you, I never truly saw the first time. I wish to see it. Would want to see you naked. What do you look like? Down there?" She looked down where her hands were splayed on his belly.

He was outright laughing now as she tried to push his shirt into his trousers. Her fingers explored beneath the fabric. He groaned deep and low in the back of his throat when she found what she was looking for. The palm of her small hand grazed his swelled sex. He wanted her. She sipped air then smiled a siren's smile his way. Wrapping her fingers around his member, embracing him, he groaned again. Set his hand on her wrist. He would take care of his problem later. Didn't wish to spill his seed now. If she continued much longer, he would never be able to stop.

Fox pulled her hand from beneath his trousers. With reverence he never felt before, he kissed each knuckle before doing the same to the tip of every finger. Not that he didn't want her hand caressing him. He did. A few seconds earlier he heard voices by the door. Assumed the voices belonged to Jasper and Maggie, giving them warning they would interrupt. Acknowledged the fact the two would only leave them to their devices for so long. However, his gamble did pay off.

"There, we are both dressed. You do, however, appear well and thoroughly kissed by me. Perhaps even ravished." Fox stood then set her on the chair by herself. Handed her the glass of wine he poured earlier before plopping down in the chair next to hers. "What should we talk about, sweet? The oh, so reluctant chaperones are about to arrive. We should appear to be in deep discussion."

"Chaperones?" Fannie parroted as if she was uncertain of what he was talking about, blinking a few times. "You said we wouldn't be interrupted. Did you lie? I would not have…" she paused, "Would not have let you do the things you did if I thought we'd be interrupted."

Well, he did say they were safe from interruptions. He was wrong. Fox didn't think she would have told him no even if she thought her sister might be outside the library door. "Your oldest sister along with her husband are about to walk in then tell us we've been alone for too many minutes. They will want to be seen as guardians of your innocence."

"They are? How do you know?"

"Lucky guess perhaps. But then I could be entirely wrong. Heard them talking outside in the hall."

"I didn't hear anyone."

"No, you were coming down from the inferno I fashioned in your lovely body. So, pleased with my wonderful attention to your feminine endowments, you screamed my name into my mouth. Otherwise, we might have found the pair inside before I could dress you." Inside, he was chuckling at her look of chagrin.

The following knock on the door was far from hesitant. Fox guessed Jasper was doing the knocking. He was correct in his assumption. The door opened. A thin beam of light filtered into the room from the hall to join with the meager light from the fire along with the candles.

"Come in," Fox called out, pleased he finished the scenario he planned before their private domain was interrupted. "Are the two of you in need of company?" Fox asked, a wicked smile on his expressive face.

"Decided we would visit the newly engaged couple. Engaged in conversation. Would learn more about your plans for your future," Maggie flounced inside the room in front of her husband. "What have the two of you been up to?" she asked the question with her brows drawn together as her gaze shifted from one to the other.

"Maggie," Jasper caught up to his wife before she could remark on Fannie's appearance. He held her arm as if he meant to keep her from striding into the room too fast. "They are, I'm certain, discussing their future. What else would the two be up to?" he asked with a satisfied grin on his face.

Fox realized nothing got past the man. If he wasn't mistaken, Jasper noticed her bee-stung lips along with the tangled blond hair that couldn't be missed. He saw the soft blush color Fannie's cheeks as she too believed they guessed at their activities in the library. Maggie would understand from her sister's appearance something of what they'd been doing. What man wouldn't notice the evidence of the pastime they'd been involved in?

Maggie didn't seem to notice the way her curls fell around her shoulders. Either that or she was ignoring the picture in front of her. She held up a second bottle of wine. "The two of you haven't made much progress with that bottle of wine you brought with you." It was at that flash of time she seemed to notice what her sister had been the recipient of. A tiny gasp flitted from her mouth to everyone's ears. She tilted her head a bit sideways before she lifted her very feminine shoulders then seemed to ignore her thoughts. "We won't open this one. We can discuss some of the details of the wedding. Maybe the color scheme. What flowers do you prefer. Since it is winter, we might not be able to purchase your first choice."

"May I?" Jasper didn't wait for an answer. He topped each glass off then spilled wine into his and Maggie's glasses. "Perhaps a toast to the newly engaged couple is in order. Yes, we need a toast to the happily engaged couple. Seems the two of you are enjoying each other's company."

With his words, Fannie's blush deepened.

While Maggie sat on the couch, Jasper leaned against the mantle of the fireplace, one foot resting on the hearth. He seemed to be deciding on some plan of action. Jasper hesitated for a few seconds. After that, he got straight to the point.

"We, Maggie and I, thought the two of you had been alone too long. Not right…not right a'tall, I say. While we understand the wedding now is counting down to fewer days…" Jasper left off as if he didn't know how to finish the statement.

"Yes?" Fox lifted an eyebrow toward the ceiling. Thought he would test the waters. Wished to understand the truth of Jasper's thoughts. "What is your point? Do you think we are jumping the gun on our wedding night? If we are, it's none of anyone's business but ours. All know the two of you…" Fox decided not to finish the accusation. He'd made his point when he saw the flush of red tint Jasper's cheeks. Jasper's job was to be the messenger. Seemed he didn't like his role.

Jasper cleared his throat, looking as if this was the last conversation he wished to have. For a few seconds, he stared at his wife as if asking her what should be said at this juncture. Maggie tossed him a pretty smile that said to anyone watching he was to finish what they must have discussed before confronting the soon to be wed couple. Fox felt positive the two had gone over what Jasper was instructed to say. Jasper didn't seem to be a willing participant. Looked disoriented as if he was a man about to embark on something he found quite distasteful.

"Our Fannie is a virgin, a true innocent. She would not understand…" Again, Jasper broke off at Maggie's hard stare directed his way. "She must be sheltered as well as protected."

"Jasper!" Fannie shrieked as it was clear she was mortified to the tips of her toes. "You've no business talking about me that way. The two of you, my sister along with her husband, are talking about my virtue? That's not right either. I don't wish to be discussed as if I'm not even in the room."

Fox loved the deepening of her color as she railed at the pair. Decided he would sit back then listen to what would transpire. He sipped his wine. Kept a steady gaze on his fiancée. She was lovely.

~ * ~

When Maggie and Jasper left the drawing room, Dillon was standing by the fire, shifting from one foot to the other. Nellie was sitting in a chair opposite, her gaze focused on the flames reaching into the chimney. She looked past the man she'd thought would someday be her husband. A growing despair settled in the pit of her stomach. She felt the heat of her embarrassment rise to her cheeks. She knew her face was a startling shade of red. Her hands, nay, her entire body shook. Stupidity being the major description, she'd assumed something that was not true. Dillon didn't love her. He cared for her but that wasn't enough for either of them. She wanted what Tessa and Maggie had. Love. Hoped Fannie and Fox loved each other too. She just didn't know the truth.

Dillon cleared his throat before he began to speak. Sipped a bit of the brandy that was in the crystal snifter he held. "I told you when we first met, I had no intention of marrying in the next five years. Good, God, Nellie, I'm only twenty-five. I've a wealth of life to live before I settle down to one woman along with a family. Don't want to be tied to any woman though we, the two of us, have spent a great deal of time together. You are important to me. I don't deny that. But marriage…not now…not anytime soon."

Her stomach rolled at his words. She was not usually so dense. "Yes, you told me. I heard you loud and clear. It's just that… I thought in the last few months things between us had changed. We were different together. We…we kissed, you touched me…I wouldn't have allowed you to do so if I believed…" Nellie gulped a lungful of air that caught in the back of her throat. After he touched her breasts, fondled her other places, she'd thought he had a change of plans. Maybe she just wanted to believe. She was so much in love she ignored what he explained to her months ago.

"Just that what!" he roared his anger at her. Clear to her he was furious with her assumptions. "Yes, we kissed. Yes, I've touched you intimately. Kept you pure. You are still complete. Still a virgin. Any number of times I could have taken you. You would have let me."

Dillon called her ridiculous for yearning for more. To her the two of them were far from ridiculous. She'd always believed if a man who was seeing you took liberties such as what she allowed him, they were serious about the girl. She was wrong. She needed to get out of his company. Wanted to be alone with her depression. Needed to figure out the new direction of her future. That was the problem. There was no one else in this town she wished to share her life with. Nellie knew she almost gave her innocence to

Dillion the night before last. He'd touched her, made her yell with her pleasure. The only reason she didn't lose her maidenhead was because they were interrupted. Another couple entered the small room they found empty during the ball.

"I almost gifted you with my virtue. My innocence was something I was saving for the man I married. I thought you loved me."

Setting his hands on her shoulders, Dillion gave her a curt shake. "I never lied to you, Nellie. Have always been up front with my intentions. You appreciated everything we did together. Never once heard the word no from the lips I was kissing. I've never told you or even intimated that I love you or intended to marry you. Your mind is spinning in a dream world. Thought you were more down to earth. Get real, Nellie."

"There is no reason for your anger. You don't need to yell at me or shake me. I'm the one who was misled, dishonored to the tips of my toes. You are a cad of the worst sort." Tears were sliding down her throat. The last she wished to do was cry in front of him, shedding tears of humiliation. Defeated, Nellie fought to keep the wrenching sobs at bay. "You should leave now. Don't believe we should see each other any longer."

"You're not going to cry," again his statement was harsh. "Don't care for little girls who cry when they don't get what they wish for. Grow up, Nellie. You will be happier when you understand the way of the world. If you don't wish to give yourself to a man, learn to say no!"

"What does it matter? You won't be here to listen to the sobs." Nellie stiffened her spine intent on keeping her emotions to herself. She didn't intend to give this man any more power over her. "No, Dillon, I don't intend to cry over you or in front of you. We are done here. Now leave!" She put emphasis on the last word hoping she wouldn't have to endure his company one more second. After he left, she might indulge in a few tears. She should be happy. He revealed himself before he took her innocence away from her. Nellie understood in that instant even if she became pregnant, he would never marry her.

He let out a heavy sigh. "Sorry you were disappointed. Believed we understood each other. It's obvious I was wrong. I've been up front. I have nothing to apologize for."

"I'm relieved, not disappointed. You would have made a horrible husband. I was wrong about you. You are a despicable man." Nellie fiddled with the skirt of her gown while he walked from the drawing room. She heard him put his great coat on then the door open and close behind him. He didn't say goodbye. Dillon left. The man was out of her life forever.

Nellie let out a long, slow breath of air, allowing herself to relax. She was alone in the drawing room. Earlier, Maggie and Jasper followed after Fannie and her fiancé to the library. Thank her lucky stars they weren't here to witness her embarrassment. She didn't wish to go to her room. If she was by herself, she would just mope. After a few minutes passed, she decided the best course would be to take a short walk. The night was chilly but there was no rain this evening. The gazebo was her favorite place in the summer. Perhaps she could close her eyes and relive more pleasant moments spent there. Dillion kissed her there, her first real kiss.

Yes, some of those memorable times had been with Dillon. She refused to think about the damn man. He wasn't worth her thoughts, not one. She wondered what she'd seen in him. All her sisters, including herself, decided they needed to fall in love with an older man. One who was well seasoned. She made the mistake of falling in love with a man who was barely older than she was. There was only one year difference in their ages.

The fleeting thought she shouldn't be leaving the confines of the townhouse passed through her muddled mind. The warnings from Jasper were clear as well as concise. She ignored the thought. Decided nothing could happen to her here on Kenworthy property. If they discovered what she did, both Maggie along with Jasper would scold. A scathing lecture would be in order. Nothing would happen. She was safe.

At this beat of her heart, Nellie didn't care what anyone would do. Words could be endured. Sitting alone in the drawing room could not. She needed fresh air, cold crisp fresh air to help her feel better. Could no longer breathe Dillon scented air into her lungs. What was she to do without him? She missed him and he'd only been out of her life a few minutes. Enjoyed the times he escorted her to events. Their discussions had always been lively. Many times, they agreed to disagree.

Her mind bent on a short walk to clear her senses, she told the butler where she was headed as she slipped on her cape. Walking blindly, she strode from the backdoor, headed to the gazebo at the end of Kenworthy property.

Shivering, Nellie brought her cape tight around her body. The night was colder than she thought. She followed the lantern lit path past the small fountain of cascading water, past the well-trimmed rose bushes. Everything in this garden paradise was immaculately cared for.

Tessa was in the country with Jason. Fannie was leaving her next Sunday. She would be alone as well as out of place in the big Kenworthy townhouse. On the shelf, on the shelf, that was what an unwed twenty-four-year-old woman was. She, Nellie MacRae, was on the shelf and she despised the fact.

By the time she reached the small lattice structure, her feet were freezing. Beneath one of the big chairs there were blankets. She pulled two out. Wrapped herself in both of them before she tucked her numb feet beneath her. Now, she stared out at the crisp winter night. What to do with herself? She had no idea.

The evening was eerily quiet. There were few sounds to be heard. Thought the air smelled of snowfall. Seemed all the usual animals found warm cozy places to wait out the night. Overhead there was no moon to be seen. The only light was that of the lanterns casting shadows along the path. She did hear the cascading waterfall. Noticed, when she walked by, a few icicles hanging from the rocks growing longer with each drip. This evening was devilishly cold.

While she sat staring into the black, velvet night, snow began to fall. The flakes were huge, white dots against the meager light cast from the lanterns. The sight was beautiful. She loved to watch the snow fall from the sky. She heaved in a breath of snow scented air, realizing she should return to the house before anyone missed her, before she froze to death.

When Jasper or Maggie discovered she wasn't in the house, they would look for her. That wouldn't be until the morning. All would think she had gone to her room after Dillon left. She wasn't in her room. Hands clasped tight together, a sudden shiver of fear entered into her. She tried to ignore the prickling sensation.

Nellie leaned against the outdoor couch, setting her head on the back of the chair, she closed her eyes. Listened to the soft sound of the falling snow. Thought of Dillon along with the wasted months she spent in his company. She could have been looking for an older man, one who she could fall in love with. One who would feel the same about her. Might have found someone who could love her. Instead, she let the boy-man take advantage of a few of her weaker moments.

"Look what we have here," A man sneered down at her.

The words gave her a start. "What?" Nellie bolted upright. Her eyes wide. Sudden fear inundated her.

"Seems like our little pigeon has flown the coup. Got her right where Mrs. MacRae wants her. She'll pay us for bringin' this one to heel. Get her into the carriage now before someone comes along to rescue her."

"Yeah, don't understand why she's not guarded. Where's her protector? Got to be around here somewhere."

Nellie leapt to her feet, her heart pounding. She needed to run. Didn't understand why her feet felt frozen to the ground. Didn't have time to question but she did. "Who are you?" She tried to get her feet, untangled from the blankets. Kicked at them to no avail. She couldn't get them off fast enough. Felt the man's hands on her, lifting her. Still wrapped within the blanket, she dangled off the ground.

"Careful! Don't hurt the girl. Want her in one piece when we hand her over to Halsey. That's where she's going first. Halsey wants to see if she's still a virgin. Goin' to stick his finger inside her to discover her truth. This tasty little morsel has been seein' that swaggering young buck for several months. He might have put his seed into her by now. Been with her night and day. If so, she's not worth as much to Halsey."

Before she could think to shout, she was hauled over the man's shoulders. He was striding down the path. Her head hung down his back. She tried to shake herself lose. So tied up in the blankets, she couldn't move.

She screamed then yelled again. "Help! Someone help me!" The flat of his hand came down hard on her rear. At the impact, she cried out then yelled again.

"Shut up, bitch. Soon you'll have something to scream about. Halsey will make certain you're introduced to the business in the best way possible. Your Lord Abernathy will get you first. Heard he's not a gentle man when it comes to whores."

Damn, she couldn't let them take her. What had she been thinking when she left the house? That was the trouble. She wasn't thinking. "Put me down! Jasper! Fox!" She yelled their names realizing she was too far away from the house for anyone to hear her cries for help. The man's hand came down on her again. At the brisk hard contact, she jerked.

Before she could think of something to do, she found herself tossed onto the floor of the carriage the two men brought to haul her away. *No...no, no...no!*

"Didn't think we'd ever get either one of the girls alone. Was shocked to see this one walking all by herself from the house. Halsey's going to be pleased, so is the MacRae lady." He wrapped on the carriage. Their transport began to move.

"Not as happy as the two of us. There was an extra hundred pounds offered to anyone who captured either one of the girls. Maybe we'll get lucky tomorrow and catch the other one. Halsey has plans for the two little birds to entertain his guests together. They seem quite tasty. The MacRae lady says she's goin' to watch the show. Lord Abernathy, I've been told, does get her first. Gets both lassie's before anyone else, even if they're not virgins."

"What do you think Halsey will do with her tonight?" one of the men asked. "He won't take her. Can't."

Nellie wiggled on the floor. Tried to push herself up. One of the men set his foot on the back of her neck to keep her where he wanted her. The same man bent close to her ear. She cringed when she felt the heat of his breath wash over her.

"You hearin' what's going to happen to you, little bird? Old Halsey, he'll poke his finger into you to see if you're still a virgin. Are you? Are you all sweet and innocent, never known a man? Even that fellow you've been seein'? If you are, well, Abernathy's going to pay more for you. He'll still get you first even if you've been used. If there's been another in your life...well...he'll give you back to Halsey to be put in his stable of little gals. No one will be able to get you out. Nor will they want to see you again."

"I'd like to be the one to see if she's innocent. Wouldn't stick my finger in her though. Want to listen to this pretty one howl her pleasure when my rod fills her."

"Now you know we can't sample this one's charms. Halsey will give us one of his other girls. This one goes to the Lord who's paying the groats to have her."

Nellie thought she'd be sick.

~ * ~

Dillon understood Nellie better than she probably knew herself. He'd seen the sheen of moisture in her eyes. Was worried about her. While he didn't feel a moment's guilt about telling her his true feelings, he didn't like hurting her. Whenever she was upset, she withdrew into herself then walked. Most of those times she went to the gazebo. During those times for her protection, he always shadowed her. Against his common sense, Dillon was positive she would do the same tonight. He needed to protect her one last time. Tomorrow would be soon enough for the senior Kenworthy to realize he would no longer escort her places.

He stood in the shadows of one of the lanterns. Watched her walk by him on her way to the gazebo. She was beautiful. He was sorry he couldn't be the man she yearned for. Loving this woman would not be difficult. He didn't love her. She was much too willful to take as a wife. The woman he hoped to live the rest of his life with would be easy to mold in the way he wished.

When the two men passed him, his heart flew to his throat. He understood they meant Nellie harm. They were there to kidnap her. She'd been warned not to leave the house by herself. That was in part the reason why he waited for her. Dillon meant to watch over her one last time before he washed her from his life. He watched the men carry her to the waiting carriage. To prevent a disaster of gigantic proportions, he needed to act fast.

With his heart in his throat, he ran. Jumped on the back of the moving vehicle then climbed across the top to reach the driver. With one quick jab to the man's temple the driver fell to the ground, stunned. Dillon grabbed the reins before pulling the horses to a brisk stop. Without wasting time, he jumped from the seat.

"I say, what's goin' on here?" One of the men jumped from the coach to see why the vehicle came to a jarring halt.

By the time he landed on his feet, Dillon set a left hook into the man's nose. He stumbled back, staggering and whirling his arms for balance. Blood spurted from his face. Dillon kicked him hard in the chest. He hit the ground with a loud oomph. When the second man stepped outside, Dillon sent his fist into his gut.

"Get out of here. You can't have the girl! Called the constables. They are on the way! Best you run before they get here," Dillon yelled. This was easier than he thought. The two men stumbled away from the carriage. He turned to see to Nellie, hoping she was unharmed.

Nellie poked her head from the door, scowling at him. She managed to put her feet on the ground. "Don't want anything to do with you," she proclaimed as she tripped on one of the blankets covering her.

"You don't, do you?" Dillon wished he dared shake her until her head would hold a little bit of common sense. "What the hell do you think you were doing walking in the garden by yourself? You know better than to do something so idiotic. Selfish is what you are," he was still yelling and he didn't like to yell. Only meant to rescue her, not give her a blistering reprimand. Lectures were Jasper's job, not his.

Didn't seem Nellie meant to gift him with an answer to his question. She was walking away from him, ignoring him. Until she tripped again, her chin was tilted into the air. Dillon cursed. He would need to take matters into his hands.

"Get in the carriage, Nellie. I will drive you home. You are in no condition to walk. Getting rid of the blankets will help. I will carry them for you."

"No! And no!" Nellie cried out. "I don't want your bloody help!"

Well at least she was speaking to him, even if it was in the negative. Even if she was cursing. He heaved a huge breath of air then swept her into his arms. Dillon deposited her in the carriage in much the same way her abductors did then slammed the door shut.

"Stay there. I said I'll drive you home."

Before he could lever himself onto the driver's seat, Nellie was striding down the street again. This time she limped. *Little fool! Little stubborn fool. No matter your disposition, I will get you home safe. After we finish here tonight, I won't have anything more to do with you. You are far too willful for the likes of me.*

Dillon jumped from the driver's seat, landing on the balls of his feet. With both angry as well as frustrated strides, he went after her. Caught up to her in a few beats of his heart. When he reached Nellie, he wrapped his hands around her arm then bent to speak to her. "We're going to do this my way, Nellie. Need to get you home safe and sound. After you are safe in the loving hands of your family, you will never see me again. I understand that is what you want."

She tried to jerk her arm from his grasp. "I said, no. No, Dillon. A thousand times no! Leave me alone now!"

"Don't care how furious you are with me. I intend to get you home in one piece. Those men might return for you. Do you want that?" He needed to shake Nellie until her teeth rattled. Dillon was thinking about Halsey. The man owned one of the worst whorehouses in Glasgow. The girls were all mistreated. Many died under his watch. All Halsey was after was a quick dollar at the girl's detriment. He didn't care about their health…if they lived or died. There were more where they came from, a never-ending stream of women down on their luck. When they became pregnant, they were useless to him. He put them on the street to fend for themselves.

"I can get myself home by myself, thank you. I am an adult." Again, Nellie tried to wrench her arm away from his hold. He tightened his fingers.

"Yes, and I see how well you are succeeding. You're limping. You've hurt yourself. You don't have the sense God put in your female brain to accept assistance when help is right in front of your face. I would have driven you straight to the front door. The snow is falling harder. The temperature is dropping. If you don't get inside soon, you will freeze." With each passing second, his annoyance with her was growing.

"Don't touch me!" One more time, Nellie tried to break free of his hold.

Before she could protest, Dillon swept her into his arms. To keep from falling, she clung to his shoulders. "Believe me, I don't want to touch you. Stayed behind because I know you as well as how you think. Realized the moment I watched you leave the backdoor, I was right. Not going to put you down until I can hand you over to Jasper then explain your foolishness." He jiggled her in his arms. "Stop squirming!" If she didn't, he was going to drop her on her little butt then haul her over his shoulder. Decided her abductor had the right idea. The easiest way to carry this squirming mass of female trouble, was over his shoulder.

Dillon heard the sob then the hiccup. What the devil? He rescued her. She didn't have anything to cry about. Felt her push her wet face against his neck. Attempted to ignore the sobs that were now growing in intensity.

"You've nothing to cry about. I'm not going to hurt you. Just stop it!" He didn't have the patience for female tears. Though he still harbored tender feelings for Nellie MacRae. She was a beautiful woman. Tonight, he'd both hurt her as well as rescued her. Damn her, he saved her lily-white hide. He saved her from herself. This was how she was thanking him.

"What do you know? For me, it's been a horrible night. If you think I want to cry, you're wrong. All I want is to be left alone. That's why I went outside."

"As soon as I get you inside the townhouse where it's warm then explain your foolishness to Jasper and Maggie, you won't see me again."

"Promise?"

"Aye, that's a vow I mean to keep. You're a danger to yourself as well as anyone who is near you."

They were standing in front of the big front door. Dillon didn't bother to knock. He walked inside. "Jasper! Somebody! You need to get down here this instant. Halsey almost succeeded in abducting this silly twit!"

"Master Dillon," Keir spoke up. "What is going on?"

"If you know where Jasper is, get him."

Dillon plopped her down on the sofa in the drawing room before leaning against the mantle. Decided he needed to help himself to a brandy. Might need more than one drink. Poured a full glass then resumed his position. A few minutes later Jasper along with Maggie appeared. A few blinks later, Fannie, accompanied by Fox, entered the room.

"No need for that. What's happened?" Jasper asked, seeming to eye Nellie with skepticism. Maggie stood behind him.

Her clothing was askew. She looked as if she'd been through hell and survived to return. In short, Nellie was a mess. "I'll let Nellie explain. Plan to fill in the details if she leaves out anything important, which she will." Nellie shot him a furious glare. He sent her a mocking grin. "When I'm satisfied all the truth has been told, I'll take my leave. Go on Nellie, tell them about all your stupidity."

Chapter Five

This night was growing longer by the second. Fannie remembered those moments with great clarity. Silver tears streaked down Nellie's face when Dillon brought her into the room. Keir was on their heels yelling for Jasper and Maggie. With that first sight of her sister then the ensuing conversation, Fannie realized there was more going on than just the kidnapping of her sister. Her sister would never cry her heart out over an aborted abduction. She was strong, resilient in the face of adversity.

Nellie stiffened her shoulders along with her back. Next, she stuck her chin in the air then shot Dillon a furious glare. She appeared to have an agenda all her own. Her sister seemed to be digging in her heels in order to brace herself for something horrible. For what, Fannie didn't know. Nellie didn't appear pleased with her beau. With instinct born from years of shared confidence, she decided they must have separated. They were acting distinctly aloof from each other. Nellie told her she was in love with the man. What she figured out without anyone saying the words was that Nellie had been outside with Dillon. Probably at the gazebo. Something happened. Did he try to do something…did he take liberties her sister didn't welcome?

Maybe not.

Her boyfriend appeared to want to strangle her or shake her teeth lose. The set to his jaw was hard, so hard the muscle jerked. The clock in the hallway ticked. The sound seeming the only one in the drawing room except an odd pop or two of the embers in the fireplace. Jasper and Maggie waited for Nellie to tell her story. Fox stood behind her, his hand settling on her shoulder. He gave a gentle squeeze as if he meant to reassure. Fannie sipped in tension scented air. Maggie's brows were creased together. The line of Nellie's lips were set. Jasper looked to be the only relaxed person within the confines of the walls. It seemed her sister wasn't going to enlighten them as to her adventure any time soon.

Fluffing her skirts for a few seconds, Nellie looked up then into Maggie's eyes as if she was the only one she meant to speak with. "I needed to be alone. That's all. Is there some crime in that?" Nellie told the group then stared at Dillon for a blink before she turned her head in a different direction. "Nothing wrong with that except I walked outside to the gazebo. Forgot about all the words of warning that have been swirling around all of us for over a year. I shouldn't have to be confined to the house unless I have a chaperone. Too late, I realized I made a mistake that I couldn't take back. If I could have walked backward in time, I would have done so."

"Nellie!" Dillon thundered as if he couldn't believe what she was saying. He appeared as if he lost control with her vagueness, acting as if nothing untoward happened. With an abbreviated snort of what sounded to be disapproval, he turned to Jasper. "Since Nellie is reluctant, suppose I'll start this story. To me," Dillon pointed at Nellie, "it's obvious the girl is still pouting. When Nellie brought up the idea of marriage this evening, I reminded her about what I told her a couple of months in the past when I first began to escort her to the events our little group orchestrated. Seems she forgot what I said. Either that or turned my words around so she no longer believed I meant them. I have never lied to her about my intentions. She has known the truth from the first day we decided to be a couple."

"What is that supposed to mean?" Jasper's voice was calmer than the stress lines around his eyes as well as his mouth indicated. Her brother-in-law was also catching the foul mood in the air. "Seems to me you are also wallowing in a vague quagmire. Will you elaborate? Do we need to continue to make stabs in the dark about the ambiguity of your words. If I'm not mistaken the two of you are at odds. While that is your business, not mine, I would like to understand what happened to Nellie this evening."

Dillon sipped on the brandy he poured earlier. Gave the liquid time to warm him before he expounded. He set the glass down then stared at it briefly. "From the beginning of our relationship, I told Nellie I wouldn't marry her any time soon if at all. I'm not ready to tie the knot with anyone. I like as well as care for Nellie which is why I stayed around tonight to make certain she got back to the house in one piece. Which I did. From the moment I left the townhouse, I believed she would do something stupid. Wish she'd disappointed me. Her foolishness knows no end."

"Nellie?" The question came from Maggie whose brows were furrowed into deep creases. She pointed a finger at her younger sibling. As if to give solace, Jasper set his hand on her shoulder assuming a pose similar to Fox's. "You need to be forthright with us. You were outside but not with Dillon. Am I right? Why? You are not a silly twit. We've known for a long time Anice has all of us watched. She won't hesitate to take advantage of any situation."

Fannie watched Nellie suck in a gulp of oxygen, her face turning the color of cold ashes. She stared at the fire for a few seconds, her shoulders shaking. Fannie wished she could fix this with Nellie. She understood Nellie thought herself in love with Dillon. By the words he spoke, it was obvious he didn't return the sentiment. For Nellie, it seemed so much had gone awry this evening.

Dillon wasn't in love with her. Never would be. How would she feel in her sister's position? Fox didn't love her. She was going to marry the man. Move away from her homeland to a different country. How did she feel? Fannie didn't know anything except the one major fact she had no choice. She was more than six weeks gone with her pregnancy. By the time they sailed for New York she would be seven weeks. After they reached the continent, she would have a small baby bump.

"Are you going to tell them or do I need to do it for you?" Dillon asked with a harsh tone to his question. "Thought you had more courage. Guess I was wrong about that also. Been wrong about a lot of things lately." Dillon waited for a reply that didn't seem to be forthcoming. If anything, Nellie's nose traveled higher into the air.

Seconds passed while all in the room seemed to be holding their breaths. As if in slow motion, Nellie turned to look at Dillion. She lifted her glass to him as if toasting him. "Why don't you tell my family about the events of this evening. I'm certain you will take umbrage with my rendition of the incidents and correct me. I dare say, you will chime in your opinion even when it's not warranted." Nellie folded her hands in her lap, closing her eyes for a few seconds. Appeared as if Nellie was finished speaking for the evening.

"Very well," Dillon cleared his throat then began the tale all were holding their breath waiting to hear.

When he finished all in the room were frowning with concern. Dillon downed the rest of his brandy. Looked around the room as if hoping for a comment or two. The silence seemed tense. Nellie was biting her lip. Fannie realized at this point Anice would never give up, never stop trying to hurt the two of them. She felt relief she was departing the country. With Fox by her side, Anice would never find her easy prey.

"You escaped with your life along with your virtue intact. For me the fact is a relief. Did you thank Dillon? From what he has told us this evening, your former beau had no reason to shadow you, to protect you. Dillon could have washed his hands of you. Instead, he fought two men to save you. Carried you back to the house because you refused to remain in the coach. If there has not been a thank you, you should do so now," Maggie told Nellie as if playing the mother. "If he wasn't there to give aide, you would be in Lord Abernathy's hands at this very moment."

Fannie understood neither of them thought of Maggie as a mother to them. She was only a few years older. Maggie was right. Nellie should feel a wealth of gratitude for Dillon. He had no reason to wait outside in the cold to protect her.

"Thank you," Nellie told Dillon in a prim voice. Seemed obvious to her, Nellie didn't mean what she spoke. Must still be angry with the man. "You may leave now. I don't want you here. Believe as a family we have some conversation remaining. Tomorrow there will be four days until the wedding, then five until my sister leaves with her new husband. We do have plans to make."

Dillon nodded then took his leave. Keir escorted him to the door. The entire situation seemed surreal to Fannie. Nothing would ever be the same. They would all need to take grave care over the next days. For Nellie, those precautions would not end after she left Glasgow. What then? What did Nellie have to look forward to? She would need a constant guard, either that or stay in the townhouse nursing her wounds. The country home wouldn't be safer. Even living there, isolated, she would need to live with the ever-present threat of abduction.

"Seems Anice will never let up when it comes to her children," Fox pointed out from his vantage point behind her. "I don't understand why she dislikes her daughters with such intensity she would see them made prostitutes. Why couldn't you prosecute when Abernathy abducted Tessa? Were there no witnesses?"

On her shoulders, Fox's hands were warm, gentle. Fannie recalled how they felt other places, how he held her breasts in his hands, touched her with intimate care in the most secret part of her. Unable to help herself, a small whimper left her. Fox's fingers pressed. Fannie turned to look at him. "I'm glad I do not have to worry about Anice the rest of my days. Doubt if she will ever travel across the ocean to try to find me. From all you've told me about the overland trip, she would have a rough time traveling through Michigan to our home. Thank you for taking me away from all this."

"Eventually, Anice will succeed. It's just a matter of time. Nellie would need to marry soon if she is to escape your mother's wrath. After you leave, she will have only one daughter to follow. Anice will be more determined than ever to procure her for Abernathy. Whatever the two of them bargained must be costly," Jasper said, his words solemn. "We cannot protect you from yourself, Nellie. You must step up then make wise decisions."

"I don't wish to spend the rest of my life a prisoner in your home, Jasper. I have friends. There are balls to attend along with other events. I understand I'm alone now. Changing Mother is impossible. Nor do I wish to become Lord Abernathy's newest playmate." Nellie sounded adamant with the statements. "I don't know what to do."

"What can we do?" Maggie asked, shooting her younger sister a sympathetic look. "Nellie is right. A young girl cannot be expected to remain in her home for the rest of her life. She cannot be separated from her friends. We must think of something."

"Nor should she need to have bodyguards shadowing her everywhere she goes outside the home. The gazebo should have been safe. It's on Kenworthy property," Fannie said in sympathy with her older sister. "There has got to be something you can do, Jasper. Maybe Judge Seymore will have some idea how to put a stop to this."

"We could ask him," Jasper agreed with a simple frown that didn't bode well for her suggestion. "Nonetheless, doubt if he can do anything. So far, there has been no crime we can prove beyond a doubt."

Maggie's expression changed. Fannie's oldest sister stared at Fox. Her fingers were tapping on the arm of her chair. Jasper looked at her as if he knew she had an idea yet she wasn't saying anything. Tension in the room mounted.

"Out with it, Mags," Jasper ordered, his voice a bit harsh. Maggie jerked from the command. "You've got something up your sleeve. Anyone who knows you can tell by that look on your lovely face. What is it that your agile mind is plotting?"

"Doubt that," Maggie told him deadpan. "Only you would think I've got some idea as to how to solve the problem of our mother's creation." Maggie seemed to be hesitating which made Fannie think Nellie would never appreciate the suggestion.

"What are you thinking? Am I going to like what you've thought of doing?" Nellie asked as she realized the same thing she did.

Air slipped from behind Maggie's lips. She spoke with a soft voice. "Most likely not. However, I believe it's our only hope to keep you out of Anice's and Abernathy's hands. Perhaps in a few years you could return here."

"Return!" Nellie stood so fast the chair she was sitting on rocked. Threatened to teeter to the floor. "Where the devil are you planning to send me? As you've guessed I don't want to be anywhere but here. Would not be pleased if you sent me to Edinburgh or Inverness, even a smaller city. The devil, where do you have in mind?"

Jasper seemed to be reading his wife's mind. His hands were behind his back while he swayed on his heels, he began. "Believe Maggie thinks you should depart with your sister. Go to Michigan. Meet new people. Make new friends. Think Fox has room in his house for you. You would be comfortable there. Your sister would be with you." For another period of time, silence hung heavy in the drawing room.

"No! I won't go. You can't make me." With each sentence, her voice died. Resting on the arm of her chair, Nellie's hands were fisted.

"Yes," Jasper replied with a calmness that surprised Fannie. "You're right. I cannot make you go with your sister, but I can make life uncomfortable for you if you remain. I will confine you to the country home. Will not allow you to leave the house by yourself. You will be a virtual prisoner there."

Fannie felt a wave of pleasure for herself sweep through her so deep the feeling reached to her soul. After that the pain Nellie must be feeling simmered to the top of her thoughts. There was no other viable choice for Nellie. Maggie's idea was the perfect solution. She turned to look at Fox's reaction. He was frowning. His fingers tightened on her shoulders. Fox must be thinking over the plan, evaluating the pros along with the cons. He needed to agree with Maggie's idea.

"If Fox concurs and passage can be arranged, believe this is the only way for you to live a normal life. Don't wish to uproot you for no reason. Think about it," Maggie said, her voice gentle as she looked at her younger sister. "You have a few days left for you to decide. You're right, this is your decision to make. In time, you might be able to return to Glasgow. On the other hand, you might find you like Michigan."

"Can you arrange passage, Fox?" Jasper asked. "A ticket is one major blockage standing in our way. If the ship is full, we will need to find another avenue to keep you from falling into Anice's plans."

"Tomorrow morning, I'll go to the docks to see if there is a room available. I am in agreement with this plan. This arrangement will be best for Nellie. Fannie will not be so lonely with her sister along for the duration of the trip to the states. I understand she was missing Nellie even today. Even before we were meant to leave. Believe this a perfect solution to the problem of Anice MacRae. All of you have been relieved by the reality Fannie will no longer need to look over her shoulder all the time. Now, there will be no more worries about Nellie."

Shocked to the tips of her toes, Fannie was surprised by Fox's statement. She was astonished he would agree with the idea. He would need to make a home for Nellie too. Nellie would become a third wheel in his life. Fannie reached up to place her hand on top of his. Turning to face him again, she mouthed the words, "Thank you." For the first time, she was beginning to fall in love with Fox, for real. She realized her love for him would have to be enough for both of them.

"You're welcome," he mouthed back, a broad smile endearing him even more to her.

"I won't go!" Nellie stamped her foot in a childish display of hostility. Nellie sounded adamant, beyond immovable. Her hands were still fisted at her sides. Her mouth was set in a firm line. "You can't make me…"

her voice died down as she searched around the room for someone, anyone to agree with her. All were looking at her as if she'd gone mad. There was no other choice for Nellie.

"Again, in this proposal, you are right," Jasper began looking as if he was striving for patience he didn't possess. "We cannot or will not make you leave. If you don't, you will become Lord Abernathy's plaything before the end of the year. He almost got his hands on you tonight. All it will take is one mistake by you. Can you guarantee to yourself that you won't be impulsive one day? Can you be positive that you will always make sensible decisions about your actions?" All in the room understood she could not.

"No…I would have found a way to escape. Just like Tessa escaped him. He would never have been able to keep me wherever it was he was taking me. I'm not submissive. I would fight," Nellie wasn't planning to back down, the stubborn woman.

Seemed to be the pattern of the evening. Once again, the room was filled with silence. There wasn't one voice to change that circumstance. Nellie was breathing hard, little puffs of air wheezing from her throat.

As was the usual, Jasper's voice broke the all-encompassing quiet. "You could have tried." He lifted his broad, arrogant shoulders. "You might have succeeded. The odds are against success. What then?"

"Tessa got away from him," Nellie shot out a second time. "She fought with her mind. Found a means to leave the house."

"Only because the Duke of Southcliff intervened on her behalf. Doubt if the luck will hold a second time or a third time. Yes, today Dillion saved your lovely hide. That man will no longer be around for you. From the looks of this evening's events, your young man will no longer be by your side when you become spontaneous. Tonight, you dodged a bullet. How long do you think your luck will hold?"

"Can you begin to imagine a life with Nelson Abernathy?" Maggie cut into the conversation while shaking her head. "I've firsthand knowledge the way his touch makes a woman feel. The sensation felt as if bugs were crawling on me. Tessa didn't like his attention any better. You would die inside if confined within his home, made to dance to his every whim. He would rape you anytime he wished."

"Because of careless mistakes he made with Tessa, he will not take any chances if he catches you. He will be certain to lock you away where you cannot escape. Abernathy will remove your clothing so you don't dare leave. Are you willing to allow him to touch you intimately? Do you have any notion of what intimate touches mean? No, don't answer my question. Believe I don't wish to know," Jasper said leaving off on a thoughtful note.

Nellie's arms were wrapped around herself, her shoulders bent, trembling. Tears slipped from her eyes, sliding down her white cheeks. When she looked up, Nellie appeared determined. "How long will I need to stay away?"

Seemed Jasper had made his point. Fannie understood Jasper didn't like having to say the things he did. At each word, Fannie shuddered deep inside unable to image the depth of evil encompassing both Lord Abernathy as well as their mother. At the words, her stomach rolled with aversion.

Jasper stroked his chin as he seemed to think of an answer. When he directed his attention back to Nellie, he began, "There is no way to know how long you would need to remain in Michigan. If you were to return too soon…" He shook his head, his eyes narrowing. "Doubt if you could come back to Glasgow without a husband. If you did return as a single woman, you would be vulnerable again. Suppose both Abernathy along with Anice would have to pass on to their maker for you to return without a husband. They are both young. Doubt if their deaths will happen anytime soon."

"I will check on passage first thing in the morning. If there is no room on the passenger ship, this is all a moot point. While I could meet her in New York, the next ship doesn't leave until March." Pausing in thought, "However, the ship is large. I'm certain there will be at least one available room that will do for Nellie." Fox held up his hands when Fannie began to speak. "No, I won't share my room with Fannie's big sister. Nor will I sleep on the deck leaving my new wife to spend her nights alone without her husband. We will be newlyweds. The time on board the ship is precious to me. Need to learn more about Fannie, her likes as well as her dislikes. Won't be separated for any reason."

Fannie glared at him. His words were both pleasant as well as unpleasant. Jasper hooted at the words Fox spoke, coupled with the look she sent her soon to be husband. Maggie directed a scowl toward Jasper. Fannie liked the idea that Fox wished to get to know her better. She wanted to learn more about him too. She also wanted to make sure her sister was able to travel with them.

"You will make certain there is a space for Nellie," Fannie told him, her words tinged with some of the frustration they were all feeling. "You must be able to talk to the captain. Finagle something."

"Yes. I will promise you that I will do my best. I can be persuasive. You're right about the need as well as the fact I know the man. The captain is a friend of mine. Seems I can come up with something. Perhaps call in a favor he does owe me."

"Now that this little contretemps is settled, we need to get to bed. It's been a long night. The next few days will be hectic. I'm pleased this has been settled," Maggie said, smiling at the two sisters. "The three of us will go wedding gown shopping first thing in the morning," Maggie said with the first smile of the night since Dillon revealed what happened at the Kenworthy gazebo.

"No," Fox said, his voice filling the room as if he didn't expect anyone to listen. He brought into his lungs a deep breath of air. To Fannie, he looked as if prepared to go into battle. "The three of you will wait until I return from the docks before leaving this home. Don't intend to let Fannie out of my sight and out of the house without me, bodyguards or no bodyguards in attendance. As for this evening along with the following nights, I'm sleeping here. Positive you've an extra room or two in this big house. The closer I am to Fannie's bedroom the better."

No one replied to Fox for a few seconds. "Sounds as if your mind is made up," Jasper spoke, a small smile forming on his lips. "Believe yours is a fine idea. Don't wish for anything to happen to Fannie before the wedding. You can have Tessa's old room. It's adjacent to Fannie's. I trust you won't slip into her bed once the house is quiet."

"What if I did?" Fox responded with a wry grin as if he meant to hear how Jasper or Maggie would respond. "What would you do? Fannie would be even safer if she slept in my arms. Don't you think?"

Fannie tossed a pillow at him. With a bold hoot, he caught the missile. "You are rushing things. We are not wed. I've a mind to…" She didn't know what she had a mind to do. After his seduction of her this evening, she wouldn't mind sleeping next to him. Looked forward to sleeping with him after the marriage. In her mind, their unwed status was the crux of the problem.

Fox laughed at her look of puzzlement. When his gaze focused on her, Fannie saw the same heated shimmer in his eyes she witnessed when he kissed her, touched her in intimate places. Her breasts were heaving. That was where his gaze was focused.

"The only way you'll find me in your bedroom tonight is if you need me," Fox admitted with some reluctance, yet it seemed his mind was spinning in a different direction while he spoke those words. "Though I am eager for the wedding night. Don't plan on rushing the event. You will remain as you are until then."

Fannie wanted to laugh at his statement. Jasper along with Maggie would think one thing while she understood what he meant. His meaning had nothing to do with keeping her virginity intact which he took weeks ago.

"I will, however, walk Fannie to her door. Perhaps steal a good night kiss before the door closes in my face."

"Do we have your word that you won't bring Fannie to your bed?" Maggie asked as if she was reading this new twist to his mind.

Fannie was standing now, watching the expressions flit across Fox's face. He must have thought along those lines as well. He waited a few beats of her heart before he responded. "No, no you don't," he said, his voice soft as his gaze caressed her. "Won't lie to any of you. I've only a few days to wait until Fannie is legally mine. Don't intend to lose her before we marry, before I can get her out of Glasgow and this dangerous situation she is in. I protect what is mine. Even if it means she must compromise." His honesty surprised her. She didn't understand why.

At his words, heat flushed her face. She drew in as much air as possible. Set her hands against her hot cheeks to cool them. Fannie didn't feel as if she had control of any part of her life. What she didn't want to admit, even to herself, was she would love to sleep with Fox. She remembered his warmth. How his big body fit next to hers, helped her feel safe. The crazy night in the brothel he protected her. He would do so the rest of her life. Even though he didn't love her, was marrying her only to protect his child, she had no regrets.

"Come," Fox extended his hand. Waited while she debated with herself whether to do his bidding or refuse. "All here understand my intentions. We have no secrets tonight. We will share a bed this evening. In the morning, you will still be with me, under my protection as you will for the rest of our lives together. Don't be afraid. Fear is not warranted here. I promise never to hurt you." His words gentled while he spoke, his eyes tender.

She moistened her dry lips. He watched her tongue sweep across her mouth. Needed a drink of wine. Before she accepted his hand, she downed the glass of wine sitting beside her. The alcohol was liquid courage. With a look of indulgence, he smiled at her, understanding her mindset. Her brain was a befuddled mess of contradicting emotions.

"Are you ready, now? I am. Tomorrow appears to be a long day. We have much to do. We will sleep tonight," he spoke with a soft, compassionate voice, sensitive to her needs. "Vow to keep my eyes closed when you are picking out fabrics along with fashion plates for the dress. Wouldn't wish to see the dress before the ceremony."

Fannie set her hand in his, wondering if sleep was all the man meant to do. His hand was warm in contrast to her cold one. At the mercuric contact, a little rush of excitement dashed through her. He helped her to her feet. Holding hands they walked from the drawing room. She felt as if all there stared at her back, judged. She inhaled for courage as her stomach flipped. Her feet wobbled when one foot hit the first step. He held her, wrapping his hand around her waist. Bent to speak for her ears only.

"No one is judging you, sweet. I understand it's what you must think. We all realize the risks at hand. Understand within the house you should be safe. It might not be true. I'm not taking the gamble that anyone will try to steal you from me before the wedding can take place. If you're within my strong arms, there is little chance of anything untoward happening to you. Nellie did tell us Anice along with Lord Abernathy offered one hundred pounds for each of you. That's a sizeable chunk of money. Vile men would risk a lot for the amount of groats offered. Will speak with Jasper. Nellie should sleep in a different bedroom. Don't know how Anice would know what rooms the two of you occupy. Nevertheless, I'm not willing to put anything past your mother."

Turning, she stared into his somber face. Touched his chin with the tip of her finger. "That much…my mother is crazy to think she can get away with abducting either of us right out of the Kenworthy home. Have someone come into this private house then seize me or Nellie? Wouldn't there be evidence then to prosecute?"

"Yes, it would be crazy or desperate. Only a mad woman would do something so wild. From all my research, I've learned it's impossible for a woman to escape Halsey unless she is of no more value to him. He makes a woman's life a living hell. The pimp buries the women so deep within his organization, she cannot claw her way free. Tessa was lucky to get away from Abernathy. Learning about the alliance, I'm positive Tessa would have ended up in his stable as soon as Lord Abernathy tired of her. You were lucky when you out ran the man to find yourself at Hannah's brothel. Hannah is honorable. She has always treated her girls well. Any woman in her establishment who finds a way out is allowed to leave. Believe you must have taken Halsey by surprise. Do you dare test your luck a second time?"

Fox's words made her shiver as she tried to bring air into her lungs. They stopped in front of her door. "I don't… Nellie was lucky too. This evening she still held on to Dillon's protection. Now the safeguard he offered is no longer hers."

"I understand you don't wish for your sisters to think ill of you. They won't judge you, especially not Maggie. Who knows about Nellie? Tonight must have given her a terrible fright. As you pointed out, she was lucky Dillion cared enough about her to stick around." He placed a gentle kiss on her forehead. "Go in your room. Get what you will need for the night. I will wait here, keeping the door wide open." Fox stood in the open door, leaning against the frame, his arms crossed over his chest. He didn't appear to have a care in the world while he was watching her retreat into the bedroom. She didn't understand what was happening.

Fannie wasn't at all certain what to think or do. How to react to his bold proposal. Didn't know if she should protest. For now, she was both eager to follow his instructions as well as terrified. During her time at the brothel, she was not totally cognizant. Part of her mind was in a drug induced haze. With a hesitant nod to Fox, she walked inside her room. Her heart raced as she thought about the night in front of her. Once before, weeks ago, she spent the night in his arms. They made love twice. What would happen tonight? Fannie had no idea. There was more than one possible scenario.

She rummaged around in her armoire. Picked up essentials. She would need to brush her teeth. Wash her face. He would be there when she put on her nightdress. Fannie believed she had a few days to come to terms with the notion he would always be by her side at night. He would see her naked. Touch her just as he caressed her before. Because of that one crazy night, she understood he would want her naked in his bed. She would see him without clothes too. Her memories of his body were not vivid in her head.

When she reached him, a little bundle of her possession in her arms, he stooped to kiss her. The kiss was a light brush of his mouth on her lips, nothing more. "There won't be any more of that tonight. Wish to save our lovemaking for the wedding night. Hope to make that evening special in every way possible."

Hearing his words, Fannie felt a wave of intense disappointment crash through her all the way to the tips of her toes. She wanted another climax like the one this evening in the library. Wished to touch him, taste him more. Wanted to watch him reach his pleasure. She wished to protest his ultimatum.

"Why? Does it make that much difference what we do tonight? We've already…" Fannie paused, placing her hands on her still flat belly. "I would like to see you. Would like to continue what was begun in the library."

He pinched the bridge of his nose then heaved out a rush of air. It seemed he gave his words a second thought. "I don't know. Perhaps I could give you a woman's pleasure. With this conversation, coupled with thinking about you in my arms, I've swelled, grown hard in anticipation. I've promised Jasper to keep an eye on your bedchamber. We're not expecting visitors but we mean to be prepared."

Fannie wasn't certain of his reluctance, no longer felt comfortable with this line of conversation. "Fox, thank you for accepting the task of finding Nellie a place on our ship. You were right when you told everyone I was already missing my family. Moving so far away from everything I know and love is terrifying. We barely know each other. This is not as if we'd been courting, as if we understood what the other was thinking as some couples do. I've no idea about your thoughts. Don't know what life will be like when we reach your home."

"Our home," he corrected with a stubborn set to his jaw.

"Our home," Fannie whispered, her voice soft.

"Yes, well, I do suppose I owe you a favor. Let's see what the rest of the night brings. Maggie was right when she said it was late. It is after midnight. Tomorrow will be busy as will the following days. If we spend the night seeing to our intimate needs you might not have enough energy to deal with all the details of the wedding. Mother used to tell me how exhausting it was to spend an hour at the dressmakers. Always said she'd rather ride the trails all day."

"I think," Fannie paused, reaching her hand to touch Fox's lips, "We should talk to that minister you told us about. You and I should marry tomorrow." Yes, Fannie thought that to be a very good idea.

Fox sucked air at her statement. "Marrying tomorrow would be a splendid idea. As far as I'm concerned the sooner we are bound together for life the better. Do you think Jasper and Maggie would agree to a wedding on much shorter notice? The minister wouldn't be particular. There would be no chance of your mother getting wind of the ceremony. As the seconds slip by, I'm agreeing with you about the benefits." Fox paused, thinking of Fannie in his arms.

"First thing tomorrow morning, before I leave for the shipyard, I will speak with Jasper. Given the urgency of these events, I'm certain he will agree to a hastier marriage. Jasper can send a message to the minister along with a monetary notion of thanks. Want you to pick out a favorite gown." He brushed his knuckles along her cheek. "I'm sorry you will not have a beautiful wedding gown. Do you care?"

She tossed him the best smile she could, then told him with blunt honesty, "You were not in Ireland when Maggie and Jasper married. They waited so she could have all these things for a wedding that any woman would wish for, the gown, the flowers, along with all of us. The entire affair was a disaster."

"Jasper waited to marry Maggie, hmm… He seems to me to be a man of action," Fox told her while she tried to think of all the right things to say.

"Jasper didn't wish to wait. He had an agenda. Nonetheless, he did because he couldn't tell Maggie no to anything she asked for."

"Believe I will have the devil's own time telling you no, also." He slipped his arm through hers then started for the door to their new bedroom.

"Maggie almost died because of his inability to tell her she couldn't have the wedding of her dreams. Since then, I've realized sometimes orchestrating events can cause problems. Maggie almost died. She took a bullet meant for Jasper."

"That was very brave of her. I take it, she did so on purpose."

"Yes." Fannie bent her head, sipping air as they walked into the bedroom where she would spend the night with this man. "She loved him so much she stepped in front of him. Will you see to a wedding tomorrow? Anice won't learn of our plans. She won't be there to disrupt." Fannie liked the thought of being this man's wife.

"I promise we will have a grand celebration of our nuptials in Michigan after we arrive. Dancing, food, all the people who work for me as well as the members of the little town nearby. Everyone will be there."

She lowered her head before she looked at him again. "I *dinna* need anything grand. We can have a small celebration Saturday night. I'm certain Mags will want to do something for us in light of the fact we are marrying sooner than expected."

"Will she be disappointed? There will be no wedding planning? No new gowns for the three of you?" Fox asked as he closed the door behind him then leaned against it.

"Hope not. I fully intend to remind her about her wedding. If she's forgotten, that is."

~ * ~

"Why don't you slip into your nightdress. Though I doubt if you will be wearing it for long. Get ready for bed as if I'm not in the same room with you."

Fannie held the gown to her chest, her eyes huge. He saw the trembling of her shoulders. Her breasts were rising then falling at an alarming pace. "This was easier when I thought you were a doctor and I was dosed with laudanum."

"Don't forget the brandy I treated you with. Brandy, a sure cure for whatever ails you," Fox volunteered while he enjoyed the splendid view, she graced him with.

"The brandy too," she agreed, nodding her head.

"I'm certain it was easier. You do remember I never pretended to be a doctor. Was quite taken aback when you stuck your tongue out then said, ah." He untied his cravat then proceeded to disrobe. Fannie was watching him as he undressed. She never removed her gaze from him. If possible, her eyes grew bigger with each item he removed and folded his clothing to set on the chair. He would need to go to his home in the morning for clean clothes before he went to the docks. Would have to tell his father about the change of plans. Jake might not be pleased at the haste. When given the relevant information, his father would understand.

Naked, he turned so she could see him. Her focus riveted on his swelled sex, anxious for her. He grew harder. Tonight, if all went as planned, he would make love to her. Fox walked through the room, turning down the lights that were set in various places. Some he turned off. After he finished, he pulled back the covers on the bed.

In bed, the covers around his waist, Fox leaned against the backboard, his hands behind his head. The light was dim in the room. There was no moonlight to add to the ambiance he'd arranged. The scene reminded him of the room in the brothel. That evening, he watched her take a bath. His first thought was the truth. She was too damn lovely to be a whore. After he broke through her maiden's shield, he wondered what brought her to this low point in her life.

Yes, in those first moments with her, he'd thought she was beautiful. Fannie had been shy yet also agreeable. In that situation she thought his intentions were honorable. They weren't. Now knowing he impregnated her, he wanted to see a bump where his child grew. Fannie's little belly was still flat. He realized she wasn't even beginning to show when he placed his hand on her belly. Spread his finger from hipbone to hipbone. So far, she showed no signs of a pregnancy. To his knowledge, she'd not been sick. He couldn't be certain if her breasts were larger or more sensitive. He touched them when they were at the brothel. Those caresses were weeks ago. Too damn much time passed from then until now.

Perhaps he should wait until tomorrow evening to make love to her.

He did wish to have a real wedding night. One they would both remember with fondness. Tomorrow, when he was again at his father's home, he would ask him to reserve a room at the Hotel Du Vin Glasgow. It was one of the best hotels in the city. He would ask the hotel to supply wine along with food to their room. They would be alone for all the days left before the ship's departure. No family to make demands on their time. Less fear that Anice or one of Halsey's men would interfere during the night. He would make sure the announcement of their wedding was in the Glasgow Herald as soon as possible.

His father would wish to do something for them. Perhaps keeping Beryl from intruding on their evening would be sufficient. Beryl would never be pleased to hear he was marrying Fannie. Too bad. She needed to be content with his father, having married him. Fox was certainly pleased he wasn't the one leg-shackled to the woman. Once he fell out of love with Beryl, he realized the shortcomings of her personality. While he hoped Beryl loved his father, he wasn't going to hold his breath waiting for the answer.

Beryl had always disliked his home in the Michigan wilderness. She was never happy while she visited him. Told him she detested the weather, the hot sun in the summer, the freezing cold in the winter. Didn't like being so far away from the cities where there were things for her to do. A small noise brought his attention back to Fannie.

He smiled at the view in front of him. Pleased with what he saw. Fannie's back was to him. He could see her hands shaking while it appeared she was fumbling with the buttons on the front of her dress. This might be easier for her if he seduced her, charmed her socks off along with the rest of her clothing. She had yet to remove her stockings or the dress. Her shoes were on the floor in front of her. Fox started to rise. Stopped himself. He meant to show a small modicum of patience. Wished to see what she would do.

"Do you need help, sweet?" Fox called to her while his gaze continued to evaluate the scenario in front of him. "My fingers are very willing to unfasten those tiny buttons of yours. Seems I was a success earlier in the evening. We could accomplish this much faster if I stepped in with my nimble fingers."

A startled gasp whispered in the room. Fannie turned sideways. He caught a glimpse of her bared chest, nothing more. He was eager to see all of her. More than likely she would keep her back to him. That was fine with him. He would also enjoy the view of her beautiful backside. In her modesty, Fannie was adorable. He wondered when she would get used to being naked in front of him.

"I'm…a…" Fannie turned away from him. "Having trouble with these damn little buttons. They won't come undone. My fingers are shaking." She looked as if she meant to stamp one pretty foot on the blue, Aubusson carpet. "No, I don't want help." Her voice resonated with what sounded like frustration. She could use some aide. Didn't appear she would relent on her solid no.

Fox swallowed his hoot of laughter. Her swearing was precious. In his very male mind, everything about her was adorable. "I didn't have trouble when we were kissing in the library. They came unfastened for me."

"No, no you didn't have a problem."

Still didn't seem she intended to invite him to help her with the 'damn' buttons. That was fine with him. He enjoyed watching the process. Fox had the best seat in the room. He sipped on the wine he poured earlier. Fox let out a long slow breath of air.

"Let me know if you change your mind." Fox flexed his fingers, then wished this was his wedding night right now. If it was, he wouldn't hesitate to lend a hand. Wouldn't give her a choice. He would rain kisses down upon the back of her neck. Touch tender places while he removed her clothing. He realized she might say she wanted him to make love to her. At this instant, she didn't appear too eager. What she looked to be was shy. Hesitant to reveal herself to him. Of course, she would be modest. They'd been together naked one time, weeks ago. Even though he saw her breasts earlier, touched her intimately, she wasn't naked.

The little sigh he heard, the one that told him she was doing better with the buttons running down the front of her dress, didn't escape him. Neither did the sight of her gown pooling around her waist then her feet. When she bent over to take it off the floor her exquisite rump still covered with her chemise and petticoats pointed into the air. He thought of coming into her from behind. His breath shuddered from his lungs.

Fascinated, he continued to observe. Her back was still to him when the last article of clothing was whisked away. She was naked. This view of her backside caused his breath to hitch in the back of his throat and his heart to thunder against his ribs. He ached to caress her, kiss her delicious backside. The length of Fannie's back was long and sleek. With his gaze he traced the vertebrae running down her back to her sweet rump. Wished his lips were doing the tracing. Delighted in the feminine curves of her hips which he thought to caress. White legs were sleek, trim, perfect to wrap around his flanks. Was disappointed when the stark white gown she brought over her head covered all of her.

A few filmy gowns for bedtime were in order. He had a couple of days before their departure to visit the dressmaker and purchase a few for the trip to the states. He meant to spend most of their time on board the ship in his cabin. Ah, light blue would bring out the color of her eyes. Lavender would look splendid against her snow-white skin. When she turned, her hands were clasped tight in front of her just beneath her chin. She peered over the top of white knuckles with huge blue eyes. Fannie appeared terrified. He didn't like seeing fear in her eyes.

He meant to make changing the fear to sexual urgency a top priority. Fox patted the spot on the bed beside him. "Come here, sweet. We can discuss what you wish to do or not to do tonight. Know everything is your choice. Though I would try to sway you to my thoughts with a few well-placed kisses."

"D...dis...discus," Fannie seemed to be having trouble forming words. "Discuss what we are going to do? Thought we were sleeping."

"Sit by me. I'll abide by your wishes. Yes, plan to sleep tonight as well as play if you are willing. Maybe recreate what we did in the library. We can't jump the gun on the wedding night because we already did that." Fox patted the bed again, smiling at his soon to be wife. He flipped open the covers. "We can start with a bedtime kiss. I'll let you decide what kind of bedtime kiss it will be. What would you like, deep, probing where you open yourself to me and I to you?"

"Open?" Fannie questioned with innocence.

Even though she wasn't a virgin, Fannie was still innocent in too many ways to count. Watching the changing expressions flash across her delicate features gave him a wealth of information. She was thinking about his tongue gliding inside her, exploring. Fannie might also be thinking about other parts of her opening for him. On this she wasn't ignorant unless she forgot how they played together in the brothel as well as in the library. Maybe she didn't remember.

"Yes, Fannie. I would enjoy you opening for me. You can part your lips, let me glide inside your delicate warmth."

"My mouth?"

"As you did in the library a short while ago," Fox reminded her, his voice resonating with soft vibrations. "Yes, that's exactly what I mean. You could also open your heart to me. I wouldn't mind having your love."

"Y…you don't love me," Fannie blurted the last part then tossed him a scowl, the lines across her forehead deep.

"That is an assumption left for a different time to explain. Also," Fox let his gaze roam the length of her, "wish that nightdress of yours wasn't opaque." He grinned a devil's grin. "Do you recall when you parted your legs for me? I found all of you beautiful. I fondled those parts of you that you opened for me. I know you enjoyed what I did with your feminine endowments. If you're willing, we could do so again." With every word he spoke, he found he was torturing himself.

She dipped her head. Fox wondered if the tilt was a nod that meant yes. He wondered if Fannie recalled when she'd opened herself completely for him. The urgency he felt told him it would be in his best interest if she wanted him as much as he did her.

"If you sit by me, we can begin with a kiss. A small kiss. I would touch your mouth with mine then my tongue. I'll even let you say…ah…if you wish. The rest is up to you. If you separate your lips for me the action would tell me how to proceed. Fannie, do you want that kiss then one after that? I'm more than willing to kiss you everywhere you ask. You must be explicit."

Appearing to be walking to the gallows, Fannie made her way to the bed. She did sit down next to him when he lifted the covers again. Her face pale, her lips mushing together she made a pretty picture of insecurity. Fox knew she saw his arousal when he gave her room to slide beneath the sheets.

"You can kiss me," Fannie's voice was very proper, stiff in the extreme. "Anywhere you like. I do enjoy your kisses."

"In the library you enjoyed kissing, yes. Where would you like me to kiss you first? Don't wish to make mistakes." Fannie wasn't at all with him. Seemed she changed her mind. If he insisted she explain what she wanted, she might balk. She shook her head at him. Stole a swift breath of air. "Very well, we should go to sleep without benefit of a good night kiss. It is after one o'clock. As you told me, we must be up early. Tomorrow is a busy day as well as the ones after that. Don't wish to end up with shadows under my eyes on my wedding day."

Fox thought he saw her let out a long breath of relieved air when she finished spouting her little bit of nonsense. What would tomorrow night be like if she came to him this reluctant? He supposed he should insist on a kiss then another one after that. They'd had so little time together. She was uneasy. He reminded himself again, Fannie was practically a virgin. Except for the two times with him over six weeks ago, she had little to no experience.

Fannie set her small hand on his chest. Her fingers spread wide. "Fox, I would enjoy a kiss. Enjoyed everything else you've done. I do want to touch you." The palm of one hand floated across his chest, touching on his nipples." She still sounded as if she was on the way to the gallows. Erasing that tone was imperative.

"You don't sound as if you want a kiss. To me, you sound terrified," Fox said as he caressed her neck with the tip of his finger. Heard her little exhalation of pleasure at the light unintimidating caress.

She'd closed her eyes. Now, they were wide open. The palms of her hands continued to stroke his chest, flitted over his nipples, first one then the other. With the gentle contact he continued to harden, swell with need. "You aren't wearing anything. Is that the way you always sleep?" Fannie seemed to have regained her voice. Her roaming hand drifted south. Caressed his belly. He sipped air.

"Yes, except when the temperature drops below zero. At those times I wear my long johns. In the future, I'll have the sweetness of your body to keep me warm. So, I don't know what I will wear. Prefer nothing at all. Would you sleep nude with me? Would you?" He thought to give her a taste of their future. Wanted to sweep the gown she wore over her head.

Holding her shoulders, Fox placed a tender kiss on her mouth. She parted her lips for his entrance. Inside her sultry heat, he tasted the mint she used to freshen her breath. Caught the lavender scent of Fannie. Without hesitating, Fannie met his tongue with hers. Played. He savored the sensations as he stroked her arms. Wished the bloody gown was pooled around her waist or on the floor which would be the best place for the damn thing. In the damn armoire was where it belonged. When she packed for the hotel, he'd make certain the nightgown didn't go with her. Her fingers wound into his hair as she held his head in her hands. He wished he could bury his face between her breasts.

Fannie's clothed breasts pushed against his chest. Even with the fabric in the way, he felt the hardened tips. Wished to suckle. Needed to devour the soft globes. A low groan of need rasped from the back of his throat. As long as she was willing, he needed to taste more of her. He played with the line of buttons along the front of the gown, unfastening then revealing tender white flesh. The gown was open to her navel. Fannie never protested. A little feminine whimper floated in a soft ribbon from her lips.

Fox moved back to look at her. Needed to see all of her he'd exposed to his view. Pushed the fabric from her shoulders then down her arms. Now, the gown was almost where he wished it to be, on the floor. With tender reverence, he cupped one breast in his hand. Bent to suckle. Rubbed his thumb across the other one.

After he finished attending to the first beautiful breast, Fox smiled at her. "You taste wonderful. Makes me think of winter then how the season turns to spring. Cold then warming with the sun's attention. Wish to set you on fire as if the summer sun brought heat to all your parts." He did the same with the other breast, tasted, suckled with reverence.

She ran her hands along his shoulders. Arched into his mouth when the fiery suck of his lips pulled at her breast brought it deep within. Fox bit with gentle care on the tip. Swirled his tongue on the sensitive bud. He wanted to lay her back on the bed. Pull the gown from her hips then look at all of her.

The pounding on the steps brought Fox to attention. His heart thundered, warning him of eminent danger. When he stopped to look at Fannie, her eyes were dazed. She was just as he wished her to be. A vague look of arousal was in her eyes.

"What? She asked her voice soft with the question.

"Lord Kenworthy! Mister Taggart… Help! Someone is trying to break into the house. Come quick! I've locked the door but they might try to shatter the glass. Need help!" Keir was panting. The last words were a jumbled mess. By the time he reached the top of the stairs, Fox could hear Keir dragging air into his lungs.

Fox figured everything out that Keir was trying to say. "No! This shouldn't be happening." Fox's instincts ran heavy. He'd half expected something like this to happen tonight. It was one of the reasons why he insisted Fannie sleep in his room. "Come with me, Fannie. Get your nightgown on. I will not leave you here, alone," Fox yelled at her. His worst nightmare was coming true. The bounty on the girls must have grown enough to make stupid men attempt to break into the townhouse. He tossed her gown to her. "Hurry, sweet. Keir is panicked. Don't know if Jasper heard his cries for help."

"Fox what is it? What's going on?" She slipped her gown over her head, Fannie's fingers fumbling with the buttons.

"You're coming with me." He pulled on his trousers, heading for the door and fastening them as he raced. "Seems someone broke into the townhouse. The voice you heard was Keir calling out for help. Yelling loud enough to wake the dead. Hope Jasper heard the commotion."

"I…wouldn't it be better if I stayed here?" She stumbled into him, falling forward. Fox caught her. "Don't wish to be…" she left off with the statement as if she realized in that moment, she'd be more vulnerable if left alone in the bedroom. It might be the ploy of the men who were trying to kidnap her.

After Fox righted her then made certain she was fine, he held her hand before pushing her behind his back. "No, want you beside me. Need your body to be shielded by mine." Fox wished he had a gun or some weapon. Jasper might have one in his room.

Opening the door, he peered into the hall. Saw nothing. Keir most likely frightened the intruders away. He would have liked to have caught them, questioned them. He didn't know if Nellie was safe in her room. They needed to bring Nellie with them.

"Where is Nellie's bedroom?"

"On the other side of mine. Why?" she asked.

Fannie pressed herself against him. He felt the hard tips of her breasts. Fox prayed she would do everything he told her. Obedience would serve her well in the wilderness where they were headed. "Need to keep your sister safe also." They stopped in front of the door. "Here we are."

Fox pounded hard. If Nellie slept soundly, she might be difficult to wake. He pounded while he yelled her name. "Nellie! Nellie, it's Fox and your sister. Open the door! We've got intruders in the house. Come, open up!"

Seconds passed. Fox's heart surged to his throat. He turned the knob then stepped inside. Nellie was standing in the middle of the room, her hair tumbling around her shoulders. Her face was as white at the nightdress she wore. Her hands were clasped in front of her. When he saw her eyes, Fox found she appeared terrified.

"Are you alright?" Fox asked as he peered into the darkness of the room. Some light filtered in from the hallway. "Is there anyone in here with you?"

Nellie shook her head then nodded. "I'm alright. No one is in here. How could anyone get into the house?"

Hers was a good question. Was positive Keir scared the intruders off. Didn't believe anyone was in the home. "Doubt if there is anyone inside the townhouse. Not willing to take chances. I'm going to look around. Both of you are coming with me."

"Oh, Nellie, there might be someone in the house. Keir ran up the steps yelling for help. I hate this."

"Both of you come with me. Stay behind me but keep close." Fox started down the hallway. Listened to every creak of the structure. He heard nothing. Saw nothing. The silence seemed to cry out that Keir scared the kidnappers away. This was another victory of sorts. There would be no relief for any of them until their ship left the harbor.

They both nodded. Fannie asked, "Where are we going?"

"To the drawing room to wait for Jasper if he isn't there before us." Fox wasn't certain of anything. While he would like to throttle anyone who threatened Fannie, he didn't need to question the intruders to know who sent them. Had to be one or all of the three people who had been these girl's nemesis since their sister, Maggie refused marriage to Nelson Abernathy. The main question reverberated in his head. How could a mother treat her flesh and blood this way? Imagined he would never have the answer.

In the drawing room, Jasper along with Maggie and Keir were talking, waiting for them to appear. Jasper's gun rested on the table near him. They all turned to watch them when they walked through the door.

"You didn't catch the men. How many?" Fox asked, searching Jasper's face for some sign he could grab onto.

Keir's head jerked up. He held his hand behind his back "There were three men in total. I saw them when I walked down the servants' stairs. They weren't expecting anyone to be up and about. Needed to check the doors one last time. I know I locked them. It's a simple precaution I take every night before I retire. I was up late finalizing plans for the wedding celebration. Saw the shadows on the back porch. Knew what I saw meant no good for the little ladies. Didn't wish to open the door to go after them so I ran up the staircase shouting for help."

Fox stuffed his hands through his hair. "You did the right thing. This won't be the last time someone tries to break into the house in order to grab the girls. We've got to take stiffer precautions to protect them. They shouldn't be terrified in their home."

"I'll hire men to watch the doors as well as have the house guarded at night and during the daytime. I'll go to the Duke of Southcliff. He can recommend a few men to be hired," Jasper said as he held tight to Maggie's hand. "First thing in the morning, I will see to this. Need the place guarded until the three of you sail for the States."

"You all should know; Fannie and I discussed the situation before all the uproar took place this evening. We've decided to tie the knot tomorrow. No matter what it takes. If the minister can't do the job, we will go to Judge Seymore. Believe Tessa's uncle would enjoy marrying us."

Fannie spoke up then, "I don't care about a wedding dress. Recall your wedding, Mags. Fox says he will take care of the small details before the afternoon. Contact the minister and such after he sees to Nellie's room on the ship. Keir," she turned to the butler, "thank you for being there for us."

"I'll make certain the cook puts together a feast for the occasion. We will have a wedding cake baked by the time all of you return from the church. Is Lord Kenworthy giving away the bride?" Kier asked with a smile.

"Yes, I believe we talked about that particular task before. My father will serve as my best man," Fox said his gaze focused on Fannie. He knew she wore nothing beneath the gown. Realized he would need to let her sleep tonight. The play they'd been involved in before all hell broke loose would need to wait for the wedding night.

"Nellie will be my maid of honor," Fannie added looking at her older sister. "All I want now is to be Fox's wife, the sooner the better," she added with a little flutter of her hand. "A few days ago, I didn't know I would feel this way."

At the paling face of Jasper's wife, nothing more needed to be said. Fox went on to describe everything the two of them talked about. When they started speaking of tomorrow's event, Fannie along with Maggie collapsed on a chair. The both appeared exhausted. Fannie would more than likely fall asleep as soon as her head hit the pillow.

"It's best for the two of us to marry as soon as possible. That way, the only sister unprotected is Nellie," Fox said his voice tender when he glanced Nellie's way. She was winding her fingers in then out of her nightgown.

"Good Lord, what did we ever do to deserve all this?" Maggie asked while she leaned into Jasper. His arms wrapped around her, holding her close.

"Fannie and I are going up to bed. We need to sleep. It's time everyone else retired." Fox looked at the clock on the mantle. It was almost three o'clock. They had not yet slept. "I will check out Nellie's room. Is there any way into it from below?"

"If a man has suction cups for feet and hands, I suppose there is," Jasper answered on a bland note. "I'll check the locks on all the doors then remain up until six. Once the sun starts to come up, it will be too light out for anyone to sneak into the house. Servants who don't live here will begin to arrive. If it's alright once there are more servants in the home, I'll go to sleep for a few hours. Need to be refreshed to help direct the celebration."

Feeling as if Nellie's room was secure, Fox along with Fannie left to find their bed. Closing the door to their room, Fox leaned against the wood, watching. Fannie ran into his arms. Tears slid down her cheeks. Against him, she was trembling.

"All I want is to be safe. Married to you. I find now, with all the turmoil, I'm eager to leave for your home. Didn't think I would ever feel that way. Only a few hours ago I was dreading the future in a new country."

Fox kissed her tears away, tasting the salt on his tongue. "No more bed-play tonight. You've shadows beneath your eyes. Want them gone for our wedding tomorrow afternoon. Sleep as long as you need. When you wake up, I'll be gone, running the errands we talked about."

"Whatever you say."

Her words didn't bode well for his intended abstinence. If it weren't for the fact she was a virtual innocent, they could have sex fast. He understood where to touch.

~ * ~

Anice paced the drawing room of Nelson's country estate. The home he bought to place Nellie or Fannie, maybe both of them when he acquired her daughters. The home was a distance from Glasgow. Far away from the city. The closest neighbors were five miles away. He told her he didn't want to risk interference from any of the neighbors.

Anice knew the Duke of Southcliff was the sole reason Tessa got away from him. The duke interfered when Tessa's guard was dragging her back to the house. Now this man by the name of Dillon Montrose was the sole reason Nellie escaped. She wasn't pleased with the outcome of tonight's work.

"Is the room secure?" Anice asked as she began to form more opinions, tried to think of some way to call her daughters home. She knew they wouldn't come to her. She tried that ploy too many times to succeed another time.

"Yes, more so than you can imagine. The third-floor room has been made up special for the girls. The lock on the one door into as well as out of the room is secure. Neither lady would ever be able to force her way out. The window is bolted as well as painted shut. It is a third-floor room. I doubt if even your intrepid daughters would risk their necks jumping or tying sheets together in order to scurry down the straight wall. It's more than a thirty-foot drop. If they tried, they would break their pretty lily-white necks."

"Give her one sheet and no blankets. I would never under judge what they are capable of doing," Anice said through clenched teeth. Fisting then unfisting her hands, she was furious the two attempts to secure Nellie failed this evening. Weeks ago, she missed Fannie by a hair's breath. Fannie ended up in Hannah's brothel for the night. The damn Madame even sent for a doctor. She hit the palm of her hand with her fist. "Halsey, you will find a means to get both my daughters before the end of the week. God knows I'm paying you more than you're worth! Don't make any more mistakes."

"What do you plan next?" Nelson shot his question to Halsey as he sipped on his brandy appearing content to keep his gaze focused on her breasts. Anice was certain Nelson had ideas in his head. "I'm beginning to lose my patience. Feel the same as Anice. You should at least have made it here with Nellie. What the devil happened? One man against two managed to rescue her. If you count the driver, there were three men."

"Dillon overpowered the men who were doing their best. Can't say that either are bright. The *lass* has got to make a mistake sometime. Her luck can't hold much longer. Seems her beau stepped in to rescue her. My men saw him leave the premises," Halsey told him. "I've men waiting for the same mistake to be made again. As I said, your offer of a hundred pounds for each girl has brought men panting to be the one to capture them."

"Let me see the room." Anice stepped toward the door leading to the foyer. Turned to see if Nelson was following. "Do you have a peep hole for me to look through. I want to see you take Nellie's along with Fannie's virginity. Need to see my daughter's legs spread wide to accept you into her. Wish to hear her cry of pain when you take her virgin's shield." She always despised the father of her three oldest daughters. The man felt the same about her. No love was lost between them. When he died, she was pleased. That was when she dallied with the oldest Seymore twin. The ongoing affair lasted a little over one year.

"That beau of hers might have beaten me to her virginity," Nelson said his voice holding a hint of disappointment. "In which case I won't need to be gentle with the lass. I can find out if she's a virgin before I thrust into her." He grinned as if he was seeing in his mind as well as feeling the deed.

"Bah," Anice waved her hand in the air. "You are never gentle with a girl. You like sex rough as well as messy. Don't mince words."

Nelson lifted his shoulders, a smile on his face directed her way. "Just the way you like your sex too, madam. Should we initiate her room? Partake in a quick bout of sex. Perhaps Halsey would like to join us in a threesome. We've done it before to enjoyable ends. Together we won't leave a part of you untouched."

"No. Not this evening. I'm going home. Have some sleuthing of my own to do tomorrow. Don't trust Fox Taggart farther than I can toss that man, which is not far at all. He's got something up his sleeve. Didn't you tell me one of your men followed him to a church the other day? Do you think he has plans to marry Fannie? If so, we've got to collect her before a marriage can take place. This situation becomes more urgent with each passing second."

"Yes," Nelson said as he flicked imaginary lint from his jacket. "I did hear from one of my employees that noxious fact. When he confronted the minister, the minister wouldn't tell my man anything. Said he'd been sworn to secrecy."

Anice was shaking her head, repeating herself. "You don't think Taggart is planning to wed Fannie? To the best of my knowledge the two don't know each other. If they do know each other it has been less than a week." Anice lost the breath she'd been holding. "That can't be. He lives on the other side of the world in that savage place they call the United States. If they marry, he will take her with him. Wouldn't leave his wife in Glasgow. If that happens, she will be gone from us for good."

Anice lifted her shoulders with an all-female delicate shrug that didn't go unnoticed by Nelson. Anice knew her unfettered breasts would entice Nelson. Staring at Nelson she confirmed her words. "Might be for real. Don't know why. As I said the two don't know each other." At least Anice didn't believe they met before a week ago. A week's courtship? Anice never believed in love at first sight. For that matter, she didn't believe in love. Love was for fools.

"Maybe tomorrow I'll visit the church. Tell me where it is located. I'll go in the afternoon. I'm certain I can figure out a way to loosen the minister's tongue. Might entice him, with thoughts of carnal pleasures. I do have my ways of offering my body to learn what I'd like to know."

"Yeah, undo a few buttons on your gown. Let him catch the rounded globes you always flaunt. Give him enough to see the pink of your nipples. Don't have one doubt you'll catch his eye. Probably be drooling out the side of his mouth when he sees a few of your assets," Halsey said with a snigger. "You're welcome to work for me anytime you feel up to it. Got rooms reserved special for the women who prove they deserve them. You could get enough sex even for you. In addition, you would be paid handsomely."

Anice shot him a disgusted look. "Never," she smoothed the fabric of her skirt. "Not on your life. I like my men clean. Not going to pick up some rotten disease in your whorehouse."

"You don't care if your daughter gets one of those rotten diseases?" His eyebrows lifted toward the ceiling. "No, of course you don't. You despise your daughters."

"Bastard daughters every one of them," Anice corrected with evident distaste. Thinking about her bastards brought a sour taste to her mouth. "They are all bastards, all four of them. Their father left me before he married me then he died. Called me a whore to my face." Anice strode to the sideboard then poured herself a drink. She downed the contents in one gulp before pouring another. "Take me to the room where Nellie or Fannie or perhaps both will live until you grow bored with their charms. Want to see where they will reside until you get uninterested then sell them to Halsey. They will bring a pretty penny."

Nelson barked a quick chortle. "Follow me." Nelson led her through the house to the back stairway. "Think you will appreciate the room."

The walls were narrow, closing in on her as she walked up the two flights of stairs. She shivered from the cold air sifting downward from what must be some type of hole in the ceiling. There were no windows. They reached a door that opened into a small walkway. Nelson unlocked it. Anice saw only two doors. One must be for the girls. The other would lead into the viewing room. Thrilled with this, she grinned.

"Here it is," Nelson said as the door swung open into a single room. "Believe this is perfect for my intentions. Neither will be able to leave or call for help. The place is unescapable. Once inside they are here for as long as I wish them to be my playthings."

"You didn't say anything about steel bars on the window," Anice said as she walked around the room. "Or chains on the bed. To my mind those are fine touches, adequate, more than acceptable. The ambiance of this room will defeat the girls. Give them no hope of escape. Looks as if you learned your lesson with Tessa."

In a shrug of nonchalance, Nelson lifted his broad shoulders. "Don't wish for the girls to get away from me. Plan on taking every precaution necessary. Would you like to try out the bed? You could put your hands over your head. With your wrists locked, I could have you here first before your girls. As we said earlier, initiate this room. We both realize it is just a matter of time until I have them beneath me. Lord Kenworthy will never be able to protect your dear little sweethearts every waking hour. Right now, it's been luck on the girls' part that has kept them from my grasp. Every day I have to wait, what happens will go worse for them. When my wishes are defied, I'm not an easy man nor patient. I've hungered for them for far too long."

"Told you I didn't wish to participate in your sex games tonight. I'm going home. You can always call on one of Halsey ladies to initiate the room." When she turned to leave, Halsey stopped her. He held his hand on her shoulders. She tried to shake off his fingers which were biting into her. His grip grew tighter. "Let me go!"

"Not so fast, little lady. I've a hankerin' to taste your sweetest places. You are not going anywhere until I'm ready to take you."

"What! No!"

Nelson picked her up then dumped her on the bed. Before she could do anything to stop them the two men had her hands bound above her head then her legs were separated and locked to the chains at the base. Anice shrieked then she laughed. Just to add to the scenario as well as please the men, she wiggled, tried to dislodge her bindings. Tugged then pulled. Moaned. Knew they grew harder watching her. Both men loved the fight. "You bastards! Go ahead. Take what you want then let me go. I've work to do for all of us tomorrow. Wish for a good night's sleep. Make it fast."

Nelson turned to Halsey. "Do we want Anice naked? What do you think? We could just…" He ran his hands along her legs, pushing up her gown. He hooted a laugh of pleasure, "How naughty. You aren't wearing underwear. You wanted us to take you. Saying no was a tiny show of defiance. You will have to pay for misleading us."

"Yeah, we could toss her skirts. Will be easy without underwear. Ah, but her breasts…we need to be able to fondle those soft, round globes of male pleasure. Her breasts are almost my favorite part of her. You've bound her ankles as well as her wrists. She's as helpless as a newborn babe. We can do whatever pleases us." Halsey was rubbing his hands together. His grin gave Anice reason to shudder. While she enjoyed Nelson, Halsey wasn't a man she would pick to have sex with. Now, with Nelson, he was part of the package deal. From the beginning, she realized her girls, if given a choice, would choose Nelson over Halsey any time they were given a choice. Maybe that was what Nelson planned, a choice. Nelson would lie. In time he would do this threesome act with them. Maybe even from the very beginning. He would say one thing then do the opposite. Her girls would learn they couldn't believe him.

"Suppose that would be fun. Just a bit of practice before we have Nellie along with Fannie locked in these chains then beneath us. Would rather have Anice naked. Without clothing there are so many more possibilities."

Before he locked her to the base, she kicked out at them, seconds later she was spread wide for their viewing pleasure. Nelson liked a woman with fight in her. Anice hoped her daughters would battle the chains along with the men. Knew their fear would encourage both men.

Nelson sat down on the bed. Pulled out a small knife. Slit her gown from the hem to the top of her corsage. Pushed the fabric aside revealing all of her charms. He palmed one breast then the other. Bent to taste. She shrieked then moaned her pleasure.

"Bastard!" she cried out.

"Bitch," Nelson responded.

"Whoresons!"

"Harlot."

Anice laughed, her breasts dancing for their enjoyment. Needing to get this over with she cried out, "Have at it, boys! Touch me however you like. One at a time or at the same time. Whatever pleases the two of you will please me."

Chapter Six

By noon, Fox accomplished everything he set out to do. He met Jasper in his office to go over the details for the upcoming wedding along with the departure in less than five days. They would leave with the tide next Sunday. Sail down the firth of Clyde to the Atlantic. It would take about a month to reach New York, depending on the weather. While he was looking forward to the voyage because he was headed home, he didn't yet know how Fannie felt. What he did understand was that she would be relieved to be far away from her mother.

This day was unseasonably warm for a day nearing the end of February. It was a fine day for a wedding. Standing in the foyer, he gazed up the stairs where his bride would be dressing. In a couple of hours, he'd be a married man. When he entered the house, an unknown man met him at the door. Keir stood beside this stranger, his hands behind his back rocking on his heels. Keir greeted him with a nod of his head.

Keir stepped beside the big man with the dour expression, he was known for. He directed his attention between the two of them. "Believe introductions are in order, sir," Keir said with a broad smile his eyes sparkling. "This man is one of the new guards. He has been assigned to the house by the Duke of Southcliff. His name is Seumas. There is a guard at the backdoor, whose name is Calum as well as two who are working the grounds, Martin and Iain. These four were the first to arrive. There will be another four coming in three hours. They will be alternating shifts during the day as well as the night; on three hours, off six. When the men are off duty, they will use the time to eat as well as sleep when needed. They are all trained in the martial arts as well as weaponry of many different kinds. Believe the girls will be well-protected with these men standing guard. No man or woman will get to the ladies." Keir seemed to preen when he introduced the man along with all his capabilities.

In other words, they spied for the duke. Were trained by the duke or men handpicked by the duke. "I'm impressed at how fast this was accomplished," Fox said as he introduced himself. "I'm Fox Taggart. The girls who you are assigned to guard are precious to all of us. One is to become my wife this afternoon. The other sister will travel with us when we depart for my home in the States. We don't wish for anything to happen to them. They've been lucky so far. Their luck won't hold forever."

"No one will get past us. I personally guarantee that," Seumas said while he held out his hand. They shook. Took the measure of each other. Seumas seemed satisfied as did Fox. "The men assigned here are among the best in Scotland. The duke knows us along with our capabilities."

"Good, I won't detain you any longer. Thank you for being here for us." He was certain Jasper was paying a small fortune for the men assigned to his home. Maybe not. The duke would want to find some way to prosecute Lord Abernathy, Halsey as well. If he could obtain proof against the men as well as irrefutable evidence, the prosecution would be easier. Jasper mentioned how much he despised Lord Abernathy. The man was a blight on his neighborhood. Wished he'd been able to prosecute the man. Even Tessa's testimony wouldn't put him away. Her word against Lord Abernathy's. At the time of the incident, the duke didn't see a crime committed. Perhaps they stepped in with aide too soon.

"Keir, is Jasper here? We need to speak about the next few days. I've ironed out a few details for this afternoon as well as the day we sail." Fox was ready to sit down with a good hot cup of coffee then discuss his morning.

An hour ago, he sent word the wedding would be at two o'clock this afternoon. Fox held his hand around the little box which housed the wedding band he brought for Fannie. He hoped she liked it. Would have liked to have had the time for Fannie to pick out both her rings. Refused to get married without rings.

The reverend was more than happy to perform the ceremony ahead of schedule. After hearing part of their story, he told him he would be here for him. Would help in any way possible. He apprised him of the man who questioned him about the ceremony and how he didn't like the look of the outsider. Told Fox, he didn't give out any information concerning him.

"Yes, sir, Lord Kenworthy waits for you in his office. Should I tell him you've arrived?" Keir asked as he stepped back to let Fox walk by seeming to know what his answer would be. "By the way, congratulations on the upcoming nuptials."

Fox nodded his thanks before answering the question. "No, Jasper expects me." Fox strode to Jasper's office where they decided to meet when they both returned from their responsibilities. When he reached the office, the door was open. Jasper sat at his desk, pen in hand, pouring over papers. He looked up from his task. Smiled.

Fox began, "Jasper, I see your visit with the duke paid off. I feel some relief speaking with Seumas as well as knowing he is not the only guard. Don't see how anyone will get passed these men. Now, we need only make certain the ladies don't do anything foolish." What he knew was that Fannie would never be foolish. For the time being she was ensconced in the house. She wouldn't be out of his sight after the wedding. After the feast being prepared by the Kenworthy cook, he would take her to their hotel suite. Fannie wouldn't be going anywhere alone, doubted if Nellie would either.

Jasper set his pen down before straightening the papers in front of him. Shot him another wide smile. "Yes, Leslie was more than willing to lead me in the right direction when it came to procuring the guards. You know, he was there when Tessa escaped Lord Abernathy. Without his interference, well, I hate to think what would have happened to Jason's wife. Leslie is a good friend. Solid. Reliable in the extreme."

"Pleased you know him well enough to ask for the favors. How much did this cost? My guess would be quite a bit. From what Keir told me we're employing eight men until Sunday when we sail."

"Nothing, this isn't costing us a penny. This is all being paid for by the Scottish government who would more than anything like to put an end to Halsey's organization. He's been a thorn in their side for years. If Lord Abernathy goes down in the process all the better." Jasper poured from a pot. Looked like coffee. Fox wasn't certain. When he caught the aroma, his mouth watered. The preferred drink in this household was either brandy or tea. Coffee, strong and bitter was his favorite. "Yes. I'm pleased to say. Nothing a'tall. Leslie told me it was a public service to try to eliminate Halsey from the streets. As for Lord Abernathy, there isn't much he can do unless he does succeed in his endeavors. Coffee?" Jasper held up the cup he poured.

"I was wishing for a hot cup when I walked into the house. It's nice you recalled my favorite brew. I was going to offer to pay half the cost of the guards." Pausing for a few seconds, he asked the next important topic on his mind. "Where are the girls?" He hoped they were getting ready for the wedding.

Jasper leaned back in his chair; his hands clasped in front of him. Fox picked up the cup then sipped. Sighed from the pleasure. He needed the drink. Felt a jolt of energy surge through him with the second sip. Realized he was tired. Last night had been long as well as exhausting. Fannie tossed and turned seeming unable to fall asleep. When she finally drifted off the sun was rising. Without waking her he rose, looked at her wishing the scenario for this morning was different. Ah, he had tonight as well as tomorrow to look forward to.

"Fannie is upstairs with her two sisters getting ready for the ceremony this afternoon as I'm certain you suspected. Maggie met me in the foyer after I returned from seeing the duke. She told me to tell you she isn't going to allow you to see Fannie until she walks down the aisle to become your wife. Bad luck and all, she told me. Under these circumstances, don't want to take any chances with lady luck. Two of the guards will accompany us to the church this afternoon. The other two will remain to guard the doors."

"No, we certainly don't need bad luck of any kind. Though I've never understood how seeing a bride before the ceremony can result in bad luck. Seems to me to be a bit of superstitious rubbish. However, I will hold to the wishes of your wife. Undoubtedly Fannie will be in agreement."

"Do you mean to risk superstitions?" Jasper let out a hoot of laughter. "Take a chance on seeing her just to prove the opposite?" One of his dark eyebrows arched upward. "Besides, think of that first sight of your bride when she steps into your view." That from Jasper a wry smile on his face as if he recalled that first sight of Maggie in her wedding finery.

"No, not going to take any chances. You're right. Besides, seems I might need to spend some time getting ready myself. Can't go to church dressed in my buckskins. While I've no reservations about this wedding. Wish we could have spent more time together. The six weeks between meeting her and now were wasted. This all happened too fast."

"Changing the subject, did you get passage on your ship for Nellie? Believe the girls are on tenterhooks with anticipation. At times Nellie even seems eager to put Glasgow along with Dillon Montrose behind her. At other moments the opposite. Nellie has come to realize she doesn't see a future for herself here," Jasper said as he sat forward, his forearms resting on the desk. "I hope so. We don't want to have these guards surrounding the house forever. Already had one neighbor stop by to ask me what was going on in our home. Don't need the added interest in the goings on around my townhouse."

"Nellie's passage has been booked as well as paid for. She has a nice cabin with a window that will look out over the ocean. Her room is two doors down from Fannie's and mine. She will be comfortable for the duration unless she gets seasick." Fox sat down in the chair in front of Jasper's desk. "I hope the guards plan to accompany us to the ship. Don't wish to have a confrontation between here and there."

"Thank, God," Jasper muttered relief written clearly on his face. "I know she is not liking the idea of leaving Scotland. It's the fear of the unknown that has her holding back. However, from what Mags has told me, Nellie is resigned to going on this new adventure. As I said, she doesn't wish to see Dillon again. Their friends are the same, so outings would be a problem if she remained in the city."

"If she gives Michigan a chance she will love the countryside. It is an opportunity for Nellie to begin over, to meet new people. There are a lot of reliable single men in the logging camp. They are rugged men but tamable." With that said, Fox gave a soft chuckle. He'd like to see his best friend Roric Haraldsson tamed by a lovely woman. Didn't think his taming would ever happen. Rory was an avowed bachelor. Nellie was a lovely innocent woman. Together the pair could set the forest a flame. Fox doubted if that would happen.

"I agree with your statement. Though this morning there were tears in her eyes while she spoke with her sisters. I don't like the sadness on a day that should be filled with happiness. Mags has had moisture in her eyes also. The sisters have been inseparable their entire lives. The separation will be difficult but they understand distance from Glasgow is necessary for her sisters. Don't like this a'tall. Hope she is happy going with you. Maybe she will find a new man to fall in love with. Understand she is also mourning the loss of Dillon. All this happening at once cannot be easy for Nellie."

"Yes, maybe she will find someone she can love where we are going. Heard her tell Fannie there was no one of interest here. Also heard she would never trust a man again. Never give her heart to someone who would shatter her love into thousands of tiny pieces." Fox hoped with all his heart she would find happiness with them. For now, he needed to concentrate on the wedding as well as keeping his wife safe. Fannie was, after all, his main concern. He wished for her happiness above everything.

"One finds love when least expecting it," Jasper said as he looked up to the second floor, a pensive expression on his face.

"You are thinking about how you met Maggie. Fannie has told me part of the story. Seems to have been an opportunity that was thrown in your lap."

"Yes, to both statements, the meeting was quite by accident. Fell in love with the precious woman the moment she buried her adorable little nose in my chest. She was hiding from Lord Abernathy. Decided I was the lesser of the two possible evils. Seems she traded her beautiful ballgown along with her matching slippers for rags." Jasper slapped him on the shoulder. "What do you think? Should we dress for your wedding? We've a half hour before it is time to leave for the church. Your buckskins won't do. No, they won't do a'tall. Not if you are hoping to impress the bride with impeccable wedding finery."

"Better. I brought my best clothing from Father's home. Beryl made a point of telling me she was far from pleased that we moved up the date. Jake was grinning from ear to ear, delighted with the new scenario. This wedding gives him everything he wished for. Hoped I would marry a girl from this city. So, I am." Fox never intended to wed a city girl. He also sent his gaze up to the second floor. Thinking of his soon to be wife. Fannie would need to do a lot of adjusting in her immediate future.

"You can dress in the room you shared with Fannie last night. She and her sisters are in Fannie's room until it is time to come down to catch the carriage to the church. When I'm ready, I'll tell the ladies. After that, I'll join you in our conveyance. Wish to make certain we are not far behind them.

Need to be able to keep another set of eyes on their transport. Two of our guards will be driving their vehicle. Our driver is also one of the duke's men hired for this one occasion. He will drive the wedding party minus the bride and groom back to this house."

The words gave Fox more reassurance. There was little chance of being waylaid on the way to the church. He grabbed the valise with his clothing for the wedding as well as the next day before heading to his room. His mind was on Fannie. Fox realized he was eager for the ceremony to be finished. Fox ached for the wedding night. He instructed the good reverend to make the ceremony short, the faster the better. Yes, Fox thought, the shorter the better. Only the necessary words would be said. A sinking feeling caused him to shudder. Some instinct, a premonition of sorts, warned him Anice would somehow put a damper on today. How, he didn't know? A shuddering breath of air slipped into his lungs.

During the wedding, Fox thought to say something as to why he wished to marry Fannie. Held words in his head he'd like to tell her. Needed to give her reasons other than the child she carried. Wished for her to understand this wasn't all about the baby. If he didn't wish for Fannie to become his wife, he would have figured out some other way. Decided against that course which would leave him far too vulnerable. Perhaps someday in their future he would speak the words to her.

Once they were on their way and had some level of privacy, he would explain to her about his mother including the fact Jake divorced her. His mother loved the land as much as she loved his father. The divorce slowly killed her. Jake wanted nothing to do with living in Michigan. His father needed the city. Despised the lumber business which was their way of life. Fox grew up with his mother after Jake returned to Scotland. Developed the same love of the land that his mother felt. They both held the forests, the lakes, the rolling hills in reverence. He would never survive if he lived somewhere else.

Ah, his mother mourned the loss of her husband the few years she lived after Jake returned to Scotland to pursue his livelihood. When she died, Fox felt certain her death was caused from a broken heart. She was never the same after her husband left. He wasn't going to allow anything to stand in the way of his marriage to Fannie. He intended to give her a life filled with happiness along with as many children as she wished. Fox prayed she would like to have more than the one she carried in her womb. He wished for heirs. Hoped to see little boys as well as girls growing up to love the land as much as he did.

He owned almost twenty-four thousand acres of timber. Had the foresight to replant the tracts of land they cut. Others in the business spurned him, telling him replanting was a waste of time when there were millions of acres of timber land in the United States. In order to harvest the timber, if he didn't replant, he would need to move. He didn't wish to leave his home. This land where he built his home was all he ever wanted if one included a family. If he didn't replant, there would come a time when he was left with nothing. Wished to leave a dynasty for his children. Bought land that had been overharvested, planted more trees. Understood years from now the timber would be money in hand.

Studying himself in the mirror, he adjusted his cravat, smoothed the front of his vest. Believed he looked the part of the groom. Even if he said so himself, he thought he cut a dashing figure. Fannie would be pleased. Ah, the wedding night was ahead of him. Her image along with her scent was strong in his head. The way she felt beneath his fingers was heaven sent. Tonight, this time when he came inside her, he wouldn't hurt her. That was one advantage to putting the bedding before the wedding. He didn't plan the events that way. Though he appreciated the fact.

Fox walked down the steps to the drawing room. Jasper beat him there. He was sipping a brandy. Handed him a snifter that was already filled.

"Just a bit of prewedding courage. Are you nervous?" Jasper asked before he drank. "I recall my wedding day. Was nervous as hell. Knew Anice would be at the ceremony along with the man pretending to be the father of the girls. Hell, I didn't know what would happen. Had the distinct feeling the ceremony wasn't going to proceed as planned. I underestimated the ensuing events. Learned a lesson about Anice MacRae. Never take anything for granted where the woman is concerned."

"I've heard part of the story. Anice won't be at Fannie's and my wedding, thank God. That is one event I don't need to worry about. The plans for this have all gone too fast for her to get wind of the occasion."

"Don't underestimate the woman as I did. Until the ceremony is finished, you cannot be positive she won't turn up unannounced. She could object to stall the ceremony. The woman has an uncanny way of discovering things about her daughters then turning up at the most inconvenient of times."

"You're right. If she hears about our little celebration afterward, I trust the guards will see to it she will not be allowed into this house. Don't wish Anice to be anywhere near Fannie. I will give them permission to use bodily force to keep her outside the door. She will not be able to interfere."

"The men will be given the order. I'm in agreement. We don't want the woman anywhere near her daughters," Jasper reassured. "By the way, I invited the Duck of Southcliff along with his wife to the celebration afterward. They agreed. Lacie has taken a particular interest in Mags along with her sisters. I hope my invitation is alright with you."

"I'm pleased you had the foresight to do so, thank you. My father along with Beryl will attend. Don't believe there is anyone else who will witness our marriage. Fannie has no friends. At least that is what she has told me. Any friends I would wish to invite are more than an ocean away from here. For Fannie's sake it would be nice if Tessa along with Jason were there." Fox couldn't imagine growing up with no friends. "Thought she would have met a few people during this last year. She and Nellie attended a lot of events."

"For the most part, Fannie followed her older sister. Nellie is the more vivacious of the girls. Many times, Fannie would have rather stayed at home and read one of those romantic novels she is fond of. The library is her favorite part of my home. Many nights she would curl up in her nightclothes then read for hours."

"I enjoy the quiet side to Fannie." She would not be quiet though when he made love to her this evening. Tonight, he meant to teach her more about lovemaking. She was an avid learner. Her raw passion was undeniable. This urgency he felt for her was irrefutable. The first night he was with her, she said only a handful of words. He'd asked for one of Hannah's girls who was not a chatterbox.

"Finish your brandy. I just heard the girl's babble as they filed out of the house. We need to be one step behind them far enough so you won't see your bride but close enough we can see the transport. Even now Lord

Abernathy or Anice might have men watching for anyone to leave. The women are an easy target."

The pair were in their vehicle. Jasper tapped on the roof to signal they were ready. Fox's gut tightened. Nerves, for the first time, appeared to sidetrack him. He brought a deep breath of air into his lungs. Jasper hooted, his laughter echoing in the cab. Fox reacted with a glower.

"See you're finally acting like a normal groom. Nerves talking to you, old man? Suppose it might have been a good idea to bring the bottle of brandy along with us. Could have eased your way a bit more."

"Nerves, yes, but no more brandy. Need a clear head right now. A brandy fog would not be good." Fox spread his arms across the seat before closing his eyes. Heard Jasper's soft chuckle then the rumble of the wheels on the road. He slowed his breathing, drinking in everything he'd learned about Fannie. Realized he was going to come to know a lot more about his delightful woman in the weeks to come. Ah, he could hardly wait until her belly rounded then the babe would kick. His imagination went into overdrive. Found he was looking forward to the next months of her pregnancy.

When the transport rolled to a stop, Fox jerked to attention. This was it. Almost the moment when he became a husband. He assumed the women would be in the church now waiting for them to do their duty.

"We will go in through the side door, by passing the entrance so there is no chance of seeing Fannie. Not going to take any chances," Fox told Jasper though he was certain he would realize the scenario.

"Yes, Mags said the girls would go to a special dressing room in the front where they will make sure Fannie is all put together in a fashion that will please you." The father of the groom opened the door. Jake waited for Fox to leave first. A huge smile reaching from one ear to the other was plastered on his face.

"'Bout time the two of you showed up. Just follow me. Beryl and I have been here for ten minutes. I'll show you where to go. Beryl is in the church sitting in the front row, fuming that she couldn't be in the wedding. She doesn't appreciate sitting alone. Since I won't be joining her until afterward, she is in a terror of a mood. I do enjoy taming her rages as well as her pouts."

After Fox jumped to the ground, his father swatted him on the back, hard enough to make him stagger. "You're an eager groom I see. No nerves? Ah, but I see that you are sweating. That's good. A man about to get married should have a bit of apprehension about the ensuing events."

Fox needed to ignore his father. His mind was on Fannie. Didn't care about much else except doing this before Anice heard the news. Decided to go to safe territory. "How's Beryl? Still acting as if she has a thorn stuck in her side? Wasn't pleased with the change of plans."

Jake chuckled seeming amused with his wife's snit. "Beryl will get over this diversion. Didn't I just say she was fuming. Well, no matter. You probably didn't hear me since I'm positive your mind is on other matters."

"I'll go in through the front door." Jasper said. "Talk to Maggie. She'll let us know when Fannie is ready. Should only be a few more minutes. I'll walk Fannie down the aisle right into your waiting arms. Never played the father of the bride before. Practice, I suppose. When Mag's and I have a darling girl, I will need to know what to do when the time comes."

Father and son walked to the side of the church then entered into a small room. The door Fox saw was the one leading to the nave. There would be few people in attendance. Most everyone was in the wedding party. Beryl would be there. Maggie would sit on the other side. In reality, she played the mother of the bride.

Fox laughed. He should have invited Hannah and Angus to attend. It was Hannah's inability to tell her right from her left that brought this wedding about. He should have thanked her. Angus would have served as another bodyguard. Even if Jason along with Tessa wouldn't be in attendance there would only be a handful of people. The two wouldn't be here, not unless Jasper wrote to his twin yesterday when all of this was decided.

After they were home in Michigan, Fox planned another celebration with all his friends coupled with the lumberjacks who worked for him in the lumber camp. His best friend, Rorik, was taking care of business in the hills where they were working. When the two of them returned, they could have a dance. Old Sam, his cook, would create a feast, slaughter a cow for the occasion. Everyone in the nearby village would be invited. Found he was looking forward to that celebration more than the one this evening.

Stunned when his father slapped him on the back again, he jerked back to the present. "Time to go, son. You've been in another world. Thinking about the wedding night?" Jake had the audacity to waggle his eyebrows at him. Did a father do that? Fox knew his best friends would jest with him. Do more than waggle eyebrows. His father?

"Yes, to both." The sound of the organ caught his attention. The music changed. Seemed the change was a signal.

The minister stood in front of them, holding a bible, smiling. "Your father is right. It's time to pay attention to what's going on around you. Fox, walk in behind me. Jake, behind your son. Once we're inside the church, Rosy will start the wedding march. Rest assured, this ceremony will be performed in record time. I made a point of outlining all the pertinent phrases. You will be wed in minutes flat."

His stomach flipped. When he held out his hand, it was shaking. He dosed himself with as much oxygen as he could. Heard his father's laughter behind him. "Step lively now, son. Got to be in the church before anything can happen."

Fox swallowed down the lump in his throat. He'd not thought he would feel this way, nervous. "Do you have the ring?"

"Of course, don't worry about anything. We've got this. I won't let you down."

They stood in the front of the church, looking down the aisle. His sweating hands were clasped behind his back. Now Fox discovered he held his breath. Beryl sat in the front row with a glower on her face. To his surprise, Jason along with Tessa sat on the other side of the row. Maggie walked down the aisle to the music then sat beside her sister. Four witnesses. Fox understood, Fannie would be pleased to see Tessa. None had dared to expect them to arrive in time for the hasty wedding ceremony.

Nellie, with a bouquet in her hands slow-walked to the front. Took a place opposite his father. Fannie escorted by Jasper would be the next to walk down the aisle. Again, he found he held his breath. Swallowed hard as the cadence of his heart jumped to the beat of the organ music. At a nod from the good reverend, the music changed again.

They appeared in the doorway, held motionless for a few seconds. Her smile was hesitant, shy. Damn, she was beautiful. Wheat-blond hair flowed free of constraints down her back. A small circlet of flowers adorned her hair. Maggie must have thought of the flowers. Fannie's bouquet was larger than Nellie's but fashioned from the same flowers. Seemed everyone had been busy this morning. He had a wedding gift for her, tucked into his valise back at the house. The wedding ring was in Jake's pocket along with all the aspirations for their future. He swept a huge gulp of air into his lungs.

The gown she wore, he was told by Jasper was the one Maggie wore to their wedding. Fox was not certain if the reality was good or bad. Even though it had been repaired, wearing the same gown Maggie had been shot in might not be wise. No, he wasn't about to think anything negative. The dress was beautiful. The sisters must have considered all the pros along with the cons of wearing the same wedding finery. Fannie deserved a real gown. They'd not had the time. Fannie told him she didn't mind.

When Fannie reached them with a hesitant smile on her sweet lips, she handed her bouquet to her sister then Fox accepted her hands into his. They were cold. He felt the fine trembling reach from Fannie into him. She was more nervous than he was. With a gentle squeeze then a smile, he gave reassurance. The next minutes passed. He knew nothing more. Fox heard the low rumble of the minister's voice. Was positive he responded at the right time. The 'I do's' were all said. He placed her wedding ring on her finger. They were announced as husband and wife.

"You may kiss the bride."

Those words were his prompt. Fox lifted her veil. Placed a gentle kiss on her mouth. Sensed her tongue sweep across her lips. Adored the slight contact between them. Swelled with his need for her. He savored the moment, letting his hand settle around her waist to bring them closer. His mind spun in a haze of pleasurable fantasies.

"I object! Stop this fiasco immediately! Stop it now!" The shrill voice coming from the inner door of the church jerked everyone's head in the direction of the strident noise. With her fists clenched, Anice stormed down the aisle to them. Her face was a mask of outrage. Reached out as if to wrench Fannie away from him. The woman's cheeks flamed red with fury.

Fox stepped in front of Fannie. "That's enough!" he roared, unwilling to allow this woman to harm his wife in any way.

Anice shook her fist at him. "My daughter doesn't have permission to marry. A child needs parental permission to participate in this sort of thing."

"Mother?" The whispered word from Fannie died in the ensuing turmoil. "I'm twenty-four years old. You have no right to object to anything I do. I'm no longer a child."

Fox stepped forward blocking the walkway. His feet braced apart, hands on his hips, he spoke. "There is nothing to object to, Anice. As Fannie just said, she is old enough to decide what she wants."

Jasper rose from his seat to refute Anice's claims. "Fox and Fannie are married. In this case, you are too late to object or stop anything. As you well know, I have guardianship of the girls. I approve of this marriage. There is nothing you can do even if I didn't have control of this situation. Fannie has reached her majority. She doesn't need or want your permission."

One of the guards stepped forward. Moving with practiced speed, he brought the newlyweds to the book where they needed to sign their names to make all that was vowed here official. The second guard placed his hand on Anice's elbow as he escorted her from the church. Fox assumed the man would make certain she was put in her coach then sent away.

Knew she would run to Lord Abernathy with the news of the marriage. Well, what did he expect from this day? Jasper told him to stay cautious. With a blink of an eye, the papers were signed. Fox heaved a huge sigh of relieved air. The marriage was legal in every way. Now, all they needed to accomplish was the consummation. He looked forward to that part of his duties. Ah, tonight would be filled with marital bliss.

They were ushered to their carriage. Fox helped Fannie inside. One guard drove. The other two accompanied the carriage that Nellie rode in. Now, Nellie was more at risk. Needed constant protection. Nellie was Lord Abernathy's last chance for one of Anice's daughters to become his playmate.

"Do you recall anything of the ceremony?" Fox asked smiling at her dazed look. Wasn't certain if it was Anice who caused her hazy appearance or the fact they were wed. "I don't. Seemed my mind wandered everywhere, mostly to you as well as all you were feeling. Wished I could be inside your head."

"No, not much. Seems the reverend didn't spend very many minutes on the ceremony. Was that your doing? For the entire time I worried about mother showing up uninvited. She has this way of sticking her nose into places where it doesn't belong. How did she know we were getting married today?"

Fox spread his arms wide, relaxed now that this part was finished. He wanted his wife sitting beside him. Needed her close. Wished for a few kisses before they reached their destination. Maybe a feel here or one there. "Don't believe Anice knew for certain. The minister told me a man talked to him yesterday after I left. At the time, we were still planning on a Saturday wedding. The good reverend told me he didn't say anything to the man. Didn't like the way he looked. Was positive he was up to no good."

The vehicle lurched as Fannie was moving to his side. She fell into him with an umph. Her hands were pressed against his chest. Her mouth so close to his, he saw the moisture on her lips. He tossed his head back laughing. "This is where I want you, sweet. Sit on my lap. Let's see if I can make you wet while we ride back to the Kenworthy townhouse. Wish to see to the flowing of your nectar. Let's have a bit of pre-consummation fun. What do you think? Would you like to see what we can achieve before we reach our destination? Once we get to our room tonight, you won't be able to wait."

"You know I would…but?"

"But what?" Fox found himself laughing inside. She was too passionate to protest. Fannie wanted this as much as he did. Perhaps more.

His hands embraced her waist. Held still for a few seconds until he decided he wished to explore the curve of her hip. Fannie turned to look at him, her breasts brushing across his chest. A slight tilt to her head, she asked, "You're going to do this in the…here? I don't think…"

Not needing conversation when he could show her, his mouth captured hers with a fierce yet gentle caress while his hand traveled along her leg, reaching all the way to her tiny ankle. "I love the way you feel, so soft. Want to see if you're as aroused as I am. Learn if you are damp for the wanting."

~ * ~

"I must be…" Fannie decided to let him have his way in the carriage, having thought of little else since last night when their loving was aborted by the intruder. She made it easy for him, her legs moving apart as his fingers traveled along the inside of her thigh. A shudder of pleasure ripped through her with the contact. His roaming hands passed by her knee. Found bare skin. Traveled higher. Met no resistance.

"You're wicked," he hooted with laughter when he discovered she wore nothing beneath her wedding gown. "What made you think of this? All night long I will know what you are not wearing." He brought her hand to feel him. Placed her palm on top of his sex. "This is me, swelled with an urgent need for you, growing harder with each second. I have been in this state since I saw you walking down the aisle to me, sinful promises in your eyes."

"I…" she pushed a slight distance from him. Tried to gift him with a siren's smile. Didn't know if she succeeded. Did appreciate the male groan she heard. "Maggie told me about Tessa's wedding celebration. She told me Tessa didn't wear undergarments and neither did she. Said that doing so would be a nice touch to the evening for you. Supposed you would appreciate the gesture. Do you?" Fannie watched his brows crease together. Saw the line of intense concentration. Felt a moment's set back then a *wee* bit sick to her stomach. "You don't like this? I'm sorry. I'm too forward. My mother would call me a brazen hussy." Fannie tried to wriggle off his thighs. At her waist, his hands tightened, holding her still. Her voice wobbled with insecurity. She'd argued against doing this. Maggie persisted.

"That's not the emotions I'm feeling. Your mother knows nothing about you. You would never be able to guess why my brows drew together. So, I will tell you. First, I'm shocked. Never expected my Fannie to be so bold and audacious. Second, I'm so pleased I am having trouble sucking air into my lungs or thinking for that matter. Third, I've swelled so much I ache at the thought of what isn't beneath your beautiful wedding gown then how I would feel deep inside your heat. I'm bound to be in this state of arousal for the entire night, knowing how easy it will be to touch you where you are wet with your need for my most randy male parts."

He leaned back then closed his eyes. "You will need to give your poor husband a moment to acclimate. I'm too stunned to say anything more. Indeed, I'm surprised I got those words delivered." His hand traveled along the ladder of her ribs. The other continued his sweet assault upon her in even more dark sensitive places.

"What are those words supposed to mean? I'm not certain of anything you've said just now. Do you like what I've done? If the answer is no, as soon as we are at the house, I will put on my pantalettes." Fannie felt as if she should apologize. Didn't wish to say she was sorry. "Well? Are you pleased or not? Do you want me to put underwear on before we celebrate?" So forlorn, she looked away from his simmering brown eyes. "I'm feeling uncomfortable. Maybe we should speak about something else."

"Like what?"

"Mother?"

"No…we will continue to consider the culmination of this newfound knowledge I have about what you are not wearing. This is something I would wish to ponder for a bit longer. No, I wish to explore beneath your gown." His fingers caressed the top of her thigh. After that he spread his hand on her belly. Allowed his explorations to turn south. He cupped her mound. One bold finger slipped between her legs. Touched the most sensitive part of her. Found the small pearl of her pleasure.

"Oh… You should forget. I…?" Fannie felt the slow rise of desire as heat pulsed with quicksilver speed. Oh, my, even her ears were hot. His mouth crashed down on hers as his fingers worked their mercuric magic in the softest part of her. His tongue parroted the movement of his two fingers as he thrust inside her. Penetrate then retreat. He continued the play. Heat spiraled within. In a few seconds she thought she would splinter into oblivion. She recalled how it felt to reach for the sun then discover mercuric pleasure so hot the sensation scalded her.

He stopped the kiss to her little mewl of displeasure. She opened eyes that had been closed. His fingers were still deep inside her, moving. She knew his sex would fill her more. This was what she wanted. Needed in the deepest, darkest part of her.

"No, don't wish to ever forget this moment. Would like to think you will continue this habit for at least the next five years, maybe longer. If so, I would be able to give you pleasure with much more ease. I could have you sitting on my lap while you straddle me or on my desk with your long white legs wrapped around my flanks. All this without having to disrobe you.

Could take you from behind while you were cooking dinner or doing the dishes. This has more possibilities to ascertain. Being newlyweds, we can do whatever it is we wish to do. I for one, want to know there isn't anything beneath your dresses all the time."

"Uh, I don't know how to cook."

"Doesn't matter. I'll teach you everything you need to learn."

"I couldn't do that. A year of going without underwear? What would people think? She wished to make a good impression at her new home. "It's…it's decadent," she finished. Oh…he found more dark sensitive places, intimate secrets. She arched, her breasts pushing against his chest.

As if nothing was happening to her beneath the wedding gown, he tapped her on the nose. "Of course you could. No one with the exception of me would know what you weren't wearing. They better not." He kissed her again. Opened her mouth with the swift movement of his tongue. Pushed his inside to dance with hers. At the contact, she lost conscious thought. She was in a different world, melting. One she didn't understand.

"No…" Fox withdrew from her, his fingers, his tongue. He pushed her skirt back to her ankles.

"Sorry, sweet, we have arrived. You need a few seconds to comport yourself. I will wait." He smoothed her hair, ran the length between his fingers. "I intend to keep you in such an aroused state that when the time comes to go to our lodgings, you will splinter into millions of pleasurable shards on the way. I regret that didn't happen this last time. There wasn't enough time to gift you with all the ecstasy I intend for you. This ride was too short."

"You stopped…that's why." Fannie was so frustrated with need, she wanted to weep. Wished she could do the same to him. "I want to touch you," she whispered to Fox, hoping he would grow hot from the words. "Touch your lips. They are beautiful. Maybe not as lovely as your belly. I recall your stomach. It is beautiful. Hard. All of you is hard."

Fox groaned low in the back of his throat. To make a point, sent his fingers in then out, faster until she panted, her head tossed back. "You do not play fair," he growled. "I want to suck on your breasts."

"And you do?" She liked the way his voice turned husky. Fannie was positive the sound meant something. Thought the rasp might mean he wanted her as much as she did him. "You never play fair."

"Always play fair. Now," he looked her over, "are you ready to make an entrance? Your hair is almost in place. The little ring of flowers is a bit lopsided. Maybe we should remove the circlet otherwise all will believe we were dallying on the way here."

Her mouth fell open, surprised. She touched the top of her head. Removed the pins along with the flowers. Set the little circlet of blue and white flowers on top of Fox's head. Smiled. "This looks lovely here atop your head. I should pin this little bouquet so it won't fall off. Do you think this will begin a new fashion trend?" Unable to help herself, she giggled. "Did I ever tell you that you please me. You are handsome as sin. I do love the way the hair on your chest crinkles around my fingers."

He sucked air. His stomach tightened. Grimaced at the words she uttered as if he was a drowning man. "No, not before this moment." Fox removed the flowers. Looked at her with a pensive expression on his indomitable face.

Her mind dashed through a million secret scenarios. Some she would never venture to tell this man of hers. "Fox, I dare you to wear them into the house." Placing a finger to her lips, thinking, "You must wear it through dinner to win the challenge." She watched the changing expression on his face. "I mean what I say. Can you do something so outrageous? I would like to see the side of you telling everyone you don't give a fig for what they think."

"I am a gambling man. Have rarely refused to accept a dare. This one is nothing I can't handle. Pin the circlet on my head. I will put on a brave face when we go inside. Perhaps pretend that I don't know what everyone is sniggering about behind my back." He set his hand on her breast, leisurely rubbing his palm across the nipple, raising the tip to a hard bud that was clear and pressing against her gown. This was her turn to suck air. Fannie understood somehow, he would return the embarrassment ten-fold.

"Perhaps you shouldn't…" her voice faded when he bit her nipple, wetting the fabric around the tip. She arched into him, her hands on his shoulders. He did the same to the other one. "We can't…"

"Are you afraid of retaliation. No? Let me see. What will the winner of this dare receive?"

"I didn't think of anything like that, Fox. What is there to win or lose?"

"Seems I should think about the prize. You, my sweet, are the ultimate prize. Nevertheless, win or lose, you are mine at the end of the night."

Fannie reached up to undo the pins. Fox stopped her. "We will both think on the prize." He snapped his fingers. "I know! If I win tonight, I will undress you, touch you as I like. Where I like. How I like. If you win, you will undress me with the same caveats. What do you say? The prize will be a fitting beginning to our wedding night."

She nodded. "I suppose so…" Fannie did wish for him to touch her, to undress her. Perhaps she should hope he would win. Believed if he wished it hard enough, he would keep the circlet of flowers on his head for as long as necessary. The outcome was up to him. She would have nothing to do with the ending.

"Good, then the prize is decided upon. Now, since our transport has come to a rumbling halt, we should vacate the vehicle. You appear put back together. You will do."

As she walked into the foyer of the Kenworthy townhouse, Fannie felt both dazed as well as content. Fox treated her with a special kind of ease. His actions during the ride from the church aroused her to a point where she wanted to grab his hand then run upstairs to his room, tossing clothing aside as she raced.

From the precious night in the brothel, Fannie recalled some of the pleasure along with the pain that first time he came inside her. She knew tonight there would be no pain just pleasure. Last night he almost brought her to that place she remembered where the sun met the stars. At the time she didn't feel the earth beneath her feet.

"Welcome," Keir met them in the hallway, stared at Fox with a befuddled grin on his aging features. "You are looking flushed just like a new bride should look," the butler told her. "And you, Fox…the wreathe is becoming. Would look better on the bride if you don't mind my saying so."

Fox barked a short laugh. "What would a confirmed bachelor know about the way a new bride should look? As to the flowers on my head. I'm collecting on a dare. Do say, I will win the ultimate prize."

"Well, Sir," With his hands behind his back, he had a smug expression on his crinkled face, rocking on his heels. "Nothing, except I did see Tessa after she was married to Jason. Saw her sister that same night," he paused, "…and…yes, there is Lady Maggie, she always has that flushed look on her face after they've returned in one of the Lord's carriages. Don't know what it is about those rides. They do bring color to a lady's cheeks."

Fannie flushed to the roots of her hair. She was mortified he would understand what they'd been doing. "Oh," Fannie said as she followed Keir into the drawing room.

Keir gestured to the sideboard. "We've pre-dinner drinks including a few bottles of France's finest champagne. I assume the others will be here shortly. Would you like me to assist in pouring?"

"I'll take care of it," Fox said, stepping forward. He grinned at her, his smile stretching to his eyes. "Believe you will be fun a wee bit tipsy. Should be different than drugged on laudanum laced with brandy." He handed her a glass of celebratory champagne.

"I didn't think Keir would say a word about your charming adornment. He surprised me. The man is always so stoic. Don't think I've ever seen him blink." She giggled, thinking she was already a bit high in the sky.

"No, even if he hadn't mentioned the flowers, I would never have forgotten the circlet was there except for the pins digging into my scalp. If I can't keep this thing on my head until after dinner, it will be because of the pain not the embarrassment. How do you stand these things?"

First Fannie sipped, bubbles hitting her nose then she giggled. "I guess we don't notice the pain. Goes with the territory. We believe men like to see women wearing these adornments." She lifted her shoulders as if questioning. "Do they? Men? You do look quite adorable. So much so, I would love to kiss you."

"Kiss me anytime you feel the urge. Can't speak for anyone except myself. The flowers looked beautiful with you wearing them. I would never wish this pain on you. You're beautiful without embellishments. I like you best wearing nothing at all."

Again, Fannie felt the fast rise of color to her cheeks. "Thank you, but you aren't obligated to compliment me. The rest of what you said…well…" She wanted to give back "I do enjoy you best when you are wearing nothing."

A bit of champagne sputtered from his mouth at her bold words. There was even a light rise of color to his cheeks. He shook his head then said as if nothing affected him, "I know. You are beautiful inside as well as out, just as your sisters are. Come, sip your champagne while I think about your feminine endowments that are naked beneath your wedding gown."

She sucked champagne into her mouth, coughed when the liquid wasn't obeying. Bubbles slipped into her nose. After she stopped wheezing, "You are doing that on purpose."

"Never."

Again, the champagne sliding down her throat tumbled in the wrong direction. Fannie sputtered, tiny droplets flying from her mouth. With her fingertips, she wiped at her gown.

Fox took the opportunity to grab one of the nearby napkins then seemed to change his mind. He set her glass on a nearby table. Pulled her into his arms to sip the drops from her chin then a few that landed at the tops of her breasts. In his arms she shuddered at the brazen contact. Her body flamed to life. Behind her, someone cleared his throat. Fannie pushed on Fox. He didn't budge.

"Dear boy, can't you wait until you are alone with your new bride?" Jake stepped into the room, Beryl on his arm.

"That's quite inappropriate," Beryl sniffed her nose in the air, a foul look on her face. "Can't you wait for the end of the festivities?" Beryl parroted Jakes voice. "Those flowers look ridiculous on your head."

Fox smiled then patted the circlet. "A dare. I'm planning on winning the prize."

"Not inappropriate for newlyweds, m'dear. Do you remember our celebrations after the wedding? I did more than a few kisses above your lush breasts," Jake reminded her with a pointed look that brought a blush to Beryl's cheeks. "Almost unveiled you, I was so besotted with your charms. As to your headdress, son, it suits you."

Beryl shot Jake a quelling glance. "Yes, I was mortified to the tips of my toes. You took horrible advantage of me. In a secluded corner, you did more than sip champagne." She nodded her head toward the balcony.

"You loved every minute. Champagne?" Jake queried. "Maybe I can get you a bit tipsy then we can relive the moment."

"Yes, after seeing that unseemly show of affection I will need an entire bottle," Beryl retorted as she accepted a brimming glass. "We are not going to relive any moments. Get that out of your head this instant." Her actions seemed to contradict her words.

Jake reached out to touch her cheek with the back of his hand. "We will see, my dear. We will see."

"Tessa! You managed to get here on time." Fannie rushed forward to meet her sister with a huge hug. "I was so thrilled to see you in the church. How?"

"Yes. We did." She hugged her sister back. Air kissed. "I convinced Jason I would forever be angry with him if I had to miss your wedding. Since he didn't appreciate the sound of my threat, he got me here on time. You were beautiful walking down the aisle."

Jason stepped up beside his wife, wrapping an arm around her. He brought her close. Turning to Fox, "Congratulations are in order. Hear the three of you will set your course to New York in a few days. Would love some adventure of my own. I've promised Tessa we'll come see the two of you in a year. Not going to comment on the flowers. Heard there was a dare in there somewhere. You are a brave man, Fox."

"As you know, I'm eager to return. Been gone from the lumber camp for more than six months. Not worried about the operations. Have a good man in charge. In fact, we use the same crew to work his land along with mine. Still, I long to be home. Need to smell the crisp mountain air."

The rest of the wedding party arrived, bodyguards following behind. The next set of four were on duty now. All was in order. There was no way Anice could crash this private party.

Keir appeared in the room. "Dinner is ready to be served."

In the dining room, the first course was served. Fannie found she was too nervous to eat much. She drank all the wine Fox poured into her glass. She wished for the evening celebration to end. Needed to be alone with her husband. She closed her eyes to lean against his arm. Fox seduced, his hand splaying on her mound, his fingers exploring intimate territory. He kept her aroused, wet as well as ready for anything he might decide.

"Don't want any more wine. Do you want me to be sick?" Two fingers were sliding into her as she parted her legs for him.

Fox set a finger beneath her chin, lifted. Kissed her lips to conceal the sweet moan of pleasure. Swept his tongue along the bottom then pushed inside. He pulled back to look into her eyes. "No, you're right. We should wait until later. Don't want you to fall asleep before we can consummate this day."

Later they retired to the third floor for dancing, along with the cutting of the cake. The sisters were chatting, laughing as well as reminiscing about the past. They'd spent so much time together they were everything to each other. Fox left her with her sisters. Last she saw him, he was speaking with the twins. Thought they might be planning the visit the summer after this one.

"Are you afraid of traveling to this Michigan place?" Tessa asked. "I had to find a map in Jason's library to see where the two of you would be going. Had no idea where this territory was. Do you know if it's safe?"

"Yes and no," Fannie said, as she looked at Nellie who said little during the evening. "I'm eager to find out what my new home will be like. Fox has told me a million stories about the land. He has described the huge lake on his property. Vows he will teach me how to swim as well as ride a horse. I'd like to learn both. As things stand, I'm useless. Can't even cook. Good thing he has one, a cook. His name is Sam. Sometimes he calls him Ol' Sam."

"Jason is teaching me as Jasper is teaching Maggie about all kinds of things," Tessa said. "Mother neglected much of our education."

"Who will teach me?" Nellie asked, sounding more forlorn than ever. "I'd like to learn too. Though I don't want a man in my life. Men cannot be trusted. They tend to be horrible creatures who want only one thing from a woman." Her voice of discontent held a wealth of unconcealed venom.

Fannie didn't know what to say at that blanket statement about men. The words were so unlike her sister. Nellie was still suffering. It had only been twenty-four hours since Dillon delivered the devastating news that he would never marry her. "Perhaps you will find someone to trust. Maybe men are different in Michigan."

"Don't think so. Not going to give out my heart on a silver platter to have it ripped to shreds as I did with Dillon. I've learned my lesson. Don't wish to be hurt again."

"You can't give up on love," Maggie said. "I'm certain there is someone for you out there."

"In Michigan?" Nellie asked with a snort as if no one lived there.

"Fox told me there are more men than women where he lives," Fannie hoped to reassure. Saw by the frown lines marring Nellie's delicate features, she wasn't helping.

The sisters chatted for several more minutes, continuing to reminisce then adding comments about the future. Fannie was ready to dance then cut the cake. She wanted to be alone with Fox. Their first dance would be soon. She'd never danced with Fox. Never swayed in his arms to music. He'd never held her close while music played. Tonight, would be the first of many new experiences.

"I'm going to find Fox. We have a few days to talk before we're on board the ship. I'll be over first thing in the morning," Fannie said. "We will continue this conversation or anything else you might wish to talk about."

Maggie's laughter echoed in the room. A few sets of eyes turned in their direction. "I doubt if Fox will let you out of the marriage bed first thing tomorrow morning or any of the other mornings before the two of you sail to parts unknown. At least they are unknown to us. A new groom likes to learn as much as possible about his wife."

Tilting her head a little sideways she frowned. Fannie questioned. "Whyever not? Learn more about me? In bed?"

"Because he will wish to keep you in his big bed for as long as possible. Men like to play in the morning when sunlight is streaming through the windows. When they can see what is theirs. That's why. Men wish for sons. Staying in bed is one way to achieve that wish," Tessa gave her input with an impish smile on her lips. "I do enjoy the mornings with Jason. Without giving anything away, believe you might appreciate them too."

Inadvertently, Fannie's hand settled on her stomach. Fox didn't have to keep her in bed to impregnate her. With only one try, he'd done the job. She wanted to ignore all the innuendos. "I'm going to find Fox. Dance, then cut the cake, he said we needed to leave early."

Fannie wandered around the outside of the ballroom. Stood on her tiptoes to look over the heads of the taller people, hoping to find him. She heard voices on the balcony overlooking the Kenworthy garden. When she stepped outside, lanterns left a warm glow across the scene. A couple were embracing. The woman with her arms wrapped around the man was pulling him close. They were kissing. She started to turn away, deciding to give these two lovers the privacy they deserved.

"Beryl. Not now…" The woman stumbled backward. Caught herself then stiffened. She grabbed onto the man's arms. Pushed her chest against him. Ran her hand down his body to stop at his sex. The man grabbed her wrist. Brought her fingers to his chest. Said something close to her mouth.

"Fox?" Fannie knew she whispered his name. Thought she recognized his voice. Knew she had to be wrong. Was watching the two lovers in a horrified trance. Needed to run from the home, from Fox. Didn't want to be anywhere near him. Needed to breathe. Couldn't catch air. The man she married didn't want her. He wanted the woman his father stole from him. A woman he couldn't have. Her hand to her mouth, she turned to race away. Needed time to herself before she spoke to him. Understood they would have to talk sometime. She was having his baby.

"Fannie?"

Her husband didn't want her. He married her because he had to. Because of the baby. Overwhelmed by what she witnessed, Fannie didn't run. Instead, she walked with slow measured steps unwilling to garner everyone's attention. Needed to pretend she wasn't mortified to the tips of her toes. Didn't want anyone to stop or question her. When she passed by a guest, she nodded and smiled as if nothing was wrong, even while her heart was breaking.

Hoping she left the horrible scene unnoticed, Fannie slipped out the door. She picked up her skirts then raced down the steps to the first floor. Breathing hard, she paused for a moment, frantic to find a way to escape this debilitating humiliation at her wedding reception no less. Stopping at the back door, she counted to ten. Brought in several long deep breaths of air while she tried to decide what to do. The house was guarded well. She had nothing to worry about if she left. There would be someone there to protect her.

I shouldn't leave the house.

More than anything she needed to be alone. Couldn't face her sisters or Fox. Wouldn't know what to say. She was married to a man who didn't want her. Wanted a different woman. She was going to have his child. No one would believe they didn't consummate the marriage. She could pray he would divorce her.

Her head held high, Fannie walked past the first guard who stood outside the back door. She tried to pretend there was nothing unusual about her actions.

"Miss?" the guard questioned, his voice urgent as well as wary. "You shouldn't be leaving the house. It's dangerous out there. I can't leave my post. You must wait here until I can call for another guard to escort you. It's not safe outside tonight, not for you or your sister. Your enemy might not realize you are now a married woman."

She tried to shoot him a bright smile. One that would tell this man he needn't worry. "It's alright. There is another one of you out there. Right? He is walking the perimeter. There can't possibly be anyone out here to harm me. No one would dare. Not even my mother." Fannie kept walking, hoping the guard would believe her. The need to be alone so she could cry was growing faster with each step.

"You should wait, Mrs. Taggert. Someone will be here before you can blink."

Ignoring the man, Fannie continued to walk, realizing this guard would never lay a hand on her. There wasn't anything he could do if she didn't obey his commands. She strode down the path, making her way from the house, from Fox. She didn't think he would follow her. He was with Beryl, kissing her. Oh, God… Just like her sister, Nellie, she'd been such a fool in regard to Fox. Men were faithless creatures. They were horrible people.

A loud sharp whistle sent a shiver of fear inside. She stiffened. Her startled response left her quivering. A man emerged, walking down the lighted path leading to the gazebo. That was where she wished to seek solace. He was a big man, tall, broad shoulders. She saw he carried a gun. A shiver of fear swept through her. The dangers of the evening becoming more real.

"What is it?" He called out to the guard at the back door.

"This little lady won't heed my commands. I can't follow her. Must remain at my post. You will need to stay by her side. Go wherever she goes. Don't let her out of your sight. Make certain she doesn't get into trouble."

"Yes, sir."

He didn't say another word. For a few tense seconds they stared at each other. They stood face to face. He wasn't going to move. She lifted her shoulders to show her indifference then walked around him. Started down the rock lined path, trying to remove the sight of her husband kissing Beryl from her head. Why? She thought he was happy with her. Knew he wanted her in his bed. Yet…Fox couldn't wait to kiss Beryl. Fannie heard the guard's footsteps behind her. Seemed he meant to keep his distance. Thank God, he was giving her space.

Tears slid down her cheeks as she thought of all she gained then lost. For a few hours she believed the two of them might be able to build a life together. Still, she had no choice but to follow Fox wherever he went. They were going to another country. There would be no one except Nellie to call friend. She would have nothing. There was no hope of love. With the backs of her hands, she pushed the tears aside. Walked past the cascading waterfall she always adored, past the roses she loved to smell. Walked until she stood inside the gazebo. Found a pillow to hold to her breasts.

Fannie heard shouts from the main house. Another sharp whistle told her the guard at the back door was summoning someone else. Sitting down she pulled the pillow closer, tighter, she tried not to wallow in self-pity. Couldn't help herself. This was all too much for her to take in. Closing her eyes wouldn't help ease the pain.

A few minutes ago, she'd been over-the-top happy about her new life along with her new husband. How was she going to deal with this new situation? Beryl wouldn't be with them where they were going. There would be no competition for his love.

I saw my husband kissing his father's wife.

I don't understand. Believed he wanted me. Supposed he was pleased I was his wife. I was so wrong. He still wants the woman he fell in love with before he met me…in a brothel.

A noise from the side of the gazebo startled her. Fannie looked into eyes she dreaded to ever see again. Recalled the night when he tried to get her to go with him. Halsey stood in the shadows, a devil's grin on his face.

She felt certain Anice must be close by, Lord Abernathy as well. Halsey had other men working for him. Where were they?

What have I done? I might not be pleased with Fox. Nonetheless, he is a far sight better than Nelson Abernathy or my mother's retainer, Halsey. Don't want Abernathy to touch me the way Fox does. I would fight. The man would rape me. Fannie shuddered at the thought of anyone else touching her, forcing her to his whim.

"Miss...can't leave you alone. Sorry. Must guard you." Having sensed the noise, the guard looked to the shadows. Saw the man pull out a gun.

"No!"

The moment was over before she could blink. Halsey was on the ground, bleeding, holding his arm, rolling. Moaning in pain like a baby who didn't get what he wanted, pretty boy's knees were brought to his chest. Her guard stood in front of her, his gun now pointed into the shadows.

"Best you come out here where I can see you or run for your life in the other direction. You won't get your hands on this lovely lady. Not on my watch." The words he spoke were calm as if he'd said as well as done the same upon numerous occasions.

"What the hell are you doing?" Fox stood in front of her, lifting her off the sofa in the gazebo. He shook her until she thought her teeth would rattle out of her head. "You could have been kidnapped. Why? There is no reason for this stupidity. What the hell is going on?"

Fannie didn't know when or where he'd come from. He was there as if a few minutes ago he hadn't been kissing his stepmother. She looked to the guard who didn't appear to be going anywhere, then to Fox. His eyes were wild, glimmering with the light from the lanterns. He was angry. Well, she was angry as well as hurt. She understood why Nellie didn't trust men.

He shook her again so hard her teeth rattled. He set her down but kept his hands on her shoulders. "What is wrong with you? If not for the guard, that man could have taken you. I wasn't here in time to stop your kidnapping. God knows I followed as soon as I realized you were about to do something foolish."

"You were kissing Beryl. Saw her hand on...where it should not have been." That was all she could say. Didn't wish to tell him anything else. The sight was stuck in her mind. Frozen in time. She wanted to slap him. Fannie did nothing except look at him, her eyes crammed with pain along with the humiliation she felt. Moisture filled them.

"She kissed me!"

Fox let her go. She sank down on the couch behind her. "What's the difference? You were both kissing." Fannie didn't understand what happened then or what he was trying to tell her now.

The duke was there, striding to them, "Abernathy has Nellie. Get Fannie inside the house. Now! Don't leave her alone. Tie her down if you have to. Seumas is going after the carriage. They won't get away."

Holding out his hand, Fox waited for her to take it. "There is a hell of a lot of difference. We can talk semantics when you are safe inside. Thank God for the guards. The two of you are impulsive as wells as reckless. Nellie followed you outside because she saw you leave. I saw you leave also. Took me too long to pry Beryl loose to stop you before you created this disaster. Once that woman sets her claws into a man, he doesn't stand a chance."

~ * ~

"We've got her. We've got one of them. The one who isn't married," Nelson said with relish coating his voice. In his mind he could taste Nellie, savor her feminine endowments. He licked his lips. Thoughts of the big bed that would be hers for as long as he wished rushed to his head. The ways he could use the chains to subdue to tame.

He stroked Nellie's cheek where he hit her. Knocked her unconscious so she wouldn't fight. He didn't mind a good fight when he had the time to conquer a female the way he liked. She would wake up naked in the third story bedroom chained to the bed, spread wide open to him. All of her feminine beauty for his eyes only. He was pleased for the first time in what seemed like years. Anice would also relish the chance to watch their sexual play. The viewing room was ready for her use. In anticipation the place was decked out with food and wine.

"One daughter will have to be enough for tonight unless Halsey was able to nab Fannie. My girls aren't stupid but they are impulsive. Don't often think of all the consequences before they act. Someone will follow us. Do you think you can elude the would-be rescuers?"

Nelson chortled, thinking about the diversions he set up in case he was lucky enough to capture either or both of the women. There were several places along the way where he would be able to out distance the pursuers. It would take years for anyone to find this new home of his. By then the Kenworthy's would have given up ever getting Nellie back. By then she might be in Halsey's possession.

"I've planned for everything. In fact, the first distraction is coming up in a couple of blocks. Hang on." The carriage swerved around a corner. Nellie fell to the side banging against Nelson. "She's out cold. We'll be there in about twenty minutes. Perhaps I will begin her unveiling. Would like to see what I've purchased."

Anice looked out the window. "I see what is happening. A large wagon filled to the brim with what appears to be garbage is blocking the road. Nice. It will take whoever is following us too many minutes to get around the wagon. Our pursuers will lose us."

They turned again, then another time. "Believe we've lost the men who are following. Though, while there is still the chance of these agents overtaking us, we will need to use a different transport. Something they won't be looking for."

The vehicle stopped. "Quickly now, no time to dawdle." Nelson carried Nellie in his arms to the waiting hack. It was small but would suit his purpose. The man driving waited until all three were in the back. Nellie remained within his arms, her head lolling to the side.

When she moaned, he laughed. Pleased with the soft sound of pain. Her jaw would hurt for a few days. Nellie might wake with an aching head. That would be the least of her worries. He sat back, thinking of the evening to come. The delights he would share with the little lady. Realized he didn't wish to take her right away. He would have more fun if he waited, if he left her wondering what he was going to do. Playing with her, toying with her fears would delight him. He would taste her then show her off. No one would discover his little hideaway.

Nellie was beautiful and she was his…all his. With a gentle touch, he brushed hair from her face. Ran his knuckles along the long, white column of her neck. She was pale. He wanted to look into her eyes. Wished he could undress her here. Didn't wish to share the private moment with the mother sitting across from him.

Much to his great relief, no one dogged his hack. His distractions seemed to have worked. No one would discover the home in the country. He also planned the purchase well. The name on the title was not his. Was fictitious. The Duke of Southcliff could sleuth all he wished. He would never discover this home. Let alone rescue Nellie MacRae from his ownership. She was his. A delight he'd been waiting for. Patience paid off.

He cupped her breast with his hand. The globe was large, rounded just as he liked his women. Nelson kissed her. Bit her lip. Not hard enough to draw blood but if Nellie had been awake, she would have cried out with the pain. He knew he would have to teach her if she disobeyed there would be discomfort. Sometimes more than others. Would depend on the level of her disobedience.

What was it about the MacRae ladies that interested him so much? Even the sight of the mother aroused him. She was more than willing to allow him what he wanted. Anice even had a few ideas of her own when it came to sexual dalliances.

Flicking open the first few buttons of Nellie's gown gave him better access to her female charms. He pushed open the fabric then undid the laces of her chemise and corset. Bit her nipple. Even in her unconscious state she cried out. Whimpered with the suffering he caused. He was pleased.

Anice laughed at the sound of the agony. Nelson covered her. He could hold out until he had her in her new accommodations. There would be so much more fun waiting for him in the privacy of the bedchamber. He wanted privacy for this first encounter though he didn't care if Anice was in the room with the peep hole. He didn't want her present in the main room.

The driver brought the transport to the back of the house. Nelson hefted Nellie over his shoulder, Anice following behind them. He climbed the three flights to the third floor. This was Nellie's new home. His grin broadened.

Without him saying anything, Anice walked into the viewing room. Nelson had his servant leave her a bottle of wine along with different types of food. He wanted Anice pleased with the service. He might take her after he had Nellie. There was a bed in the viewing room that would accommodate them if he wished. If he waited for Nellie to wake then to wonder when he would come to her, he would have more than enough time for a fast frenzied round with the mother.

Slowly, so as to memorize Nellie, he began to undress her. Starting with her shoes along with her stockings he relieved her of the clothing, stroking the unveiled flesh. She was beginning to wake. Her small, tempting body moved restlessly. She whimpered with each touch. He needed to hurry. No longer had the time to do this with the leisurely thoroughness he wished for. Needed to prolong the moments to his satisfaction. Once she was bound, he could relish her with slow, intimate precision. If he wished, he could caress with tenderness. Fondle the most sensitive parts of her. Nelson knew she would taste sweet. He wished to savor all of her. If she rejected him in any way, there were punishments he had in mind.

As he planned, by the time she was naked, her eyes were beginning to blink. She moaned then closed her eyes as if she didn't like what she was seeing. "Little princess, you will discover how wonderful sex can be with me. I am your new owner. You, my sex slave."

First, he bound her ankles to the sides of the bed then stretched her arms over her head. He sat beside her, stroking her breasts then her belly. He would wait until she was fully cognizant to fondle her more private places. Wished to see the expression on her lovely face when she realized what happened to her when he stroked her feminine endowments. He walked around the edge of the bed, memorizing her. Lit another sconce. Enjoyed the play of the light across her slender, white form.

While she was waking, he poured himself a glass of wine. Drank long and deep of the red Bordeaux. Nelson stood at the end of the bed savoring the view which he appreciated more than he was willing to admit. Realized the moment Nellie understood what was happening to her. Her eyes were wide with both defiance as well as terror. To no avail, she tugged on her bindings. The two reactions pleased him to no end. He wished he could burrow into her head to better understand her thoughts. Burrowing between her parted thighs would be more fun.

"See you are awake, my sweet. I'm enthused you are with me tonight and tomorrow night as well as many more nights to come. You will enjoy your new position in my household. You, my dear, are the main attraction."

Nellie didn't say a word. Nelson saw the wheels spinning in her head. Understood what she was thinking. "The chains will not come off until I've tamed you to my desires, until there is no more fight in you. There is no escaping me. No savior to come to your rescue this time. You are mine to do with as I please, Nellie. Mine until I no longer wish to have you. That won't be for a very long time. You are lovely. Don't know if I'm going to taste your sweet, feminine charms tonight or wait until the morning sun peeks its head out from the craigs. We will see. What would you like? Do you wish for me to wait a few hours or steal your virginity right now?"

Nelson rubbed his cheek across her breasts. Felt her flinch of distaste at his touch. Twirled his tongue around her hard nipple, sucked until it was elongated. The hard bud couldn't help responding to the hot suction of his mouth. He bit. Crying out, she arched, bucked, trying to move away from him.

"Your chains are secure. All your fighting will do is rub your wrists as well as your ankles raw. Lie still. This will be much easier on you if you accept the inevitable."

The room was chilled. He left the window open. A small array of goose bumps decorated her arms. He appreciated the chill in the air. She closed her eyes. Nelson decided he wished to prolong this event. He was having too much fun seeing terror in her eyes along with the revulsion she felt for him. After all, this was a special occasion. Nellie would lose her virginity tonight or tomorrow morning. The when depended on how he felt. She would no longer be a chaste maiden. He wished for her to think about what he planned for her. Wanted her to worry as well as hope for a rescue that wouldn't happen.

"I'll be back." He kissed her hard. Forced his tongue deep inside her mouth. Escaped before she could bite him. Laughed. Whistling, he left the room to join Anice. He hoped to get some insight into the beautiful lady on the bed.

Watching her through the viewing glass, he tossed his head back and laughed with the sheer pleasure of the night ahead of him. He had not thought to abduct either girl this evening. The Kenworthy townhouse was too heavily guarded. He stopped by with Anice just so she could hope as well as imagine these delights. This unplanned visit went off beyond his expectations.

"What are you doing here?" Anice asked, "Don't you want her? Thought by now you would be deep inside the silly chit. Her virginity gone."

"Ah, you are impatient to see the deflowering of your daughter. So am I. However, if she worries and frets, thinks of escape, this will be more fun. I've all night to torture Nellie by doing nothing. From time to time, I will visit. Taste different parts of her. Show her some of what she has to look forward to learning. I will have her in the next twenty-four hours, more than once. Perhaps on the third or fourth time, you can connect with us. Might bring up my guard to join in the fun. What do you think?"

"Where is Halsey? He should be here by now."

"I would suspect the gunshot we heard stopped him cold. He might be dead. Now watch." They looked at Nellie while she tugged on her chains. Her head thrashed across the pillow. From this vantage point he could see her soft pink folds, damp from his fondling. The girl was not immune to his attentions. If she continued the way she was, her wrists and ankles would be raw. Ah, he couldn't leave her any other way. He couldn't trust her. Didn't wish to lose her as he lost Tessa. Maybe he could find something softer to bind her with. The only reasons he chained her ankles apart was for the view as well as to keep her from kicking him. Perhaps the fight would be more fun than the vision she was treating him with.

Seconds ticked by. He enjoyed a glass of wine with Anice. They ate a bit of the meat and cheeses that were on the tray. "It's your turn, Anice." He needed relief. He was hard, engorged with his need. Nelson ripped Anice's clothing. She moaned her pleasure. He cradled her breasts in his hands then turned her on her hands and knees. Thrust inside her. Anice cried out with delight. Emptied himself inside her hot channel. He was appeased for the moment. Thought to visit Nellie to continue the slow torture he planned.

"Watch now. I'm going to touch Nellie until she is squirming with her pleasure. I'll leave her then. In time she will beg for me to relieve her," Nelson said while he fastened his trousers.

Inside the room that was Nellie's cell, Nelson sat down beside her. Set his hand on her breast. Twisted her nipple until she whimpered. Kissed her then sent his tongue inside her mouth. Nellie tried to bite him again. He slapped her hard. At impact, the jerk of her head gave him reason to grin.

Her eyes blazed with her hatred, with revulsion. He needed to subdue her. Tame her to his ways.

"If you bite me, it will go bad for you. I always retaliate. My retribution is always worse than what the woman did to me. Do you understand?"

"I hate you!"

"You can hate me all you want, Nellie. However, you will come to realize I am your master. You will obey me. I will possess you any time I wish. You no longer have a say in what happens to you."

He needed to teach her who was the boss. Decided he would keep her like this for longer than his original plans. Wanted Nellie to beg him for food as well as water. She would be cold. He would see to that. She would remain naked. He might have his guard fondle her. Until she became more placid, he would withhold nourishment from her.

Chapter Seven

Fannie didn't want to let Fox touch her. She walked beside him back to the house because he insisted. On the way, Fox wrapped his arm around her, holding her against him. He didn't know how to combat the fury that seemed to rage within her. She'd withdrawn from him. What had been a night of great expectations a few minutes ago turned to one of fear as well as abandonment. When they returned to the house there was chaos in the home. People were shouting. Maggie and Tessa were crying. Lacie was trying to calm the sisters. Fox didn't like the fact this happened. Believed their precautions would keep the girls safe. Keir seemed to be uttering directions no one listened to.

Keir stood in front of him. With a deep breath, the butler began, "Thank God, Fannie is safe. Lord Abernathy snatched Nellie right off the path to the gazebo. She was on her way to find her sister. The guard at the back door whistled for another guard to follow her. The man wasn't fast enough. Couldn't get to her before Abernathy grabbed her." Keir was giving a breakdown of what had been going on for the last few minutes.

He was beside himself. He thought only of Fannie. Everything that happened must have gone over his head. "What are you saying? Abernathy has Nellie? I think I knew that." Fox's gut turned sour. His fingers tightened on Fannie's waist as she seemed to wilt next to him. "We will find her," he whispered to Fannie, hoping to reassure.

"No…" she moaned, the sound deep and raw nestling into his soul. "This is my fault."

Fox understood the desperate pain she must feel. He saw moisture shimmer in her eyes. This wasn't supposed to be happening. Tonight was about celebrating their nuptials.

"Yes. Everything happened so fast. One minute the wedding celebration was going full swing. Dancing would begin. The cake was about to be cut. You would have your first dance as husband and wife." Keir sat down on the first step leading to the upstairs rooms, his head in his hands. "I don't understand how all this came crashing down on our heads. There were guards to prevent this. The duke is beside himself with worry. I sent one of the other servants for the magistrate. Apparently, Halsey is tied up still in the gazebo with one of the guards standing over him."

"Abernathy has Nellie?" The stark fear in Fannie's voice terrified him. "That can't be." Fannie seemed to be in a state of denial. "Why?"

Fox saw the same emotion in her eyes. Fannie blamed herself. She said as much a few seconds ago. Didn't make a difference who was at fault here. They needed to find out where Abernathy took Nellie before he had time to hurt her. How? Fox understood the duke had men everywhere. Maybe he had people watching Abernathy. Doing so would be prudent as well as wise. The duke was both.

Keir looked up, blinking tears away then rubbing at the moisture still falling. The elder butler seemed to age in front of them. The crease lines around his eyes and mouth grew. With each passing moment, his hair seemed to turn from grey to white. Through the moisture clogging his throat, Keir spoke again. "Lord Kenworthy, along with his twin, went after the vehicle. Oh, Jake went too. Said he didn't wish to wait at the house without doing something to help. The duke is taking care of Halsey. He's sent more men to look for the carriage. They are on horseback. Will be easier to keep track of the transport. Said there could never be too many rescuers. The duke said both Fannie along with Maggie and Tessa must stay in the house. He sent for the magistrate since he captured Halsey." Keir paused long enough to inhale. "Oh, I'm repeating myself. Halsey was bleeding from his arm, saying the duke's man meant to kill him. The bullet went straight through the fleshy part of his arm just as the duke's man planned." He seemed to search the room as if he would discover Nellie. "They are well-trained, you know."

"My other sisters? Where are they. I have to go to them." Now the words Fannie spoke sounded frantic. Fox wanted to find a way to calm her. Until the sisters had Nellie back in their arms, nothing would relax her. They were all so close.

"No, don't wish to allow you out of my sight. You are not going to them. Who can predict what the three of you will do?" Fox's words rumbled from his throat. Seemed to think better of his statement. "I will take you to them. All three of you will remain in the room. Promise you won't go anywhere."

With his command still on his lips, he felt her bristle then give in to his demand. She would realize he was right. "Promise."

Fox focused on Keir. "Beryl? Is she alright? Nothing has happened to her? She would not wish to be with the sisters." With his questions, he felt Fannie stiffen again, withdraw more deeply before she looked away from him.

"Beryl is fine," Keir said. "She is having something to drink in the drawing room."

When he turned to Fannie, she had an expression on her face he'd never seen before. He couldn't read her. She did look determined to have her way. "You have an hour to reassure each other. When the hour is up, we are going to the hotel. This is our wedding night. That fact won't change for me or for you. The marriage must be consummated."

"No…you can't mean…not tonight. Not after what has happened, after what you did."

"Yes. If not, your mother might find a means to have the marriage annulled. Not going to risk your life with an annulment. Nothing important happened with Beryl." When she started to protest, he held up his hand. "If there is too much discussion on this topic, we will leave now. Take the time with your sisters I am giving you. Use the seconds with wisdom. We will return tomorrow sometime. Can't or won't predict when."

"You have to let me stay until Nellie is returned."

"We don't know if they will even find her tonight let alone be able to bring her home. No, we will do this my way."

Fox walked behind her up the stairs then down the long hallway. He wondered how all went so wrong between them. She saw him kissing Beryl. He wasn't. He was trying to pry her away from him. Attempting to do so without attracting unwanted attention. He'd looked for Jake. Didn't wish for his father to see Beryl flaunting her attentions on him. He never thought Fannie would believe he was kissing the pretentious woman he disliked with an intensity surprising him.

Once she thought on it, Fannie would blame herself for Nellie's capture. No, she didn't need to think about what happened, she already blamed herself. All understood Nellie would not have been vulnerable except for her. Fannie would never have needed to be alone, if not for Beryl's actions. Fox had no idea how Beryl cornered him on the balcony. He couldn't remember why he followed her outside. He shook his head as if the rattling of his head would give him the insight he needed. What was it Beryl said? His muddled mind couldn't remember.

At the door to Maggie's room, he opened it for Fannie. Nodded, then watched her walk into the room. The sisters hugged. Tears flowed. After he surveyed the room for a few seconds, satisfied the chamber was safe, he closed the door. Thought on the wedding night he planned. Didn't see his dreams as being fulfilled. She was no longer a willing bride. Fannie believed he kissed another woman tonight. Hell's teeth.

How to explain Beryl away? He didn't have one idea as to go about doing so. He would never initiate a kiss with the viper who was his stepmother. The woman was detestable. He'd been blessed when she turned her attention to Jake. His father loved the conniving little witch. Why, he couldn't fathom. If for no other reason, he wouldn't kiss her because he loved his father even though he disagreed with him about most things. Beryl didn't care about the kiss. What she wished for was to hurt Fannie. Wanted her confused about his feelings toward her. Beryl was a jealous bitch. She planned the episode on the balcony. Plotted for Fannie to find them. How she managed this, Fox didn't know.

Pulling out his pocket watch, Fox noted the time was just after eight thirty. Fannie had an hour to visit, an hour to come to terms with the fact she would accompany him to the hotel. If she was still unwilling by the time they reached their lodging, he didn't have a clue as to how to proceed with the wedding night. She deserved the time with her sisters. They would be terrified for Nellie. He wanted to strangle Beryl. This fiasco was her fault, not Fannie's. Fox wanted to put this incident in the proper perspective, at Beryl's doorstep.

In the drawing room, he found Beryl sipping champagne as if the world had not turned upside down. As if she didn't instigate the scenario they were living. "Witch," he snarled at her. "You caused enough trouble tonight. Are you proud of yourself? Does Jake know what you did to start this fiasco?

You do realize Nellie was kidnapped by a maniac. The man is crazy. An entitled lord of the realm, a man who believes he is permitted to do what he wants to women. Abernathy will rape Nellie. After that he will continue in the same vein for as long as doing so pleases him. She won't come to him with willing open arms. Are you proud of yourself?"

Beryl lifted her glass in salute but she wasn't smiling. "I didn't know Nellie would be kidnapped. You can't put the blame on me. This was all a misunderstanding. Now, Jake is risking his life for the little trollop. I don't like the fact he volunteered to be part of the rescue party. The girl should have stayed in the townhouse where she would be safe. Where she was told to be. We were all advised not to leave. With guards at the doors, she must have known better."

He downed half his glass of wine. "I can do whatever the hell I want! You're a petty woman, pretentious. You believe the world revolves around you. I was never more blessed than when you decided you wanted father's money more than you wanted me. I'd been blinded by the Beryl you presented to me, a kind loving woman. What you showed me was not the woman you are but the woman you wished for me to see. With single handed finesse, you set this in motion." He rubbed his hand across the back of his neck, muscles strained. He felt on edge. "What I cannot figure out is how you managed to get Fannie to the balcony the very moment you kissed me. How?"

Beryl lifted her shoulders in a 'I'll never say' pose. The expression she sent him was a smirk. "I didn't plan anything. What happened was a coincidence. You should not have been kissing your father's wife. Everything that happened you deserved. Kissing another man's wife is frowned upon by most societies."

Fox didn't believe he could stay here in the drawing room with this woman. There was nothing more he could say. The air was filled with hatred. Understood she would deny everything, all the truths that were laid at her doorstep. "Don't want excuses. Realize you would never tell the truth. Not going to listen to more of your lies."

He strode to the back door. One of the two main house guards was there; the man who whistled for the other guard to follow Fannie. It was his intervention that saved her from Halsey. Otherwise, Abernathy might have both girls in his possession. He needed to thank him. If not for this man, Abernathy would have Fannie also. He would be beside himself with worry. Halsey would have grabbed her. Would have knocked her out to keep her quiet. She wouldn't have made a sound. No one would have learned she was missing until it was too late.

"What's your name?" Fox rarely smoked. Tonight, he lit a cheroot then offered one to the man who saved his wife. The smoke inside his lungs was almost as relaxing as a full snifter of brandy. "Would you like one? Need something to calm my nerves, a distraction so I don't think about how close Fannie came to being in the same predicament as her sister. Thank you," he said again, realizing there weren't enough words in his vocabulary to tell this man how he felt. Comprehended he could never say the two words enough. "How long are you on duty?"

"Mhàrtainn, and no smokes or drinks for me. Not while I'm standing guard. Smoking is kind of like drinking. Can be a distraction as you said. There are still ladies upstairs who are in jeopardy. Got to keep a clear head. The duke would not be pleased if anything else happens tonight. None of this should have played out the way it did. We thought we had control of the grounds. Turns out we didn't."

"When you are not on duty, I'll offer again."

"I'll be here at this door until the others return. Doubt if they'll come back empty handed. The duke has feelers out as we speak. He'll figure out where they've gone. We've been on both Abernathy's as well as MacRae's tail ever since Lord Abernathy kidnapped Tessa. Seems he sold the townhouse in the duke's neighborhood before buying himself a new one. The duke knows where this new place is located."

The relief he felt at the guards' words was restorative. "Leslie Stewart has men working on this? The location? Should have guessed as much. Jasper explained to me how he and his wife helped Tessa. Abernathy would never return to the house where he brought Tessa. Doing so would be foolhardy. You say he purchased another place?" Fox asked, encouraged by the news.

"As I said, the boss has been working on that matter for over a year now. Before he assigned me to guard duty here, I followed Anice MacRae. Been tailing the lady for a number of days now. Know what she does as well as where she goes. I was just put on her surveillance. Until this last week there's been little activity. The duke is a persistent man. Tonight, Lord Abernathy ran out of patience. This lack of control will cost him."

"I suppose Leslie had someone following Lord Abernathy as well. He will know where Nellie is kept."

"As we speak. The men he sent to get Nellie have the address of this new place Lord Abernathy purchased. Must have thought he was outsmarting the duke when he used a fake name. It won't be long before the little lady is returned. Can't say what condition she will be in, poor little thing. Frightened, mistreated as well. Hope she is in one piece. Pray they will get to her before that crazy man can hurt her."

Fox drew on the cheroot. Let the smoke flow into his lungs. Held the fumes there for a few seconds before the blue smoke drifted out into the cold night air. Mist still hovered close to the ground. "That's good to know." He felt relieved. Still, what would they be able to do? Would they have entrance to a private home. Fox imagined the duke could arrange most anything he wished.

Mhàrtainn continued. "The men who have gone after Nellie have authorization to arrest in the name of the Scottish government whoever is involved. As I said, this will all be over soon. The little gal will be back in loving arms before the sun rises."

"I should tell the sisters." Fox looked to the upstairs window where he knew the girls to be. Perhaps he would give this more than an hour. He hoped to bring Fannie back to the hotel this evening. If her sister was returned all in one piece, she would feel much better. Maybe they would have the night he dreamt of.

No, Beryl still stood between them. Would until he could convince Fannie he didn't want anything to do with the woman who was his father's wife. Fannie didn't know him well enough to understand he would never dally with another man's wife, especially not his father's.

"I wouldn't do that, sir."

"What?"

"Don't tell the ladies what I just told you. The words were privileged information. Under the circumstances, thought you should know the truth. Believed you would realize nothing is a sure thing until it is done. Nellie might not be in any shape to see her sisters tonight or anytime soon. It might be best for the girl to not need to explain what the man did to her. Rape is cruel. She will need the duchess not her sisters if that is what happened to her. Though…" Mhàrtainn paused for a few beats, "I believe the duke's men will reach her in time. The location is known. As I said, Abernathy thought he was sneaky when he used a fictitious name to purchase the home. In the end, the name didn't matter. Anice led us straight to the new country estate as did he. Seems he's been preparing the home for its initiation for a few months now. The men that went on the mission do have the authority to storm the house."

"If that is what the duke wishes, I'll abide by them. Where is Lacie?"

"As of the last time I saw her, the duchess was with her husband. Seems he was wary of letting her out of his sight. Just as you are with your wife. Once Nellie is brought back into the fold, they will go home. The duchess will see to the girl's needs. She is truly very good with hostages. She has had more than one experience."

Fox wasn't surprised when nine thirty drifted by, then turned to ten. He was loath to tear Fannie away from her sisters. He paced the foyer, hoping to hear the sounds of the men returning. Every time he turned at the stairs leading to the second floor, his gaze drifted up to the rooms. He needed to see Fannie, to hold her in his arms, to reassure her.

After the guards changed, he heard from Mhàrtainn that Lacie returned with Leslie by her side to their home.

"They found Nellie chained to a bed, a spectacle for Abernathy's viewing pleasure. Also found Anice along with Abernathy in a room where Nellie's room could be watched. I wouldn't mention Nellie's condition to her sisters. They will be terrified for her. Let them know she is safe and at the duke's home. Lord Abernathy was having his way with Anice when they caught the two. Had to give them time to dress, though seems Jason wanted to haul them both to jail stark naked. He said it was what they deserved."

"Where is Nellie now?" Fox shook his head. He was certain Mhàrtainn told him. He couldn't remember the answer. He'd been thinking about Fannie. His wife of a few hours was all he could think about.

"At the duke's townhouse," he said again. "The duchess is seeing to her needs. Nellie was naked when they found her. Jasper gave her his coat to wear. She wasn't raped. At least that is what she told them."

The sigh of relief slowly left his lungs. "Abernathy and Anice?"

"They are in a holding cell in the Glasgow jail. Kidnapping charges are being brought against the two of them. Will most likely spend some time imprisoned. Don't believe they can beat the charges. Sometimes juries can be manipulated. They both have the funds to attempt bribery. There was a guard at the place who was also charged. He claimed he had no idea what Abernathy was doing on the third floor. Told us he thought it was a playroom for him whenever Anice came to visit."

"That man will probably go free."

"Yes, that's unfortunate because we all believe he played a more intricate role than he admitted."

"Would like to tell the sisters then collect my wife. We have a wedding night ahead of us." Fox waited for the answer. While he didn't believe the night would go as he planned, he intended to sleep with Fannie. Hold her in his arms. Reassure her that Nellie would be fine. He also needed to plead his case about Beryl.

"Our duke said you would want to go to the hotel. There is a guard waiting to leave with you even though the danger seems to have passed. Don't wish to take chances at this stage. Everyone we know who were involved with the plot are behind bars."

"I'm going to share the news with the sisters then leave for the hotel."

Fox walked up the steps then straight to Maggie's room. He knocked but didn't wait for an answer. He would have Fannie's obedience in this matter. Didn't wish for an argument in front of her sisters. The hour was nearing ten thirty. Nellie was rescued. It was time for the two of them to iron out their differences, to figure out a way to move forward. Before they could attend to their future, they would need to rehash this evening.

As he stepped inside the room, he heard Maggie ask who was there. The eyes of all three were focused on him. He cleared his throat thinking the next few minutes were all important for he and Fannie. "It's me, Fox," he said the obvious. Saw the look of distaste flit across Fannie's face. He couldn't help but grimace. In the last two hours, she had not softened toward him. She would not have discussed their new situation with her sisters.

He held out his hand. "Come here, Fannie. We are going to the hotel."

At the stiffening of Fannie's shoulders, Fox realized he should have begun with Nellie's rescue rather than an ultimatum she would look on with distaste.

"No!"

So much for keeping their disagreement private.

Ignoring her adamant statement, he proceeded with the relevant news. "Nellie is found. She was not hurt physically. Though, the kidnapping will play havoc with her head. The duke's men along with your husband's knew where to find her. I won't go into the particulars now. Jasper as well as Jason will discuss this with their wives."

"Where is Nellie?" Maggie asked as she stood, concern as wells as fear, evident on her beautiful face. "Jasper? I would know where everyone is. Are they all safe? We need to see to Nellie."

"I'm certain," Fox looked at both Maggie as well as Tessa, "Your men will be here soon ready to explain what is happening. As to Nellie, the duke is having her brought to his home. Lacie will take care of her just as she took care of Tessa in her need. The duke thought it the best scenario."

"No!" Maggie said as she protested, "She should be with us. We're her sisters. We understand her."

"No, I know what it is like to be kidnapped. Given no choices. Understand how it feels when you believe you will be forced. Lacie can help her more," Tessa added. "She will be calm, caring but also detached in a way none of us can be."

Fox didn't wish to explain. He tended to agree with two of the sisters. In this matter he wasn't in command. The duke was overseeing the rescue along with the recovery. "According to the duke, Nellie needs a mother figure. It is the belief of the duke along with the twins the best place for her to heal will be with the duchess. With Lacie, there will be no expectations."

"He's right," Tessa spoke up again. Her fingers in front of her, laced tight. Fox saw the fine trembling. "Lacie soothed all my shattered nerves. She is very good at listening. Helped me understand that given time I would feel whole again. We don't know what Lord Abernathy did to our sister. I do understand what he wanted to do with me. The man is repulsive. Nellie would never wish to confide in us what happened to her. Lacie will be a neutral companion. Something none of us could be in this situation."

"I've been told Nellie wasn't raped. The rescue party reached her before that could happen. Now, if she wishes to remain in Glasgow, she has the choice. Both Abernathy along with your mother are incarcerated. They were caught stark naked in the room built to view the room Nellie was taken to. They will be charged with kidnapping. Though with good lawyers, they might beat the charge. Under the circumstances, I rather doubt that will happen. In any case, there will be no more fear."

Fox chose not to elaborate on how Nellie was found. For Fannie's sake, he hoped Nellie would choose to go with them when they left for Michigan. She didn't need all these bad memories to float around her, to haunt her. What Nellie needed was a new beginning. She would never find a fresh start at this home.

"Come, Fannie." Fox held out his hand again. "We have our wedding night to look forward to enjoying."

At the mention of the wedding night, frown lines creased her forehead. She shot him an expression he wasn't certain about.

Jasper, along with Jason, chose that moment to burst into the room. He'd thought he heard the thundering of their booted feet as the pair raced upstairs. Chose to ignore the noise. He needed Fannie to come willingly with him. His hand was still held out for her to take, to accept him the way she used to accede. Trust was illusive. He needed her faith in his word.

"Maggie!"

She ran into Jasper's outstretched arm. Their lips met then seemed to devour as he watched.

"Tessa!"

She did the same with Jason. He whirled her around in a circle, her feet never touching the ground.

"They will all be busy. There is no place for you here. There will be no more chatter between the sisters this evening. The twins will seek their beds with their wives. Nellie is at the duke's townhouse." Fox nodded to her. Tried to encourage her. "Come with me. We need to figure out what went wrong tonight. Why you left our celebration to put yourself in jeopardy." His hand was still outstretched waiting for her. "Trust me."

Jason held Tessa in his arms. He was striding from Maggie and Jasper's room to find his. Jasper's mouth was fused solidly with Maggie's.

Her arms were wrapped around his neck. The couples needed privacy just as they did. With the two of them standing in the middle of the bedroom, there would be none.

Fannie walked past him, her shoulders stiff. She didn't look at him or take the offered hand.

"The carriage waits for us outside the front door. We will have a guard at the hotel." Fox walked behind her trying to decide on a plan for the rest of the evening. Nothing came into his muddled head. Felt as if straw filled his skull not brains. He didn't know how to remove the starch from her back. Fox realized Fannie was jealous. Perhaps jealousy wasn't so bad. Gave them something to begin with.

In the carriage, Fannie remained silent, staring out the window as the city passed by. Fox decided not to try for conversation. If he did, he would find himself speaking to her back. He wished he understood what was in her head. A mist was falling when the transport came to a stop in front of the hotel. She pulled her hood up then allowed the driver to assist her to the street. Seemed she was waiting for him.

"Allow me," Fox took her elbow in his hand. Felt the never-ending warmth from her small body. She could heat him to a fever pitch. Ever since the near kidnapping, he'd wanted to touch her. Fannie should be in his arms, melting, absorbing his strength. He should be able to give solace. Understanding her grief for her sister was overpowering. The little incident with Beryl should not get in their way. It did.

Fox guided her to the front desk where he picked up his key. "We are on the third floor. All your things have been moved to our suite of rooms. Tomorrow we will spend time with your sisters. I'm certain there will be a great deal to talk about. We have three days left to us. You should be able to see them as much as you like." Hell, if Fannie's attitude didn't change, this was going to be a silent, long night. Didn't seem as if there would be pleasure for either of them.

Damn!

Explaining Beryl away seemed next to impossible. Fannie was so positive she knew what happened she wouldn't listen. Her mind was set. Stubborn woman. For the sake of his marriage, he would give the explanation his best tries. Maybe he should start at the beginning. Return to the day he met Beryl. The day was a beautiful one, sunny as well as warm. At first sight he'd been besotted with her. Besotted until he discovered her beauty didn't go soul deep. The beauty was only in the mirror she looked into.

So far, he never told Fannie much about the woman his father eventually married. She did know they'd been engaged at one point. The engagement never seemed quite right. Neither wanted to set a date. Fox imagined he understood soon after putting a diamond on her finger this relationship wasn't working. It would never serve his motives if he told Fannie that Beryl broke off the engagement in favor of his father. She would believe he was still smitten with her. He wasn't. Seemed he wasn't infatuated for more than a month. By the culmination of a few weeks, Fox realized her character did not match her outward beauty.

He understood he needed to be blunt as well as honest with Fannie. The truth was the only way he could dig himself out of this grave he fell into.

Inside their rooms, he poured them both a glass of wine. With her legs tucked tight beneath her as well as her spine rigid, she sat on a large chair staring into the fire, doing her best to ignore him. Fox sat down in the chair next to hers. Stared at her profile for a few beats of his racing heart. Lord, he didn't want to mess up this conversation.

He offered her the tray that held an assortment of food. "Are you hungry? I am." Fox was hungrier for Fannie than he was for the food on the tray. While he sipped wine, he tried to put everything into perspective.

Fannie picked up a slice of meat then paired it with one of the cheeses. "A little," she said then turned to him, her big blue eyes shining with intensity. "Thank you for letting me have more time with my sisters. That was nice of you. I knew you wanted to be alone with me. Privacy too." She tossed up her hands looking frustrated. "You were going to lecture me about leaving the house. I deserved a lecture but it's unnecessary. After that you want to make sure I know you weren't kissing Beryl. I lost my head with jealousy. It isn't as if you love me. I should have expected something like that to happen. You must still love her. Should have never reacted the way I did."

Fox choked on the wine. A few drops flew into the air. He was surprised at the statements which showed a softening toward him. He shouldn't let a simple thank you get ahead of his thoughts. Fannie still believed he kissed his father's wife. The fact Beryl was his father's wife should be enough for her to trust him not to trespass on Jake's territory.

"You're welcome. I came to realize you would need the comfort of your sisters. Understood, throughout your lives, all you had were each other. Anice has put the four of you through so much. How do you feel about Nellie coming with us now? With your mother, along with Lord Abernathy facing charges, she will have a choice as to where she would like to live."

Fannie lifted slim white shoulders. "I want Nellie to be happy. Don't think she can be content living here with the shadow of Dillon haunting her. Every time she saw him, she would remember how he broke things off with her. Then…" she paused to sip her wine. Remained silent for some time gazing into the fire.

"Then?" Fox needed her to finish the statement.

"Memories of Mother and Abernathy will linger. She won't be able to go anywhere the awful man has been without recalling this nightmare he put her through. They both have wealth at their disposal. Lord Abernathy also has power. They might not remain incarcerated for very long. What did he do to Nellie? He is evil, as is Mother. What happened could not have been pleasant."

"No, I'm positive what happened wasn't nice in any way." Fox brought her free hand into his. Was pleased when she allowed the contact. Her fingers were cold as ice. "I don't know details. Nothing was explained to me." Fox didn't like the lie. Nonetheless, he felt as if the misstatement was important to Nellie's well-being as well as his wife's. No one else needed to learn of her state of dishabille when they found her. The facts were Nellie's to reveal or keep them secret.

"You know more than you're telling me. I wish this night never happened. It was my fault she was kidnapped. I shouldn't be so impulsive. Did believe the guards would protect me. For me, they did their job. But Nellie…for Nellie the man who was supposed to protect her was not with her soon enough. She was bent on getting to me to offer solace even though she didn't know what troubled me. Nellie sensed I was in need."

Fox meant to ignore the first statement. There wasn't anything he could tell her about Nellie's plight that would make her feel better. While she was receptive to him, it was time to tell her a bit about his history with Beryl.

"For me, until what you believed you saw sent you into danger, the night was wonderful. One of the best in my life. I was looking forward to our first dance. Wanted to put a bit of icing on your lips so I could savor the sweet confection when I kissed you. Never wished for the evening to end. What do you suppose happened to our cake? Is it still sitting on the table on the third floor waiting for us? No, would guess Keir took care of the dessert." He paused then to watch the expressions on her face change. "If you are willing to listen, I would tell you some of the story between Beryl and me."

"You don't need to say anything. I was stupid. Still…watching you kiss that woman sent a knife into my heart. I…" she broke off with a soft sound of regret. "I am willing to listen. For me, there is too much at stake not to let you explain. For our baby's sake and even though we don't love each other, I want the marriage to work."

His heart lurched when she said she didn't love him. He wasn't certain why her words mattered to him yet what she said did. "This man would love to have his wife trust him as well as love him. Imagine faith in one's husband takes time. You are too important to me to squander on kissing a woman I dislike. I do dislike Beryl. Perhaps dislike is not a strong enough word." Fox reached out to caress Fannie's cheek. She leaned into him. "You see, I met Beryl when she was just twenty. Thought she was the prettiest little gal I ever saw. Fell head over heels for her. That was more than six years ago. I was only twenty-two, too young to understand a woman such as Beryl. Too young to think about marriage. I did. Now I see the infatuation was lust, nothing more. She was no different then than she is now."

"Younger than I am now," Fannie seemed to think the information over for more than a second.

"Yes. Beryl wanted a rich man. She saw me as her savior. You see, she grew up poor. Used men to buy her things. While she never opened her legs for the man to gain her end, she still, in a way, prostituted herself with any man willing to indulge her whims."

"Fox, you don't…"

"Hush. I have to make my feelings clear. I didn't stand a chance against her provocative ways. I was too young as well as naïve. She knew just what to do as well as what to say to a man to get this trinket or a new bonnet or whatever else she wanted. At first, I wanted to give her the world. Gave her a diamond ring when I asked her to marry me. Thought I was the luckiest man in the world when she said yes."

"Fox…" He set a finger on her mouth.

"I have to finish. She was mine until my father visited. Beryl saw right away he was richer than Midas. Within days of his arrival, I found her in Jake's arms. He had his hand on her breast. Something I never did. I was very careful of her. Treated her like fine bone China. To give my father credit, Beryl had taken off the ring I gave her. He didn't know we were engaged when I found them kissing, her bodice askew and Jake's hand beneath her dress. It was then I realized how she used me. To Beryl, I was just a stepping stone on her way to greater riches. Still, I was afraid she would hurt Father."

"Why would you kiss her tonight? Not to get even with your father? Did you want him to stumble across the two of you?" Fannie let out a puffy little sigh, lifting her slim shoulders. "I don't understand."

"Well," Fox paused, listening to the clock tick. "First, as I said before, I didn't kiss the woman. Beryl kissed me. I pushed her away. Second, I would never stoop to something so underhanded as to get even. I'm loyal to my father. Would never kiss the woman he is wed to. Third, it was Beryl who wanted you to run into us not the other way around."

"Is all that true?" Her wide-eyed look of wonder told him he was making progress. Wasn't there, just yet, but getting closer.

"I wouldn't lie to you about something so important. I dislike my father's wife with an intensity you wouldn't understand. You've probably…no I would guess you feel the same about Lord Abernathy. She wished to marry money and so she did. Beryl is beautiful on the outside but not the inside where it counts the most. Father understands there is no love from her for him. Though I do believe Jake loves her. It is too bad she cannot return the sentiment. Father deserves love in his life."

"I don't like Beryl. She seems to have a mean streak in her. Her soul is dark. You truly weren't kissing her? It looked so much as if you were."

He found himself shaking his head, a slow smile forming as he began to believe he made progress with the short explanation. Perhaps the night was not lost. "I would not kiss that viper, not willingly. She caught me by surprise. What you saw was me trying to get away from her. Do you believe me?"

"I'm mortified at what I thought then did. I believe you. All this time, you've had my interest at heart. When I saw the two of you together, I thought you didn't want me. Imagined the wedding was forced upon you by the baby." She set his hand flat on her belly. "I'm still not rounded. I've no symptoms. For a few beats of my broken heart, I felt certain you thought I lied about the pregnancy. I didn't."

"Soon," he told her, bringing her hand to his lips for a kiss on the palm. He touched the middle of her hand with his tongue. Her little whimper of pleasure gave him more hope for the evening.

~ * ~

Fannie acknowledged the fact she'd been injudicious in her accusation. Her actions caused Nellie pain. No, according to what Fox explained, she'd been manipulated by a woman with no scruples, a pretentious woman. Fell into Beryl's plans like an untried virgin. Despite growing up with her mother, Fannie realized she trusted people. She always expected them to be honest in their dealings. Fannie wasn't positive why. Her mother was far from truthful. Lied as well as manipulated all who ventured into her path. Despised all four of her daughters. Until recent events, she always trusted her mother.

"Would you like more wine? Your glass is empty. You should eat something. Don't think you ate much at the wedding." He was observing her, anticipation in the shimmering brown of his eyes that seemed to darken as he watched.

"More wine, please." She did pick out a piece of cheese. Bit. Chewed then swallowed. Realized she wasn't hungry. Her stomach seemed to be doing somersaults. All she could think about was being in his arms. She needed a distraction. Didn't know if she was willing to let him make love to her. Understood her emotions were vacillating. One second, she wanted him to do all those delicious things to her body that he did just last night. The next moment, she was afraid to make herself more vulnerable.

"You may have anything you would like." His smile while he poured melted her heart. "My plan this evening is to please you. Want to give you satisfaction. Would see to other needs too if doing so is acceptable."

She did wish to forgive him. If she believed what he told her, there was nothing to forgive. Fox did nothing wrong. He tried to get himself out of a horrid situation that she walked in on. Did hope to forget how the evening was ruined.

More thoughts of Nellie along with her turmoil surfaced to take over other considerations. "When will we visit the house tomorrow? I'm eager. In a few days… Do you think Nellie will be there?" Fannie had a myriad of questions for him. She was well aware he lied to her about Nellie. Fox knew more than it seemed he was willing to admit. Perhaps it was better if she didn't learn the details. With Abernathy anything could happen. The man was pure evil. Her mother wasn't any better. After Tessa got away from him, he would take extreme precautions to keep Nellie. She would not have been placed in a second-floor bedroom with a balcony. Nor would this house be near others.

Fox lifted broad shoulders that seemed strong enough to hold the world. Fannie understood she could rely on Fox. Found she wanted what they shared last night. Needed Fox to hold her, touch her in all those places that heated her from the inside out. In addition, she needed to caress her husband. Wished to feel all the different textures of his body. His day-old stubble was rough to her fingertips. The hard planes of his body fascinated her. His muscles rippled when she touched his stomach. The crisp hair growing on his chest intrigued. She needed to run the palms of her hands across him. He could help her forget what happened to Nellie. She wished for new memories to begin a different part of her life.

"Depends on when we retire for the night as well as when we rise. The time is dependent on you. If you will allow me to make love to my wife, I'd be a pleased man. Wish to consummate our marriage. Would you like me to see to your pleasure?"

Feeling shy, she looked down before she brought her gaze back to meet Fox. "I would like all of that…all of what you said. Though I do wish to be at the Kenworthy townhouse first thing in the morning," she paused to tuck a breath of air into her lungs. "Is all that possible?"

"What is your definition of first thing in the morning? Are you in such a hurry to get away from me that you wish to rush from my arms? As to Nellie, I've no idea what she will do. Believe the duke and duchess will provide a safe haven for her. My guess is that she will stay with them at least one more day. Nellie will not want to answer questions or face her sisters with what happened to her." Fox ran his knuckles along her arm, making goosebumps rise. "Our conversation now would be better suited to what we want. Are you telling me you would like more of what we did last night. You do know, if we had not been interrupted, we would have made love."

"I'm not in a hurry to get away from you. From the first time I met you, from the beginning, at the brothel, I felt something deep within me when I touched you. Something about you moved me. I know we are meant to be together. Fear of losing you coupled with a too healthy dose of jealousy has a way of tangling my thoughts. I don't wish to be vulnerable. Afraid to care so much it hurts." Fannie was also terrified of telling Fox she loved him.

"Fear? There is no reason to be afraid of losing me. You have this man for life. I will never hurt you. The pain you felt this evening was there because of Beryl's machinations." He touched beneath her chin, lifted until her gaze met the darkening of his eyes. For a few frantic beats of her heart, he seemed to study her. Reached into her soul with the piercing darkness of his eyes. "As to the jealousy, you have no reason to be envious of that woman. Do you think making love with me will cause vulnerability?" He was questioning her.

No, she could never tell him she was in love with him. He married her because of the baby. Would never explain the defenseless part. She should have never spoken the words out loud. Should have kept her thoughts in her head. "I understand. Accept it as well." Fannie stared at this man who crashed into her life like a lightning bolt. She was looking over the rim of the wine glass while she held the crystal at her lips. Her heart beat harder when he took the glass from her then set it on the table between the two chairs.

"Would you like to begin now where we left off last night? If not for the intrusion, we would have made love." Fox reminded her with the steadiness of his words. "Even though you are no longer a virgin, you are still more innocent than I would have thought. Before the night that forever changed our lives, had you ever been kissed? No?" A half-smile formed on his mouth. "You've only been with me once. You remained in the Kenworthy townhouse not venturing outside."

"Yes."

"You've only felt my lips caress yours."

With a fingertip, she touched his mouth. "Yes." Loved the smoothness she found there. "Your lips are soft. I think it is the only place on all of you that is soft to the touch. Everywhere else you are hard. I adore all your different textures. You are the only person to kiss me. Touch me. I would that it stays that way." With the touch to his lips, she found her urgency for him growing. Fannie wanted to join with him, to be one with him. So close within each other they would feel as if they belonged to each other.

At the culmination of her words, Fox groaned. "I do want you now. Don't know if I can wait. Wish you were ready for me this instant." His tongue touched her fingertip. He bit with gentle precision.

Her body pulsed to life. Frantic with the pleasure of his simple caress. "Oh! Fox." She inhaled a deep poignant breath of air. Understood the night was just beginning. Remembered they could make love more than once. She recalled the second time he came inside her, so sweet and moving, even the memory stole her breath.

Fox brought her fingers to his lips. Sucked each one into his mouth. As he sipped, his actions heated her. She was on fire. Flames were fanned to life with each gentle caress. Inside the deepest part of her, those sparks grew more intense. He did the same to the other hand. "Where did we leave off last night? Do you remember? No, believe we should start from the beginning. Wouldn't wish to miss out on something important. No rushing. Not tonight. I will have a slow hand. Will be a considerate lover. We are going to do this slow…easy. Want to see to your pleasure."

"I want to start at the beginning too. Can I touch you anywhere?"

"If you do, this joining won't be slow or easy. Maybe the second time around. We will see."

Fannie didn't care about slow and easy. She needed him now. Wanted to touch all of him. Fannie pushed on the lapels of his coat. Smoothed her hand beneath the fabric. Pushed the jacket from his shoulders. Fox shrugged out of his coat before tossing it to the floor. Her fingers fumbled with the buttons on his shirt. She was shaking so hard she couldn't get them through the little button holes. Closing her eyes, Fannie set her head on his chest. Drew in gulps of air, hoping to settle her raging desire to have this man. She felt frustrated as well as anxious.

She looked into his eyes. "Fox, I want to touch you. Can't get the damn little things out of their holes."

His swift inhalation left her breathless too. His eyes darkened to warm brown, simmering with heat from the moment. At the dark, piercing look Fox sent her way, her breath caught in the back of her throat. Her mouth felt parched. She reached for her wine. Missed the stem. He sipped on her neck, his tongue smoothing the skin. When she couldn't get the buttons undone, she whimpered with the annoyance.

His bark of laughter surprised her. He tapped her nose before smoothing her brows. "I will do the honors, sweet. I like the notion you are impatient, no eager, to get me out of my clothing. I wish to touch you also. Test the weight of your breasts in my hands. I need to taste you on my lips." Fox pushed her hands to the side as he shrugged out of his shirt, letting the fabric fall to the floor along with his coat.

She was thankful he could do the deed because she could not. One more time she tried to pick up her glass. She needed to drink to wet her parched throat. Her hand shook while she brought it to her lips. Tiny drops slid over the top then onto Fox's shoulders. Without conscious thought, she licked the tiny droplets away. Heard his husky groan emanate from the back of his throat. Startled, she looked at him. Didn't realize such a small thing would affect him in such a way.

The sound made her smile. "Umm…the wine tastes better this way…part wine, part Fox. I could drip some other places. Where? I suppose here." She licked a bead at the base of his neck. Sat up. Let her tongue travel across her lips savoring the taste of Fox coupled with the sweet Bordeaux.

"Two can play this game you began. I would do the same to you. A little bit Fannie and a little bit wine." Fox took the glass. Held it to her mouth. "Sip." She did but he let the edge rest barely touching her mouth. Some of the wine splashed down her chin then onto her neck. He sucked on the tiny beads. Nibbled on the tip of her chin.

She whimpered with the sensations he created. Her heart pounded as each breath heaved into her lungs. The beats of her heart were now frantic with her urgent need.

"Fox, please…"

"You taste good. Better than the wine. Now…" His mouth hurtled down on hers. He kissed her hard then slow. Played with her lips. Delved inside the dark secret heat of her to dance with her tongue. She opened for him, wishing he would bring her closer. They still sat opposite each other in two different chairs. Last night she sat on his lap. That time he swept his hand beneath her gown; touched intimate, secret places. Tonight, she wore nothing under her wedding gown, no chemise, no pantalettes, no corset. Nothing except herself.

Fannie never wanted Fox to stop kissing her. Wished this moment to go on forever. This kiss was hotter than ever before. Mercuric desire ripped through her. Little ribbons of pleasure filled sounds floated from between her lips. Fannie ran the tips of her fingers along his shoulders then down his arms. His texture was heavenly to her touch.

Felt his shudder at the light contact. He pulled her up so she straddled him. Felt contact on her bare thighs. The fabric of his trouser brushed on sensitive flesh. Fannie squirmed against him in an attempt to get closer. He was covered. She didn't like having the clothing between them. "You need to take off your trousers." She noticed the hard bulge of his sex nestled at the apex of her thighs. She felt the moisture from within. She was wet. Needed him to touch her.

He might remember she wore no underwear. There was nothing beneath her gown except herself. Fannie wanted to touch all of him. Needed him to caress all of her. Her palms brushed across his small nipples. She let her fingers sift through the hair on his chest, winding around the strands. Her hands explored south. Followed the trail of his dark hair to his waistband. Tried to unfasten his trousers. Fannie wanted to wrap her fingers around his sex. Hold him in her hands. She wanted him to touch her between her thighs.

His fingers wound around her neck, his thumbs pushing her chin up. Fox deepened the kiss, thrust between her parted lips until she thought she would burn into cinders. Her lips were swollen. Mercuric magic swept within. He created a raging inferno of flames.

Before she realized what was happening, her bodice was at her waist.

There was nothing covering her. The globes swayed as she moved. He held her a small distance away from him, watching with hungry eyes. After he looked his fill, he lowered his head. Fox rubbed the tips of her breast against his face, once then twice more. She arched to meet him, to give him more of herself.

The day-old stubble intensified the pleasure, made her flesh tingle with need. "Do you know how beautiful you are to me. No, don't suppose you do. Your breasts are so soft and white, the tips a rosy shade that beckons to me. Wish to taste then savor all of you." His mouth closed over one hard crest. When he sucked, she jerked then arched with the contact. Hot aching pleasure grew between her thighs. With unconscious need, she parted them for his further exploration.

"Oh...my..." she purred when his hand slid beneath her gown. Found unclothed territory. Fannie felt the caress of his fingers. Noticed the calluses on his hands as they caressed with gentle finesse.

"Forgot you weren't wearing anything but your gown. Was going to play with you when we were eating dinner. Seemed nothing about this night is going the way we planned. I like knowing how easy it is for me to find your hidden secrets, treasures that are meant for me alone."

His fingers parted her. Slipped between the folds while he continued to play with her breasts. "Oh..." Felt her muscles clench at the contact. Deep inside her dark interior, she pulsed. Let her head fall back, encouraging him to taste more of her.

"We need the bed," he whispered, as he brought his mouth to savor the taste of her lips again. "Want the first time on our wedding night to be done right. Won't take you straddling me until we've made love a few more times." He sent his tongue across her mouth. Swept inside with his tongue. She sucked on him, brought him deeper. Felt the velvet texture of his against hers. Fox was everything to her. The only man she would ever want.

Fox lifted her. Swept the gown down her body to pool on the floor next to his clothing. "You aren't naked yet," Fannie told him, wishing to see the evidence of his arousal. The first times she'd been too drugged to remember all his dark splendor. Last night they were interrupted before she could truly see him.

"Neither are you," he mentioned with a dry chuckle. "Neither are you but for all practical purposes for making love, there is nothing that will hinder me. Nothing between us to get in the way."

"Yes. In all the ways that count, I am naked," she retorted, feeling heat rush through her. "I've only my stocking and slippers on."

"You are blushing. I do like the way pink looks on you. The tops of your breasts have changed to a pretty rose. You are very adorable wearing this lovely shade of blushing color."

"Fox, you need to…"

As if he read her mind, he answered, "I will be naked in a few seconds," Fox assured her. He strode to the bed. "This is where I want you. Lying on my…our bed…naked as the day you were born. Don't want to let you out of this bed until we are both too weak to move. We will sleep then make love again. We will eat to keep our strength. All night is how I want you…all night long. Not one second without you."

After setting her on the bed, he rid himself of the rest of his clothing. She braced herself with her elbows so she could see all of him. Still wearing her stockings and slippers, she parted her legs encouraging him to come to her. She could not take her gaze from that part of him, jutting from his groin. Fox was her dream come true. "You are beautiful. I…" Fannie wished she dared touch him. Would he let her? "I want to wrap my fingers around the part of you that gives me so much pleasure. Need to kiss you, suck as if you were my favorite candy. Are you as hard as you look? May I hold you?"

"Harder," he told her, his voice low, rich with dark consistency that made her feel hotter everywhere. "Harder than you can image. You can touch me later. Don't wish to explode before I'm part of you."

"Later…I will hold you to that."

In a voice sounding husky with need, he came down between her legs. Separated them farther then brought her knees up. As if savoring her with his eyes, he studied her longer. His expression flaming. His eyes so dark they were almost black.

"You are ready for me. I see the sweet nectar between your legs. Your honey is creamy and white. Did you know that? No, probably not." He kissed her again on the mouth. Found the small pearl that would send her higher than ever when he touched her. She recalled the intense feeling from the night in the brothel.

"No…" she told him. "White?" Fannie didn't understand.

"Don't think I can be slow right now, sweet. My hands are shaking. My sex is needing to sink into your velvet softness. Want you too damn much. An hour ago, I didn't think this would be happening. Believed the bed would be cold. Tonight, we will both go up in flames if we continue in this manner."

"Please." Fannie held her hands out to him. "You won't hurt me."

"You're right. Did that weeks ago. I broke through your maidenhead. Called you a virgin whore. Knowing what I know now, the words were not well done of me. Should have realized how much I changed your life."

"What are you waiting for?" When she watched his expression change, she smiled. "I need you more than I can tell you."

"Damned if I know. I do understand why I'm waiting. Want to taste your sweetness, savor your most private parts. Want to see you reach the sun before I come inside you."

"Oh!" With his hand beneath her hips, he raised her. Set his mouth on the most intimate part of her. Pressed against the hard nub with his tongue. She bucked with the pleasure. "Oh! Fox!" She cried out, her body jumped with shock as well as pleasure. She felt beyond herself. Floated to the stars. Lost conscious thought. As he savored her, his other hand played with the tips of her breasts. Dragons roared to life between her parted legs, shooting flames of urgent passion to extreme heights.

Her fingers wound into his hair, pressing him closer urging him to do more. She felt as if she was outside her body when everything exploded inside.

"Fox!" Fannie's body writhed. Whimpers of ecstasy floated around them, winding in ribbons to bind her to him. She was beside herself as it seemed the sun and the stars collided in a blinding inferno of frenzy. The sensations didn't stop. Seemed to go on and on until she had no more strength.

A moment later he was inside her, thrusting deep, then it seemed deeper still. Fannie clung to him. Her nails bit into his shoulders as she reached that pinnacle again, screaming her pleasure into his mouth. Felt the wet warmth of his seed fill her. Floated on a cloud down to earth. He covered her. His forehead touched upon hers. His deep ragged breaths told her he was just as completed.

Closing her eyes, she was limp. Her muscles jelly while her body shook with the amazing fulfilment, he gifted her. Braced on his forearms, he pushed damp hair from her face. "You were wonderful," Fox told her, before rolling to his side and pulling her with him.

he nestled her head in the hollow of his shoulder. "Me? I didn't do anything special. You orchestrated everything. You were magnificent."

"Ah, but you did. You're remarkable. How do you feel?" He ran a fingertip along her eyebrows then down her nose. "Are you sore? Did I hurt you?"

"I had two…"

"Climaxes," he told her when she paused.

"In almost the same time. How does that happen?" She felt as if she just gave him reason to applaud himself. She didn't care. He could pat himself on the back all he wanted. Now, she was replete, filled with happiness.

Instead, he grunted then rose from the bed. She watched as he walked naked to the tray of food. Brought both the food as well as their wine back to the bed. Fox splashed more wine into her glass then did the same with his.

Fox was naked. He looked splendid to her. He wasn't embarrassed to show himself. Fannie wasn't certain about her nakedness. She scooted under the covers then pulled them up to cover her breasts. It was one thing to be uncovered when she was in the throes of passion. Something else when he wasn't kissing her.

He grinned at her as if he realized what she was thinking "Sustenance. You will need to regain your strength for the next round. Finish the glass of wine. There is more where this came from. My father stocked the room for our basic needs. Did you notice all the flowers? I believe the decorations must have been your sisters doing. They would wish to please your other senses. Jake would have never thought of flowers. Food and drink however, is right up his line of expertise."

Fox sat down beside her. Tugged her into his arms. The back of her head rested on his shoulder. He slipped his hands beneath the blanket covering her. Held her breast in his hands. She sipped air as she found her body quickening once more. It was too soon for the next round, as he told her.

"Until you mentioned it, I didn't notice the decorations. Was looking at you. The flowers are beautiful. Not as beautiful as you. The wine is delicious. The food, there is plenty." Fannie closed her eyes, reveling in the gentle caresses that were igniting her once again.

"Not as delicious as your breasts." He uncovered her. Fox tipped his glass so a drop hit the tip of one. Turned her to give him access to the succulent wine. "Need to taste you again." He licked the wine off then repeated on her other breast.

Her heart began a frantic dance. Heat raged with each minor caress. Soft and gentle then he nipped the crest. She thought she would jump out of her skin. "Don't think I can do this again right now. Fox…" She moaned. Her breath hitched in the back of her throat when he sipped again then again.

"I will give you time to recover. Perhaps you are right. This is far too soon to play with all your delicious parts. You need to catch your breath, gain your strength as do I." Fox brought a piece of cheese to her mouth. "Bite then chew. Wash it down with more wine. We've plenty for the evening. You can have as much as you like. Maybe a bit tipsy would be nice for you as well as fun for me."

"Don't wish to wake up with a headache," she murmured, then drank wine.

"Oh? You've been tipsy before? When did Miss Fannie drink too much? Would be interesting to learn," Fox asked, while he continued to run his hands along the ladder of her ribs, higher to her breasts then weighing the tender globes with his hands. "There is so much I don't know about you."

Fannie didn't wish to answer. Decided why not? "It was a party that Nellie was invited to. I was nervous. She was flirting. We both drank too freely of the punch. Didn't know until later someone spiked the drink. Learned my lesson that one time. Don't wish to do the same again. What do you think Nellie is doing now?" It was hard to keep her sister from her head. She missed her so much. Over the last year, with Maggie and Tessa married, they grew closer.

"Sleeping or trying to go to sleep," Fox replied, while one large hand settled on her belly. "Maybe she and the duchess are chatting."

"Yes, maybe she is pouring her heart out to the duchess. She should be talking with her sisters."

"Who are far too close to her. In time she might reveal her truths. Don't be surprised if she masks what truly happened to her with half truths."

Fannie turned. The tips of her breasts tripped across his chest. She felt the crisp dark hair. She sucked in a gasp of startled air. "Fox, what happened to Nellie? Yes, I might be disturbed by what you tell me. True, the story is hers to tell. Nonetheless, you, a stranger knows what that horrible man did to her. That's not right." She pressed the palm of her hand to his cheek. "I need to learn. Need the information before I see her tomorrow or the next day. Need to understand."

Fannie was upset when he turned away from her, blocking her from seeing his expression. "Let's just say what was told to me was not nice. For Nellie it could have been worse. Nelson didn't have time to do what he must have been planning. Anice was there too."

"What does that mean? It could have been worse." Her brows drew together in a frown directed his way. "What you said was vague. You're dancing around the truth. I don't like guessing games. Tell me. What she experienced wasn't anything like Tessa endured. Was it? He compensated by being brutal. We all know the man has treated his mistresses with contempt. While he keeps them under the guise of making love, rumor has it that he hurts them. The man enjoys hurting women. Did Abernathy hurt Nellie?"

"No, not in the physical variety of causing pain. Mentally, he did quite the job on her. Any woman would be a mess after enduring the hours of not knowing when or what was going to happen to them."

"Tell me, please. You're still ambiguous." Fannie wanted to learn more, then she didn't want to know what happened.

Fox sifted a huge breath of air into his lungs while seeming to think about what he could and could not tell her. "Abernathy made certain there would be no escape for Nellie. He along with Anice brought her to a third story room in a house far outside of Glasgow. The windows were barred. There were no sheets or blankets on the bed. But there were other things."

"He thought she would get through the bars then tie them together making a rope ladder? From the third floor. How absurd." Fannie felt more contempt than she ever thought possible. "What else?"

"When they found her, she was almost naked. All she wore was her shift. I'm certain that was going to come off her sooner than later. Her clothing was shredded and left in a pile on the floor."

"She would be freezing. Left with no clothing." Abernathy would have done to Nellie what Fox did to her. It would have been in the guise of lovemaking but the act would have been force. He intended to rape Nellie while understanding her sister didn't want anything to do with him. He would have forced Tessa too.

"Yes, I'm certain she was cold?" Fox turned away again, his focus seemed to be out the window. He didn't like omitting some of the truth. There were things he just couldn't tell her. Some outright lies he would need to tell her. When he turned back then spoke, his voice broke, "That could have been you. If it had been, I would have killed the man."

"No, you can't mean…no." She found she was shaking her head.

"He didn't chain Nellie to the bed but there were chains lying on the mattress." The half-truth had to be enough. The fact Abernathy chained her as well as how would devastate Fannie. "Abernathy told her he wouldn't use them if she did everything he demanded. If not, he would chain her hands to the headboard and her feet to either post at the other end. This time he would not leave her with the shift covering her. She would be naked. The man is sick."

Fannie felt rage build then a slow sickness enveloped her. Her stomach churned. For a few seconds she was afraid she would lose what she ate. "That still isn't all of it. Where was Mother? You said she was there."

"You shouldn't call that woman mother. Call her Anice or whore. Because she is a whore to the tips of her toes. No, Fannie, what I told you isn't everything. Abernathy had a viewing room where a person could watch what was happening in the bedroom. Anice watched him disrobe her daughter until she was wearing nothing but the chemise. She was going to watch Abernathy rape Nellie. The woman enjoys voyeurism. Especially when her daughters are involved."

"Thank god they got there in time to stop him." Her heart thundered beneath his hand. A wave of dizziness assailed her. "They did get there in time?"

He nodded. "The only reason the duke's men got there before she was forced was because Abernathy wanted Nellie to worry about what he intended to do with her. He meant to tease her with words along with caresses that she would despise. He wanted her to fret about the when of her rape. He didn't believe anyone knew where this new house of his was. I'm so glad the duke is smart as well as meticulous in what he does. He has been following both Anice along with Abernathy since he kidnapped Tessa. For the last year, the duke has made it his mission to catch Lord Abernathy at his foul pastimes then prosecute."

"I'm glad he caught them."

~ * ~

"What do you mean neither man will see me?" Anice raged. Frustration hit her so hard, she needed to scream her outrage. This wasn't fair. Her hands clutched the bars of her cell so tight her knuckles were turning white. She'd never been incarcerated. What the hell was anyone thinking? She was innocent of the kidnapping charge. Nelson was the guilty party. She was a model citizen. Always had been.

This time she was stupid. Wasn't used to being in the wrong place. She trusted a man with an ego that was far too big. Thought he was smarter than everyone. Believed he could get away with anything. When she heard how easy it was for the duke to find his location, she understood they'd never had a chance. Neither she nor Nelson attempted to hide their destination when they left their homes. She spent weeks helping him fix up the little love nest.

The guard cleared his throat a couple of times before he spoke. "Miles Seymore sent the message that as far as he cared you could rot in hell. Hoped you never were able to breathe a drop of fresh clean air in this lifetime. His twin said nearly the same word for word. Wrote that you were never a mother to your children. Armstrong went even farther in the denunciation to say he despised you." The man in charge of the prison told her all the details of the Seymore twins' reaction to her confinement.

"How dare he? The nerve of the man! He owes me. Both the judge along with his twin owe me some time. I gave both of them some of my best years. I was the mother of his daughter! This is how he repays me." Good God, she despised men, all men. They believed they owned the world. Men were only good for one thing.

Anice admitted to herself the truth, she needed to find a good lawyer. Needed to sit down on the dirty mattress and think. Miles was a judge. Wasting her time on him was a mistake. She knew he couldn't be bought for any amount of money, neither could Armstrong. The two were most likely celebrating her captivity. What the devil was she going to do now? Staying in this place was out of the question. The cell they put her in was filthy, reeked of sweat and urine. If or when she left this horrid place, she would figure out a way to seek her revenge on both Nellie along with Fannie. There would be a time as well as a means. Even if she had to travel to that savage land they called the United States, she would make her daughters pay for their disobedience. Daughters were supposed to mind their mothers. Do as directed. The disobedience started with Maggie. The girl should be the first to feel her retribution. Maggie was protected by a wealthy and powerful man as was Tessa. Her two daughters also had the protection of the Duke of Southcliff.

No one would help her out of this predicament. As usual she needed to rely on herself. She was the only person she could count on. If she sent a plea for help to either Kenworthy or Fox Taggart the men would laugh in her face. While she realized The Duke of Southcliff was after Lord Abernathy, the duke also knew what she'd done to her daughters. After he helped Tessa escape, a bond was formed between them all. He would never be helpful. No one else knew.

While she didn't kidnap her girls…how could she be accused of kidnapping? They were her daughters, her children. She could do as she pleased with them since they were hers. The arranged marriage of Lord Abernathy to Maggie, was a good negotiation. From there all of her plans went awry.

Anice intended to find a way to freedom. How? Her liberation might take some time. This place was grimy. She couldn't abide dirt. When she had to relieve herself, she could be seen by anyone who happened to be in the vicinity. Granted, she was the only female in jail at the moment. The guards were male. They could come into this area anytime they pleased. Two of the guards made lewd gestures to her. Told her they could have her anytime they wished. In here and alone she had no defense against those men. If either man tried to take her, the act would be force.

The cot where she was expected to sleep was infected with vermin. The mattress made of straw poked her tender flesh. She didn't want to lie down on the bed. All the blankets they gave her had holes. She cringed at the thought of sleeping on that place they called her bed. Told her she was lucky. There was no alternative. Sleep was necessary.

This was the third day of her detention. Fannie was set to leave today or was her departure tomorrow? Fannie was going to a place called Michigan. Anice had intended to be at the boat when the ship left port. That wasn't going to happen. Now that she and Nelson were restrained, Nellie would stay in Glasgow. As soon as she got out of this place, she would make certain Nellie never saw the light of day again. She would purchase a home far in the highlands. The duke would never follow her there. Anice meant to leave Nellie with a caretaker who could do whatever he pleased with her. She wouldn't tell Abernathy where Nellie was either. The duke would have him followed.

Anice began to make plans, unshakable plans. Plans that would never be destroyed, not even by the Duke of Southcliff.

~ * ~

In another jail cell, Lord Nelson Abernathy was having more luck with the negotiation of his release. While the duke provided irrefutable evidence of his guilt, Nelson had a good lawyer waiting in the wings. The man was smart. If he couldn't get the charges dropped, the sentence would be reduced. After all, he was a lord. He had the money to pay the guards. With money in hand, he would have clean clothes along with better food. He might even be provided with a woman for his entertainment. He would need to pay enough to be certain the lady was clean. Life wouldn't be too bad until he could get out. Once out he intended to seek retribution to the crimes committed against him.

What he hadn't decided yet was if he was going to have the lawyer help Anice. He smiled at the thought of the lady rotting in here. She would be forced to have sex with the guards more than once. Even for a woman of Anice's ilk, she did pick her lovers with meticulous care. Appreciating any of these course jailers and enjoying the sex was absurd. Anice would be certain to fight. Ah, perhaps he could take pity on the woman. When it came to her daughters, she was a better friend than foe. When he didn't have a young lady at his whim, he could always have Anice. Seemed she was always open to his impulses.

Nelson leaned back against the wall, his fingers laced together behind his head. The devil, he'd been in here three long days. The major question in his mind was whether or not Nellie would leave with her sister. If she was to please him, she would remain in this city. Once he got out, after a few months passed, he meant to figure out a way to get to Nellie without being caught. Thought if Nellie left with her sister, he would follow them to this savage land. He would have both Nellie along with Fannie if possible. Nellie would be without protection. It would be more difficult to take Fannie. He should, perhaps, temper his wishes. Either one of the ladies would be enough for his needs.

He'd heard the country was rugged, lots of lakes and forests. Places where a man could lose himself if that was what he wished. A snug log cabin in the wilderness somewhere would be perfect to hide her. No one would find them. When he finished with Nellie or Fannie, he would leave her at the cabin.

There would be fun along this journey he intended. Maybe he'd visit his favorite little whorehouse in London before he left for the states. Wished he could recall the two girls' names who entertained him for a week of mutual pleasures. Taught him about the uses of cocaine. Still used the drug. Gave it to his mistress so she would want him over then over then over again. He liked her insatiable. Would need him until she blacked out with fatigue. He liked the surge of power the drug created. Making love continually until all one could do was crash into a heap on the floor invigorated his senses.

"Nelson," Clive stood outside the bars looking inside, a scowl on his rugged features. Clive was slim. His moustache was impeccably groomed, curling on the ends. His dark red hair showed a bit of gray on the sides. "You got yourself into deep trouble this time, my friend. Don't know how I'm going to get you out of this mess. The judge assigned to your case is none other than Miles Seymore. I can't bribe him. Believe he's already decided you are guilty of the crime. Kidnapping," he stroked his chin while seeming to think. "Did you do it? Kidnap the chit? Need that bit of information first. When I know the truth, I will be better able to defend you. After this one is answered, I've got a couple more questions."

"What do you think? Of course I didn't do it. Women come to me, eager to throw themselves at my feet. You have always understood my position. I'm a good lover and protector. They are after a title. The Duke of Southcliff has trumped up charges against me because he doesn't like me. His men entered my home without my permission. Isn't that against the law?"

"They had papers from the government that gave them authorization. They didn't need yours. Now, did you have the girl locked in the third-floor bedroom?" Clive asked with no emotion in his voice.

"Yes," Nelson understood he couldn't deny this little fact. Her would be rescuers caught him with Nellie locked inside the room. At least he'd not forced her yet. He'd waited. Believed he was in control. The men broke the door down. Took the door right off its hinges. "The Kenworthy twins were there along with a few of the duke's men. Nellie MacRae was willing to have sex with me. She begged me to make love to her in that very room so we could have privacy. The twins wouldn't allow her to be with me. Nellie wanted sex. Lots of sex. She begged. Under those circumstances, what's a poor man to do?" He poked his thumb into his chest. "With me she's a wild creature. Can't ever give her enough. Nellie is just like her mother, voracious in her needs. She spreads her legs for any man who shows interest in her. I wasn't going to be her first lover."

"Will she testify to that fact? What if she says different?"

"Yes, why would she lie? Unless she didn't want her sisters to know what she did then she might not tell the truth." Nelson pondered the questions even though he understood Nellie would say no. She would tell the world she wasn't willing if she was asked. Maybe this time it would serve him best if she left today along with her sister. Later, when he had the upper hand, he could find her. Once on trial, it would be his word against the missing woman's. The duke could not testify that she wasn't willing. He didn't know.

"To save face."

Nelson lifted his shoulders in a masculine gesture of indifference. Setting a lazy half grin on his face, he spoke, "True, a female lies to save her reputation. She would not want the truth known. She went with me and wanted me more than I wanted her. Would never wish for her peers to learn she was willing to open herself up to me."

"Heard there were chains on the bed to keep her pinned down, to spread her legs. She was found wearing her chemise and nothing else."

"That's true. She wasn't naked though she told me she wanted me to strip her, touch her everywhere. It was Nellie who shredded her clothing. When I was arrested, she wasn't chained. Nellie asked me to buy the shackles. She wanted me to make her feel helpless. I am always ready to do whatever the woman I'm with would like even if I dislike the idea. The thought of chaining her to the bed with her legs sprawled apart was repulsive to me. She also told me she wished I would spank her. Bend her over my thighs and hit her little bottom until her butt was red with the print of my hands. Yes, Nellie said corporal punishment would make her more…excited." He'd never spanked Anice. That was something he might enjoy. Didn't care if she would like to be hit or not. Anice did enjoy rough sex. She would probably howl with delight.

"I will tell you the truth. This doesn't look good for either you or the mother. If Miles were not the judge assigned to your case, we would have more wiggle room. His brother, Armstrong, legitimatized Tessa. The Seymore twins consider themselves part of the Kenworthy clan. Right now, from my perspective, you are looking forward to at least a year in jail if not more. Anice will receive less if she finds a good lawyer. I would take her case if that is what you would like."

"Yes, well, let me think about this. If I'm in jail for a year or so, shouldn't she be incarcerated the same amount of time? No, from the outside she might be able to use some of my connections to smooth the way to a shorter sentence for me. I am a lord of the realm. Go see her. Tell her what I expect of her."

If either one of the Seymore's had an accident, nothing lethal, just something that would keep him out of the courts for a few months, his fate would improve. Perhaps he could arrange a disaster. Yes, but he couldn't tell his lawyer.

Clive needed to be above reproach.

Chapter Eight

"We are here." Fox helped Fannie then Nellie down from the wagon. The threesome stood in front of his home.

Fannie's hands were set beneath her chin as she gazed upon her new home. "This is a lot more than I expected," she grinned at him. "Thought your house might be made of logs. Didn't expect a porch going around the outside, chairs on the veranda too. I'll bet in the summer; the breeze is beautiful. Do you like to sit on the terrace at night to look at the stars? Are they the same here? I used to stand on the balcony to look for different constellations. Can you see the big dipper and the north star and…"

Fox set his finger to her lips. "Too many questions sweet. Yes, to all of them."

"Tonight, can we sit on the porch and look at the sky? Feel the soft breeze coming down from the hills."

"Whatever you would like." Fox hoped Fannie love the land, his house, along with the men he employed. The porch excited her. She was precious. He wanted to tell her he would make love to her there.

A little over two months passed while they journeyed to his home. She'd been sick on the ship. Fox didn't know if was because of seasickness or the baby. Though both scenarios might have been at play. He felt sorry for her. Sometimes the only thing that kept food in her belly was when she stood at the bow staring at the horizon.

"You are proud of this place. You love the land. I'm certain I will too," Fannie said looking at her husband, her eyes alight with happiness. "I see why. Your home is beautiful. You will treat us to a tour? I'd like to see everything including the outbuildings. You never told me anything about the rest of your place. It's huge. Is there a room close to the master where we can put the baby when he arrives."

Fannie always called the baby he. Fox wondered if that was true. Did a mother have this sixth sense about the gender of their baby? He placed her hand in his before he spoke from the heart. "This place is part of my soul. I grew up in this home. Of course, I've expanded the main building, built on. Added the upstairs." Fox pulled Fannie into his arms. Wanted this first kiss in the clean air of his homeland. His lips met hers with a gentle touch before he deepened the kiss. Parted her lips so he could delve inside her warmth. She whimpered. Her fingers wound into his hair.

"Fox," she whispered his name as he claimed her as his in front of his people. She was soft as well as willing to kiss him with his employees looking on. That fact pleased him. Before he pulled her into his arms, he saw Ol' Sam along with Rory. There were others watching, all friends. The men he worked with. They would know what this woman meant to him.

She opened for him. Touched her tongue with his. With a solid groan of desire, he closed his eyes. Splayed his hand on her back then lower to cup her delicious little fanny with his hand. He was sending an irrevocable message.

This woman is mine.

"Fox…" she moaned as he pushed away to look at her. Kissed the tip of her nose, her mouth, then traced the line of her brows with the tip of his finger.

"Fannie," he spoke with a soft sound to his voice. He let her go. Turned her to meet his friends. Fox held out his hand. The man who strode to him, accepted the greeting then hit him on his back. Fox grinned, pleased with the homecoming. More men were gathering. "Rorik, how the hell have you been? Trust the men are prepared to start cutting timber. I will be ready before the end of the week. Damn, I've missed this place. Missed everyone here."

He didn't want to leave Fannie at the house when he left for the lumber camp. Hell, they were still newlyweds. Thought he would bring her with him to the base camp if she was willing. On off hours, they could explore the places he liked the best. He could teach her how to swim as well as fish. Perhaps she could learn to ride. Horses were the best means of transportation in these parts. May was fast approaching. She was due the end of august or the first of September. Would she be willing to leave Nellie alone? They would need to discuss this plan of his. Nellie could come if she wanted to live in a tent in the wilderness. That was fine with him. She would need to sleep in a different tent. He wasn't going to share the tiny space with Fannie's sister.

"Everything is a go on my end. We can start tomorrow or next week. Whatever you like." He looked from one lady to the other. "Who is this?" Rorik looked at her again then appeared to study her sister. Nellie caught his attention. He smiled at Nellie, tipping his hat. Nellie looked away, a frown marring her lovely face. Appeared Nellie didn't want anything to do with this handsome man who seemed besotted with her at first sight. "Who are these two beautiful ladies? Appears as if one has been claimed. You didn't waste any time, Fox. When is the babe due?"

"You noticed," Fox said deadpan, knowing the man watched them kiss. Would see the beginning swell of her belly which he adored touching. He could hardly wait until she waddled and he had to help her rise from the chair where she was sitting. Fox wrapped his arm around her, pulling her next to him. Felt the heat of her small form. Set his hand on the curve of her hip. "Nothing gets by you, Rory. What a good eye you have for the obvious." Keeping his arm around Fannie, Fox did the introductions. "Fannie Taggart this is Rorik Haraldsson. We call him Rory. He is a friend as well as a partner. A lady's man from the top of his blond head and clear blue eyes to the tips of his huge feet."

Rory grunted.

"Fannie, nice to meet you. And who is this other exceptionally lovely lady? Not another wife I pray." Rory winked, his grin bordering on little boy mischievous. Fox realized he was setting his sights on Nellie. He would have a hell of a wall to break down. If anyone could shatter the barricade she wrapped around herself, Rory could.

"Nellie MacRae, this is Rory. Nellie is Fannie's sister. She traveled with us. Seems she was eager to visit this beautiful land of all the lakes. She is single but not available." Fox shot out the last part in hopes Rory would not set his sights on Nellie. He would only hurt her. Rory wasn't a man ready to settle down with one woman. If he was, Rory was perfect for Fannie's sister.

"Enchanted," Rory picked up her hand then placed a kiss on the back. "It's nice to meet you, Miss Nellie."

Nellie pulled away from him frowning, sticking her hand in the pocket of her gown. She let out an unladylike snort before she spoke. "You are rude, sir. I did not ask to be manhandled. You have no right to touch me without my permission." Nellie picked up her skirts as she walked to the front porch. Not going inside, she sat on one of the chairs on the front porch.

Rory tipped back his hat then watched, grinning as if pleased by the first encounter with a shrew. He let out a low whistle that sounded much like astonishment. "She's got a lot of starch and vinegar, that one. Beautiful but untouchable and not available is what she shouted to me loud and clear. We will see how that goes. While I've been known to be rude a time or two, wasn't impolite this go-around. What's wrong with her?" Rory asked, still watching Nellie as if fascinated by the vision in front of him. She was in the rocking chair, her hands on the arm rest.

Fox didn't know what was going through Rory's head. Whatever it was, the challenge Nellie issued was obvious. Rory looked as if he meant to address the test, meet the challenge head on.

His money was on Rory. "It's a long story. Nothing wrong that time won't heal. We hope with passage of days it will help her get over the past. I will tell you part of her story tomorrow when we ride out to take a look at the lumber camp. Otherwise, it is up to Nellie to tell the tale."

"Would you like to start at dawn as usual?" Rory was laughing inside. Fox knew it.

The man would understand he'd be seeing to his wife at dawn, maybe even an hour later. "No, going to initiate my wife to our big bed. Give me an extra two hours for my enjoyment. We are newlyweds. Also wish to make certain everyone is introduced to her. She will be mistress here. The men will be expected to take orders from her."

"Imagine if I had a pretty little gal such as this one for my wife, I'd be thinking along the same lines." Rory was still watching Nellie. She wasn't sitting in the rocking chair now. Nellie leaned against the railing, waiting for them to finish the business at hand.

Seemed she was always waiting for something. On the trip she said few words. Spent the majority of her time in her cabin, either that or staring out at the ocean. One of the lieutenants onboard tried to make conversation. Nellie walked away from the lad. The lass wasn't playing hard to get. This person was who she was now, not who she used to be.

"You're a partner?" Fannie asked Rory, as if trying to change the conversation from Nellie to something mundane. Fannie would not wish to drag Nellie into this man's attention. "Do you live as well as work here?" She was looking at the house then back to him. "Where do you stay?"

"If you're worried about your sister's virtue, don't be. Don't make a habit of pursuing women who aren't willing. Especially women who don't like me. Seems as if your sister has been worked over pretty hard then laid down cheap. Don't burrow into other's privacy either. If she has secrets, they are hers to keep or to share. The choice to do so is up to her." Rory lifted his broad shoulders in what appeared to be an indifferent shrug, all the while looking at Nellie.

"Does that mean you live here?" Fannie asked, her curiosity was bound to get the best of her if she continued the pursuit.

"No, I've got a home about twenty miles north of here. My property line starts where Fox's ends. We cut lumber both places. Logs we cut float down the river to the mill in the village you must have ridden through on your way here. However, at the moment I am living in this house. My friend is kind. He is letting me stay until I can get my place fixed up enough to move into. The home is bare of essentials. Needs a woman's touch." Again, he looked in Nellie's direction.

Fox was intrigued by the expressions floating on Rory's face every time Nellie was brought up. He was trying not to show interest in the lass. His friend wasn't fooling him. If Nellie showed any softening toward him, she would find herself being courted by the big man. As far as he knew, Rory had never courted a woman in his life. "Rory is fixing up the house. 'Bout all it has inside is a stove, a big table, two chairs in case he has company, along with a big soft bed."

"I see," Fannie said on a laugh, her eyes twinkling at Rory before her humorous gaze returned to light on him.

"Doubt it," Fox told her as he kept his hoot of laughter behind his teeth. Fannie was playing right into his hands. Hands that would enjoy exploring all of her soft body.

Fox felt a tightening in his loins. Maybe before they turned their attention to mundane life, they would try out that bed he needed to initiate.

Rory could keep himself company. Nellie would find a way to amuse herself. They had a good hour before dinner.

"I'm ready to start that tour of my new home. Afterward, suppose I'll have to see if I can find something to burn for dinner. We could have tea. I don't scald water. If I'm to be the cook around here, someone will need to teach me. If not, we will all starve," Fannie said with a little snort of laughter.

It wasn't just food she burned. His Fannie burned him to a crisp every time they were close enough to touch. Scorched him from the inside out. Sometimes they didn't even need to touch to set fire roaring in his loins. "She can't cook worth a damn but that isn't why I married the little lady. She's pretty fine at other endeavors necessary to keep a husband pleased." Fox winked, a devilish grin on his face while he watched her color turn brighter.

Fannie elbowed him in the stomach. He made an obliging grunt for her benefit. Then she spoke with a sweet pure voice coated with sugar. "You must have a cook. Fox, you didn't tell me if you can cook or not. If you can, maybe I should oversee the cutting of the timber and you can do the wifely duties around the house. Believe an apron would become you. Perhaps one that is a soft rose color."

"Whoo…eee! I can see Fox now, wearing just a bright pink apron. You might freeze your big butt off. Bet this pretty little lady of yours will keep you warm all night long." Rory said as he looked from his longtime friend to the new wife. "You can dish it out. Is your sister as adept?" His gaze shot back to the woman ignoring him.

"I wouldn't know about that. Perhaps if you get to know her better, you will bring her out of the shell she has enclosed herself within. However, if you hurt her, you'll have me to deal with. At the moment, Nellie is fragile. She is an innocent. However, she has been treated to more than a dose of what most women can endure. You strike me as a man who has been around the block a few times. Seen as well as done most anything."

Hearing the exchange between his wife and his friend, Fox decided he needed to bring the conversation back to them. He didn't mind sparring with his wife. As far as he was concerned, Nellie was off limits to Rory. "Not in this life will I wear an apron." Couldn't picture himself wearing only an apron. Might prove interesting if his wife was dressed the same. Her fanny was delicious. Tasty. A little morsel of delight. Her beautiful breasts would round out the picture.

"I might need to make you eat those words." Her voice was still filled with syrupy sweetness. "Believe if that was all…" she stopped, forgetting they were not alone. She'd said too much already.

"Have a housekeeper. If you would like to keep the woman in your employ, this is your choice. Also, a cook who does well enough." He turned to direct his next comments to Rory. "My wife, Fannie, is worth her weight in gold. With what she can do in that big bed of mine I will be a satisfied man every night as well as every morning. Pleased even if she burns my meals." He laughed when this time he received a scowl from her pretty pink face. "Always tell you the truth. You look pretty wearing pink. This particular shade becomes you. The rose is a perfect match to other…" He left off, knowing he was treading in dangerous territory. If they continued in this vein, she might never forgive him. Not that he needed forgiveness to seduce her.

Her back just as stiff as Nellie's had been, she picked up her skirts to march to the house. Seemed to have had enough of the sexual banter. She could never win that game. Didn't have enough experience with verbal teasing. He would remind her later tonight.

Rory's bark of laughter seemed to have caught her attention. If possible, Fannie stiffened even more. She didn't turn to look back. Fox understood Fannie needed to get away from male dominated territory. She needed a respite to lick her wounds, battle scars he would attend to later.

"Believe I will see to my horse." Rory made the comment, Fox felt positive, to give them some time to explore the house as well as the big bed upstairs. While Fox didn't believe Fannie was angry, she did need her temper soothed a bit. He would kiss her until she sighed into his mouth with the enjoyment he gave her. Perhaps caress a few of her most sensitive places. He did enjoy pleasing his woman.

When he entered, Fannie was standing in the parlor speaking with Nellie in hushed voices. They were so intent, neither noticed his entrance. Nellie's face was too pale. Fannie's sister needed to forget the past. Should forge a new future. For a few skips of his heart, he thought to turn around then walk outside. He could join Rory seeing to his horse. Not that either mount needed attention. His stable hands were good at their jobs.

Something untoward affected Nellie. All he could assume was Rory was the reason for Nellie's discomfort along with the sudden withdrawal. He wasn't positive what to do. Rory was always welcome at his home. He wasn't going to change his friend's status because Rory made Nellie uncomfortable. She would need to find a way to get used to the big man.

"Fox?" Nellie noticed him first. She spoke to him with a clear even voice. "Your friend is rude. I don't wish to see him again. You…" she quit speaking, seeming to realize she infringed on his territory. She was a guest in his home. She had only the rights he wished to dole out.

If Nellie was giving him an ultimatum, he wouldn't deliver on her request. "Rory is staying for dinner as well as the night. He brought down the buck we are going to eat. That venison is going to be in a stew to be served here. If you don't wish to join us, you can have dinner in your room. I'm sorry, Nellie. You will need to get used to his company. Rory is a fixture here in my home. His own home is not ready yet to live in except for a night or two when he is delivering supplies. With the trees needing to be cut, he must stay here. The land we are working on is too far from his place to travel daily." Fox drug in a deep breath of air. They needed to discuss what would be happening when he lived at the camp. Bottom line, Fox wanted his wife with him. Fannie wouldn't wish to leave Nellie alone. Well, hell, Nellie could come too.

"Very well, tonight I will have dinner in my room. I've thought about this. I would like the one bedroom on the first floor if that meets with your approval."

"That's fine with me," Fox told her.

"Any reason why?" Fannie asked. "Seems as if you might be more comfortable in one of the larger rooms on the second floor. Fox did tell me the one you've asked for is the smallest one available. There is no reason for you to take the smallest."

With a quick tilt to her head, Nellie explained, directing her words in Fox's direction. "You and Fannie deserve privacy. It won't be that much longer when there will be an addition to your family. I'm a third wheel. Maybe if I'm in the bedroom downstairs, I won't be in the way."

"Oh, you're not in the way. We wanted you to come with us. I would have missed you more than you would have known if you stayed in Glasgow.

Besides, there was nothing there for you. You said those words yourself. Didn't wish to see Dillon or your friends who believed the two of you would marry soon."

"I am a third wheel everywhere I go. Enjoy your dinner." Her voice along with her back were stiff, starched to the extreme. She started toward the downstairs room.

Fox's next words stopped her. "I will have your trunks brought to your room. If there is anything you need, let me know." Worried about her, Fox watched her walk away. Nellie's face was so white it frightened him. She wasn't making a smooth adjustment to this new living situation. More than two months had passed since they left Glasgow, since her kidnapping, since the breakup. Seemed Nellie still mourned the loss of Dillon. She needed to begin a new chapter to her life. If she remained in her bedroom, a new beginning would never happen. A person needed fresh air and sunlight, people around them to blossom.

"She should be eating with us. Don't want her to slip inside herself," Fannie said, the sound of her voice hollow. "I'm worried she will never be her vivacious self again. Want to hear her laughter. A giggle or two wouldn't be out of order. For some reason Rory seems to frighten her. He is a large man. Though… it must have something to do with what she went through with Lord Abernathy. She's never told me the entire story. Keeps what happened to her in that third-floor bedroom bottled up inside."

"Why doesn't she like Rory? That is a good question. It's passing strange. Everyone likes him. Never seen a woman turn away. He wasn't rude to her. We both know the truth of the matter." Fox asked but he was pretty darn certain he knew the answer to his question. "Nothing is making sense. Rory attracts women as if he is a magnet."

"He's a man. A man who doesn't have a wife. The twinkle in his eyes when he looked at her spoke volumes. There is more. Positive I don't need to elaborate. She must be frightened of meeting another Dillon or a Lord Abernathy. Both those men are handsome. However, Rory outshines all men except you."

"I understand. She can't be afraid of single men all her life. If she is, she will never find someone for herself. She is beautiful. There are a lot of men who will find her attractive, a woman worth courting." If something or some man didn't happen along to change her perspective on life, she would never come out of her shell.

"It's only been a couple of months since the kidnapping along with the dissolution of a relationship she thought would last a lifetime," Fox said as he tried to think of the words to coax Nellie out of her bedroom to have dinner with the family.

"You're asking me to give her time," Fannie murmured her voice soft. "I'm trying. I've come to realize moments alone with her thoughts is what she needs. Doing so is hard."

"Yes. That's what I'm asking." Fox was immersed in the conversation. He didn't hear the two people they were talking about enter the room.

"Am I interrupting?" Rory stood in the doorway, his hat in his big hands. His attention was on the woman standing behind them. "I don't wish to frighten you. If that's what my presence does, I apologize. I'll try to stay away from you so you're not scared." His pause spoke volumes when he voiced aloud what he was thinking. "Never, ever, met a woman who was afraid of me."

"We were talking about Nellie's aversion to you," Fox offered while he rubbed his hand on the back of his neck. "Don't understand why."

Tension seemed to be radiating from the big man. "Ah…I've never had a female take an intense as well as sudden dislike to me. Don't understand either. Was it something I said?" Rory appeared baffled. He was still looking at Nellie.

"No…" Fannie offered. "I'm afraid we can't talk about what happened to my sister. Before we left Scotland Nellie had one bad encounter with a young man who she was fond of then another horrific confrontation with a man who we all detest. The healing appears to be taking longer than any of us expected. Nellie is free to speak of what happened if she chooses but we are not."

"It's nothing you did," Fox told him, in another attempt to explain as well as reassure. "Maybe you do terrify her. All that golden hair atop your outrageously tall body. A person who is too handsome might frighten women. Perhaps it's the width of your shoulders that scares her witless. You could try to stoop down a little. Make yourself smaller. Walk like an old man.

Doing so might help render you less harmless in her eyes."

Fannie tossed a pillow at him. Fox ducked. The pillow landed on the floor behind him. "You are almost as large a man as Rory. The twins are big too. Nellie was never afraid of a large man. Dillon wasn't quite as big. Nonetheless, one could never call him a small man. You, my dear husband, are climbing up the wrong tree."

Nellie appeared in front of the tossed pillow. After picking it up then holding the pillow against her chest, she stood stiff with her hands clasped tight on the pillow. "You all are talking about me. I heard every word. Don't appreciate you speaking about me behind my back."

"Oh, Nellie, I'm sorry. I didn't mean anything by it. Nothing we said was untrue. What we all want is for you to be more like yourself. Didn't know you were there," she said with an apologetic note. "Don't imagine my ignorance makes a bit of difference."

"I know. To set the record straight. I'm not afraid of Rorik. I don't like him. That's all." With that said, she left the room again.

Fox watched Rory sift in a deep breath of air. "She's got backbone. I like fortitude in a woman. She is beautiful as well as fascinating." Then in a quieter voice. "I like Nellie. I'm making it my mission to discover her truths then change her mind about me. Believe we could be good together." Held up his hands to stop Fannie from sharing her next opinion. "Promise I won't hurt her. As you say, she is fragile. Never harmed a woman in my life. Also…I won't make false promises to her. She will always know where our relationship stands…if we have a relationship."

"Dinner is ready." Ol' Sam stood in the drawing room, a large spoon in his hands with the announcement. "Got venison stew along with the best biscuits you've ever eaten. Everything is hot. Best the two of you come along now before it gets cold. Don't like cold food."

His biscuits were always good. "Be right there. Will you take a plate to Nellie. She doesn't wish to eat with us."

"Yes, sir."

After they finished eating, Fox and Fannie sat on the porch swing in the front of the house looking at the stars. Rory left them alone. He decided to walk down to the stream that flowed by the house. Told them he needed to plot his strategy. Fox didn't know what Rory meant by plotting strategy except what he was thinking would revolve around courting Nellie. If Nellie never came out of her room, Rory would never get a chance to use this so-called stratagem on her. She would never fall for his dashing good looks or his fatal charm.

Fannie let out a long slow breath of air. "The stars are so bright. I feel as if I can reach out to touch each one." Fannie set her head on Fox's shoulder. Her body pressed against his. "They are much brighter than in Glasgow."

"That's because there are no city lights to dim them." Fox pointed into the sky then let his hand slip beneath the blanket covering them. He never found a chance this afternoon to try out the bed. "Can you find the big dipper and the north star?"

Fannie's giggle was soft. "Yes, they are up there in the sky, all connected." She turned to Fox, "What is going to happen to Nellie? I'm so frustrated I want to shake her until she returns to her old self."

"I don't know. I believe Rory will be good for her. Don't think he'll allow her to wrap herself up so tight she becomes a shallow version of herself. That man could be her new beginning." Fox traced Fannie's eyebrows, something he enjoyed doing almost as much as making love to her. Well, maybe not almost. "Do you wish to come with me to the lumber camp? I would like for you to do so. We will be there for the next month. The work doesn't ever seem to stop. If you don't, might not see you except a couple of times during the month."

"Your work is dangerous. Isn't it?" Fannie's fingers were playing with the blanket covering them. "I don't like to know you are in danger."

Fox needed to still those nervous fingers, give her a different direction to think. She was anxious. He didn't blame her. "Yes, however, I seldom do the cutting of the big trees. The lumberjacks are skilled in a lot of different areas. Rory and I oversee the work, give directions. After the orders are given, we stay out of the way of the falling trees." His little bit of humor didn't seem to be appreciated.

She sucked air then glowered his way. "If I go with you, what will I do while you are working?" His fingers enclosed hers. "I would be bored to tears if all I can do is sit in the tent worrying about you. Did you think about what I would do?"

He brought them to his mouth. Kissed the knuckles. Opened her hand so he could trace the lines in her palm with the tip of his finger. "Whatever you would like. Ol' Sam could start teaching you how to cook. Meridith, Paul's wife, can teach you about herbs as well as other foods that can be collected from the land. She knows the perfect mushrooms that will delight the taste buds of even the pickiest eaters."

"When will I see you? You will be busy. Wouldn't it be better to stay here with Nellie? We could chat. Talk about…" she lifted her shoulders. "Don't know what we would discuss. Certainly not our past."

"We will have the nights all to ourselves. During the day, there will be some time for us since we work in shifts. I'm going to teach you how to swim as well as fish. Paul oversees the logs going into the river. They will float downstream to the mill. We have a holding tank or sometimes we call it a log pond, where they gather until there are enough to send all at once. The pond can be dangerous if a person gets in the way of the logs that are floating downriver."

She tilted her head, seeming to digest what he told her. "I'm not certain. Swimming…you say. If you are teaching me to swim, what am I wearing?" His hands settled on her belly. He massaged the bump, wishing the babe would move.

Fox didn't want to answer knowing she would balk with his answer. He didn't need to close his eyes to visualize her breasts swaying with the movement of the water. Clearing his throat, he forged ahead. "Nothing. You cannot swim in a dress. You would sink. A person is supposed to float on top of the water. The extra fabric would send you under. A chemise might work. Nonetheless the fabric, once wetted, would hide nothing. You might as well swim in the buff. If you did, you would still have dry clothing to put on when we finished the lesson. Your choice." Fox brought his hand higher to cup her breast. "I love the feel of your breasts in my hands. They are larger now, more sensitive." Sighing with pleasure he ran his palm along the hard crest. He liked the change of subject. Fannie was mulling over his suggestion. He didn't know what she'd decide. Whatever her decision, she would be naked by the time the lesson ended. Might as well start that way.

"We can't make love out here in the moonlight even though this setting is romantic. Someone might see us." Disregarding her words,

Fannie's nimble fingers played with the top button on his shirt.

Fox chuckled, his voice soft with a husky cadence. He felt her shiver of pleasure as he continued to caress. "Who will stop us? I don't see anyone around. Rory has gone for a walk. He enjoys watching the little stream behind the house rush by. Moonlight will play on the water. He might even be swimming naked. The rushing stream now is frigid. Comes from snow melt. Refreshing. Would you like to take a dip in the stream?"

"What I would like is to learn to do something practical. I feel useless. Have no skills. Can't sew a straight seam. Cooking seems to be my nemesis. Besides, you have people to do all the tasks I mentioned as well as everything else. I've wracked my brain trying to think of what I could do." Fannie let out a puffy little sigh of displeasure.

"No one else can please me as you do. Don't want anyone else in our bed, beneath me, part of me. In a short time, you will be busy with the baby. Believe rearing the child is beneficial. The baby will take up most of your time." Fox didn't like the fact she felt useless. Anice's daughters were taught nothing useful. She did have an extensive education. She could speak three languages. "Let me see, you could have women friends. There are wives of the men who work for me. Most of them come to the camp. They don't wish to be away from their men. Would you like to get to know more than Meridith? Believe all the wives will be thrilled to meet the bosses' wife. My housekeeper loves to chat up a storm. Tells everyone she is better at listening than talking."

"Yes, maybe Nellie would enjoy having a few friends. Female companionship would be nice for both of us. We did make friends in Glasgow in that year when Tessa tormented Jason to the point he didn't know what to do about her. Nellie was always on the go. There was never a night except on Sundays that she wasn't out and about flitting with her friends. She was popular."

Fannie turned. Placed her hands on either side of Fox's face. "Kiss me. I want you to make love to me. Now!"

Her urgency astonished him. To his delight, she was losing her shyness. He was surprised as well as very pleased by the invitation. "Here? On the front porch? Where anyone tripping along that path might see us?" he asked, while he looked into the clear blue of her beautiful eyes.

"Yes. How? Don't wish anyone to stumble upon us. Maybe we should go upstairs to the bedroom. If we stayed here, Nellie could come out of her room. Rory could return. Ol' Sam might wander from the bunkhouse to have a smoke."

"They won't. Even if they do, they won't see anything. There is strategy in this. Since you asked, yes, I will delight in the lovemaking on the porch. As you said the setting is romantic. Want to see your lovely features when you reach your climax, moonlight glowing on your cheeks, on the tops of your breasts, reflecting in your eyes."

Reaching beneath her gown, Fox was surprised to find nothing there except his warm wife. "Naughty. You are not wearing a stitch beneath your dress. I like that. Just like the night of our wedding." Fox pushed the small sleeves down her arms, freeing her breasts. She wasn't wearing a chemise either. He touched the hard tip with his tongue. At the first contact, the little ripple of feminine pleasure delighted his male instincts.

"Yes, knew the idea would please you."

"Your suggestion does." He picked her up, turning her. She straddled him. Her gown flowed over her legs. If anyone came upon them, they might guess what they were doing. They would see nothing except her breasts. He would cover them.

With a husky groan, he freed himself from his trousers. In the next instant Fannie was part of him. "This is going to be fast and messy. Hold on." His mouth closed over hers. He massaged the small knot.

Fannie obeyed. She clung to his shoulders. Her head was thrown back seeking her pleasure. "This is wonderful."

He was deep inside her. The muscles of her core kissed his length. "Now!" Fox thrust once then twice. Again, he covered her mouth with his as he spilled his seed inside her and she fragmented, bucking on him, crying out her pleasure.

She calmed. Her forehead rested against his. She was breathing in quick little spurts of air. "Fox…" she managed to say.

"You're going to be the death of me. Next time I will have a slow hand. Promise. The loving will be the first time in our bed. I will make certain it lasts and lasts then lasts some more." He was thinking of the way she would look with the length of her golden hair spilled across his pillow.

She would be naked, her legs parted for him. The small bump that was his child would please him. He didn't want to hurt her. Talking to the midwife was imperative to her well-being. Must do that as soon as possible. Maybe tomorrow if they returned soon enough.

"I don't care about slow. You…" Didn't seem she could say what was on her mind.

"Let's go up to bed. It's getting late. Tomorrow, Rory and I are going to ride up to the lumber camp. Check out the place. I would take you except…"

"I can't ride a horse." Fannie ran her fingers through his hair, her nails scraping across his scalp. "We have all our clothes on. That doesn't seem right."

"Best way to make love in public…with clothing on. Unless you are an exhibitionist, it's the best way. I want to touch your breasts, taste as well as explore you everywhere. Best we go to the room now. Don't want anyone but me seeing your beautiful breasts."

"Alright. I want that too. Need to taste you too. Suck you into my mouth. Can I pretend you are my favorite candy?"

"Enchantress."

~ * ~

The next day, Fannie sat in the kitchen sipping strong black coffee. This drink was what her husband preferred. Tea was her preference. She put so much milk and sugar in her cup the coffee was pale not black as it was when she poured the liquid into her cup. With each sip she grimaced. Fox told her she would come to enjoy the coffee. Always gave him an extra boost in the morning. She didn't think so.

"I'm Agnes. Mr. Taggart told me you wish to have people to chat with, your sister too. Your husband doesn't want you to be lonely." She paused long enough to give her a look from the top of her head to the tips of her toes. "I'm not much of a chinwagger. Nonetheless, I fancy myself a good listener. What would you like to know about these parts? Ask me anything. I will do my best to answer. I have lived in this piece of Michigan all my life, born as well as raised here."

Setting the cup down, she smiled at the older lady with the hugest bosom she'd ever seen, coupled with well-rounded plump hips. Her smile lit up the room. Agnes' hair was graying. It was pulled back in a tight bun. Her brown eyes twinkled with unsaid humor. The apron she wore was pink, of all colors.

The fact made her think about her conversation with her husband the night before. Fox would look delicious wearing a pink apron and nothing else. With the wicked thought hovering in her mind, her body thrummed to life. The nothing else part was Rory's addition to the conversation. After he mentioned it, he winked at her.

Unable to stop herself, her hand on her lips to stifle the sound, Fannie giggled. "Oh my…" she murmured at the vision filling her head.

Agnes cast her a glance that asked what was so funny. She didn't use words to ask her the question. Imagined she was coming to conclusions. Sending her a frown, she spoke, "Now, you won't be doing any cleaning on my watch. You're the mistress of this house. You give me directions then I follow them. If I disagree, I will tell you why. What happens next will still be your decision." She reached into the pocket of the apron to bring out a dust rag. "Right now, I intend to dust the shelves. We can talk while I am working."

Fannie cast the older woman a half-smile. Agnes intrigued her, understanding she would speak her mind. "I want to be honest with you. You won't ask but I imagine you wondered what I was giggling at." Trying to tell her without telling her everything, she used a few moments to put her thoughts in order.

"You can speak your mind on any subject. Told you I was a good listener. Don't ever judge or spread gossip." Picking up a vase she wiped it down before setting it back in its place.

"It is funny. You might get a giggle out of the story." Fannie truly didn't understand how she had the nerve to speak up. Casting a quick look at her cooling coffee, she began, "Yesterday, I told my husband I should take care of his lumber camp and he should do all my duties. Told him how good he would look in a pink apron. Now, you are wearing a pink apron. Wish I could borrow it for the evening. Rory said…" She stopped herself before she spoke of Fox modeling the apron naked.

Agnes waved the dust rag at her. "I can well imagine what that young pup said. Rory can be a scoundrel. Suppose he intimated that the apron was all your husband would be wearing. That young whipper snapper has a one-track mind. All the girls swoon after him. He soaks up all they wish to give him. Never tells a lady no."

"How did you know?" Fannie found herself giggling again. "How did you guess that is what he said? I would have never…not in a million years think of something like that."

The housekeeper waggled a pudgy finger in her direction, coupled with an all-knowing smile that enhanced her plump cheeks. "Now, if I had a husband as well-put-together as yours, I would wish to see him wearing this apron and nothing else. Believe he would be a tasty morsel to a beautiful young woman. My man would have never complied with my request. He could be a real prude at times. After we were married for a while, I felt it was my duty to loosen him up. Neither Rory or Fox are prudes. They would be thrilled to prance around wearing nothing but an apron in front of their woman. Mind you…they would never want anyone else to see them."

The coffee Fannie just sipped sputtered from her mouth in all directions. Little droplets all over the tablecloth. She would never be able to imagine Fox prancing. "I'm surprised. Nay shocked. You read my mind. the prancing part…it…well…I don't have words. Don't believe either Fox or Rory are capable of prancing." With her words, Fannie felt the heat of her embarrassment rise to the roots of her hair. She never expected her imagination to be so obvious.

"Not hard. You might not believe this but I was young once." Agnes got a dreamy expression on her cheeks that also appeared to have a rosy glow of embarrassment about them. "My husband was also a handsome man; a prude, yes, but a handsome man. Wish he were still with me. Tell you what, tomorrow I'll have this apron of mine laundered. You can have it for the week, longer if you wish. Might be too much fun for you young newlyweds." Agnes held up her hand to stop her. Fannie closed her mouth. "Besides, I've got plenty of aprons. See if he'll do your bidding. If I was a gambling woman, I'd bet my last dollar he would do whatever you ask as long as the doing is kept in the bedroom as well as the telling of the deed behind your teeth."

Fannie was mopping up the milky coffee that spattered across the table top. She smiled at her. "You would do that for me? I promise I will let you know if he puts the apron on for me." Fannie knew she had a dreamy expression on her face. The image Agnes created was too poignant. Agnes would be a good friend. She was certain of the fact.

"Of course, dear, you are such a sweetling. You will have to tell me as much as you dare as to what he did. In turn, I promise never to say anything." She set her finger against her lips. "Mums the word. His reaction when you show this to him then make your request will no doubt be precious. True, it would be nice to learn what happens. I'll bet after the two of you laugh your heads off, he'll make you wear the apron naked. He will also see to your pleasure. The night won't be wasted. Will be one you all will remember for the rest of your lives though the evening will not be one you tell your children or grandchildren about."

"Yes, I would guess you are right in your assumptions. He does enjoy compromising me. Would wear it for me if he gets a promise from me in return. You know, he thinks when he teaches me to swim, I should wear nothing." Fannie blurted the next piece of information. Seemed it had been a deuced long time since she spoke so openly with anyone except her sisters.

"Of course, he will wish to make love to you in the water. Why would you wear clothing that needs to be removed? There is nothing better than when there is nothing between you and your man than a thin film of liquid."

"What if someone comes along? I would be mortified to the tips of my toes. No, best to keep my chemise on while he is teaching. Truly, he would want to make love in the lake?" She didn't know about doing that. Seemed Fox liked to make love in all kinds of different places. A lake? She would need to think about that prospect. "I'm glad you mentioned about the lovemaking to me. Now, at least, I'm prepared."

"Believe if your man is willing to wear a pink apron, he will wish to make love in the lake," Agnes paused for a few blinks, "If the water is warm enough, that is. This time of year, the lake is still a bit chilly."

"Oh?" They were grazing into unfamiliar territory. This wasn't something she understood. Last night on the porch was risky. She wasn't positive about anything else he might come up with. "I don't know," she finished on a lame note.

"Your man will find a means to take the choice from you. He will seduce you until you don't possess a coherent thought in your beautiful head. All men seemed to be born understanding how to seduce a woman to get their way. Mark my words." She waved a finger at her. "You will see. The two of you have only been wed a short time. Understand you left for here almost the day after you were wed…" Agnes paused then as if she was speculating about something.

Fannie sipped air. "Yes, we were rushed. Fox needed to return. Said he'd been away for far too long. We couldn't wait to plan a large wedding. Anyway, it was best we do it without my mother learning. She would have caused a scene." Fannie knew she said too much. Didn't wish for anyone to learn the babe was conceived weeks before the wedding. Imagined Rory guessed at that fact. The man wouldn't care. Agnes might take exception.

"When is your wee babe due? I'm also the midwife around here. You must take care of yourself. Don't do anything too strenuous. While love making is fine there are other activities that might need to be avoided."

"Such as?" Fannie understood she needed to protect her child.

"Well, you shouldn't be lifting heavy objects. That is what you have me for as well as the other people Mr. Taggart employs. Nothing over twenty pounds, give or take a few. I will make certain everyone understands you are not to lift anything heavy. If he has his way, Ol' Sam won't let you do anything in the kitchen. He will insist on doing all the cooking as well as all the chores I leave for him."

The question about the baby was far too perceptive for Fannie's piece of mind. Agnes might just be curious. That was a possibility. If she told her the due date, Agnus would learn the child wasn't conceived on the wedding night. "Can I learn to ride a horse? Fox wants to teach me how to ride too. Is riding too strenuous?" Fannie understood she could wait until after the birth of the child. She didn't want to wait.

Agnes gave a little cackle of delight then snorted. "Not unless you fall off the animal. I'm certain your young man will be careful with you. Will give you the most docile mare of all the horses he can choose from. That man of yours does love his horses as well as his wife. Now, when is this baby due to see the world?"

She supposed the tale might as well get out. Since Agnes was the midwife, she would need to know the approximate time. She let out a puff of frustrated air. Agonized for a few beats of her racing heart. With a deep breath, Fannie blurted, "The end of August or the first of September."

Agnes tapped a finger to her chin. Cocked her head to one side before she asked. "You are certain about this date? You are still small. Not much of a bulge. But then…this is your first child. Is it not?"

"We know the exact date this one was conceived," she divulged without thinking. As soon as she realized what she'd said, more heat rose to her cheeks. Fannie covered them with her cool hands, relishing the cold.

"Oh my, the exact date you say? How can that be? One can rarely be certain of the exact time of conception. Oh my… How? I won't judge. Things happen. Your man is a lusty one. Imagine he couldn't keep his hands off you."

Agnes asked, made a few comments. Nonetheless, Fannie was certain she knew the answer. "Yes, I can't explain. Shouldn't. Just understand what I said is true." Fannie was positive Agnes comprehended the conception came before the wedding night. Many babies were conceived before the wedding night. She wouldn't be the first woman to get pregnant before she was married. Might be the first to conceive in a brothel with a partner she didn't know. "It's a long story. One that, well, one that doesn't bare repeating. I'm not proud of what happened. Can't change the circumstance. Yet it resulted in the happiest days of my life."

"You've got a randy man. He couldn't wait for the wedding. Nothing wrong with that. Seems you must have been over a month and a half pregnant before the wedding night." With her hands on her hips, she looked outside as if she wanted to see Fox then give him a good solid lecture. "It's not your fault. That man of yours wanted you bad. Couldn't wait. That's fine. He stepped up then did the right thing by you. Fox is going to give his son or daughter his name. Doesn't hurt that he loves you."

"You don't know the half of it. What happened isn't at all the way you are imagining," Fannie sighed, the soft breath rippling into the coffee scented air. "I was sick that night. We didn't know each other at the time. When I saw him, believed he was a doctor come to help me. Fox carried one of those little black bags doctors carry. Only it was brown. Hannah told me she would send for a doctor because I was so sick I couldn't talk." She looked to Nellie who walked into the room. "Was on a scavenger hunt with my sister Nellie." Fannie waved her hand in the air. Her face heated. She didn't understand what was getting into her. "Oh my, said too much. Don't repeat any of this, please."

"Fannie, you shouldn't speak of that night. You do know I'm sorry about what happened to you, the pimp and all. The other men who thought you were a whore. Wanted to be alone with Dillon," Nellie paused, her eyes flaming with her anger. She seemed to appear out of nowhere. "The cad. I despise that man. He stole all my dreams."

Fannie hoped Agnes wasn't paying attention to Nellie. Her words were even more condemning. "Nellie? Didn't expect to see you this morning." She pulled in a big breath of air. "Glad you aren't staying in your room. Did you sleep well?" Fannie felt a small measure of relief. Nellie could be a buffer. Agnes had this way of getting her to say things that should remain private. Of course, Nellie just shouted out more damning information.

"I slept. Now I'm hungry. Rory is not around this morning so I felt as if I could come out from my room. Neither is Fox. What are they doing?" She poured herself a cup of coffee then cut herself a slice of bread. Sitting down, she bit then chewed as if she was thinking.

"The two of them rode out to look at the lumber camp. We will be joining the crew in less than a week. Fox wanted to see what they needed to bring with them. He has a team out there right now. Is eager to get started."

"We?" Nellie lifted a blond eyebrow. "I'm not going anywhere Rorik will be. Why would I leave this house? Why would I wish to camp out? Live in a tent?"

"To be with me," Fannie was quick to say. She wanted her sister along so she would have someone to talk to when Fox wasn't around. "This is Agnes. Fox's housekeeper. You can do anything you wish. If you decide to remain, she is a good listener." …and she gets a person to say things about herself that are better left private. "You might enjoy her company."

"Why were you telling her about your encounter with Fox at Hannah's brothel. Seems a bit strange. Thought you would rather keep the information private." She sipped the black coffee then made a face. "Is there any tea?"

The grunt Agnes made with Nellie's words told her there would need to be more explanations. The woman was good at listening. If Nellie stayed here, she might get everything that was bothering her off her chest. At the moment, it appeared Nellie was willing to expound on her secrets. She'd not mentioned the brothel.

"No, to the tea. Fox has it on his list next time anyone goes into the village. At least one person makes the trip each week. For the time being, you will need to make do with what we have on hand."

"This stuff is horrible." Nellie made a face at her cup of coffee.

"It's drinkable with lots of milk and sugar," Fannie offered, wondering when Agnes was going to ask the next questions.

Agnes stared again. Stroked her chin. "You met Mr. Taggart at a brothel? How interesting? I would have never guessed that bit of information." Agnes shook her head. Examined a figurine of a dog for a few seconds before she turned back to face her. "No explanations need to be made to me. You're not a whore. Anyone with eyes can see the truth. While I can believe your husband visited a whorehouse, I don't believe you would be working in one. So, if you met him there…" she paused again tilting her head to the side. A gesture Agnes seemed fond of doing. "Why were you…mentioned you were sick. What was this about a scavenger hunt and a pimp? Other men who attacked you? Details only if you wish to fill me in."

Nellie held her cup up to her lips. Sipped then stared at her for the longest time. Fannie didn't wish to speak of the incident. Nellie knew few of the details.

She wasn't about to throw her sister under the carriage. "We were looking for objects, asking people if they would give up this or that to our game. I wished to be with Dillion without my chaperone, Fannie. Maneuvered as well as plotted to get time alone with the man I thought I loved. Believed with my whole heart to live the rest of my life with. Unfortunate for Fannie, she got lost. That shouldn't have happened. Ended up in a dangerous part of the city."

"I was supposed to find a monogrammed handkerchief." Fannie finished with the story, including the part Halsey played. How she escaped the pimp to end up in a brothel. "Fox was not supposed to go to my room.

Hannah doesn't know her right from her left. She gave him the wrong directions. The rest is history."

Nellie continued with more pertinent information. "They met six weeks later quite by accident. Fox thought she stole his money. Fannie knew she was pregnant with his child because she'd never been with any other man. As you said earlier, Fox did the right thing. He offered marriage."

"Odd, the two of you love each other. Can see the truth in your eyes when you are looking at each other," Agnes pointed out, looking pleased with her conjecture.

Fannie was quick to deny Agnes' statement. "He doesn't love me. Fox cares for me as well as what happens to me. He will protect me. Might love his baby." She set her hands on her roundness. "Nothing more as I decided I must live with what I have," Fannie said as she watched the expressions on Agnes' face change. Her mind was racing through the story she was told.

The housekeeper snorted again. "Believe what you will. I know what I see as well as hear. Been livin' a long time. If he hasn't told you how he feels, he will soon. You love him. Tell the man how you feel about him. A man needs to hear these things. Makes him open up when he's afraid to do the same. Men don't like to be rejected," she added with a sniff.

"Telling him something like that would make me too vulnerable. If there is love in his eyes, I don't see it."

"I believe the truth I see, nothing more nothing less," Agnes finished, still proclaiming his love.

"Fox will break your heart," Nellie warned, shaking a finger at her. "Men do break hearts without thinking or caring. You'll do something wrong. He'll tell you he doesn't want you any longer then put you aside, or worse send you back to Glasgow." As if she didn't just spout such incredible nonsense, Nellie sipped her coffee, grimacing as she did.

Fannie had no clue as to how to combat Nellie's dire forecast. She didn't think Fox would set her aside. Nevertheless, he might. She was useless except in his bed. He did tell her she pleased him.

Agnes shook her dust rag at Nellie. "Now, you've no reason to be so down in the dumps. You're young with your entire life ahead of you. No one has the right to spread their nastiness to other people. You've been hurt, that is obvious. Don't make your sister worry or feel bad because you can't get over what happened to you."

With the onslaught of Agnes' words, Nellie stiffened, her eyes narrowing. She shook her head before she spoke. "You have no idea what I've been through. Don't cast judgement on me unless you understand the reasons."

"Well, didn't I just say the same? You are judging your sister from your experiences with men. You are forecasting dire circumstances for her. Fox will never set this pretty lady aside. Never." Agnes stole a breath of air before she began again. "All men are not cast from the same mold as your Dillion. So, you ran into a bad one. The man broke your heart. Move on. There is a man out there who will love you with all his heart. Trouble is, before that can happen, a woman has to give the man a chance." With that said, Agnes turned back to her dusting. She hummed as if there was no simmering anger in the kitchen.

For several ticks of the clock on the mantel in the parlor, Nellie remained silent. Her face was pale, mouth set in a grim line. Fannie wasn't certain how to move forward. Nellie did have a chip on her shoulder.

"He told me he loved me. More than once. What should a girl believe?" Nellie asked as she lifted her too thin shoulders. "I'm never going to believe another man when he's got his hand up my skirt..." No longer pale, Nellie's face flushed crimson.

Fannie didn't notice the loss of weight before. She'd been too involved in her life to pay much attention. Nellie was thin, too thin. She'd not been eating enough. Until they found their sea legs, they'd both been sick on the way here. Fannie's sickness might have been because of the baby. Nellie's wasn't.

"So, the man was a cad of the first order. Get over it," Agnus said, her voice soft as well as gentle. "There are good men out there. How did this guy, Dillon? How did he get you to forget the first thing mothers teach their daughters."

"Yes, Dillon Montrose. If we hadn't been interrupted, I would have let him have my virginity that night. Think he was going for that all along. Thought he was entitled to have it just as Lord Nelson Abernathy believed. I might be pregnant now too. The difference is Dillon would have never stepped up. He would never offer to marry me."

Fannie was stunned by that announcement about Dillon. She looked to Agnes who didn't see anything unusual in the revelation. "Then you should thank the man who interrupted his conquest of you."

"How did you know it was a man?" Nellie's blue eyes were wide with wonder. "Yes, I should thank him. At the time, I was too mortified to say anything. Dillion merely grinned as he brought his hand out from under my gown."

"Agnes has this way of seeing through what a person says then getting at the truth. Either that or it's just dumb luck," Fannie muttered.

"There is nothing dumb about me. Always have been lucky. Lucky to have had my husband. Lucky to get this job. Lucky to get to know you two charming girls," Agnus cackled with delight. "You've got the right of it. Did tell you I was a good listener. Can see through all the blarney then get down to the cold hard facts. What about this other guy who hurt you, Lord Abernathy? What did he do?"

"The man kidnapped me twice. The first time, Dillon saved me. The second time there was no one there for me." She slanted a pointed look to her. "My sister was moping about. Left the townhouse when she knew she shouldn't."

"This time it was my fault," Fannie admitted. "Thought I saw something. I was wrong about what was happening." Fannie knew she would at some time tell Agnes about the kiss between Beryl and Fox. How she misconstrued what she saw. "Do you know Beryl?" Fannie blurted the question. Caught the frown on Agnes' face.

Fannie went on to explain what happened the second night which sent all their lives into more turmoil. Everything except the reason why she left the house. Under the circumstances, she should have never thought Fox was kissing the woman. Should have been able to see more clearly the fact he was trying to disentangle himself from her.

"Has something to do with Fox." Agnes set her hands on her ample hips. "Bet that Beryl was part of your problem. How that man ever fell for the little witch is beyond me. When she first arrived here, she was all sweetness coupled with smiles."

A startled gasp was all that left Fannie's lips. "You did it again. Yes, you are right about the cause of my mope. Thought I saw Fox kissing Beryl. Was so jealous I couldn't think straight. Was green with envy. Had to be alone. Was wrong about the situation. Fox was trying to get away from her. She was holding him to her. Her arms wrapped around him as if they were snakes. She is poisonous. He didn't want to hurt her."

"Hah! Except for the first infatuation, Mr. Taggart never wanted anything to do with her. He was a lucky man when his father asked Beryl to marry him. Did you know she took the engagement ring Mr. Taggert gave her off that first day she saw Jake." Agnes tsked for a few seconds. Pointed her finger at Fannie. "He's got you now. Yes, he is a fortunate man." She turned her attention back to Nellie. "What happened with this lord after he kidnapped you. Did he hurt you?"

She could tell Nellie wanted to reach out to this motherly woman. Nellie's lips were moving but no sound was coming out. The memories were harsh for her sister.

Nellie brought in a big mouthful of air, her bosom rising with the input. "Abernathy meant to force me. He was going to do whatever he wished. He and Mother…"

"Your mother is part of this? Who ever heard of such a thing?"

"Yes, they took me to a place way out of town. So far away they didn't think anyone would find me. Brought me up to a third-floor bedroom." A tear slid down her face. With the back of her hand, she wiped the moisture away. Sniffed.

"What happened next?" Agnes sat down beside Nellie, held her in her arms. Nellie's face pressed against her magnificent bosom. "If it hurts too much to remember, you needn't tell me. Sometimes it feels better to get the horrible thoughts off your chest."

"I've had a long time to think about what happened. There were bars on the window. Chains on the bed. Abernathy told me what he would do with the chains if I disobeyed him. Didn't want him to spread me out like I wasn't human, as if I was a slave to him. He could have me anytime he felt the urge. I was terrified."

"Bet you were frightened near to death."

"Told him I would do anything he wanted. He laughed at my fear. He ripped my gown into shreds. Left me wearing only my chemise. I was cold but thankful I wasn't naked. Not that it mattered. He could see all of me."

Fannie was appalled at what Nellie was telling her. Hearing the story one more time didn't make the details sound better. This was too much for her to take in. Nonetheless, Fannie realized Nellie needed to talk. Wasn't at all certain she was telling the absolute truth. Knowing Abernathy, he would have stripped her as well as chained her. If he did, could Nellie say the words?

Agnes was good for her. "You don't need to say anything else. I'm so sorry. I was stupid that night. It could have been me. Could have been both of us. Halsey was shot by the guard who followed me to the gazebo. I was safe. Fox was there for me too. You had no one."

"Before... Before he...he restrain... Abernathy brought mother into the bedroom, laughing. She stripped right in front of me before she sat on the bed. Abernathy did the same. He showed me what he was going to do to me. He chained her legs apart then her hands to the head board. Mother was laughing, telling him how she wanted him. He took her. She moaned but it wasn't the sound of pain. After that another man appeared in the room. They took turns with mother. She loved every second. Abernathy told me there was a room where mother could watch when he had sex with me. When the other man did the same."

Fannie felt mortified. Didn't know the half of what happened. Fox never told her what Nellie just admitted.

"Before the two left, they stripped me of the chemise then...then..."

"Mother was part of it," Fannie said. "She touched me."

"Yes. When the twins along with Jake rescued me, Jasper gave me his coat to wear. They took mother and Abernathy away as well as the other man."

"You poor dear," Agnes stroked her hair, cradling Nellie in her arms while she sobbed into her huge bosom.

"What's happening?" Fox asked as he and Rory stepped into the room.

Nellie stiffened when she saw the men. Her eyes huge. "What did you hear?"

"Nothing," Rory said, his voice soft.

~ * ~

Three months later.

"This cabin is perfect," Lord Nelson Abernathy told his guide. "You delivered. I'll pay you the going rate plus toss in another fifty because I'm pleased."

His getting out of jail card was played with expertise. He spent less than two weeks incarcerated. Anice topped off her in jail time with two weeks behind bars. They laughed together when freed. With her last day finished, Nelson escorted her to the country home. Halsey was there waiting for her. They both enjoyed all her charms there in that third-floor bedroom that had been meant for her girls. Now, he had a cabin waiting. The only person who would be missing from the equation was Anice. Ah, he would miss her, Halsey too when he thought about him. They both declined his invitation to travel to America with him.

"Soon as you told me what you wanted, I thought of the old Cooper place. It's miles away from everything. The old man was pretty much self-sufficient. Hunted as well as grew his vegetables. Came into town once a month to see to his needs with one of the ladies who lives above the saloon. He died three months ago. Always kept the homestead in good condition. The bedroom will be perfect for you and the misses. See you had a new feather filled mattress brought there. When did you say the little lady would be arriving? I can meet her in the village. Bring her out here if you like."

"No, that won't be necessary. I'm going to see to her arrival myself. Want to surprise her. Got a few plans for the little lady. Those ideas must have privacy. Need to be alone with her. She should be along in another day or two."

"Well." The man tipped his hat back while he rocked on his heels. "If you need anything else you know where to find me. Been thinking I'd like to find a new lady for myself. Tired of the whores in town. One's old as sin with graying hair along with sagging breasts. The other one's a timid little creature. If a man gets too rough with her, she sobs. Tears role down her cheeks. Sometimes all she does is just lie on the bed like a statue, nothing more. Want a woman with a bit of spunk. If you understand what I mean."

"I might need more of your help. Also agree with you about needing a woman who responds one way or the other. Don't mind a little resistance. A bit of fight in a woman is always fun. Like to tame my woman to my hand. My women need to learn what I like as well as what I don't." Abernathy poked at the fire burning in the fireplace. "Perhaps after a month or so, I'll come by to see you. Might arrange something for you to have a little plaything if you wish. If all goes well with this first little lady, could have a second woman to dally with. They both have spirit. Known them for a couple of years."

"Plaything? This woman isn't your misses?" he asked, looking more interested than before. "Not a whore either? Could come to appreciate that fact. Have had my fill of whores. Never know if you're going get some disease from them."

"No, deep down in her soul, this little lady is a whore. One who likes my attentions. Likes her sex rough as well as down and dirty. Can use a strap on her if I like. Chain her to the bed and she cries out with all the pleasure I give her. What do you say? Once I've had my fill of either lass, do you wish to join me?"

"Can't say as I would or wouldn't. Don't share my women. Stay with them until we've both had enough fun then agree to move on to a new plaything." He paused in what appeared to be thoughtful thinking. "You say the lady is a whore but not like a whore. Would I have to pay her?"

"Said she is a whore in her soul. No need to give the slut money. These ladies, if I retrieve both, give their favors away for free."

Abernathy lifted his shoulders. The shrug, he knew was deceptive. Was certain Maurice would change his mind if he got a good look at either girl. They were both lovely. "In truth, as I said there are two of them. I don't mind sharing either girl. You can have your pick. Sometimes wish to take them at the same time. Once I've taught the lass she has no choice, she falls into my plans."

"Two women?" He questioned. "At the same time, you say. Might enjoy having a double whammy. Don't know. Never tried before."

"At least I'm setting my sights on two little gals. Hope there will be two. They are sisters. Pretty little things. No bigger than a mite, either of them."

"Never been into threesomes or foursomes. Just like one woman at my beck and call." Maurice rubbed his jaw. "On the other hand, two gals at the same time might be fun, a new thrill. You must show me how to do that."

"You can have either girl any way you want after I've had them. Doesn't matter much to me. Join me or not." Nelson shrugged with an air of indifference. What he needed was to seal this man's lips with satisfaction so deep there would be no way he would give him away.

Maurice left, mumbling beneath his breath about having two gals at the same time. Needed to think the idea over. Seemed wrong. Nelson wondered if he showed his true intentions too soon. Maurice didn't strike him as being overly honest. He was a man. A big man. What did it matter? He shouldn't have said anything. Ah well, what was done was done. He would deal with anything that came of his words.

If Maurice wanted a piece of the action, he deserved to have whatever he wished.

Chapter Nine

Fox delighted in watching her. Three months had gone by since they first arrived at his home. He found a private place where they could play without anyone coming upon them. It was a secluded spot he'd known about for many years. Never seen anyone in the vicinity. Leaning back on his elbows, he watched Fannie frolic. She was no longer shy in front of him.

Stark naked, just the way he liked her, Fannie kicked at the water. Her rounded belly was beautiful. Larger breasts, swayed with the little dance she performed for his viewing pleasure. She learned to swim as if she was part fish. Rode the little mare he gave her with ease. Almost as if she'd been riding before she could walk.

He was proud of his wife. Fannie was adapting well to this life. She was stronger than he expected. At first, he'd been afraid a gently born woman from Scotland would never be able to assimilate into the more rugged lifestyle he lived. He did need to admit, his home contained most modern conveniences. Yet they spent a lot of time at the logging camp without those amenities.

Despite Rory's efforts to get to know Fannie's sister, Nellie still held herself aloof. Around him, she was stiff as well as unbending. The girl never smiled. She continued to tell him she didn't like him. Didn't appreciate his efforts to speak with her. Wanted to be left alone. Fox was afraid Rory was smitten with Nellie. Didn't wish for his friend to be hurt. This was the first time Rory showed more than passing attention to a female. He didn't believe Nellie would ever soften toward Rory or any man.

Memories with his Fannie were building one day at a time. With fondness, he recalled the apron incident. Naked wearing only a pink apron, Fannie minced from behind the bathing screen, surprising him. He'd been relaxing, his hands behind his head when he first saw her. Realized his jaw dropped at the sight in front of him. His entire body jerked to attention at the lovely vision she presented. His sex swelled with need. He lost his breath. Gasped. Believed he'd died and gone to heaven. After the first few seconds, his heart began to beat again.

Standing in front of him, so close he could reach out then touch her, she twirled, her breast dancing with the movement, jiggling delightfully. He adored the way her jewels bounced. She tantalized every masculine sense he possessed. For a few seconds, he didn't know what to think or do. Fox felt as if time froze. In all his days with Fannie, he never thought she would show herself this way. He was a man well pleased.

Fannie was graceful, her movements fluid. He loved seeing her naked. That evening, she was bare except for the pink apron tied around her waist. At the time she had a tiny bump that was the babe. Nothing like she was now. She had three months left before the child would be born. He could hardly wait to hold his son or daughter in his arms.

When Fannie issued the challenge for him to wear nothing but this other pink apron she waved through the air. He swore. Sat up with a start. He eyed the scrap of material. He would be wearing less than a loincloth.

He growled at her. "Told you no one would catch me wearing an apron. I'm not going to humiliate myself." He was acting the prude. They both understood he was also a coward. Though by wrapping the rose-colored fabric around his waist, only a few seconds would pass before he was deep inside her heat.

"That's not the point," she told him, tilting her head so her hair fell over her shoulders. The long blond strands covered then played peekaboo with one nipple. She tossed her hair back while she slowly walked toward him, holding another pink apron in front of her. The delicious sway of her breasts along with her hips held his undivided attention. Believed he might drool. He wished to taste them so much.

"What is your point? I'm not a coward or a prude. We both understand, your challenge must be met. Not going to allow my brazen woman to outdo me. Told you once I am a gambling man. Imagine now is the time to show you the proof of my words. Even if it means wearing women's clothing." Within a couple of seconds his shirt was over his head then tossed on to the floor. He was hopping from foot to foot to rid himself of his boots as well as his socks. After that, his buckskins met the floor.

Naked, hands on his hips, he stood in front of Fannie. The huge grin she graced him with showed him an adorable façade. Found he grew harder with each passing moment. This was going to end on his terms. Not hers.

"Give me the damn apron! Why does it have to be pink of all colors? You look amazing wearing pink. Pink is not a man's color." He grumbled about nothing important. What the hell were they going to do once he wore the apron? Did his Fannie have something in mind besides making love?"

He'd take hers off first. Not that he needed to remove the simple barrier, to get what he wanted.

After that she would untie his. When she reached around him, the tips of her breasts would sweep across his chest. His imagination was running wild with all the possibilities. Heat rumbled through him. He'd rather not wear anything at all.

She laughed, smiling at him as he grabbed the apron from her. "Think of the color as rose not pink. Do you want me to tie it around your waist? No, you will have to tie it around your hips. Might not be able to keep it on. That would be fun." She touched her finger to her mouth. Allowed her gaze to travel down to the huge part of him that needed her sweetness.

He growled low in the back of his throat. After the growl he held out his arms. Before he said another word, he turned in a full circle. "Tie the apron, sweet, then we can play this game my way. I'm going to be certain this challenge you've issued is met with perfection. You will get what you want as will I."

They played. He swatted her on her delicious butt. She shrieked. Fondled as well as caressed every sensitive part of her. She found him beneath the apron. Ran her hands along his sex. Purred as he caught a nipple with his teeth. She was magical, enchanting all his senses. Didn't wish to wait another second for what they both wanted.

Fannie giggled, her delicate blue-veined breasts tempting him. He pulled her to him, kissed her until she whimpered then sighed a soft feminine sound he loved to hear. Fox didn't know what he would do without her. If she wasn't in his life, he would be lost.

Still wearing the aprons, he took her with her legs wrapped around his flanks while she was against the door. After they both climaxed, Fox brought her to the big bed where he loved to play with her, dally with every sensitive spot on her beautiful body. Tonight, he meant to taste every delicious part of her.

This second time he took his time with her, teased all the sensitive hollows, all the soft parts of her until she was writhing beneath him. She begged him with soft words. Called out his name more than once. When they finished, he pulled her against him. Her head rested in the hollow of his shoulder. When she closed her eyes, he felt the sweep of her lashes against his chest. Ran his hand along her back to soothe her. Knew contentment.

This time when she giggled, he understood there was a reason. "Fox…"

"What is it? What thought has you giggling like an untried schoolgirl? Tell me." He cupped her rump with one hand. Tugged her until their hips met. She set her hand on his belly. Spread her fingers.

"Um… Agnes and I had a bet of sorts. You're not going to like what I have to say. Thought you should know." Fannie ran the tip of her finger up then down his chest. She stopped just shy of his sex. Splayed her hand across his belly again. She was a little tease. With the delicate contact, his muscles contracted. "Don't think I will ever get enough of you. Want to feel all of you all the time."

"Yes?" he reciprocated. Trailed a fingertip down her arm just to feel her shiver with the pleasure. His hand strayed to one breast where he teased her, his finger moving around her aureole but never touching. "I understand. A bet? Imagine the wager had something to do with a pink apron. Did my housekeeper also have a wager with Rory? He is the one who brought up the topic."

"No wager," she was quick to point out. "I said of sorts. We never bet anything except whether or not I could get you to wear a pink apron when you were so adamant against doing so. Didn't have any problem. Did I? Believe you saw all the decadent possibilities." Fannie pushed up on her arms. Her breasts floated across his chest. He felt the tightening of his body coupled with the swelling of his sex. Good God, he needed her again. He should be satisfied. He'd had her against the door then on the bed. "Agnes bet that you would wear the apron naked if I did too. She said you would do anything I wished."

"I would. Wish to keep you happy." The words were true. Did he love her? His love for her was something he needed to contemplate.

Love? Has a nice ring to it.

"You did what we both excepted." She bit his shoulder, smoothed the spot with her tongue. Rubbed her cheek across one of his nipples before sipping for a few seconds. "I can hear the beat of your heart. It is beating at the same pace as mine."

"Why? Seems a bit strange. Why were you talking about something like that with my housekeeper? Agnes, what else does she know about us?" The notion brought him back to reality as if cold water was splashed across his face. "You haven't told her anything else? Anything damaging?"

Fannie grimaced then nodded. In response to the look of chagrin on her face, he frowned. "I might have. She has this way about her. When she asks a question, she is so sincere. I blurt things I should not. Did tell her how we met. How I came to be pregnant before the wedding night."

He groaned again, realizing the story was now out in the open. Hoped Agnes would never mention what she learned to anyone. "So, Agnes knows all about Hannah and the brothel? Can't believe you would reveal something like that." He held up his hand to stop her protest. "I'm not angry. Just seems strange."

"I didn't, Nellie did. Agnes also knows all about what happened to Nellie when she was kidnapped. Most of what happened. Don't believe anyone except Nellie along with Abernathy and my mother know everything. Realize for her piece of mind, Nellie keeps details to herself. As I told you, your housekeeper has this way of discovering secrets. We were both caught up in the moment. She is so sweet as well as kind. The woman is easy to confide in. She even learned a little about Mother."

All that sharing of information happened three months ago. He never saw a problem with Agnes knowing all those secrets. She was a good sort. His housekeeper would never tell anyone what she discovered that day. Agnes was a goodhearted woman. She liked his wife. The girls needed to talk. Perhaps all was for the best.

He brought his attention back to Fannie. She still needed protection. Hadn't heard from the Kenworthys about Lord Abernathy or Anice. Last he knew they were both incarcerated, waiting for their trials. No one believed either would travel this far then into the wilderness for revenge. He didn't want to believe they would do something so out of character. He couldn't forget the evil in these two people.

Rory knew about the night when Nellie was kidnapped. Didn't know any specifics as to what Nellie endured. Fox wanted his friend to help protect Nellie. Doing so was near impossible since she still wanted nothing to do with him. Fox didn't believe Rory would give up on Nellie. His friend thrived on challenges. He seemed smitten with the girl. He'd never seem Rory besotted before.

"Come in the water with me," Fannie called out, beckoning to him with her arms. "The water is warm. You will enjoy a swim."

'You're a crazy woman. The water is freezing. Is always cold this time of year. Will give me goosebumps on my arms." After a little more bantering, they would swim. After that he would make love to her in the lake. Thinking about thrusting inside her heat warmed him all over. When he stood, he was hard. He strode to the water's edge. Stopped with ripples of liquid caressing his toes.

"You're a coward," Fannie taunted, staring at that part of him that was telling her how much he needed her. "Afraid of a little cold water. What's a girl to do?" She turned then dove into the lake.

At the edge of the water, he watched her surface a few feet away. When she swam underwater, he was always worried. He tried to follow her progress by the tiny ripples on the surface above. She'd not been swimming very long. Fannie liked to swim beneath the surface best. Her doing so terrified him. He was always afraid she would never come up.

"Little minx," he said, after her head popped above the water. When he could see her, his breathing was easier.

"Are you coming?" she asked, still watching, waiting. "Time doesn't stand still. Ah, you're still afraid of the cold."

"Wouldn't miss this for the world." His gaze met hers. "I'm going to make love to you in the lake. That's what you want. I know you."

With measured steps, Fox waded into the lake. Felt the cold glide of the liquid on his skin. Fannie was right. It wasn't all that cold. She stood, the water reaching just above her breasts. When the chilled liquid hit his belly then his back, he grimaced, sucking air. Dove. Wasn't about to complain about the temperature when Fannie waited for him.

When they first started the lessons, the lake had been colder. The snow melt from the mountains made the water almost unbearable. They'd been able to stay in the water for a short amount of time. He would have waited for the temperature to warm. Fannie was eager. As she should be, she was proud of all her accomplishments.

He reached her with a few strong kicks. Set his hands around her waist. Smoothed her belly. Kissed. Sipped on one hard crest then the other.

"I want you, now! Can't wait for one more second," he told her as he brought her legs around his waist.

Fannie purred her satisfaction when he entered her, little whimpers of delight following. This was one of those times where the lovemaking was fast. She accepted him inside her body. Ready for him. She bit his chin then his shoulder. He shuddered, spilling his seed inside her when she cried out, splintering with her need. She collapsed on him. Her head rested against his chest. He felt her breaths even out as he smoothed her back.

"This was too fast," he told her, wishing he could control his needs better. "Next time I will have a slow hand." *Next time.*

"Doesn't matter to me," she whispered against his neck.

"Ah, you just like to feel me inside your hot little channel."

"Yes, you're right," Fannie admitted with the breathy little sigh Fox loved to hear.

He carried her to the grassy knoll where he'd been watching her frolic in the water. Dried her off, making sure to touch her everywhere. He dressed her, pulled on his buckskins then his shirt.

Fannie finished fastening his shirt for him. Ran her hands along his shoulders. "You need to return to the logging camp. Always the lumber. The trees are always so important," she giggled then grinned at him. "Will you take me with you sometime? I'd like to see what goes on."

"I'll think about it. Don't know if it would be safe for you. You're right though. I do need to go."

The time he spent with Fannie had been more than he planned. She was always on his mind. He didn't like leaving her alone at the base camp. Seemed he was always afraid for her. Today there had been more fear than normal. Fox didn't understand the gut instinct that had him looking over his shoulder every few minutes. Was taught to never underestimate his instincts.

His breath caught in his throat. For the last few months, he felt free of fear. Doubted anyone would wish Fannie harm. Abernathy was still out there, still a threat. So was her mother. They didn't know if he was in jail or was able to find a way out. They could not relax.

He didn't need to remind himself of the fact Lord Nelson Abernathy was a dangerous man. He possessed enough wealth to live as he pleased. Nelson Abernathy sought revenge against his wife as well as Nellie.

Damn the consequences. The man seemed bent on pleasing himself. He was petty as well as self-indulgent. Was unaccustomed to anyone gainsaying him. Lord Abernathy would always do as he liked.

"Yes, I've got to return you to the base camp. Today, there is no option for me. You've made friends, I know. What will you do this afternoon?" He set her between his legs, combing her damp hair. Worked on the tangles. Touched soft skin whenever he could manage. Let the back of his hands skim the tips of her breasts. With each pass Fannie purred with the pleasure he gave her.

Damn, he didn't wish to leave her. He needed to return her to the base camp then be on his way back up the mountain.

While she leaned against him, she sighed her voice soft. "Meridith said she would show me where to look for wild onions and potatoes, mushrooms as well. We plan to add them to the venison stew Ol' Sam is making. Meridith planted some herbs when we first arrived this spring. Suppose we will see what we can collect that will add flavor to your dinner."

Fox found himself nodding, still thinking about the danger which might wait for her. He didn't wish to frighten her. Fannie needed to understand some of his fears. Over the last few months, they'd both been lax. "Don't go far from camp today. If Rory is around, take him with you, or Paul. I'll send them both back to base. If I'm at the logging camp, the two men are not needed." He brought in a deep breath of air, telling himself he was acting ridiculous. Abernathy was in Glasgow, no threat to them. If that was true, why were the small hairs on the back of his neck standing on end? What didn't he know that he should?

"I promise. After finding out how Abernathy treated Nellie, I will never take chances with my life. Don't want to become his plaything. If Rory is not there, we will bring Paul along for the adventure. He's even larger than

Rory." She turned around to look at him. "Wouldn't Abernathy still be in jail? No one would have let him out this soon. Would they?"

"It's possible he didn't stay incarcerated long. Money combined with titles can accomplish a lot in a short amount of time. I can't shake the feeling something isn't right. Every time I look over my shoulder at the shadow that seems to be following me, I'm reminded of Lord Abernathy. I shudder to think about him being here, in Michigan. Can't dismiss the notion from my head. Despite the fact we haven't heard about Abernathy's status from Jasper, maybe because we haven't heard, we need to be more vigilant. Letters get lost."

Before they left a few months ago for the base camp, he told Agnes to watch out for Nellie. His housekeeper agreed. Rory spent two days a week at his house despite Nellie's objections. He and Fannie came home on off days whenever he felt he could leave for two days.

If Abernathy wanted Nellie, he would snatch her without anyone knowing. Nellie was so reclusive, he would have trouble finding her outside the house, alone. Abernathy would figure out a way. Would do the same with Fannie. He should take more precautions.

"Still, don't go far from the camp. Stay within shouting distance. If Abernathy has come for either of you, he will use stealth. If you see anything strange, run, then don't stop yelling. Scream until someone comes to help."

Fannie turned back around. Fox drew the comb through her hair a few more times. When he set the comb aside, she leaned against him. "We both know he isn't in Michigan. Lord Nelson Abernathy would never deign to get his hands dirty in these mountains. There are a lot of women who would accept a position as his mistress who are not as difficult to get to," Fannie said, her tone light, disbelieving.

Fox understood she was giving herself a confidence boost. Doing so was fine. Nonetheless, she needed to understand this lord who persisted when he lost. The man didn't like to lose to anyone, let alone a female. Now, he would be seeking revenge. "I don't think he will ever let this go. Doubt if your mother will either. Abernathy is not a reasonable man. He wanted Maggie then Tessa. Because of his loss, he wants to hurt both you along with your sister."

He helped her stand. Tucked a few drying strands of her hair behind her ears. "You are beautiful. I would always come after you, no matter the odds. Let's get you back to base then me to the logging camp. We've got logs to send down the river to the mill."

Hand in hand they walked back. He kissed her before he left. The premonition of doom continued in his mind. Every second, he wanted to turn around then race back to Fannie, shielding her from any harm that might come her way. Needed to hold her. Make certain she was safe. Once at the lumber sight he spoke to both Rory along with Paul, telling them both of his fears.

"Believe I should check out your house. As we both know, Nellie and your housekeeper are there alone. They've no protection. I would stay the next two nights. Nellie won't appreciate the company. Too bad." Rory told him as he pinched the bridge of his nose. "I am worried about both the ladies. Did Abernathy know Fannie was pregnant? If he discovers that little fact, he will be furious. The man could use the unborn child's life to make her do what he demands."

"No, no one knew. Not even the immediate family. Fannie and I chose not to say anything as to why we didn't see each other for six weeks or the happenstance meeting at the brothel that brought all of this about. She didn't wish for her sisters to be upset. They were all brought up to remain chaste until the night of their wedding. What happened at the brothel was out of her hands." Fox found himself shaking his head. "Fannie might have told me no. She couldn't because she was too drugged with laudanum combined with the brandy, I gave her to be able to think straight."

"This Abernathy fella won't be pleased to see Fannie swelled with your child. Does he know the two of you are married?"

"True to the first statement, yes to the second. It was during the celebration of our marriage when he kidnapped Nellie. He knew what was going on in the Kenworthy townhouse. We didn't announce our marriage. Didn't keep it a secret either. Anice has her ways of discovering what her daughters are doing."

"Nellie is the most vulnerable. She won't be pleased to have me ghosting her. The girl has no say in this. I won't leave her alone. Are you certain Abernathy is here?"

"No, can't be positive about anything. Do believe Jake would have let me know if Abernathy was released. I've heard nothing."

"Takes time to get letters from across the Atlantic. Sometimes they get lost. He might have written the day the man was released. Even so, Abernathy would have needed to depart at the same time."

"There has been no softening to you by Nellie?" Fox asked, wishing these two would find a way to close the huge gap separating them. "Is she still turning her back on you when you appear?"

"No softening. That little gal still has a huge chip of dislike for all males on her tiny shoulders. Agnes explained some of what happened. Not the horrid details as she told me. Your housekeeper said the rest is up to Nellie to say if and when she wishes to do so. Women! I would like to know what occurred. Learning would help me understand her better." Rory rubbed the back of his neck. Now, he was shaking his head. "She still insists on calling me Rorik. No one except my mother calls me by that name." He paused, his thoughts seeming to spin. "…only when she's angry with me."

"Can't say as I blame her feelings. While I wasn't part of the rescue, Fannie told me what she learned about the abduction the day Agnes caught the girls off guard with her listening skills. The day they both blurted without thinking things that should have remained private. Still believe there are untold facts concerning this matter."

"You won't tell me anything either." Rory let out a long slow breath of air sounding a lot frustrated. "Wouldn't I be better able to protect her from this Abernathy guy if I understood some of his motivation?"

"Revenge is part of the scenario. Sex is another factor. Abernathy thinks he is entitled to everything he wants. Anice, their mother, has made him feel that way. Fannie tells me Anice gave him *carte blanch* with Tessa when he snatched her off the bakery porch. Probably did the same with Nellie after they trapped her in his third-floor bedroom. For some reason, she detests her daughters. All of them, all four are bastards."

"Hell! I'm leaving now. I'll stay the night even if Nellie protests. We've got to come up with some plan. The man might not even be in the States. We can't be afraid of shadows. In a way, I hope he is here where we can deal with him. Don't like shadows ghosting us." Rory stuffed both hands through his hair. Cursed.

"My gut tells me different. He is here, waiting for a golden opportunity. I'll send Ol' Sam into the village to see what he can discover. A Scottish gentleman would stand out as much as a sore thumb. He wouldn't be able to keep people from commenting on his appearance then talking about him. Should know within a few hours. I'll also have him check the post office. Maybe Jasper or my father has sent a warning letter. I know the Duke of Southcliff will have the man watched. That's how we were able to get to Nellie so fast the night of her abduction."

Feet braced apart; Fox watched Rory gallop out of the logging camp. His friend wasn't wasting time. Now, he needed to get Paul back to base camp. His wife must have protection. If Meridith and Fannie were together, Abernathy might snatch both women. Since he couldn't safeguard the two women himself, he felt a hollow pit in his stomach grow to gigantic proportions.

"Paul," Fox waved his friend to his side. "Have a proposition for you. One you can't say no to. I won't allow it." Fox was trying to figure out how to explain what was happening. Until now, the only people who knew anything about the sisters past life were his housekeeper along with Rory. In this situation, he believed the best tact was honesty.

With a smile on his handsome features, Paul strode his way. "Yes, what do you need? Can do anything you wish. The timber they brought down this morning is now being dumped in the holding tank ready to be sent down stream. Brought in three wagons full. It's a good haul." Paul pushed his hat back revealing his dark brown eyes. Eyes that were so deep a color they were almost black. His biceps were as large as a tree trunk. His massive thighs even larger. Paul would be an asset to his plans.

"What I need is some help safeguarding my wife from a past enemy." Fox went on to relate a brief history of the MacRae girls with Lord Nelson Abernathy. Gave him a brief description.

"Hell!"

"Yes, I've said worse."

"You must be terrified for the misses. You're telling me Fannie is with my Meridith. Is my wife in trouble too?"

"Yes, if the man can't get Meridith away from Fannie, he will take both girls." Fox pinched the bridge of his nose. "Keep in mind, none of us know if Abernathy is here. It's the gut of mine joined with the feeling I've been watched. If so, the man knows I'm not with Fannie. He will believe she is an easy mark."

"If there is trouble, Meridith won't leave your wife's side. She carries a gun with her. Knows how to use the weapon. I taught her. She's a better shot than me. Hits everything she shoots at," Paul said with an eager smile, looking proud.

"Has she ever pulled a trigger on anything living?" Fox hoped so. If she hunted with Paul, Meridith might be able to shoot a man.

"Yes, of course she has. Not often though. Brought down a deer last fall with the rifle I bought for her."

"Good, I've got to stay here. Can't ride down the mountain to base camp. Sent Rory to watch over Nellie. You have the same job with your wife and Fannie. The ladies, your wife and mine, were going to do a bit of collecting for dinner. Told Fannie not to go any farther than shouting distance from the others. Abernathy is sly. He'll think of some way to lure the ladies away. Don't doubt it."

Fox went on to explain more of his fears. Handed him a little more information about Lord Abernathy's shenanigans in Glasgow before he returned with his wife. Finished with, "Both ladies could be in danger. Your wife because of her association with mine."

"I'm going. Don't need to ask me twice."

~ * ~

"What do you want me to do first?" Fannie grinned at Meridith. It was obvious what they would do first. Fannie was thinking about Fox's fears. She didn't believe Abernathy was here in Michigan. Why would he come after a married woman? After Maggie then Tessa married, he left them alone. His wanting her made no sense. It was also a long way for him to go to retrieve Nellie. In the rugged Michigan countryside, he would be out of his element.

With an exasperated whoof of air, she reminded herself she promised Fox she would take care. Would do nothing to put herself in danger. She would do all Fox suggested, take every precaution. Would remain close to camp. Hoped Nellie would agree. Rory wouldn't let her out of his sight. His constant presence was good. Fannie wanted Nellie to fall in love with Rory. As Fox along with Agnes pointed out, he was smitten with her sister. He was giving her time to heal. Maybe, he should try a different tactic. Shock her out of her bad humor.

When they celebrated their wedding here in Michigan, Rory danced with Nellie. Throughout one entire song, she was stiff. Held herself away from him. For the whole waltz, her lips were set in a thin straight line. The sight was almost laughable. She found out later, Rory offered Nellie a challenge. Called her a coward who was too afraid of her own shadow to take a risk. His dare had not been well done of him. Nonetheless, he got a chance to dance with her. For a few minutes, he held her in his arms.

During the party, she learned how to square dance, which left her breathless. When the first waltz played and Fox swept her into his arms, she was breathless for other reasons. He made a point to tease her with words as well as his lips. Held her too close. Kissed her ear as well as let his hand drift to her fanny when he didn't think anyone looked. She loved the way he danced as well as the way he made her feel. Fannie wasn't positive when she fell in love with Fox. Perhaps she had been in love with him from the very beginning.

I'm in love.

"What's got you looking so dreamy-eyed? You thinking about that good looking husband of yours?" Meridith asked as she patted the earth down around one of her plants.

"Yes. I am," she admitted. "He is the most fascinating man I've ever known." Fannie shook her head to return to the present. Wondered how much she should tell her new friend. "Was remembering when we cut the cake the night when my husband invited everyone to come celebrate our marriage with us. He smeared icing on my nose then licked the sweet confections off." She shuddered remembering the heat that rushed through her with the sensuous contact. At that point all she wanted was to race to their bedroom dragging Fox along behind her. If he realized her intent, he would have swept her into his arms then carried her there.

Meridith was a pretty woman of remarkable height, sweet as well as gentle. Her hair was a rich, dark auburn. She possessed eyes the color of the Irish moss that Anice had in the walkway leading to her home. They were a soft green. Her bosom was impressive. She was perfect for Paul who Fannie knew adored his wife. Today, her hair was pulled back in a tight bun with tiny tendrils escaping to frame her delicate face. She blew a strand off the tip of her nose which was tipped up a *wee* bit.

"Seems you did just the same with the icing when it was your turn to feed him the cake. The women were all laughing and cheering you on. Wanted you to put more of the icing on him. When the men called for a kiss, your man stepped up. Fox kissed you until you gasped for air. We all saw the way you were panting after he finished. Knew he helped you to a bit of his tongue."

Fannie made a face. "We didn't do any of that in Glasgow after we were married. Jasper procured the best musicians who would have played the pipes while we danced. Something happened then that had me so jealous, I forgot the dangers of leaving the house. Just knew I needed to be alone with my simmering suspicions. Going against everything I knew wasn't right, I marched outside." She waved her hand in the air. "None of what happened then matters now. We should get busy. Want the venison stew that Ol' Sam will have bubbling over the fire to be tasty tonight. The men will all be starving by the time they come in from the logging camp."

"Tasty, yes…some of these herbs will be a good addition to his stew." Meridith stood up, her hands on the small of her back to stretch out kinks before returning to her precious herbs.

"Tell me which ones you will use. I hope to learn as much as possible. Want to be helpful. I came to Fox with no skills that are needed here. I'm educated. Fluent in French as well as Italian. Can speak a smattering of Scottish Gaelic. I can dance. Don't sing well. Don't need any of these skills where I live now. He tells me I please him in other…" Fannie stopped with her hands to her heated cheeks. "I shouldn't be saying anything more."

Meridith stopped pulling weeds around the herbs she'd planted this spring to look at her with an all-knowing smile on her upturned face. She tended them with loving care. Her hands were dirty with the rich dark loam. There was a streak of dirt on her cheek. Fannie didn't appreciate dirt under her nails. Meridith seemed to thrive in that condition.

Tossing back the grin, that formed on her face, she cleared her throat then began to speak, "Now, Mrs. Taggart—"

Interrupting her, Fannie needed to make something clear to Meridith, "Call me Fannie. I'd like that." She didn't like the formality of the last name with Mrs. in front of it. Understood when it came to Fox's men, his employees, that was the right way to address him. "I insist," she added when it seemed Meridith would object. "Truly, I do insist. Won't speak to you again if you continue calling me in that formal manner. I'm just Fannie." Fannie laughed at the look of chagrin on her friend's face. "Say my name, Meridith. The more often you do the easier it will become."

"Fannie," she bit out with a begrudging sigh. "Fannie," she said her name again. "You shouldn't be embarrassed that your husband appreciates your other skills." With the finishing of her statement joined with the mention of the undefined skill, red rushed to Meridith's cheeks.

"I wouldn't say I was skilled in that… don't know what to call it. Fox tells me I please him in bed. He taught me what I know. I should hope I please him. He orchestrates everything we do." Except for the time with the aprons, that was my doing. "We should not be talking of things like pleasing our men in bed." Fannie felt the same dreamy eyed reaction wash over her again, her hands resting on her protruding belly. Oh, she seemed to be growing larger by the day.

"Fannie…don't be embarrassed. My Paul says much the same to me. It's a good thing. We women need to satisfy our men on all levels. The men work so hard to put food on the table. Paul used to shimmy up to the tops of the trees to cut away limbs that would get in the way when the tree falls. It's dangerous work. He loves the danger. Shrugs his shoulders then tells me he knows what he is doing then tells me I'm not to worry. Can't help but fear. Hold my breath every day until I see him walking into the tent."

She grinned. "Now that that's settled, about my name. Fox tells me he doesn't do anything hazardous. Mostly supervises the crew." By the expression on Meridith's face Fannie realized Fox lied to her. She needed to shrug off the fear. Would need to figure out a way to live with the risk every day for the rest of her life. To look the other way would be difficult. "So, what can I do to help?"

Meridith sat back on her legs. Pushed some of those little pieces of hair that were delicately framing her face behind her ears. "I'm almost finished with the weeding. Go to my tent. On the table by the entrance there is a basket along with a trowel. Bring them back here. We can start to look for our tasty additions to the venison stew Ol' Sam is fixing as we speak. I'll show you how to find the wild onions and potatoes. The mushrooms…well…you need to be careful. Until I'm positive you know which ones to avoid, don't do any mushroom hunting on your own. That might be chancier than climbing trees. Morels are easy to identify. You can stick with the collection of those for now."

"Done. You will be my fountain of knowledge here in this wilderness. Teach me everything you know about plants. Wonder if there is anything I could teach you. I'd like to repay the learning."

"You can tell me all about Glasgow. Could you teach me French? You said French was a language you speak. I'd like to learn more about the entire country of Scotland. Fox's tales have inspired me. He prefers life here in America."

"*Oui,* and I'm beginning to understand why. I'll be right back." Fannie skipped off in the direction of the tent to retrieve the objects Meridith asked for.

Just as Meridith told her, Fannie found the required equipment at the entrance. When she returned, Meridith was wiping her hands with her apron then pointing. "Look. Wonder what Paul is doing back so early. Hope nothing happened up at the logging camp."

Paul was smiling. A grin was a good sign that nothing was wrong. "Me too." A little shiver of fear swept through her. Thoughts of Abernathy surged inside, turning her stomach. Nerves snapped as she watched Paul ride toward them. Fox did tell her he would send someone to protect her. Fannie didn't believe she needed extra protection. She planned on doing everything he told her. She wasn't about to wander off.

In a lithe graceful move, Paul leapt from his horse then strode toward them. Kissed his wife long and slow before he spoke. "Know the two of you must have some questions about why I'm home before the end of the work day. Boss sent me back here to watch over the two of you while you gather some tasty items for our dinner. Nothing untoward has happened. Now," he stepped back, "appears the two of you are ready to go to work. Tell me what we are looking for so I can help."

Meridith shook her finger at him. "Now, don't you be getting in the way. You know there will be no hanky panky while we're working."

"Me? Hanky panky? Never." His bark of laughter was followed by a female giggle. "I promise to keep my hands where I want them."

"Of course, you," Meridith swatted one of his large hands away from her waist. "I know you. You will do what you please when you please. If you are supposed to protect Fannie here, you will behave. Keep your mind on the business at hand."

"If you insist," he said with a complaining tone to his voice.

They spent the next half hour with Meridith giving instruction on locating the plants then showing her how to dig them up. She even allowed her to do some of the digging. They collected morels which were a tasty mushroom that was easy to recognize, more potatoes and onions than they would use in the stew. The basket was almost full to the brim. There wouldn't be room for too much more.

"We've gone too far from the camp," Fannie said, realizing with a start she couldn't hear the chatter from the campground. She didn't hear the banter between Meridith and Paul. "We should get back." When Fannie turned, she didn't see either of the two people who were supposed to be with her. Fannie's heart skipped a few beats. She sucked in a long draught of oxygen. No matter, she would head back to camp. The two were just taking a moment for themselves, to kiss. Paul did have difficulty keeping his hands to himself.

This didn't make sense. Paul wouldn't ignore an order from Fox. He would never make himself scarce if he was supposed to be watching over her.

What happened to them?

"Meridith! Paul!" Fannie called out as she looked in what she thought was the direction of the camp. She started walking then stopped. Tried to listen to the sounds. Seemed the birds as well as the bees and other insects were quiet. There was no hum of any kind. She felt very real terror slide down her spine. Forced the fear away. Reminded herself she had nothing to be afraid of. Abernathy was miles away from here.

Fannie didn't know where to go. She was lost. If she walked in the wrong direction, she would be even more lost. Her heart beat a hard staccato beneath her ribs. Fox never told her what to do if she got lost. She forced down fear joined with panic. If she didn't see Meridith or Paul soon, she was going to shriek. This wasn't supposed to happen. She was to stay within screaming distance. Turning again in a full circle, she felt certain she would see both Meridith and Paul. They would come out from behind a tree, smiles on their faces. Meridith would wear a pretty smile and her cheeks would be flushed pink. Wouldn't be surprised if her bodice was a bit askew.

All would be fine.

When he emerged from behind a clump of bushes, he walked with light steps. His smile was one that chilled her through to the bone. He was smug. Arrogant. Appeared positive all was going his way. Fannie backed up a step, her legs shaking. For too many beats of her heart she stood frozen in place. This was her imagination playing tricks on her. She should be running as well as yelling for help.

No!

She couldn't scream. When she tried, nothing came out of her mouth. Picking up her skirts she ran in the opposite direction. Fox told her to run as hard as she could toward the camp. Dear God, she didn't know where the camp was. How to find it? She didn't know. Clueless in the face of danger was not what she wanted to be. So vulnerable…

Something large got in the way of her feet. The earth rose to greet her. She fell to her hands and knees, panting with her exertion. Her hands were scratched from the tiny rocks beneath them. She heaved air into her lungs, gulping oxygen. Understood she needed to stand, to keep running. No, no…no… No! Her hair came loose from the braids she wore, spilling across her face. The ribbon landed on the ground. When she tried to stand, she caught her foot on her skirt. She fell again.

His arm circled her. "No! Leave me alone!"

"Yes! Stop running. You know you want me. I have you now. You're mine." His cry of accomplishment was triumphant. "Got you, my pretty little slut. Going to get a lot more of you. Taste all of you, every sweet feminine part of you. You've denied me too long. Made me work too hard." Abernathy hoisted her so he held her with one arm, her head and feet dangling on either side.

"Let me go! I'm married. You don't want me."

"That's where you are wrong. I do want you. Your two bodyguards won't rescue you. Caught them by surprise with my club. If the blow didn't kill him, the man you called Paul will be out for a long time. Your friend, Meridith, never knew what happened to her. She was digging something up. A hard tap to her chin caught her unaware. She's stretched out close to her man. They won't be waking up any time soon. Might be dark before anyone misses you. Thought it fortuitous when you two left the camp. Played right into my loving hands."

While she couldn't seem to scream, she struggled. Twisted in his arm trying to wrench herself from his hold. With her fists she beat against his legs and side. Tried to kick him. He tightened his hold on her, squeezing air from her lungs.

His other hand came down hard on her rump, once then twice. "Stop it this instant! You won't like it if I dump you on your pretty face. Didn't know you were pregnant. Pregnant women are ugly. Makes this all the more fun. Got leverage over your stubborn hide. Bet you'd do anything to protect the *bairn*." Lord Abernathy whistled as he strode through the trees.

Her dress caught on something. Left a scrap of fabric behind. Fannie tried to think of something she could do. Her befuddled mind was in a fog. She didn't like this feeling of helplessness. He would force her as soon as possible. This time he wouldn't wait in an attempt to torture. He must be certain no one will find wherever it is he was staying.

Fannie gathered as much courage as possible. She was furious. Couldn't seem to keep that emotion inside her chest. She cried out. Trying to get leverage, she pushed against his side. Lifted her head. "Fox will kill you!" Fannie beat her fists on his side again, not heeding his warning. "He will hang you by your scrawny neck. His employees will find you. Feed you to the bears and the wolves. They won't stop looking for me!"

"Shut up, bitch." He hit her again. Left his hand where he hit her. She flinched with the contact. "I'll show you what I do to little sluts who don't obey. Got that baby to hold over your head if you're not willing to do as I ask. I'm not an unreasonable man. You will be treated with a tender hand if you come to me willing and eager."

"I hate you. Despise the ground you walk on. I will never come to you willing, never eager." She felt her baby move. Groaned. "You're hurting me. My baby doesn't like what you are doing." Her voice was calm now.

The child growing within was more important than anything else. She would protect this little girl or boy with her life. Would have to do all he asked.

"Do you think I care if I hurt Taggart's brat? Doesn't make any difference to me if the little *bairn* lives or dies." Abernathy shifted her from his side. Set her on his horse. "We're going to take a little ride, you and me. Got a cabin up in the hills. Enough food to last a couple of weeks. By then I should have had my fill of you. I will go back to civilization when you start to bore me. All I need to do now is add Nellie to my little harem of MacRaes."

Fannie realized then she would do whatever he asked of her. Even force her. He didn't want her forever. Fox would still take her back. She prayed he would never shun her for something that was out of her control.

"Hope you can cook the food you brought with you because I can't," Fannie tossed that out to see what he would say. "Anice never taught us to cook. Don't know how to do much of anything. You'll have to see to all the chores yourself. I'm useless in every way. Fox doesn't even like to make love to me. Tells me I'm not passionate enough. Wants his woman to respond. Says I'm not to lay on the bed like a cold fish."

"Liar. You will cook. Whatever food you ruin will be yours to eat. Pretty certain you can figure something out. By now, you must have learned something. So, Fox wants a passionate woman. I don't care. You've got the parts I want. Lay on the bed like a stone. That's fine with me. Doesn't change anything I intend."

With his words, her heart sank. He would do what he said. He mounted behind her. She was sitting between his thighs. His arm was held tight around her pushing her breasts up as he pulled her against him. She was sick to her stomach. Bile threatened. She didn't think she could stay here a moment longer. The scent of him made her stomach churn. Thoughts of what he meant to do as soon as they reached the cabin turned her inside out.

'I'm going to be sick.' Frantic, Fannie pushed on his arm. She needed to get off the horse. "Sick all over your boots if you don't let me down."

"Now why would I do something so ridiculous?" Abernathy laughed then pulled her tighter. You're faking. If I let you down, you'll run again. I'll have to chase you. That would be a waste of energy. Don't like to use up valuable energy when I can be playing with you, sucking on all your sweetest parts."

"No, I'm not lying."

"Don't believe you." He spread his finger across her belly.

She felt green around the edges. Running now, the way she felt, was impossible. "Please…please let me down. I'm sick…" It was too late. As she predicted, she lost her lunch on his boots. Just as she told him she would do.

"The devil take you, bitch!" Abernathy shoved her off the horse.

As she flew through the air, she shrieked. The ground flew up to meet her. Fannie landed hard. Breath rushed from her lungs. One more time, she was on her hands and knees. She wretched again and again. There was nothing left in her stomach, but the nausea continued. She'd not had morning sickness for the last two weeks. Now, it was happening to her again. Perhaps this would work to her advantage. Abernathy wouldn't want her if she was cramping with nausea, tossing up everything she ate. He wouldn't wish to be near her. She would disgust him. Ruin his plans.

On the forest floor, she remained curled in a tight ball, moaning. "I can't get up on that big horse. It's going to keep happening." She whimpered, hoping he would leave her here.

"You are an awful lot of trouble for a little whore. Come." Abernathy grabbed her by her arm, hoisting her to her feet.

"No…" she moaned with the movement, her stomach churning and somersaulting.

A small whimper, nothing more stopped him. He held her shoulders then shook her. "You going to be sick again, girl? I won't stand for it. There is no reason. You are too far along for morning sickness. It isn't morning. You can't be sick again."

"Doesn't matter the time of day. If something bothers me, I get sick. You make me sick. The way you smell makes me sick," she added. "You'll have to take your chances. If you try to force me, I'll vomit all over that part of you. Just you wait and see."

"You didn't lose your guts on Taggart," he said. "If you did, your belly wouldn't be swelled with his child."

"No, I like him. I married Fox. He smells nice. Taggart is my name too. Not going to vomit on the man I love. You on the other hand, I detest. Vomit on your boots is too nice for you. I'm going to lose my food on your crotch."

Abernathy backhanded her. She'd not expected him to hit her. Fannie fell backward. Didn't have time to brace herself for the fall. Her head hit a rock. She moaned then the world went black. Strange, she still heard him swearing. Realized the moment when he set her on his horse. This time he didn't hold her in front of him. He put her stomach down across the animal as if she was naught but a sac of grain. The horse's back was between her breasts and the swell of her child. Her head hung on one side her feet on the other. His hand was on the small of her back holding her in place. She worried about the baby.

She didn't know if she was dreaming, her imagination working overtime. Cast adrift in blackness, she didn't comprehend if she was alive or dead. There was nothing for her to focus on except the velvet blackness she saw. Nothing for her to see or hear. No coherent thought fluttered through her muddy brain.

Fannie wanted Fox. Didn't want to die. She was too young to find out about a heaven she didn't know if she believed in. If she died, so would Fox's baby. She couldn't allow her baby to die before he was even born. Understood she needed to do what Abernathy told her no matter the personal cost.

No! She was dead, on her way to heaven. Fannie fought to climb from the darkness of her mind. Didn't know how long she'd been like this. Before she saw light, Fannie heard Abernathy muttering to himself. She heard him curse. Realized he was carrying her. Heard him kick in a door. The wood banged on the wall. If she remained in the black void, he wouldn't force her. Would give Fox along with Rory time to find her.

After he set her down, he slapped her cheeks. Yelled at her. Swore several times before walking away. She heard his booted footsteps as he strode through the home. Heard herself groan from the pain in her head. Fannie couldn't move. When she tried to open her eyes, she couldn't. Still, all she saw was darkness. She kept trying to see light.

With a slow steady effort, taking what seemed like hours, she opened her eyes. Fannie was staring at a ceiling. Pushing up on her elbows, she looked around the room. Abernathy was lighting a lantern. It was dark outside. A full moon beyond the window cast shimmering light inside the small home. Fannie fell back, closing her eyes as her head hit the pillow. The throbbing on the back of her head was horrible. She hurt everywhere. Her hands. Her knees. Most of all her head.

When he sat on the bed beside her, the cloying scent of him turned her stomach sour. Fannie knew she was going to wretch and heave again. She didn't have anything inside her. Nothing. There was nothing for her to lose.

"I know you're awake. It's about time you opened up your eyes." With the back of his hand, he caressed her cheek. She shuddered. Revulsion swept through her. "I'm going to have you now. Don't wish to wait one second more. Made that mistake with Nellie as well as Tessa. No, not going to wait to have you. Lie back and I will do everything. You don't have to move a muscle. If you don't do as I say. I'll use the straps."

"Straps?" she whispered, confused.

Rolling to the opposite side of the bed from where Abernathy sat, she vomited nothing. Dry heaves constricted her belly. She moaned then groaned again. Sickness invaded her soul. She set her hand on her aching belly. Prayed the baby was doing fine. She felt a little elbow or knee press against her hand.

"Stop pretending, you little bitch," he growled. "You are going to sit up now. You are going to be well. I'm going to take all your clothes off for you. Want to see your breasts, touch them, bite," Abernathy commanded, to no avail. "Don't want any more of this play acting. You hit your head when you fell off my horse. A little headache is the only thing wrong with you. We will do what I came all this way to do. You've been asleep. You're well rested. You'll spread your legs for me."

With all the strength she could find inside, she pulled herself up. Focused on his sneering mouth. Hated him with all her being. "You pushed me off because I vomited on your shiny black boots. I didn't fall. You are not a nice man." Her stomach so at odds with her, she rolled into a fetal position, holding her belly, groaning.

"On the contrary, I'm a very nice man to those who treat me as I deserve to be treated, with kindness. You don't act like a woman should. Females are submissive. They give themselves over to a man's better judgement. Your sisters weren't either. You along with your sister's disobedience is Anice's fault. She gave you girls too much leeway."

"I'd laugh at you if my head didn't hurt so much. I've got a splitting headache. I can't do anything you've asked." Fannie lay back on the bed, her forearm splayed over her eyes. She wanted some headache powder. Didn't suppose Abernathy had any.

Abernathy seemed to have a change of mind. He looked at her, then the kitchen, as if he wanted food more than he did her. "I'm hungry. Need for you to fix me dinner. After we eat, I'm going to play with you, toy with my sex slave. You will like me then. You will scream with your pleasure as your mother does when I take her. Anice even likes it when I spank her with my belt. Would you like me to thrash your little butt? Would you want to have me smack your little fanny?" He hooted with laughter at his witticism. "We will see."

"No. You won't do anything to me. I'm sick. I will throw up all over you. Go away." He was an arrogant beast. Fannie didn't want anything more to do with Nelson. She closed her eyes then wished herself back into oblivion. It seemed she got her wish. Blackness descended. This time Fannie knew where she was. Understood she wasn't dreaming. If she was dreaming, her dreams would be filled with Fox.

When next she woke, sunshine filled the room. She was still dressed. Abernathy didn't try anything while she was unconscious. He told her he would undress her. Leave her naked. Fox would come for her. He would discover where Abernathy took her. He would be here soon, pounding down the door with the sheriff from the village. Fannie knew Walker had a sheriff because she danced with him when all the town celebrated their wedding.

"You're awake. It's about time," Abernathy sat by the bed. He was drinking straight from a bottle. Looked like it could be brandy. There were bags under his eyes. "Time for me to dally with my little plaything. Your sickness made me wait for you. Not going to postpone this any longer."

"What time is it?"

"You fell asleep. It's the afternoon of the second day since you decided to become my next mistress. You were sleeping all that time. Wasting precious seconds we could have together," he was shaking his head and tsking. "Was not well done of you. Don't like to be ignored by my mistress. I've had to wait to have sex with you. I had no dinner except for the bread I bought in town. You will get up now and make us dinner. It is past five o'clock. I'm hungry for food as well as for you. I've had to put up with your failures." Sometime in the last day or night, he'd loosened the buttons of her shirt. He ran a fingertip along the opening, parting the fabric more with each pass.

Gulping for control, she fought the urge to bat his hand away. "I can't cook," Fannie groaned from the pain from the very real ache in her head.

"You are female. You can cook. Women are born knowing how to cook." Abernathy pulled her so she was sitting. The fabric of her blouse falling open.

She whimpered at the roaring pain in her head. When he let go of her arm, Fannie fell back on the bed. "You will have to make your own food. I don't have the strength to sit, let alone stand. Go away." She was afraid he would tie her arms as well as her legs to the bed.

Abernathy must have seen she was telling the truth. He cursed then left the room, slamming the door behind him. An eerie silence stretched her nerves. He would stay away, for how long? She didn't like feeling helpless.

Fannie wished she could fall asleep. Wished she possessed the strength to run from him. If she didn't, he would return then force her. First, he would undress her. She didn't want to be naked in front of Abernathy. Fox would find her soon. What was keeping him so long? Where did Abernathy go?

This was all too much for her. Pushing against the mattress, Fannie tried to sit up again. The effort was futile. She was thirsty. Needed water. After several tries, she managed to sit up to lean against the headboard. Saw the leather straps at the foot of the bed. Turned to see more straps attached to the headboard. Realized those were meant for her if she disobeyed his commands.

Maybe she could figure out something to cook for him. She'd watched Ol' Sam make stew enough times. Cooking couldn't be too hard. She would do what she had to in order to survive. Understood she needed something to eat.

Fox would find her.

~ * ~

315

After talking to Fox, Rory raced down the mountain, his body thrumming with pent up energy. His nerves stretched far too thin. His heart was racing with frantic need to get to Nellie, to make certain she was still in Fox's home. When he reached Fox's house, he leapt off his horse then tossed the reins to one of the stable hands. He was eager to see Nellie, to run his hands over her. He didn't want to admit his feelings for Nellie went beyond friendship. Hated she still kept her back stiff when he was near. Once, a week ago, he believed she was softening to him. Later, he decided it was wistful thinking on his part.

He tossed the reins of his horse to the stable boy. "Take care of Satan. He's been ridden hard. Give him extra feed after you've brushed him down." He strode across the yard. Heard the absolute silence surrounding the home.

"Yes, sir."

With his heart in his throat, Rory strode to the porch, two-stepping the stairs. His boots thudded against the planked wood. Afraid for what he might encounter, he didn't bother to knock. He never knocked on Fox's door. Never felt the need. Impatient with worry, he pushed the door too hard. It banged on the other side. The crash brought Agnes from the kitchen with her mouth gaping open, eyes wide with surprise. Now that she knew who caused the commotion, she stood in the doorway, drying her hands on a towel as if he hadn't barged into the house.

"You!" Nellie's startled word stopped him midstride. She sat on a chair, sewing something that was now on the floor. Her eyes were wide pools of stricken terror.

He didn't know she could sew. Her face was pale. She stared at him as if she was seeing a ghost. He'd not meant to frighten her or Agnes. Sometimes he was unthinking. He'd been in such a damn big hurry. "Me…" he told her with a voice that didn't sound calm only a bit sarcastic. He tipped his hat back. "Surprised to see me? My visit is coming early this week. I will be staying here tonight as well as tomorrow night. Longer if it becomes necessary." Setting his hat on the coat stand, he walked farther into the room.

"Why? You comprehend I don't want you here." She picked the fabric up from the floor. Didn't yet seem to realize the importance of this visit. As if it was a second thought, she asked, "What are you doing here?"

"I do understand how you feel about me. Mores the pity." He looked to Agnes then back to Nellie. "Fox has the gut feeling your favorite Lord Abernathy is in the immediate vicinity. While the boss needs to stay at the base camp with Fannie, he sent me here."

She turned whiter than new fallen snow; her beautiful green eyes looked as if they might leap from her face, they were so huge. Damn, he should have eased into the reason he was here. Should have… No there wasn't an easy way to break the news. If she was frightened, she would do as he ordered. Didn't wish to take chances with her life.

"How does he know? Did he see him? Was there a letter from Jasper?" Nellie asked, turning breathless by the end of her bumbling.

"None of the above. As I said, it's a feeling a man gets when he knows someone is watching him and he can't see the person. The little hairs on the back of his neck stand up. His belly cramps. Can't stop looking over his shoulder."

Nellie was shaking her head. "Not just a man, I've felt that way for a few days. Agnes and I don't leave the house. There is usually at least one man at each door."

"Damn! You've felt someone is watching you? Fox sent Ol' Sam into Walker to find out if anyone has seen an aristocrat speaking funny sounding English. Didn't think he could hide there. He would need directions along with a place to stay. We will know where he is at. When the people we know discover what he wants, we'll run him off. Make it so he'll never bother us again. It's an old-fashioned punishment. Meant for those with no loyalties except to themselves."

"When will we know? What kind of punishment?"

Rory watched her long slender fingers drum on the arm of the chair. Seemed she was nervous as hell. His nerves could snap at any moment. He was so damn worried about her.

"Hard to say. Sam is supposed to check if there is any mail from Jasper or the Duke of Southcliff. While I'm here, I'm not leaving your side." He realized that wasn't something he should have pointed out. Sleeping in her room was a necessity. She slept on the first floor. Easy to get at for a creative and motivated man.

Nellie sipped air, her eyes narrowing. "You are not going to be with me every moment. You understand I won't allow you in my bedroom."

Thinking remaining with her all the time was a fine idea, he realized he could not. She would need a few moments of privacy every now and then. "Don't know about that. Depends on the measure of the threat. You say you feel as if something is wrong."

"Yes. Ever since last night."

"Dinner is ready," Agnes announced, as if she wanted to stop the escalating argument. "You two can hash over the details of this visit during a good meal. We are having fish. Caught by one of the stable hands this morning. I fried them in butter."

Rory's mouth watered in anticipation. His stomach rumbled. He hadn't eaten since this morning. "Those baby potatoes too, smothered in sweet butter?" he asked, thinking this meal might be better than the one being prepared at the base camp. Agnes rarely cooked because she didn't wish to hurt Ol' Sam's feelings. Tonight, she was the chef.

"Yes, also peas in cream sauce. Made fresh bread this afternoon. It's still warm from the oven," Agnes told them.

"My mouth is watering with anticipation." Rory imagined he could taste everything she mentioned. "You are a saint, Agnes." He pulled her into his arms then whirled her around the room.

"Put me down," she wailed. "You're making me dizzy."

"Ah, Agnes, a man couldn't ask for a better woman."

In the dining room, Rory pulled out Nellie's chair for her to sit, then the chair for Agnes. He wanted to impress her with his manners. She called him rude. If he wished, he could be rude. Tonight, he was going be a gentleman.

Agnes said grace.

Between bites of food the conversation continued. "Best you think of some way I can be with you all night. I will stay in your room. Since you sleep on the first-floor, your window would be easy to access. Anyone wanting to get at you wouldn't have a speck of trouble."

He watched Nellie bristle. Saw indignation in her expression. "No! I mean it Rory. You are not sleeping in my bedroom." As if to give emphasis to her words, she pointed her fork at him.

Should have pointed her knife. A knife would have had more impact.

"You have no say in this. Your safety is more important than any missish airs you wish to put on."

"Missish!"

Agnes interrupted their argument with a plan that Nellie shouldn't refuse. "I'll have a cot brought into Nellie's room. If there is evidence your Lord Abernathy is in or near Walker, I won't be able to sleep a wink when Nellie is alone during the night. Nellie, you must realize this is not your typical situation. Common sense is what is needed here."

"No!" Nellie protested. "I won't allow him to sleep in the room with me. It's not right."

"Yes," Rory agreed with Agnes' proposition. "I will give you the time to don your night clothing. Then I will be with you. You can leave a light on if that would make you feel more comfortable. Whatever you want. Promise I won't ravish you on the spot. You will still be a virgin in the morning."

She looked perturbed then determined. Her lips were smashed together. She gulped for oxygen, looking as if she would shake him until he rattled. Understood it wouldn't be physically possible. "I have a gun. Luke bought it for me last time he was in town. I don't need…"

Before he could stop himself, his laughter hooted from him. Perhaps he should have tapped huge guffaw back a bit. She looked boiling mad, more furious than a moment ago when they were speaking of sharing a bedroom. "Do you know how to load it or shoot the damn weapon for that matter?"

"Teach me." The statement was a command not a question. Now, some of her anger flew away to be replaced with hope.

"No." He wanted to remain adamant with this stance. On the other hand, perhaps teaching her would be a way for him to win her confidence. She might soften towards him. He could touch her when he showed her how to hold the gun. He would be close to her. Wrap her in his arms while he was teaching. Then again, "Hell! You might shoot your damn little foot."

At the conclusion of his statement, she bristled, her cheeks turning rosy. "I'm not stupid or inept! Not going to shoot anyone except Abernathy. After I learn, I might shoot your foot," she retorted, her anger at his refusal appearing to grow, though there was little to no venom in her words. When she brought in a deep breath of air, her sweet breasts moved, tantalized every male part of his body. Those beautiful jewels were off limit to him.

"You couldn't. Not unless I was sleeping. The answer is no for the second time. No for a third time too."

"Reconsider, please. We both realize you cannot stay here for more than two nights. I would like to be able to defend myself against a creature like Abernathy."

He hitched in a double dose of oxygen then let the air sift through his lips while he found himself thinking. Tapping his fingers together beneath his chin, he spoke, "Suppose that's a reasonable notion. Most women living in these parts can shoot a gun as well as a rifle. Alright, tomorrow morning we will begin your lessons. You will do what I tell you without argument. In this matter, your opinions don't count for a damn thing." Rory leaned forward, his arms resting on the table. "Do you think you could shoot a man? If you were face to face with another human, could you pull the trigger?"

Nellie looked him straight in the eyes. Stole a breath of air from the room. "Lord Nelson Abernathy is not a man. He isn't human. Yes, I could shoot him with pleasure in my heart. Would never be able to kill anyone else. Abernathy is scum needing to be brought down."

For some reason, Rory was pleased with her answer. "I'm not certain…with your sweet little heart," he paused to form the right words, "don't know if you could shoot him to kill. You could aim for his foot. He'd be hoppin' mad."

"Sounds like a fine idea to me," Agnes cackled with a charmed snort at the picture he painted, seeming to delight her. "Maybe you can teach me too."

"Do you have a gun?" Rory felt as if he was about to repeat himself. Thought Agnes wouldn't have trouble shooting Lord Abernathy either.

"Have my late husband's gun at my house. You'd need to send someone to fetch it. I'm not going home as long as there is a threat to Nellie."

"Done! I'll send Luke tonight." He was pleased with the ladies. They were stepping up to face the challenge. While he still held reservations about Nellie, he was beginning to realize she wasn't the fragile piece of fluff he first thought her to be. He wasn't positive he every truly thought that about her. She seemed to have more backbone than he gave her credit for before.

The knocking on the back door caught his attention. Nellie looked up, a bite of fish on her fork. Agnes grunted when she saw Ol' Sam at the door shifting from one foot to the other, his old hat held in his hands placed on his chest.

"The boss told me I was to stop here before going on to base camp. Let you all know the news from town. May I come in?"

Rory motioned him inside, eager to learn what he discovered. "What did you find out?" Rory asked while he pointed to a place at the table. "You hungry?" he nodded.

Agnes dished a plate for him. "Sit down and enjoy. Talk with your mouth full if you like. We need to hear everything."

"Couple of things," Ol' Sam chewed then smiled. "This is darn good, Agnes," he said pointing at the fried fish. He looked to Nellie before he spoke. She gasped in a bit of air as if she knew what he would say. "Your Lord Abernathy is in these parts. He wasn't in town. Not staying there anymore. Paid for his hotel then moved on."

"You don't know where he is?" Rory asked, frustrated with the answers. They needed to locate the damn man then send him back to Scotland. "He must have bought some place that's in the wilderness. He likes to be isolated when he has a victim. Was there anything for sale?"

Ol' Sam sipped on the hot coffee Agnes handed him. After he swallowed, then sighed, with apparent satisfaction, "Ran into Maurice at the post office when I was checking to see if there was anything from Glasgow. Told me he took this Lord Abernathy fellow up to the old Cooper place. Seems Abernathy bought it. Plans on bringing the two sisters there as his playthings. Not good, not good at all. Boss is going to be madder than a hornet when he hears this bit of news."

"He's not going to take me anywhere. Rory is teaching me how to shoot. I'll shoot him in his most private parts before I let him kidnap me again."

Rory choked on his meat.

"That true?" Ol' Sam asked, wiping his mouth with his red and white checkered napkin. "You mean to teach the little gal to shoot a gun. Not a bad idea. Should have thought of it sooner. Fox should teach his missus too."

"First thing tomorrow we're starting." When he looked at Nellie, she was smiling. At the sight, his heart skipped a beat. He'd never seen her smile like that before. Wondered if her grin meant she was softening to him. Always positive, Rory decided he made progress in the softening department.

Chapter Ten

When Fox heard the bad news from Ol' Sam he cursed for a few seconds. Ol 'Sam repeated what Maurice had to say to him at the post office. Pinched the bridge of his nose while he tried to think. Halted all the work at the logging camp then raced to the base camp. Most of his men followed. He needed to find Fannie. Terrified for her, his gut soured. She would be with Paul and Meridith. They would never let her out of their sight. He was a good man, a trustworthy man. There was no reason for this unruly fear.

"Fannie!" he called out as soon as he leapt from his horse. "Fannie! Meridith! Paul! Where are you?" Pulling off his gloves, he slapped them against his legs. Called out again. Heard nothing from the three. Beneath his ribs, his heart clamored.

A few of the women came out of their tents to see what the commotion was about. They were all doing something. One held a towel in her hands, another, something she was sewing. A third held a bowl of something she stirred.

"Mr. Taggart?" one asked. "Why are you bellowing? You can't find your wife? She must be in your tent."

He felt frantic with worry. Shaking his head as he searched everyone's expression for clues. "Anyone seen my wife? Fannie is supposed to be with Paul and Meridith. They must not be here. I've found everyone except the three I'm looking for."

"Haven't seen any of them for hours."

"Didn't the women go out to get herbs and vegetables for Ol' Sam's venison stew? We ate the stew but there wasn't anything extra in it. No onions or potatoes. Not one herb was put into the dinner."

Nausea swept his belly. If he didn't keep control of himself, he would be on his knees. Useless. This couldn't be happening. No, they were all three somewhere safe. He was jumping to unfounded conclusions. "No one has seen them?" Damn, the night was dark. He'd need to gather men as well as lanterns. The old Cooper place was a good ten, fifteen miles from here. He didn't know if Fannie was missing. He couldn't just rush off without proof.

If Abernathy abducted her, Fannie would be so scared. Frightened out of her wits. What happened to all of them? Surely, Abernathy couldn't win a fight against Paul. Paul and Rory were the biggest men he knew. There must have been a gun held at Meridith's or Fannie's head. Paul wouldn't let Abernathy take them without a fight.

"Did anyone hear anything? See anything? Fighting or a gun shot?"

"No, nothing." One of the women told him. The others agreed. No one heard anything.

He wished Rory was here by his side. Wished Paul hadn't disappeared with the two women. He needed to rely on the rest of his crew. They were all good men.

Fox started shouting orders then gathering the necessary lights so they could go up the hill. "We must see if we can find them. First, we'll search the immediate area. See if we can uncover any clues. If there is nothing to discover, we will assume Lord Abernathy has all three under his control. Break up in groups. Spread out. Treat this as if we are searching for a lost child. We must cover every square inch of land. If you find anything or anyone, two shots in the air will bring me running."

Holding the lantern high, Fox found he was shaking both from fear for Fannie that he would get to her too late, as well as frustration that, despite his plans, Lord Abernathy would win this round. Abernathy would pay. After he found Fannie, he would make certain the man never tried to grab either of the women again.

An hour later, they were about to give up on the search for clues or the missing people. They needed to head straight for the Cooper place. Time seemed to be melting away. If they left now, they would get there by tomorrow afternoon. Traveling in the dark would be difficult as well as slow. As Fox saw it, there was no other choice.

The night was cloudy. There would be no extra light from the moon. From this camp there were no trails. They would need to forge one of their own making. Fox was beside himself with the impatience he felt. He needed to remind himself he was lucky Ol' Sam ran into Maurice at the post office.

If not, they would need to wait until morning to search again. Every second counted. Would still be guessing as to Fannie's whereabouts. Paul was the best outdoorsman in the group. He could track anything, read clues no one else would recognize.

A female moan caught his attention. "Over here!" he shouted. "Someone is hurt." His heart raced as he followed the small whimpers of pain. Too much time passed while trying to find the body in the dark. Seemed like it took hours to find her.

He saw the white of her petticoat peeking out from behind a bush. He bent down. Placed his hand on her forehead. "Meridith? What happened? Are you alright?" He had too many questions and no answers.

Meridith looked confused. She tried to sit. Fell back with a soft moan of pain. "Fox? Where's Paul? Fannie?"

"What happened?" Fox asked a second time. He needed to discover the truth. He could send a few men back to camp with Meridith. They could carry her.

"I was hoping you could tell me. You don't know where either Paul or Fannie are?"

He saw the bruise on her jaw. "Someone hit you. You've been out for hours. Is that what happened?"

"Paul…I need to find Paul." She tried to sit up. Failed. Tried again. This time Fox helped her to a sitting position, then to her feet.

"With help, can you walk back to camp? We'll keep looking for Paul." Fox didn't think Abernathy would be foolish enough to confront the big man. He would understand Paul would fight back. If they kept looking, he'd gamble they would find Paul close by. Abernathy would have struck him from behind.

They were not far from the base camp. He was surprised no one heard the confrontation. A skirmish of most sorts would cause noise. Fannie wouldn't keep quiet. He told her to yell if she saw Abernathy. She would have tried.

"Found Paul." The call came from about twenty feet away. "He's out cold. Got a lump the size of Texas on the back of his head."

"Is my husband alright?" Meridith managed to remain standing, clutching Fox, trying to move toward her husband. "He has to be."

"He's out cold, ma'am. It's going to take a couple of men to carry him back to camp. We'll bring him right to your tent, Meridith. No worries. He's breathing. His big heart is beating."

Together, Meridith and Fox struggled through the dark to Paul. Meridith collapsed by his side, touching him, running her hand along his face. With a sigh of relief, she found his pulse. Set her head against his cheek.

"Paul is alive, thank God. Don't know what I'd do without him. I would be lost." Tears slid down her cheeks.

Fox felt relief for Meridith sweep through him. Now they needed to find Fannie. He didn't think they should spare too much time looking for her here. With Paul out of the way, Abernathy wouldn't waste time abducting her. He would take her to the cabin. Force her. Fox's stomach churned. Felt as if his heart was in his throat.

The man couldn't think he would get away with this. Abernathy would see what vigilante justice meant. It was no longer a question of time. By now, he would have forced Fannie to his will. Fox's fists clenched then unclenched as his mind struggled with his rage. Filled with the helpless feeling he couldn't control. He hit his fist against his palm.

"Get them both back to camp. John, Harry and Thomas, we're going to make pine tar. Enough to cover Abernathy from his head to the tips of his toes. Think Ol' Sam has already started the fire going. He came back from the logging camp with the idea. Be ready by morning with what we need. We'll bring Abernathy to this camp. We will see to his punishment here."

Fierce rage boiled up in him. He set the women to locating enough feathers for their use once he was covered in tar. He meant to humiliate Abernathy as well as give him a taste of the torture he put women through with his arrogant ways. This wouldn't kill him. What the tar and feathers would do would torture, along with degrade. His flesh would be burned from the heated liquid. The pine tar had to be hot enough to melt. That was when they would pour the material over his naked body.

Once Paul, along with Meridith, were comfortable in their tent, and with five men, he set off for the Cooper place. When they left, Meridith was tending Paul. He was still unconscious. The pine tar was being cooked in a huge pit. The sun was starting to shine through the trees. He felt a rise of exhilaration. They would find Fannie then he would bring her home. He would love her until she forgot Abernathy's vile touch.

Six men rode hard through the day. Six men came upon the cabin a little after five o'clock in the afternoon. All seemed quiet. Peaceful. The men spread out. He didn't expect a show down. Abernathy would not believe they would find him. He would be caught unaware. This capture would be easy. Still, he wasn't about to take one chance with Fannie's life. They would approach with caution. There would be no mistakes.

With one of the other men, they were in front of the door. Fox nodded. Together they pushed in the door. What he saw brought bile to his throat. Nellie was lying on the bed, her skirt pushed up around her waist. She was struggling. Abernathy above her, holding her hands above her head trying to tie them to the bedframe with straps.

"Told you. You little bitch, I'll tie you if you don't behave!" He slapped her cheek. Fannie's head jerked back.

"No!" Fannie cried out. "Fox!" She saw him, her eyes widening.

"You're mine! I've got you."

Fox didn't stop to think. So, enraged, he reacted before Abernathy realized his cabin had been invaded. "You will pay for that!"

With a roar of anger, he caught Abernathy by the back of his fancy frock coat. Yanked him off his wife. "You bastard!" He slammed his fist into Abernathy's jaw. With a soft groan, Abernathy tumbled to the ground. He didn't move. Fox felt immense satisfaction at the sight of the so-called lord of the realm lying on the floor. He wiped his hands together, satisfied, then turned his attention to Fannie.

"Fox," she whispered, "I knew you would come."

Pulling her gown to her ankles, he asked, his heart racing. "Fannie?" He touched her cheek. Grimaced at the red mark on her face. His body shook with both fear as well as relief. "How are you?" He saw the silver trail of her tears sliding along her cheeks. Fox wished he could smile at her. Wished this never happened.

"I'm fine. Scared. Terrified." She reached out. Touched his face with her fingertips. "You came in time. He didn't force me."

"Doesn't matter if he did. I would still want you. You are the most precious part of my life." He bent to kiss her. Touched his tongue to her lips, tasted the salt from her tears. Felt relief at her words.

Fannie held onto his shoulders. Her fingers pressed against him. "Have to tell you why. Need to talk."

"We have time. Don't need to say anything now." He was so thankful; his body heaved a huge sigh.

"I do. You see, I was sick. Throwing up…on his shiny black boots. Abernathy was so angry, he pushed me off the horse. There were other things. I fell backward. Hit my head on a rock, I think. Was unconscious most of the time. Just woke up a little while ago. You came to me in time."

Abernathy was lying on the floor. He was a pathetic sight. "Bind him tight then toss him over his horse. We will tend to his retribution with all to see. His sentence will be just and fairly executed." Fox knelt beside his wife. Touched her gently on her bruised cheek. "He hit you, too? Meridith has a similar bruise. Did he do anything else?" Fox believed her. Abernathy had not raped her because she was in such a state he couldn't.

"He slapped me. I fought him, Fox." She set her hand on her belly. "Seems our little one here thought to help me out. I did do it. I threw up all over his boots. Was so sick, even Abernathy couldn't find joy in taking me. He was so furious because he didn't want to wait. What are you going to do with him?"

"Tar and feather him," Fox's voice was calm, pitched low, filled with anger coupled with relief. "Humiliate him until he'd like to die. He won't though, too bad. Back at camp, the men are melting the pine tar. The women are gathering feathers." He wanted to see this man degraded, brought to his knees. Just as he dishonored as well as tainted so many women, Abernathy would feel the emotion deep into his soul.

"Will that kill him? Wouldn't want for anyone to hang you for his death. The man is a worthless swine."

"No, it will burn his skin. He will have blisters that will need healing. When the pine tar is put on his body, he will scream with pain. The women will have the feathers. The best thing about this punishment, even Lord Nelson Abernathy will never dare return. Will let him know if he does come back, he will hang. I will let the women strip him of his finery. Shave him so the tar has no barriers between him and his flesh."

"You will do this to him naked?" Fannie smiled. "He deserves the punishment. If it's alright, I would help."

"No one in the camp will speak of it to the authorities. If he goes to them, we'll pretend innocence. It will be his word against ours. The punishment was Ol' Sam's idea. Agreed it would be a fine one. It goes back to the seventeen hundreds, maybe back farther than that. The colonists used to tar and feather the British tax collectors. We will leave the finer details up to you and Nellie as well as the other women if they wish to make comments."

Fox turned to Luke, "Get his bag and his horse. His possessions will go with him to camp. We will ride through the night. I'm eager to put thoughts of Abernathy behind me." Fox was impatient to have Fannie with him. He wanted to make love to her as soon as the men saw Abernathy on his way to Walker. The so-called lord of the realm would need to parade himself down the main street naked. The sight would be fine, a good one for a sunny day. Too bad he wouldn't see the event transpire.

Fox kept Fannie in front of him. He couldn't bear to let her go. Afraid he might lose her again. "Lean on me. Sleep if you like. I will be here for you. If you need anything, tell me." This trip back to base camp, they didn't ride as hard, arriving a little before the noon hour the next day. Abernathy spent the trip tossed over the saddle of his horse, his head and feet dangling on either side. His hands along with his feet were tied together beneath his horse. Most of the trip he'd been unconscious. Silent. Fox didn't question the fact when he woke they would hear quite a lot of spontaneous talk which would do him no good.

"I'd like that." He felt her snuggle against him. Knew when she drifted to sleep. Liked the idea the babe helped protect her from Abernathy. Enjoyed the fact she vomited on his boots. Was glad she'd been unconscious for the duration even though he wasn't pleased she hurt herself. Wanted to put her injury on Abernathy's shoulders. Fannie told him she fell, backing away from him.

When Abernathy woke about an hour from camp, he started cursing. Yelling at them. "Let me go! How dare you? I'm a Lord of the realm! You can't do this to me. I won't stand for this treatment. You are all peasants." He tried to rear up, to see what was going on.

"Not a Lord of this realm," one of the men called out with a yowl of laughter. "Here in America, you're nothing. Titles don't mean anything to

Americans. We fought two wars and won two wars to rid ourselves of aristocrats like you."

Fox listened to the banter between his men and Abernathy. He held his wife tight against him, resting his chin on the top of her head. As the small group closed in on the camp, he sent one of his men for Rory to bring Nellie. Fox felt certain Nellie would want to play a part in the punishment of this so called 'Lord of the realm'.

"Heard you dropped my wife over her horse. Didn't think anything of doing that. So," he paused for emphasis, "why would I care about you?

"You are positive you are fine?" He bent close to Fannie, touched the tip of her ear with his tongue. Felt the whisper of her desire twist through her small body. She would be fine. Was a fighter just as her sisters were.

She turned to caress his jaw. "You never told me you found Paul and Meridith. Abernathy told me he hit Paul with a club. Thought he might die. I prayed for him then the same for his wife. She is very nice. He loves her so much."

"Meridith woke up while we were searching the woods. Her moan of pain brought us to her. Otherwise, we might not have found her. Paul, when I left, was not awake. He must have been hit very hard." Fox feared for the man. He was sturdy and strong as an ox as well as loyal. Despite his great size, could shimmy up a tree faster than all his employees. When the logs were in the holding tank, he could stand on top, dancing with the easy roll of the logs on the water longer than anyone. He had the quickest feet backward as well as forward of anyone he knew.

"Abernathy laughed about hitting him in the back of the head so hard he might not ever wake. I think he hoped he killed the man. He did know he silenced them long enough for him to get away." Fannie rested back against Fox. He saw her lashes flutter then lie still.

"You must be exhausted. Promise you won't have to work at anything for the next week."

Fannie laughed. He loved the sound of her laughter. She set her hands on his thighs. The gesture rocked him to the core. "I never work. No one will let me close to whatever is cooking. When we need our clothing washed, we bring it back to your home. Agnes does all the laundry."

"Our home," Fox corrected.

"Our home, Agnes does the washing," she repeated. "I would like to work at something. Find something I am good at."

He cupped her breast in his hand. "I prayed for you all the time you were missing. Didn't know if I'd find you in time. Due to lady luck, I did." He ran his hand along her belly. "You are very round. I want to make love to my wife. Need to give her the pleasure she deserves. What do you say to that?" he asked, still massaging the delightful swell of her belly.

"I do believe all you just said is wonderful. You will be able to hold me, make love to me, give me my pleasure in a short time. I've no doubt you're counting the seconds. Would enjoy hearing my husband's groan of desire." Fannie placed her hands on his arms, encouraging him to keep his hands where they were. "Did Rory reach my sister? She is safe. I assume."

"Very safe."

"Don't suppose she was too pleased when he showed up early for his weekly visit. Wish Nellie would stop being such a witch where Rory is concerned. She doesn't need to be treated as if she is fragile. Nellie isn't delicate. She is a strong woman. Rory puts her on a pedestal. She takes advantage at every opportunity."

"You're right on all counts. When he got to the logging camp with the news about Abernathy, Ol' Sam told me Rory agreed to teach Nellie and Agnes to shoot a gun. Rory was worried she'd shoot her foot. What about you? Would you like to learn? Most women in these parts know how to use one. They don't shoot a foot either, unless doing so is their intent. Heard Nellie said she would shoot Lord Abernathy's foot as well as another male part of him. Too bad that's not to be his punishment. If it was, we could line up all the women. Let them hit one foot or the other with a bullet or... That won't be as much enjoyment as what we have planned. Don't wish to maim him for life. Watching the man dance might be fun. What I want is to be positive he will never return."

"Meridith knows how to use a gun. Paul taught her. Says it's an easy way for a woman to protect herself. Says it's not just the two-legged varmints that can be dangerous to a woman in these woods. There are four-legged varieties too."

"He's right on all counts."

Fannie was running her hands along his arms. She circled his wrist with her fingers. They were almost to the encampment.

Fox found he was eager for this to end. Once Abernathy was sent on his way, both Fannie along with Nellie would be free of the man. They could relax. Stop looking over their shoulder for trouble. He would never bother any of the MacRae girls again. When he reached Glasgow, he might remain subdued for a short time. Well, most likely not. Abernathy would take up his old ways. Find other women to torment.

The rescue party rode into camp amid welcoming cheers. Meridith walked from her tent, a smile on her beautiful face. She mouthed the words. "He's awake as well as feisty. Doesn't wish to stay in bed unless I'm there too." After the words everyone heard, she laughed. The sound was wonderful.

Appeared Paul didn't stay where his wife wanted him. He stood behind her, his hands on her shoulders. "You got the man!" Paul yelled, shaking his fist in the air. "I want a piece of him, as do many others in your employ. No one here likes the fact he kidnapped your wife or hurt mine."

"Yes, he's here. Because of unexpected circumstances, he didn't force my wife. For that one fact, I'm going to allow him to live. Otherwise, our vigilante justice would include a tree along with a hangman's noose. If that were the case, he wouldn't be buried in Scottish soil or his family plot. Not that I care about where the bastard is buried."

"Imagine that's the right thing to do," Paul called back. "He can live. What Ol' Sam suggested is just the thing. We will all witness his pain along with the humiliation he will feel at the hands of our women folk."

Fox hooted his laughter. Soothed Fannie's belly with the palm of his hand. Felt his *bairn* move. The day was a good one. "We're going to treat Lord Nelson Abernathy to a little Yankee hospitality along with a *wee* bit of vigilante justice. Is the pine tar ready? Teach him he can't walk over us because he thinks he is better. A title doesn't make a better man. Do you want to paint it on him or dump the whole barrel?" he asked Fannie. "It's up to you since you were the wounded party."

"Me?" Fannie pointed at herself. "I get to decide what happens? Think we should paint the man, cover every square inch of his royal flesh. The heat would be slow torture. Don't wish for this to happen all at once. All who wish can take a turn, step forward." Fannie said, a large smile on her face. "I want the first chance to brush the pine tar on his naked body. Know where I'll paint him."

"Ouch, you can be vicious. Remind me not to get on your bad side," Fox said with a bark of laughter following. "Are you thinking what I'm thinking?"

"He was going to take all my clothes off. I want a shot at that too. He is going to have the stuff all over him. Every part, even the part you and I are thinking about. What does it matter? The burns will keep him celibate for a time. He won't be forcing anyone until he heals. Could it do permanent damage?"

"No, the tar won't. Any woman who wants to participate in the disrobing can do so," Fox told her. He took the knife from his boot. This is for cutting cloth. Nothing else." He laughed at the face Fannie made for him. Was certain she would like to slice and dice Nelson's sex then stuff his manhood down his throat.

Fox supposed she might also wish to bury the point in his heart. She wouldn't. This punishment was long lasting. He would feel the pain for weeks. Might not be able to lie down or sit for the duration. There would be no sex in the forecast. A man couldn't stand forever.

Still all trussed up, Abernathy was dumped from his horse. He fell on the ground. Fox imagined he must have eaten some dirt. He sputtered. Tried to move to his knees. Fell again when Meridith shoved her foot in his back. She set her foot on his head, keeping his face buried in the dirt along with the pine needles.

"Hope you weren't planning on leaving his pants on. After what he planned on doing to Fannie, there is no other way for him except naked," Meridith said as she focused her gaze on the Lord of the Realm who was lying in the dirt.

From his horse, Fox helped Fannie slide to the earth. She strode to Abernathy. With her knife in hand, she slit the back of his trousers in strips then ripped them from him. "There, how does that feel?" He still had his small clothes on. Fannie handed the weapon to Nellie, who arrived riding in front of Rory moments before.

"You bastard!" Nellie kicked him in the side. "Take that! You miserable excuse for a man. It's my turn now. I'll never forget what you tried to do to me. Wish Mother were here to have her punishment along with you."

"Way to give it to him, Nel!" Rory applauded her. "Nice job."

"Yes, makes me feel fine." She kicked him again. Nellie did the same with his underwear, making sure he felt the cold steel of the knife on his buttocks. "Would enjoy cutting you somewhere else. That part of you that enjoys hurting women."

Men and women alike cheered her on. Both Nellie and Fannie walked around him, staring at his revealed parts. The men lifted Abernathy. Turned him so all could see his nakedness. With his hands held tight behind his back, he couldn't cover himself. All the women jeered, calling him a tiny failure of a man.

"Stop this. Stop all of you. I will have you prosecuted. You can't just disrobe a man! You can't do that other thing either." He was shaking as he shouted.

Nellie handed the knife to Meridith.

"What clothing do you wish to rid him of? His fancy frock coat was left behind at the Cooper place," Fox said, enjoying this more than anything. Abernathy was trembling in his boots. "Do you know what tarring and feathering a person entails? No, of course you don't. A little surprise never hurt anyone. Take your stab, Meridith. Don't draw blood."

The men held Abernathy while she slit his silk shirt from hem to neck. After that, she cut the sleeves off. "Once he is cowed, we will unbind him."

"You are a sorry excuse for a man." Meridith spat at him. Her spittle hit him on the cheek.

Meridith handed the knife to a friend. Each woman took a little part of his clothing away from him until he wore nothing but his boots. The women were vicious. Fox imagined he could be the same way if he feared rape.

"Do his shoes go too?" Fannie asked as she focused her curious gaze on her husband. "I want him bare…all of him. No reason to make his trip back to Walker an easy one or in any way comfortable. Besides, he does have his horse. We won't steal from him. He can ride if his buttocks aren't blistered."

"Then his boots go too, if that's what you wish. I wouldn't have this any other way." He turned to the crowd again. "What do you all say? Are you agreed with my wife?"

"He should wear nothing," Paul yelled, shaking his fist at him. "Did you have any consideration for the women you abused? No! Strip him naked. Make him pay."

"Strip him naked! Strip him! Strip him," the people yelled. The chant continued. "Strip him!"

In seconds, his boots along with his socks vanished. Abernathy slumped over, as if that would hide him from the crowd. The men holding him straightened him. He was naked for all to witness the beginning of his humiliation.

"Next, we shave him. Makes the heat of the tar all the more potent." Paul brought out a cup of shaving crème along with a straight razor. Paul began with his groin, shaving away the hair. Fannie shaved his head. Nellie his chest, then Meridith, his back. The rest of the women, in turn, got rid of the hair on his arms, as well as his legs. In no time he was hairless.

"Hand my wife the brush. She says she has a certain place she wants to paint. I told her ouch. Didn't sway her one tiny bit. When she has finished with her artistry, Nellie can be next in line, then Meridith, of course. After that, if anyone, man or woman, wishes to use the brush on our very own Lord Nelson Abernathy, they will get the chance." With a dramatic air, Fox held his hands out, making a full circle. "We won't' finish with this man until all are satisfied with his punishment."

Facing Abernathy, whose face tuned white with his fear, Fox proclaimed, "Lord Nelson Abernathy, you are hereby sentenced to tar and feathering. Go to it ladies. Do your best or your worst."

Abernathy was pushed to stand by the pit of pine tar that had been burning over the last twenty-four plus hours. Steam rose from the crater. With the first stroke to his sex, Abernathy screamed. Fannie covered his male parts in the tar. Soon he was sobbing and crying out with the agony. Nellie painted his cheeks, nose, as well as the top of his head, not missing one spot. He was covered with light brush strokes of pine tar. Once all the women were satisfied, the men brought buckets of the tar to cover him from his shoulders to his toes. No part was left untouched. He stood in a solid ring of people. The men slit the ropes securing both his feet as well as his hands.

The feathers were tossed on him. His bag was placed at his feet then his horse was brought to him.

"You are free to go," Fox pronounced. "Don't ever return. If you dare to show yourself in Walker, you will hang."

"I can't go anywhere like this?" Abernathy was shaking his head, refusing to leave. "I'm naked. You all saw to that. I would have clothes to wear."

"We won't allow you to remain here. Men, tie his valise to his horse then start toward Walker. If he wants to put clothes on, he may. He should learn they would stick to his skin. He's better off naked. Lead the animal by his reins unless Abernathy decides he wishes to ride. Maybe he can find someone to help him in town. The doc there might be the best bet. If he wants, he can ride his horse. Wonder if that would hurt more than walking on bare feet."

Fox wrapped his arms around his wife, her back pressing against his front. "Now that all the drama is over. Would like to make love to my wife."

"Umm…can we eat first. The baby is telling me he's hungry. We haven't eaten since the day I was dragged away from my husband."

~ * ~

Fox and Fannie were lying in his big feather bed in his home. Neither wished to remain at the base camp for the evening. The two rode back as soon as Abernathy headed toward Walker. Needed time alone in the privacy of his house. Wanted moments free of everyone else to heal. While Abernathy never forced her, she was terrified through the ordeal. Fannie cuddled into Fox's shoulder with a long sigh of pleasure. Kissed his neck at the base.

"It's over. It's truly over. Abernathy will never return here?" Fannie asked, needing reassurance from Fox. Under the circumstances, what man would return? Fox threatened to kill him if he ever saw him near or in Walker. All the other men felt the same.

"Would be shocked if he did. The man is no fool. Made certain Abernathy understood if he came to these parts the vigilante justice would end in his death. My crew would hang him then leave him for whatever wildlife wanted more of him. His body would never be found. After today, the man knows we are serious. He will be in pain for at least a week, perhaps longer. It will be as if he got a severe sunburn over his entire body. There might even be some permanent scarring."

"Maybe his pretty face won't be so pretty any longer. Though…some women think a scar makes a man look rugged," she said, as she smoothed her hands along his chest. "I like the way you feel. Abernathy looked pathetic after his entire body was shaved." When he stood in front of everyone, stripped of all his hair, he appeared a weak man. Not wishing to think of the man any longer, she focused her attention on Fox.

His beautiful body.

She liked winding her fingers through the hair on his chest. Thought about pink aprons. Trailed a path to his groin, first with her fingers then with her mouth. Touched him with her tongue. Nibbled on the flat planes of his hard belly. Heard the low moan of raw passion rise from his chest.

He brought her on top of him. "You wish to have me inside you again? You want me to rock you until you scream then shatter into tiny pieces? Ride me, Fannie. Let me come inside you, so deep I touch your womb."

"Yes, to everything. You are magic to my soul. Need to feel as one with you. Want you to be part of me. Wish to ride you until you groan so loud the neighbors will hear." She felt the rise of his sex touch her intimately.

"We don't have neighbors," his voice was low, intimate and dark. He ran his hands along her sides to beneath her breasts. Cupped both of them within his large hands. Brought his mouth to sip on the tender buds.

"The bunkhouse then. They might hear you. Would come running to see if you were alright." She pressed more kisses on him.

"No one would dare." Fox wound his fingers into her hair. Brought her mouth to meet his. "It is you who will scream with your pleasure, not me. My men would know what we were doing."

He made love to her for the second time since they returned home. He stopped her when she began to play again. "No," Fox didn't let her hold him as she wished. Told her he would explode if she touched him. "I know you are tired. We should see if there is any news about Abernathy. He should be in town by now. If he got lucky, Doc would have seen to his needs."

"Well…one more time would never over tax us? Would it?"

Fannie's fingers continued to roam. Fox stopped her hand, knowing what her target was. "I've created an enchanting monster. Not yet, sweet. It's too soon. I'm a weak man. Playing with one's wife could exhaust a man. We should go downstairs. Have a glass of wine. I'd like to feed you again. You didn't eat for more than a day. Agnes cooked a ham. We could make sandwiches with the ham and cheese. Didn't I hear your stomach grumbling a few seconds ago? Oh, there it goes again."

"That is your stomach. Mine doesn't rumble as loud. I want to hold you. Suck on you. Devour the best parts of you. Would you let me do that in, say an hour. After you've drunk a bit of wine to make you more compliant, you would revel in my mouth covering you. Licking you as if you were my favorite sweet treat. You need food to make you strong again. We could retrieve the pink aprons."

He groaned, then rolled over to pin her to the bed. Fox was inside her. Fannie felt the length of him slide into her. She bit his chin. Nibbled. Pleased with her accomplishment. "You have no idea how this feels to me. You are part of me again. We are one together."

"Are you always ready for me? You were wet, dripping with your nectar." The mating was over in a few seconds.

"Yes, and yes," Fannie told him with delight.

Fast. Hard. Disordered.

Yet wonderful in the culmination. He slipped from inside her. "Now, we are going to feed our other appetites. Put on your dressing gown. Agnes went home for the night. We will be alone. Maybe once I'm strong again, I'll have you on the kitchen table."

"What about Rory and Nellie? Won't they be returning here tonight?" Fannie asked, uncertain of going downstairs wearing almost nothing. "I wouldn't wish for anyone but you to see me like this."

"Rory wanted to stay at the camp. Told him he could use our tent." Fox grinned, as he rose from the bed. Turned to her so she could look at him.

Fannie sipped a breath of air. "Nellie isn't going to like that arrangement. I'll wager the pair will head here as soon as Nellie realizes she is supposed to share a tent with him." Fannie sat up with the covers around her breasts, thinking again about the situation between her sister and Rory.

The two were perfect for each other. She believed the fact with her whole heart. Nellie continued to push Rory away.

"We will be covered. Nothing to see." Fox wrapped himself in his dressing gown before holding his hand out for Fannie. "We are both hungry. I hear your stomach talking to me again. Let's not worry about an intrusion. We won't be naked. Besides, this is our house. We will do as we please."

"Don't know." She found herself shying away from this. "Thinking about the possibilities makes me uncomfortable. Ol' Sam might come by with news." Somehow Ol' Sam seeing her in her dressing gown didn't bother her a much as Rory.

"If they show up, we will bring a tray to the room. We could have our meal in privacy. What do you say? The kitchen or this room? Make a choice." Fox held out her nightgown along with the matching robe.

"I would like to talk to my sister. Positive the two will show up soon."

"And I to Rory. Maybe they've heard news. Ol' Sam was one of the men following Abernathy to town. He will report back. Stop here before he goes on to the camp. We will hear before them."

With clothing on, Fannie felt more comfortable. In the kitchen, Fox poured the wine. Fannie sliced thick slices of bread and ham. Assembled servings of cheese to be paired with the other food. At the wonderful scents, her stomach did growl.

The noise at the front of the house caught her attention. She walked to the door. "Ah, someone else at our doorstep. Seems we are destined to have company. Glad we managed a few moments alone." Fannie smoothed the folds of her robe. "Guess I've got enough on. I shouldn't be bashful."

"Never bashful, only if you were in the same state as our less than favorite Lord of the Realm," Fox barked a laugh. Kissed her hard on the mouth before wrapping his arm around her.

Rory, along with Nellie, appeared in the entrance. Nellie's hand was encompassed by Rory's. Fannie couldn't hold back her smile. This was a long time coming. "Come along to the kitchen. We were getting something to eat. There is plenty. Join us if you're hungry."

Following behind her, Nellie spoke, her voice soft. "As long as I live, I will never forget his naked image all covered with pine tar and feathers. He was so angry; thought he would shake all the pine tar off. Too bad shaking the disgusting stuff off didn't work." Nellie slipped her hand from Rory's as if she realized she was supposed to put distance between them.

He frowned at her but gave her what she silently asked for.

"Abernathy is a pathetic picture of a man. He deserved everything he got," Fannie pointed out, her voice stiff with unleashed emotion. "I also want to know how he fared, as well as be informed as to when he departs Walker. The only thing that would have made this day better was if Mother, too, had been tarred and feathered."

"True," Nellie said, agreeing with her sister. "She is more despicable than Abernathy. She sold her own daughters to that horrid man. Her punishment should be more than a little tar and feathers covering her."

Fannie let out a long slow breath of air in total agreement with her sister. "I shouldn't be so vicious toward Mother." She didn't wish to feel guilty about her thoughts. All her life, she never felt warmth from Anice. "She is a horrible person. Hope to never see her again."

Nellie rasped in a breath of air before firing out her thoughts, "Good God, Fannie, Mother gave Abernathy *carte blanch* with me. She was going to watch him rape me through a hole in the wall. She deserves everything Abernathy got as well as more. I hope she comes to visit. I believe we could manage another tar and feathering. She, just as much as Abernathy, needs to be taught a lesson. I have no mercy where she is concerned."

Rory stood with his hand on Nellies, shoulder. "Nel," he began, using a soft calm voice, "I'm in complete agreement with all you've said. If your mother shows up here, say the word. We will haul her up to camp, strip her clothing from her, shave her body, all of it…every part…then tar and feather her. Send her down the mountain naked."

"You would do that?" Nellie asked with a breathless sigh. "For me?" Looking at Rory, Nellie's eyes were wide with wonder.

What is happening here? Fannie loved the way her sister looked at this man who was the second largest man she'd ever seen. This man who had been smitten with her sister from the first moment he looked at her. Rory seemed gentle with Nellie. She needed tender. If this was a clue to the future, she was happy for her sister.

"In a heartbeat. For you along with every woman she has abused. Any mother who would do something so horrible to her flesh and blood deserves no respect, no kindness or consideration. As long as I live and breathe, Anice MacRae will never get respect from me. If you wish her punished for what she has done to all four girls, I will lead the posse."

Fox splashed wine into four glasses before handing them out. Held his up in a salute, "Here is too the MacRae ladies. May they always remain strong and never see Lord Nelson Abernathy again."

"Or their mother," Rory added on an emotional note, then sipped his wine.

"Or our mother," both girls said in agreement.

"No, believe I might be pleased if Mother dared to come here," Nellie said on a soft breath of air. "I want to see her get her due."

"I'll cut more food. Are you two hungry?" Fannie asked, she was still amazed at her sister's easy way with Rory. She didn't wish to speak about her mother even though she agreed with Nellie. If she came, Anice wouldn't come alone. Who would accompany her into the wilderness? The only person Fannie could think of was Halsey. The two deserved each other. Perhaps if they showed up, there would be two who received vigilante justice.

"Starving," was Rory's answer. "Could eat just about anything." Then he looked at Nellie as if he wished to devour her.

"Yes, hungry now that all the fanfare is done with. I believe I could eat. The wine is good," Nellie sipped, watching Rory over the rim of her glass.

Rory seemed to take notice of their state of clothing. "Did we interrupt anything? You two are…" he stopped, rubbed his hand on the back of his neck. Turned to Nellie who was turning a rosy shade.

"No," Fox said, grinning at her. "We were taking a break to put some food in our stomachs. Fannie was hungry. She doesn't have enough stamina. Needs to eat more so she can keep up with me."

Fannie hit him on the arm. Was tempted to toss her wine in his face. Didn't wish to waste it. "You…" At that point, she didn't have any idea what to say. Anything she thought of would cause her more embarrassment. More heat flooded her cheeks.

"Let's take the bottle of wine along with the food to the covered veranda. Rory, grab a couple of blankets from the cupboard. It's still sunny but it might get a bit chilly as the sun goes down," Fox said, as he looked between Rory and Nellie. Seemed Fox was also noticing the change in their demeanor together and hoped it would remain positive.

Rory looked pleased at the idea, Nellie a bit worried. Frown lines creased her forehead. While she seemed to soften toward him, she was far from at ease. Holding hands was one thing. Sitting with him, both wrapped in the same blanket seemed to intimidate her. Still, she didn't say no.

"Nel, do you want to go on the veranda to eat…with one blanket or two?" Rory asked, putting Nellie on the spot. He waited for an answer. Appeared he was going to make her answer. Had the look of an uncertain man.

Nellie flushed a delicate rose shade. "I don't know," she whispered, on a thin stream of air. "Why don't you decide?"

Rory beamed. His wide grin told everyone his answer. "Will be right back with two blankets. One for Fox and Fannie, the other for us. Are you certain?"

To Fannie that sounded like a yes, I'd like to share a blanket with Rory. That statement was coming from Nellie. Rory shouldn't have asked the next question. Nellie's hand rose then fell. Had the look of distress on her face. The smile vanished.

"If you don't want to…" Nellie looked at her feet then back to Rory with her lips thinned. "Wouldn't want to make you feel uncomfortable."

"Didn't say that now, did I? What I did was put you on the spot in front of your sister and her husband. That wasn't well done of me. Would love to share a blanket with my favorite girl."

That was a bold statement coming from Rory. Nonetheless, Fannie saw the cautious smile form on Nellie's expressive features. Could hear her questioning the 'my favorite girl' part.

"As a just in case proposition, I will bring an extra one if at some time you have a change of heart." He turned on a boot heel, whistling on a jaunty note as he left the room.

Fannie didn't know about Fox but she was holding her breath. Didn't know what the rest of the evening would bring. She was intrigued by this new set of circumstances. Would like to disappear for a few minutes with Fox to see what he thought about the conversation they heard between her sister and Rory. Later, when they were alone, they could discuss the possibilities.

After Rory returned, he sat down next to Nellie. The three blankets were piled beside the door. The food was set on a table in front of them. Fannie didn't think she'd ever felt so awkward in her life. Nellie was stiff again. Rory couldn't keep from staring at her as if he wanted to consume her rather than the food that was put in front of them. Rory topped off all the glasses. Nellie's was empty.

Fannie's sister nibbled at the sandwich she made. She gulped the wine as if the liquid was her lifeline. Rory leaned back, stretching his long legs out in front of him, his hands clasped behind his head. He seemed content as if he didn't have a care in the world. Nellie appeared as if her nerves would snap at any time. She would look at Rory then her wine.

"Nice evening," Rory said, as if he needed to make conversation. Looking as if he sensed Nellie's confusion.

"What was the mood at the camp when you left?" Fox asked, sounding curious. Needing to put their attention somewhere besides Nellie and Rory. "Would like to know how the men and their wives were feeling."

"Satisfied is the best word I have to describe the emotions. They were all horrified at what Abernathy attempted with your wife. Our crew doesn't like men who force women to their will. Two of the men followed Ol' Sam and Abernathy halfway to town. They returned hollering, as well as laughing. Seems he tried to ride the horse. Couldn't do it. His bare feet were so tender he was cursing and swearing the whole time he was walking. Says he'll come back to get his revenge on everyone involved."

Fannie gasped before inhaling the sip of wine. The liquid went down the wrong way. She sputtered a few drops slipping from her mouth. She dabbed at the wine with a napkin Fox handed her. "Do you think that's true?" she asked, hoping and praying it was not. "We won't have any respite from this nightmare. We will always be looking over our shoulder, wondering.

Fox spoke first, "No, I don't think so. The words were from an angry, as well as a humiliated, man. Abernathy is not stupid. Understands if he shows up in the area, his life won't be worth a plug nickel. He will be a dead man."

"I hope you're right," Nellie moved closer to Rory. "The man terrifies me. I hate him. Don't need to worry about him appearing out of the blue."

Rory set his arm behind her back. Seemed to be an invitation for her to move closer. One hand rested on her shoulder. "Understand, Nel, if you want, I will protect you from all the scum of the earth. Just say the word."

To Fannie's surprise, Nellie scooted even closer to him. His hand moved down to her arm. Didn't hold her too close to scare her. She appeared to be pressing against him.

"From my mother too?" She looked up at him, stars in her eyes as if she thought he could solve all the world's problems.

"Anyone, as well as everyone, who would wish you harm." He squeezed her shoulder then sat back on the porch swing, his hand on the back of it. Appearing to give Nellie a bit of distance. Rory seemed patient, willing to wait things out.

Fannie saw Ol' Sam before he could announce himself. "Sam, you're just the person we want to see." She was eager for news. All were impatient to learn about Abernathy's state of being. She hoped he was cowed. Prayed he was convinced to never return.

"Wondered why no one answered my knocking on the front door. Can I join you for a cup of hot coffee? Need something for my parched throat. After a good cup of Agnes' coffee, I'll head back to camp. As well as give them the latest news."

"If you describe in lurid details Abernathy's trip to town, you're welcome to anything you'd like. Food too, if you're hungry," Fox said, as he left the veranda for the kitchen. Came back with a steaming cup of coffee as well as a chair for Ol' Sam to sit on. "Don't know how strong the coffee is. Been brewing all day or longer."

"The coffee is from this morning," Rory said. "Agnes brewed it up around six o'clock. Probably very strong since it's been on a low simmer all day. Surprised the brew isn't sludge."

After a quick sip, Ol' Sam replied with an "Ah, this is what I need. A good jolt of energy then I'm on my way back to camp. Do you all mind if I grab a ham sandwich?" He sat down on the chair Fox offered then crossed his feet in front of him. Before he spoke, he made his sandwich.

"You must have heard from Rory the aristo wasn't pleased with the long walk he was forced into. Hurt him bad to ride his animal. Walking wasn't much better. After about an hour, he stopped hollering and cursing you and the girls. Course he used crasser terms for the little ladies here. Won't repeat what he said."

"Did you get him to Doc's place?" Fox was the first to ask the question.

Fox sat down next to Fannie. She leaned against him, needing his warmth. While she didn't wish to think about Abernathy, she needed to learn what happened. Hoped he would be able to leave soon.

"Well, that's just the thing." Ol' Sam ran his fingers through his salt and pepper hair. Looked to the sky before back to them. He cackled. "Doc wasn't there at the time. He was out seeing to little Irene's baby. She was in labor. So, his assistant saw him."

"Rosemary?" Fox hooted out his laughter. He picked up Fannie's hand. Kissed the palm, biting on the soft flesh. "Getting a little of his own medicine. Did Rosemary know why he was in the state she found him?"

"Made certain to tell her as many details as I could," Ol' Sam said with a bit more of a snigger in his voice.

Rory joined with a huge guffaw. "He had to see a female doc? That's too funny for words. She needed to see to all his parts. Wash him off with that solvent they use to get pine tar off things. Don't know what it is exactly."

"More mortification for him. Rosemary has been helping out Doc for about ten years now. She's a nurse, not a certified doc. Nonetheless she knows what to do in every situation. She's also not the type of female Abernathy is interested in. Rosemary could wrestle him and win," Fox laughed again. Pulled her close for a quick kiss on her mouth.

"What did she do for him besides wash him?" Fannie saw some humor in the situation. She didn't know how the tar would come off. Assumed the sticky stuff would need to wear off. "Doesn't the pine tar just go away with time? You say she washed the tar off?" Fannie tried to clarify.

"It might," Rory told her. "On the other hand, how long would you wish to have the tar covering you. Clothes would be impossible to wear. I'm positive Abernathy would never wish to remain naked for as long as it took for the tar to go away."

"So?" Fannie persisted, wishing he would get to the point. "The three of you can't stop laughing. Tell me or I'm going to toss my wine in your face, Fox Taggart."

"I'll toss mine in Rory's. Yours was an excellent idea, lil sis," Nellie chimed in, appearing to have the same emotions.

"Now wait a minute," Rory said, as he reached for Nellie's glass. "You won't be doing any such thing."

"Or what?" Nellie challenged, standing up to him. Appearing to be escaping the shell she surrounded herself in ever since Dillon's breakup, coupled with the near rape.

"Or you will never hear what Ol' Sam is going to tell us. I for one wish to hear the entire story. This is almost as good as the women painting the tar on him."

Nellie reached her hand out, "Give me my wine. I won't waste a good glass of wine on your face."

"Might not be wasted. I'd let you lick all the sweet red drops off," Rory said, deadpan, before waggling his eyebrows at her. It was clear Rory was enjoying Nellie's change of heart.

Fannie watched her sister's eyes cross. She pointed her finger on his chest. "You would let me do what?"

"Never mind, Nel. Licking my face is for another day. Sam, go on with the story. Tell us what the assistant did for Abernathy."

"Well, that's just the thing, Rory. No one wants to leave the tar on. I'm told it's too uncomfortable. There is this solution of some kind that takes it off. Thing is, little Rosemary had to wipe down every part of Abernathy's big body. Took some time to clean away all that tar. Had to clean all his private places the women painted. I stayed to protect Rosemary from Abernathy. Didn't know how that awful man would treat her when she started touching his male parts."

"Until today, I'd never seen…" Nellie didn't finish. "Oh my." Pink rushed to her face.

Rory placed her hand in his. Brought them back to his lips. Kissed her with a light caress. "It's alright, Nel. This is all too funny. Once he was all cleaned up, what then?"

"There were blisters on every part of him. His face was marked like he had the pox, all of him just the same. In his condition, he couldn't force a woman or even have sex with a willing lady. Decided sexual encounters weren't going to work until the blisters healed." Ol' Sam set his head back then hooted. "Rosemary wouldn't give him his clothes. Was afraid he would get an infection if he put on clothes too soon. She brought him to the backroom where he could lie down. Course, he couldn't get comfortable. Left him there with a clean sheet covering him along with one beneath him."

"How long?" Fox asked, drumming his fingers on the glass of wine he held. "I might have to make a trip into town just to clarify our intent if he ever returns."

"Tomorrow morning we will both go see how our Lord of the Realm is doing. Wish to illuminate to him that he needs to leave as soon as he is able to dress," Rory spoke up.

"That would be our second day of lessons," Nellie said, adamant with her next words. "You can't leave."

"Yes, it is. I'll be back before you can eat your breakfast. Not going to give up any time with you."

"Same for me," Fox volunteered. "Fannie is also going to learn how to shoot. However, tomorrow morning when I return, we need to get back to the base camp. Yesterday was a day off for the crew. We've a need to make up for lost time. I'm certain Meridith will want to see you."

An hour later, they excused themselves to go to their room. Fox grabbed a bottle of wine and glasses then headed upstairs.

Fannie knew he wanted to make love. She also needed to talk about her sister and Rory. She was pleased at this knew development. Inside the bedroom, she leaned against the door. "This time I'm going to seduce you, Fox Taggart."

"I'd like that, Fannie Taggart.

Epilogue

"It's been more than a year since Abernathy left," Fox said. "He hasn't been back. Your mother hasn't come to cause trouble. Maggie, as well as Tessa, write that from time to time she tries to see her grandchildren. Both your sisters refuse her admittance to the house. Do you think we can live in peace without looking over our shoulders?" He wished for his life to go on as it had been for the last year. Hoped never to see fear in Fannie's eyes. When Abernathy kidnapped her, it had been the worst moments of his life.

Jake along with Beryl came to see them the second summer they were in Michigan. Beryl seemed to be in love with his father. She gave Jake another son. Fox hoped the boy would be what Jake hoped for, a partner in his Scottish business.

To his surprise, they brought the satchel containing the fifty thousand pounds he won as well as lost in the same night. Fox couldn't believe where they found the lost bag. It had been beneath Fannie's bed, stuck in between two boards. When the bed was moved to clean the floor, the maid discovered the satchel along with the money.

"You did take my groats that night," he barked laughter at her look of chagrin. "I was right. You are a little thief. You stole my groats along with my heart."

He wasn't surprised when she turned a vivid shade of crimson. She poked him in the chest. "Thought the satchel was the one Nellie was carrying to keep the items we collected safe for the scavenger hunt. Didn't steal it. Believed the bag to be mine." Appearing perturbed, Fannie crossed her hands in front of her chest, pushing her beautiful breasts higher. Until I saw it again, I didn't remember the bag.

"Yes you did, sort of," Fox murmured as he massaged her shoulders. Fannie always loved it when he eased the tight shoulder and neck muscles. He pushed her hair aside then kissed the back of her neck. Ran the silken strands through his fingers. Loved the way her hair felt on his sensitive flesh. Wanted to make love to his wife.

Pushing away from him, she set her hands on his chest. "At the time you did. I recall that small fact. You insisted I stole your money. You should not have been gambling. You might have lost the five thousand you started with."

"Agnes has our little boy in the backyard. Bryce adores her. Calls her Mimi. I'm glad Anice isn't his grandmother. Well, officially she is. However, she hasn't seen our boy. She would never play with him or cuddle with him. Agnes is perfect grandmother material. Couldn't ask for anyone better."

"I agree. Since I did choose Agnes, I'm pleased with the outcome. Do you think our new little one will also love her to distraction?"

Fannie was pregnant again. She was due at any time now. He wished to have as many children as possible. Understood, she might put a halt to more children after three. Pregnancy was hard on a woman.

He touched her ear with his tongue. Brought his hand up to cup her breast. "Hope this one is a little girl. Not that I would mind another boy. One way or the other we should try for three. Maybe four, then we could have two of each."

She set her head on his shoulder. "I want a little girl, another boy as well. Bryce needs siblings to play with, to fight with. Laughter is what I wish to hear in this house. Love is what I want to feel."

"I will do my part. Enjoy creating little Taggarts. Not one of them will want for love. They will have everything they wish for."

"You will spoil them?"

"Always. You as well."

Fox pulled her into his arms. "I love you, Fannie. Think I have from that night I stumbled into your room at Hannah's brothel. You were so cute. When you slipped out of the red gown to step into the bath, my mouth hung open. You were so beautiful. However, you are lovelier now. When you opened your mouth and said ah…well…I knew I found the woman for me."

She batted him on the arm. "Thought you were a doctor. What did you expect me to do?"

"Not that."

"I love you too. So very much. I remember thinking how handsome you were. How brilliant your golden fox eyes were. Still do believe you are the most handsome man alive."

"Oh!"

He saw the grimace on her face. Beneath his hand, felt the cramping of her belly as she tightened. Gulped in a breath of air. "I will send Ol' Sam for the doc. Let me get you to bed then I'll tell Agnes."

"No, I'll tell Agnes. Don't want to go to bed yet. You remember how long Bryce took. Not going to be in bed for twelve hours."

"Second babes are faster," he reminded her.

"Even so…oh! Oh my…"

"Agnes!" He swooped her into his arms then headed for the bedroom.

COMING SOON
by the author
at
Rogue Phoenix Press

Nellie
Good Girls Book Ten

Chapter One

Michigan 1834

The little water sprite frolicked in the stream running behind Fox's ranch house. Her skirts were hiked up to show a nice span of white legs coupled with well-turned ankles. His gut tightened in anticipation. Sometime, she would surrender to him. Now, romping through the cool liquid, brought drops of water to other parts of her. When she tossed her head back to laugh, he viewed a sparkling glimmer sliding down her neck then downward in the valley between her breasts. He yearned to follow the path with his tongue. Taste every succulent part of her.

Rorik Haraldsson crouched about one hundred yards on a hill above the stream, twirling a blade of grass between his fingers. His intention was to see Fox Taggart, his best friend as well as business partner. On his way, he unexpectedly came across Nellie. She shouldn't be alone. Possible danger lurked even though the biggest threat returned to Glasgow one year ago. Doubted if Lord Abernathy would return to these parts. Nonetheless, neither her mother or the pimp she associated with could be counted out of the picture. Both at one time promised revenge. They were both unsavory creatures.

Nellie MacRae didn't realize as yet he observed her from a distant place on the horizon. While he'd had every intention of revealing himself, he found himself caught up in his view of the little water sprite. Frozen in time while she cavorted believing she was alone, she set his wounded heart dancing. If he had his way, he would pull her into his arms then kiss her until she was breathless. He needed more from her than a few mind shattering kisses. He wanted her for the rest of his life. She was no longer agreeable.

A little less than a year ago, Rory believed he crossed over the bridge keeping Nellie at a distance. Seemed she softened for him. Just when he thought to deepen their burgeoning relationship, she turned her back, rejecting his cautious yet hopeful advances. The action befuddled his head.

He didn't know why her behavior shifted so dramatically.

She refused to explain herself. Told him if he had any wits at all, he could figure it out.

Now, it seemed to him, he moved two steps back from the first day they met. Nellie disliked all men because of one man, a beau who rejected her. He overheard part of her story one day when she confided in Fannie, her sister. Guilt didn't play a role in his ease dropping. He would do anything to understand her revulsion toward him. Would do anything to change the feelings.

Hell, he wanted her with an urgency he didn't understand. Never before had he experienced this yearning when seeing a woman. His quicksilver rise to infatuation shocked his soul. Nellie was all woman. Now, he needed to back up a few steps. Approach the flighty woman from a different angle. For the last year, he tried giving her space. Distance was what Fannie told him her sister needed. Given time, she would come to understand he was nothing like the man who tried to take her virginity then tossed her away.

Distance didn't change their relationship for the better. Nellie was colder now than she'd ever been. Whenever he visited the ranch house where she lived, Nellie would disappear into her bedroom. Would remain hidden away until he left. Since his home was nearly finished, he seldom remained the night at Taggart's home.

As this was the end of summer, both he along with Taggart spent most of the week at the logging camp. Fannie would accompany her husband, Fox. Nellie would remain at the ranch house with the housekeeper, Agnes.

Seeming to sense his presence, Nellie put her hand to her forehead to shield the sun from her eyes. She looked at him. Unless the sunshine blinded her, Nellie would see him. He rose from his crouched position. His heart in his throat, Rory decided to meet Nellie. Face her head on. Talk to her.

When her hands dropped to her sides then tugged her skirts down to cover her legs, he stopped. With the bottom of her skirt soaking up water she walked from the stream. Stared at her shoes as if they were a mile away. If she wore her shoes, she would flee. Run to the ranch then hide from him. There was no time.

Even if she ran, he would catch her. Didn't intend to allow her to ignore him much longer. Was tired of the distance she put between them. Needed to confront her. Discover why the reversal of her feelings. "Nellie," he spoke as he approached with caution. She was too flighty. "You shouldn't be here alone. Anything could happen." Not only did he think of her mother who held no kind thoughts for any of her four daughters, his mind drifted to four legged dangers. There were wolves in the hills along with bears. He'd also heard of two lawless men who attacked unprotected homes, forced the women. Made certain they approached only when the woman was by herself.

Taggart's home was protected. Inside, Nellie would be safe. Out here in the open she was not. He didn't like to see her vulnerable.

"Go away!" Her voice was shrill. Held an edge of desperation. "Don't want to see you or talk to you."

Unable to help himself, he grimaced at her reaction. Women usually flocked around him. Wasn't used to these negative vibes when it concerned a woman. He needed to be so much more to this beautiful innocent. Over the year, he found himself falling in love with her. Would never confess his emotion. Would deny the feeling if confronted. He held out his hands. "Nellie, listen to reason."

"There is nothing you have to say I wish to hear."

"I will see you home." He continued inching forward hoping to reach her before she finished dressing. "You shouldn't be outside alone." It was then he noticed the easel, the painting supplies she laid out for her use. "You were painting. I'll stay here with you. Find a place in the shade to sit. You can finish what you started." He noticed the quick sketch of the stream. Noticed the large rock she outlined. "Is this going to a water color?"

"No, don't need or want your help. I'll send Ol' Sam back for the supplies." Nellie sat on a rock. Donned the stockings then the shoes. Stood.

Marched away from him as if he didn't intend to follow.

"We don't need to leave this behind." Torn between going after her or collecting her things, he chose Nellie. If she didn't care about her unprotected belongings, why should he?

"If you want to carry it, go ahead," she shouted as she turned to look over her shoulder.

He caught up to her. Felt her disdain as well as the cold emanating from her. Looking straight ahead, she marched down the hill to the home she'd known for a year now. At one time, he believed she would return to Glasgow. In numerous letters, her two brothers-in-law, Jasper and Justin dissuaded her. Explained that Anice was still a force to be reckoned with. She associated herself with one of the worst pimps in the city. Halsey was his name.

"You're damn well going to get my help," Rory muttered as he matched her strides. "Your sweet white hide is more important than a few paint brushes."

"No one is at home except the housekeeper. Everyone left for the lumber camp at noon. There won't be anyone for you to converse with," she said with a prim starch filled tone.

"Good, I'll have time to speak with you. I need to understand why you've been avoiding my company for the last year. For a few days, I thought we were getting along. Believed you might come to care about me." Rory wiped the sweat from his forehead. Not going to leave until I get a few answers." He reached out to her. This might be a long few days. He left the camp with the understanding he might not return within the week. Fox understood his needs where Nellie was concerned. Fannie wished him good luck. Told him perhaps giving her time had not been the best advice. Maybe he should have confronted her the moment she changed directions.

"I don't like you." Her pert little nose was tilted into the air when she spoke. She squared her shoulders as she lengthened her strides in her attempt to leave him behind. She mumbled something beneath her breath.

At her harsh words, his heart skipped a beat. Felt air rush from his lungs in an explosion of regret. Damn, he needed to fix what went awry. She liked him well enough for a few days for him to receive a kiss, one with tongues. Her female whimper at the contact entered into him. The soft sigh wrapped around him, binding her to him for a few breathless moments. What the hell made her change her mind? Before he went crazy, he needed to get to the bottom of her unexpected wrath.

"Don't feel the same sentiments. I like you," he countered wishing he dare say he loved her. At this beat of his heart, all he wanted was to pull her into his arms then kiss her soundly. The way he wanted to kiss her would be tongue on tongue. Ultimate exploration of her dark, hot secrets. If he did proceed in that direction, he was certain his efforts would be met with a resounding slap to the face. Intimate contact might be worth the ultimate retaliation. A kiss would only happen if he forced her.

"No, you don't feel the same. When will you understand, I don't want anything to do with your advances."

"What?" He wasn't truly surprised by her avid denunciation. Needed to know why. What did he do to make this so bad between them? His hand landed on her shoulder, turning her. "Explain yourself."

Nellie's eyes were wild, darkening with her anger. He might have hoped the color was due to passion. Under the circumstances he would never lie to himself.

"No! Never. If you don't know why I dislike you, you are stupid. You're just like all men. You take what you want…when you want. With no care to anyone's feelings but your own." She tried to wrest free of his grip. He didn't intend to let go yet. None of what she said was true. What the devil made her think that way? "Where you are concerned, I don't have to do anything. You're not anything to me. Not even a friend!" Blazing eyes, breasts heaving with agitation, Nellie glared at him.

That was the major problem. He wanted to be something to this beautiful, troubled woman. She was beautiful even in her anger. He could deal better with her if he understood which direction her mind was coming from. Good God, once she kissed him as if he meant something to her. A week later, she wouldn't speak to him. What the hell happened? He couldn't right something when he didn't know what went wrong.

"I told you I'm not leaving here until I understand why you did such a quick turn about. Waited a year. Been patient. All you did was drift farther away from me." He let his hands fall away. Resorting to force wouldn't get him where he hoped to go. "I'm going to shadow you night as well as day until you talk to me. If you go to the privy, I'll be at the door until you leave. When you retire at night, I'll stay in the bedroom on a cot." If she would allow, he would lie on the bed with her. They should have wed months ago. He'd yet to ask. They were so far from marriage, the thought was laughable.

Her shudder was visible. She pushed at his hand trying to dislodge his hold on her arm. This time, he allowed his hand to fall away. An unladylike snort preceded her words. "I'm talking to you now. Isn't that enough?" Moisture rimmed her beautiful green eyes. If he kept this line of questions going, tears would soon slide down her cheeks. He never intended to make her cry. Guilt had a way of intruding on his actions.

All her refusals to meet him part way were getting to him. His anger exploded. "No, not nearly enough and you damn well know it! Tell me why. If you do, I might leave you alone." He could never leave her alone.

"Cursing won't get you anywhere." She flinched away then ran. Hiked up her skirts to go faster. Stumbled. Her arms whirling, she caught her balance then continued in the same manner. If she hurt herself in her mad dash away from him, he would blame himself. A deep breath of air scorched his lungs. He would deal with the fallout. For him, there were no more choices. Whatever wound he caused festered inside her.

The view tore at his heart. Ripped it into tiny pieces. He felt as if she wrenched it from him. Shattered, he followed at a more sedate pace. She could hide in her bedroom for a short space of time. He would give her breathing room. Doing so wasn't going to make a bit of difference as to how he meant to proceed. As to how his plans would unfold. He debated with himself. Now, there was no other choice.

Agnes was on his side. If he explained his intentions, the housekeeper would do all in her power to help him with this endeavor. In fact, all were on his side. In front of him, the screen door creaked open then banged shut. Nellie disappeared inside. With the back of his arm, he wiped sweat off his forehead. Sweat caused by tension, not the heat of the summer sun. For a few beats of his heart, he thought about turning back to the stream. A dip in the cold water might be just the thing for his body as well as his disposition. Before he confronted Nellie again, he intended to possess a cool head.

Later he would take a dip in the stream beside his home.

As for now, he needed to see what Nellie was up to. Trusting her was not something he intended. He was certain she would hide in her room until he left. She would not find solace until his questions were answered to his satisfaction. As he told her, he wasn't leaving. She had no lock for her bedroom door. If she barricaded it, there was always the window. He was agile.

Just as Nellie let the door bang shut behind her, he did the same. Stepped into the cooler interior of the house. Agnes stood framed in the doorway, wiping her hands on a dishtowel. Her look of disapproval gnawed at him. She turned away from him then disappeared. He heard a few clanks as she shuffled pots around.

"Cold drink?" Agnes called out from the kitchen. "Got cold beer in the barrel. Mr. Taggart has some bottled in the ice house.

The question brought a smile to his face. Agnes always thought about a man's needs. "Yes. A cold beer if you've got one." Rory stepped into the kitchen to savor the aroma of fresh baked bread.

"Got whatever you want. See you had a little spat with your gal. What are you going to do to clear things up? Can't say as allowing Miss Nellie to hide away in her bedroom has done the trick. You need to get her to open up."

"My gal? Open up?" Rory questioned her terminology. "A year ago, thought Nellie might be my girl…my best girl. Now…thought I was ready to settle down with her." He lifted his shoulders in frustration. "We're farther apart today than ever. Can't say as if I do anything right."

"By my reasoning you gave up on her too soon. You let her little snit grow out of proportion. Should have confronted her the first time she turned away from you. Now, she's got her back against the wall. Has something to prove though I don't know what that is." Agnes shook her head. "Stubborn pride that one. Can't see what's written in your eyes as clear as day." Agnes pumped beer from the barrel Taggart kept in a cool place. "Brought it out just this afternoon."

"Don't know how to reach her." Rory sipped while he tried to digest the words spouted by Agnes. "You know what's botherin' her. Tell me."

"Not my place to say. Know just about everything concerning those two MacRae girls. All I can tell you is you've got your work cut out for you. Got to be more stubborn than Nellie. She believes you've done something you didn't."

"You're not going to tell me what she thinks I did." He knew the answer before she replied.

"Nope. Was told in confidence. Don't break those vows. A smart man could figure out how to get the truth from the little gal."

He meant to be exactly as Agnes said…more stubborn than Nellie. Once he discovered what brought the miff on, he could work to counter act whatever the problem was. Had no idea what it was she thought he did that caused her to turn against him. As things stood now, they lost a year together. He didn't intend to lose more.

"Maybe you should court her, woo her so she wants to be with you more than anything. Bring her flowers or chocolates. Girls like those things. Our Miss Nellie thinks you betrayed her trust. A girl's not likely to get over that kind of betrayal."

Rory leaned forward, his forearms on the table. Those words were more than she'd ever told him before. Betrayal? He was loyal to those he held dear. Nellie was in that list of friends.

"Say that again." Waiting for an answer his heart thundered. He was having trouble believing what she said.

Agnes was slicing pieces of warm bread. She set butter on the table then a jar of freshly made strawberry preserves. Looking up she paused. "Said too much as it is. That's what talkin' to your intended is supposed to do."

"By my mind, you haven't said enough. Couldn't you elaborate? Give me a tiny hint of what she's thinking about. Would like to comprehend what's in store for me." He thought back on events almost a year in the past. There had been a dance to celebrate Fannie's safe return. The entire town turned out for the occasion. They came to the ranch bearing all sorts of food along with drinks. A huge bonfire was set in the middle of the field. Several men playing various instrument provided the music. The party went on until near dawn.

"It's up to you to get Miss Nellie to open up to you. Sit her down. Have a long heart-to-heart. Tell her your feelings for her. She wants to give you her love. Pour Nellie is afraid to take a chance on another man. After what happened to her in Glasgow… Don't let her suffer…"

One eyebrow shot to the sky. "Let her suffer? What do you think her reticence is doing to me. I've tried to talk to her."

"No…you waited almost a year to sit her down. She gave up hope that you might care about her."

"Fannie advised me to give her space." In hindsight he understood the tactic had been all wrong.

Agnes didn't say anything more. She bustled around the room, putting a tray together containing slices of bread, a bowl of butter along with a jar of preserves. "Take this to her. I'll open the door for you. If you like I could lock the door from the outside. Seems the two of you shouldn't be able to leave until all the mess is sorted out."

"My sentiments too. If you lock the door, she'll climb out the window" Rory snorted suddenly needing to see for himself if she was still in the bedroom. "She's going to clam up as soon as I step inside her little room. What do you think? She's going to suddenly change directions. Talk? I won't hold my breath."

"Won't know unless you try. She's not had anything to eat since early this morning. If you play your cards right, you might have a chance of some private time together."

Skepticism swept through him. "Where that little gal is concerned, my luck has vanished. She controls all the moves. Checkmate has been her ploy. With her pretty little chin pointed upward, she is giving me the cold shoulder."

Agnes didn't say anything more. She handed the tray to Rory then walked through the house to Nellie's door. Opened it. The hinges creaked. Silence. The two looked at each other. The dumfounded look on the housekeeper's face must match his own. He set his finger beneath her chin then pressed her mouth closed.

Inhaling a deep breath his emotions circling, then, "Damn her!" Rory yelled. He looked out the open window toward the stream where her painting was set up. His gut told him she didn't go there. It would be the first place he would look. Where would she go? Nellie didn't know anyone. As far as the countryside was concerned, she didn't know north from south.

"After you catch up to her, don't be too harsh on her. She's hurting bad." Agnes stood behind him. "She didn't have time to take her things. Should I send someone with them?" Imagined she had the same idea in plan as he did.

"You could tell me. Yes, pack her things. Send Ol' Sam with them to my place. As soon as I find her, that's where we are headed." He persisted, wishing the housekeeper would forget her promise to keep the confidence. Too many times to count she reminded him that she vowed to remain silent no matter the cost.

"I cannot. Go…I've the feeling she rides to the camp. Must be having the same feelings as you. She must feel she has protection there. Her sister will guard her from you. You can catch her in a few minutes. She rides the most docile old mare in the stable. Still afraid of the beast, she won't run her."

"When I catch up to her, I'm not giving her a choice. I'm taking her to my home. She will remain there with me until I get to the bottom of her issues. Can't fight unless I know what the argument is about."

"You'll have to keep her locked…"

"If she leaves my ranch house, she will get herself lost in the forest. Believe she will be smarter to remain with me than brave the wild forest beyond. With Nellie one never knows what she will think or do. She's too impulsive."

"Don't count on it," Agnes muttered shaking her head at him. "I won't protest your treatment. Don't be surprised if Fannie has Taggart running after the two of you. Fox will know by Friday when he returns here where you've taken her."

"Fox won't butt into what isn't his business. Fannie isn't much better in the forests than Nellie. No one will come after her."

"Good luck," Agnes provided some encouragement with a friendly wave then a smile.

Rory stalked from the house, saddled his horse then headed toward the logging camp bent on catching Nellie before she could take refuge within her sister's tent. Once inside he didn't know if he could get her out. While Fox would look the other way, Fannie would not. He rode hard for about five minutes. Pulled up his horse to watch the steady but slow progress Nellie made. She looked uncomfortable. If the situation wasn't so serious, he would hoot with laughter at the sight in front of him. When she slipped sideways clutching the saddle horn, he cursed. Even on the old mare, she'd be lucky to survive the ride all the way to the base camp.

What the devil was in her head?

The thought she risked her life to run away from him infuriated every sinew and bone in his body.

While he studied her awkward advance down the road, he set a pace that would connect with her at the turn in the road. Wondered too if she saw him, if she would try to make the poor horse move faster. Rory didn't know who was the slowest, Nellie or the old mare. Star was the old girl's name because on her forehead was beautiful star.

Her mount heard his approach before she did. The horse turned to look at him as if she hoped he would be her way to return to the stable. At almost the same moment, Nellie looked over her shoulder. Then back to the road. Urged the mare faster. The horse stopped, rearing her head then snorting her disapproval. Again, if this wasn't such a desperate situation for him, he would have laughed. Instead of running, the mare stopped, standing her ground. Against Nellie's wishes, Star turned to wait for him.

"You!" Nellie cried out when he reached her, pointing a shaking finger at him. "Why did you come after me?"

"Me? Why did you run, sweet. You've no reason to be afraid of me," his voice was soft as he surprised her by lifting her from the mare then setting her in front of him, his arm around her waist. Rory gave Nellie's mount a swat to her rear. Star made a tiny noise before trotting in the direction of her stable. No doubt she would eat her head off.

Nellie took the brief moment to struggle, pushing on his arm. Her strength was nothing pitted against his. "Let me go! How dare you? What are you doing? You've no right."

In his mind he had every right. "Never. Never will I let you go. You and I are meant to be together." He nudged his horse forward. They picked up speed. "I gave you a year. Now, you have no more time."

Instead of trying to push herself away, Nellie clung to him. Nails bit into flesh. He relished the slight pain. Kept him feeling real. Kept the situation in the forefront of his head. Loved the feel of her back pressed against his chest. This was a heaven he believed would be a long time coming. This little piece of paradise would end soon. Once he set her feet on the ground, she would put distance between them.

"My horse?" she asked as if an afterthought.

"Is worthless for a long trip. She would balk in another few minutes just as she did for you. The little mare will be happier back in her stable. The hands will feed her as if she were a queen. Rub her down though she wouldn't have broken a sweat."

After he reached the road turning off the main one to lead into the hills, he stayed focused. Headed to his home. His change of course would come in about two miles. In his arms she stiffened. Nellie had been to base camp often enough in the last year to realize they weren't turning in that direction. His home lay north of the little camp of tents.

"Where are you going?" She let go of him long enough to point. "That's the road we need to take. Are you lost?"

"Not headed to base camp, little darlin'. No right where we are headed." Wondered when he should tell her where she would end up this evening. Let her guess. She would come to the proper conclusion sooner than later.

Nellie whirled on him. The glare her vibrant green eyes slanted him would melt ice. "I am not going with you…" she paused as if thinking for some words she could say that would get him to do her bidding. "Wherever you're headed. Put me down."

"Not on your life." He made a few tsking noises. His stallion increased his speed. Nellie melted back against him. Rory grinned. At this tick of a clock, he understood how to silence her. Soon he wished to do the opposite.

Miles passed. Nellie didn't say anything more. With her silence, he was relieved. Understood when his house came into view, she would throw a fit. He realized he played with fire. A tempest in the small fragile body he held close to him would soon flare to life. His hands would be full. The first hours between them might be harsh. Two days ago, he made a trip into town. Brought back supplies for a week. While Agnes had been teaching the girls how to cook, Nellie didn't take to the task. Fannie did much better. Of course, she had a man to please. Nellie ate little. Didn't need to learn how to cook a meal.

To his surprise when his home came into view, Nellie remained silent but stiff. For a flash of time, her fingers gripped his arm harder. Within the embrace of his arms, she quivered. Anger or fear? When the big stallion halted, he set her on the ground then slid off. She made no attempt to move.

"Go inside. Make yourself at home. I'll see to my horse." In truth, he didn't need to see to his horse, he had workers to do that. Harry stood just outside the stable door waiting for the order that wasn't going to come. He needed time to gather his wits about him. Didn't know how to handle the little lady who bedeviled his days then stole into his dreams at night. Understood he needed to use caution. Her spirit was as brittle as her small form. His agile temper could flare at any time. Anger with her wasn't going to get her to open up about his mistake. Perhaps a bit of bribery would do the trick.

Ten minutes later when he gathered enough courage to face Nellie, she sat on the porch steps a dejected look on her pretty little face. For a few seconds, guilt inundated him. Hell. He had nothing to feel guilty about. She brought this on by refusing to have a civil, adult conversation with him. She pouted when she could have explained the situation to him. He was an avid listener.

"Go inside." He gestured to the door. Didn't want to think about her refusing his home as shelter. "The night up here is almost always cold. Don't want you to take a chill."

From her perch on the step, she looked up at him. "No…" There was little to no emotion in her voice.

So, the argument would start here on his front porch. "Why not?" Rory meant to win this tiny show of defiance.

To her astonishment, he swept her into his arms before striding through the front door. If he hoped she would surrender then make this easy for him, he'd been stupid. One could drown in unfulfilled hopes. Patience with Nellie was something he needed but lacked. They would begin the conversation. What would happen next was in the air.

Rory set her on an oversized chair that pointed toward the fireplace. "I'll get dinner." There would be venison stew simmering in the kitchen. He did have a cook…a very good cook. At least he didn't need to rely on Nellie's cooking. Nor did he need to rely on his.

"Are you hungry?"

~ * ~

For Nellie the day started with promise. The sky was blue and endlessly clear. No rain threatened. She carried her paints to the spot near the stream. Set her easel up then the stretched watercolor paper. There were several landscapes she wished to portray on canvas. It was just the matter of what she wished to paint first.

Once she reached the spot, she wasn't eager to begin. She felt lethargic. Even though the easel was in the shade, the air was hot, growing hotter as the sun climbed higher. Instead, the cool water in the stream beckoned to her. For a few seconds she held back, looking over her shoulder as if Rory would appear out of nowhere. A week had passed since he last came to the ranch. Truth be told, she missed him, his smile, the way his eyes twinkled when he thought of something funny. How they darkened when he looked at her.

She wanted to see him.

Didn't want to see the blasted man.

Needed to talk to him.

Didn't think talk would solve any of their problems. He was just like all the other men she met.

Her conflicted emotions never ceased to confuse her. Rory was all man. That fact tended to unnerve her. Because of Dillion, she possessed a small sense of what he wanted. His size overwhelmed her. His kiss…she touched her mouth…astounded her. She both wanted as well as needed more from him than a mere kiss. Wished to have a promise of loyalty. Almost a year ago she thought she was falling in love with Rory. He wreaked havoc with his faithfulness to her the very night they celebrated Fannie's rescue from Lord Abernathy. The night he stole her breath with his potent kiss. At that time, she melted into the man. Yearned for more kisses, more… She wasn't certain what came next.

Nellie understood better than most everyone what the Lord of the Realm was about. He was no good. Her mother was tagged in the same vein as Abernathy. Anice was no good. Here in Michigan everyone thought they were safe from the pair. She tended to believe Anice would never lower her standards to come to the United States. She would never travel to Michigan. Her hatred of her daughters would surpass anything Nellie could understand.

With clarity, she recalled the night Lord Abernathy abducted her from her sister's wedding. Remembered how Dillon rescued her the night before when she strayed from the house. At the time, she thought she was in love with Dillon Montrose. Was willing to give her innocence to the man. He told her with quiet frankness, he was not in love with her. Had no intention of marrying her. Within a heartbeat Nellie realized Dillion used her. Tromped on her heart.

At the blunt words Dillon spoke, her heart shattered. The second time Abernathy kidnapped her, her rescue came after she'd been thoroughly humiliated at the man's hands. She was certain he would force her with her mother looking on for her own amusement. The bed he placed in her room had shackles attached to both ends of the bed.

Thoughts racing through her head, she shuddered. Moaned. Didn't want to remember those events. They happened a lifetime ago. Putting those memories behind her was imperative. Sitting by the stream she watched the water splash and tumble against the rocks. A few drops hit her face. She laughed feeling carefree for the first time in what seemed to be ages. The cool water felt good. If she waded the liquid would feel even better.

Bringing her knees to her chest, she wrapped her arms around herself trying to hold back the threatening sob. This self-pity wouldn't do. She wiped the moisture away on the fabric of her skirt. Nellie looked both ways…up then down the stream. Turned around to make certain no one was about. In a fit of boldness she rarely felt, she undid her shoes then slipped off her stockings. Wiggled her toes. Cool air caressed her bared legs.

She felt naughty.

Didn't care.

She tucked the bottom of her skirt into her waistband before dipping a toe into the cool water. Hiked the fabric higher so the water wouldn't soak through. A shiver swept through her. Stepped into the flowing water. Giggled. As she moved farther into the stream, the flowing water swirled around her legs. Carefree, she kicked at the water. Liquid splashed on her soaking her blouse. Fabric molded to her skin. She pulled the fabric away from her breasts. When it fell back into place her body was outlined.

Laughter spun from her. She could see her nipples. This was decadent. Heat stained her cheeks. Thinking about her behavior would ruin her day. Wondering what Rory would think if he saw her this way, caused her heart to leap with confusion. For her Rory no longer existed. Nothing mattered because there was no one here to see her. Fanny and Fox wouldn't be back to the ranch for another week. They came down form the logging camp during the weekends.

She was alone.

Could act anyway she wished.

Agnes would never venture this way. She would tell her it was too far to walk and it was too close to take the buggy. Slipping on a stone, her arms whirled as she tried to keep from a tumble. Nellie found the trunk of a tree to hang onto. Laughed as the water rose. Her skirt was soaked through.

"Thank goodness," she muttered, she'd not wished to fall into the water. She couldn't swim. Thought perhaps she should leave the stream behind while she was still ahead of the game.

After she waded from the brook, the beautiful and oh so perfect day changed to a nightmare. Rory was watching her from a distance. She crossed her fingers he would leave. He never acted the way she wished.

Now she was sitting on the steps of his front porch. Her mind in a jumble while her heart pounded hard as well as deep within her chest.

Nellie didn't want to think about the ride to his cabin. Not recalling how her body pressed against his was impossible. The feel of his big, warm body so close caused her heart to race. Oh, when she slipped out the window of her bedroom, she understood he would come after her. Thinking otherwise was a waste of time. At least with this distance, she would have a few minutes to think…to gather her thoughts.

Rory told her he wanted to talk. He could talk all he wanted. Her lips were sealed. There was no way she would humiliate herself by reminding him of his betrayal. If he gave himself a moment to think about the night he kissed her, he would remember the other girl. The one who received the second kiss. At the time, she believed she was falling in love with the big man. Was beginning to think he might feel the same.

Sometimes he seemed like a gentle giant to her. She loved the way their first kiss felt. The sensations were faster as well as deeper than anything she experienced before Rory. When his lips touched hers, her heart roared to life. Heat scorched her. The year she spent after the Kenworthy twins won guardianship over her, she had her share of beaus coupled with a few kisses from each one. Nothing she recalled compared. When he kissed her, she felt as if the earth moved beneath her feet.

Even Dillon's kiss didn't bring her to a heated rush in a split second. With the first contact she melted into a mindless puddle in his arms. When Rory's tongue dipped inside her mouth, she nearly jumped from her skin. His tongue rubbed on hers, danced with hers. He sucked hers into his open mouth. Her body quivered. All of her ached. Pulsed with anticipation. Her whimper floated into Rory scented air.

Now she sat in his home, gazing into an empty fireplace. The weather was too hot. There were no flames to watch dance within the grate. What did he intend? Her stomach growled. She caught the heady aroma of stew as well as biscuits. She'd had nothing to eat all day. The cup of coffee overflowing with cream and sugar didn't count as food. When he stepped from the kitchen, he caught her attention.

"Dinner is on the table. Will you eat with me? Promise I won't ask anything of you," Rory told her then walked away, heading toward the kitchen. She didn't know what to expect. Seemed at the moment he wasn't interested in talking. The fact suited her just fine. She would accept his promise of silence.

Not knowing what to anticipate, she followed him. The table was set. Two bowls filled with steaming liquid were placed opposite each other. A plate of biscuits was piled high in the middle of the table. Her stomach rumbled. Rory pulled out a chair for her. She sat. Set her hands on the table while her anxious nerves seemed to split.

Across from her Rory stared at her, waiting. Realized he waited for her to say grace. Nellie said a few words of thankfulness before she picked up her spoon. He still stared at her. Seemed he expected something more.

Frustration got the best of her. "What?" Nellie asked with an accusing tone. From a position beneath her eyelashes, she glared at him. All she wanted was to eat in peace. If this continued, she'd lose her appetite.

After her question, he lifted an eyebrow. His twinkling blue eyes seemed filled with emotion. "Don't understand what you are asking. Try to be more explicit." He dipped his spoon into the stew. Savored.

Silence still creating tension, he continued to eat. The surrounding hush was oppressive. Nellie didn't think she could stand this strangely tormenting stillness for the rest of the night. She would much rather have him yelling at her to tell him what was wrong than this eerie quiet. "I don't know what you want of me," she blurted wishing she could find a means to keep her lips sealed.

Doing so wasn't easy.

Unable to stomach the food in front of her, Nellie pushed back from the table, having more questions than she wished. This abduction was so out of the blue. She needed to understand his motive. "Where do you want me to sleep?" Her stomach rolled. Imagined she could figure out his answer.

"There is only one bed." He sat back, his hands entwined on top of his belly. Watched with what appeared to be expectation. She wasn't going to share his bed.

"Convenient."

"No, practical. You may sleep wherever you wish. Not going to tell you what to do…or what not to do."

"Oh…" She needed to interpret his statement. "If I take the one bed…?" Didn't understand why she asked since she was certain of his answer.

"I'm more than pleased to share." He sipped his coffee. Picked up a biscuit, cut it in half then lathered both sides with butter.

His hands were bronzed, fingers lean as well as long. She knew how they felt when they held her. Touched her with tenderness. Despite his size, he was a gentle man. This was all about male lust. She understood it completely. Experienced lust too many times.

"I'm not," she blurted then was met with a small twitch to his lips. He was trying not to grin. The task seemed difficult for him. She had an immediate as well as urgent need to toss her stew in his face. He wouldn't be so smug wearing venison and potatoes.

"Then…if the bed is not to your liking," he tapped his fingers on the rim of his coffee cup, "there are a number of places you may sleep. You may pick anywhere you would like to set your blanket."

"Where?" She should never ask. In defiance, she set her fisted hands on her hips.

Rory cleared his throat before he began his long, drawn-out answer. "The floor in the bedroom, the floor in the kitchen, the floor in the living room or the chair by the fire. There are places including outdoors. I shouldn't need to tell you how dangerous as well as unprotected you would be if you chose outside."

"I'll take the chair by the fireplace." She sat down in her righted chair.

"Suit yourself."

"I will," With her spoon she mixed the stew. Found a piece of potato. Ate then chewed slowly wondering what was going to happen over the next few days. She didn't enjoy what she experienced now.

With his spoon, he pointed to her barely touched bowl of stew. "You need to finish your dinner. You've scarcely touched your food."

She didn't know what to expect from Rory. At every turn he

befuddled her, acting different than she expected. The sight of the food left her nauseated. Her stomach was rumbling when she picked up her spoon in an attempt to put something in her stomach. Now she felt queasy. He wanted her to finish. Instead of eating, she cleared the table. Fetched water to heat for the dishes.

With icy disdain he watched. His silver blue eyes focused on her. "You don't need to work. I've a housekeeper."

"Where is she? We shouldn't leave the dirty dishes." Nellie meant to challenge him. She'd not seen anyone else since their arrival. "Shouldn't a servant be here?"

"Home…a cabin about a hundred yards from here. Could ring for her anytime I wish." He shrugged his shoulders as if nothing mattered.

"Is she coming back tonight?" Nellie made the sinking assumption the lady in question would not be called back for dish duty.

Rory lifted his shoulders again then let out a long sigh. "No, I gave her tonight as well as tomorrow off. Needed our privacy."

"So you could take advantage of my situation."

"Perhaps," Rory gave a grudging admittance.

There wasn't much more to say. While she never got the hang of cooking, she never did the dishes either. Nellie wasn't certain as to how much soap to use. She didn't know where he kept the soap. Rory wasn't volunteering the information. She could walk from the kitchen. The mess would still be there in the morning. For that matter, tonight's dirty dishes as well as the ones from the next day would remain.

"Soap?" she asked as the silence continued. If possible, she was determined to do something other than stand around looking useless.

Instead of answering, Rory produced the soap. Took a pot holder from a cupboard then poured the steaming water into the sink. Added soap. The water bubbled. "There you go. All is ready to be cleaned."

Now, he leaned against the counter, his booted feet crossed watching as he sipped his freshly brewed coffee. Nellie wasn't positive how to go about washing the dishes. This would be a first. Couldn't be all that difficult. Maybe a bit like taking a bath. She would pass the rag across a dish rinse then set it to dry before going on to the next one.

"There must be a sponge or a rag somewhere." She searched. In frustration, she threw down a towel. "You could help!"

Rory tipped his head to one side then the other. "More fun to watch. You remind me of a fish out of water all wiggling and waggling trying to figure out how to solve the problem." He pushed forward; strode the few steps to her. His silver-blue eyes sparkled. He nodded his head toward a table. "Go sit. Finish your coffee. Eat a biscuit. You need something in your stomach. I'll take care of the dishes. I see it's not one of your talents."

What Rory would never understand is the fact she didn't possess house-wifely talents. They were educated in the way of the affluent. Her mother never expected her to live in a small cabin in the middle of nowhere. She conceded him the job. "Do you have milk?" She needed something to dull the bitter taste of the coffee. Wished he had tea.

"No." He set the first washed then rinsed dish on a towel to dry. He offered some direction. "You can put the left-over stew in the quart jar."

"Sugar?"

"In the pantry."

Nellie looked around. Didn't know where the pantry was. Didn't want to ask. Her nerves were stretched, ready to snap. This was not going at all the way she hoped. She supposed she could drink water. Wanted a few answers to her most prevalent questions.

"When are you taking me to my home?" While she didn't expect an answer, she hoped for one. His back was to her.

He stiffened before he let out a slow breath of air. "You are home."

The chair fell on its back when she stood. Her hands were planted on the table. She wanted to refute his statement. Couldn't. All she could see was Rory's back. "No! This is not my home. What the hell do you mean!"

His slow turn coupled with a lazy smile told her she would have her work cut out for her if she thought to change his mind. She learned months ago; he was a man who made up his mind. Once he decided on a course, nothing changed.

"Yes…Nellie…this is your home from now on. When you get the burr out of your little white pantalets, we will marry. You will have my children. Until then…" He set another bowl out to dry "Until then, make yourself at home. You don't need to ask permission for anything. If you don't know where something you want is located, ask."

In other words, she wasn't going anywhere. He was a…a…she couldn't think of the word to describe him. An autocrat. A dictator. Worse, a man who took what he wanted. He was fickle. At this moment, he wanted her. What about in two months from now? She didn't wish to be with a man who changed his mind as often as the wind changed direction.

"I don't know what you want?" She refused to stomp her foot…a childish tantrum. "This is not my home. I haven't chosen this or you."

Again, one wheat blond eyebrow shot to the sky. Didn't appear he meant to answer her. Of course, she knew what he wanted. Rory wanted her in his bed. She understood the way men think. What he wished for went against everything she understood as well as wanted. Once, she had dreams. If she told him how she felt about the day she saw him kissing another woman, he would make up an excuse to appease her.

Excuses were what men did best. They blamed everything on something the woman did or said. A man would never apologize. Would set blame on someone else's shoulders.

In Glasgow, she experienced men along with their excuses. Wasn't going to tolerate a man shaking her down. Putting her chin in the air, she marched around the room while trying to memorize its contents.

"Where do you plan to sleep? If not with me, I'll get you a blanket. The nights up here get cold even when the day is hot. You would be warmer in my bed." He crossed his arms over his chest. "Where?"

The fresh clean stream tumbling its way to a bigger river then onto the ocean behind his cabin swept into her head. She wished she could have a bath. Nellie found she was hot as well as sweaty and sticky from the day's events. Asking him for a bath was out of the question. He would tell her she needed a chaperone. Danger lurked. While she understood there were both two as well as four footed dangers in the forest, she doubted one would find its way so close to his cabin.

"What is it you are thinking of now? It's not the bed." He moved closer to her. "Tell me. If it's something I can give you, I would be pleased. Wish for you to be comfortable in your new home." He stood in front of her so close she caught a spicy scent then felt his breath ruffle across her cheek. He set his finger beneath her chin. "Tell me."

She flinched away from him before stepping back. The big man was too close, too intimidating. With no distance between them he touched all her senses. His potent charm captivated. Enthralled. She didn't wish to feel this way about him. "I'll sleep on the chair."

He reached out then drew back before he touched her. "Sorry to hear you feel that way." A few minutes later he dumped a blanket along with a pillow on the chair by the fireplace. "Hope your neck fairs well. Fell asleep in the chair one night. In the morning, I couldn't move my head because my neck was stiff. If you change your mind in the middle of the night, I'll let you climb into my bed. Keep you warm. All you need do is say the word. No," Rory paused his grin growing wider, "all you need do is join me. Don't need to say anything at all."

"In your dreams," she shot back to him then felt the rise of heat to her cheeks. She shouldn't say things that were not true. Maybe they were. Rory never spoke of his feelings only his desires.

"I'm waiting on our future. Won't retaliate with the words in my head." He left her with her empty thoughts. "Coming to what will be our bed is your choice. Can happen before the vows or after. I would prefer tonight. In this my wishes don't seem to count for much."

Would it be so bad to tell him what was bothering her? The image which had been festering in her soul for the past eleven months? She didn't know. He should have apologized more than a year ago for kissing the girl. Marsali Sue was her name. Agnes told her about the girl. Tried to dispel her by telling her Marsali was the biggest flirt in the area. Forgetting how the lady clung to him was impossible. Ignoring the fact caused tears to rise in her eyes. It was impossible. She thought there was a strong connection between them. There wasn't. At least not one she would live with. If the relationship was strong, Rory would never have kissed that girl.

His reputation…yes, there was his reputation to consider. In these parts as the natives would say, he was a lady's man as well as a man's man. Women flocked around him, batting their eyelashes to gain his attention. Giving him whatever he wanted. She knew he wasn't new to sex. Could crook his little finger and women would drop their drawers for him. She didn't intend to be one of the many. At the celebration she witnessed the women. Saw how he soaked up their compliments. Grinned at their remarks.

She would never be one of his women. Intended to be the only woman for him. Now, she understood he might never change. Men don't change their true colors. The fact he kissed the lady didn't make that much difference. What mattered was the reality of his character. He would always want to test untried waters. She would never be able to trust him. Living her life wondering if there was another woman gracing his bed was horrific. A life in that manner wasn't for her.

As to becoming his wife, she shook her head. There was no way in hell she would marry a man such as Rory Haraldsson. If he wasn't in her bed, she would never know whose pillow he set his head on.

The creak of the porch swing caught her attention. She imagined she might have picked the swing for her bed. The bench on the swing was longer than the chair. Lying down might not be impossible as it was with the chair. Tossing the possibility out to him, would be her next move. Somehow, Nellie felt positive he would shoot her down. Would give her some reason she should choose elsewhere.

Holding two fresh cups of coffee along with a buttered biscuit, she opened the door to the front porch. When she stepped outside, he looked up then patted the space beside him. Nellie wasn't certain she wished to sit so close to him.

"Here, this cup of coffee is for you." The biscuit was for her. As she organized her thoughts, she began to feel hungry again.

When she didn't move to comply with the gesture, Rory lifted his broad shoulders before gazing out on the land in front of them. She picked a seat on the steps. Sipped coffee then nibbled on the biscuit. Now that her stomach was not buzzing then tumbling, she might be able to eat a bowl of stew. The meal was put away. While she brooded, Rory finished the dishes. Everything from the evening meal was cleaned up. There was nothing left for her to eat. Her stomach rumbled.

Rory swept his arm pointing to the land in front of him then to the sides. "This is my land. My future. Hope someday this will live on for my children. A dynasty." He turned to face her. His eyes deep blue in color shimmered with intensity. "Our children…our lives…wish to share all this with you."

"Why me? From the rumors abounding about you, you can have the pick of any woman in the vicinity. You've known…I wouldn't venture to guess how many women you've slept with. Why me?" Nellie believed the question to be more than relevant. Love didn't seem to be involved. While she knew she was attractive there were a lot of beautiful women to choose from.

Rory looked at her for several seconds. He rubbed his hand on the back of his neck. "Imagine to you the question is relevant. I didn't pick you. You picked me."

"Don't understand. How can you say something so absurd?" I picked him?

"Yes, understand under the current circumstances why you question my statement. Be advised, you are the only woman I've ever wanted to settle down with. You snared me from the first moment I saw you. Caught me in your feminine trap of intrigue as well as beauty. Your standoffishness inspired my quest. Once I talked to you…hell! I didn't need to talk to you. Knew you were the one the moment I saw you. You've run me a haphazard chase. My feet are tired. Need to end this pursuit soon."

"What about all your other women?" Nellie had no business asking the question. "They would scratch and claw eyes out to receive a proposal."

He barked a laugh. "An exaggeration at best."

"Don't agree."

In the last two years she'd been through more than most women. Would never forget the disgusting touch of Lord Abernathy. Lust was powerful. A motivation beyond anything she encountered. Even now so many months later when she closed her eyes, she could see the bed in the upstairs bedroom. Remembered how dirty she felt when Abernathy stripped her clothing from her body. She was left naked on the bed while she worried about what would happen next. Everyone except those who found her thought Abernathy left her with a simple covering, her chemise. No one who knew said anything different.

Her rescue was timely. If Nelson Abernathy had not taken the time to dally with her mother, he would have forced her before the men searching for her reached her. She was fortunate the Duke of Southcliff knew where the country house Nelson purchased was located. No man would have wanted her after Abernathy defiled her. Fannie advised her to tell Rory what happened. The events were too mortifying to recount.

"In my mind, there are no other women."

Blurting out what she saw, held no merit. "Another one could come along. One who would catch your eye. A girl more suitable to your needs. One who could keep house, cook, sew, the chores endless."

"I will never want anyone except you, Nellie." His voice was sincere. With all her heart, Nellie wanted to believe him.

When he picked up her hand to hold, she jerked away. "So you say." She couldn't allow trust. If she did, he would hurt her.

"Trust is powerful. Imagine I need to work harder to gain yours. Don't…" He popped all his knuckles. The sound gave Nellie reason to cringe. "Don't understand what I did to discredit myself in your eyes. I vow to work harder to change your feelings toward me. Talk to me. Give me some ideas as to how to proceed."

"Do you know why I'm here? Why I traveled with Fannie and Fox? It wasn't because I had an urge for adventure. I preferred to stay in Glasgow. All my friends lived there. Staying wasn't safe for me." She could tell him a few things. Not everything. He should understand something about her mistrust of men. He knew about Dillon but nothing else.

"In part, why don't you explain. Fox has hedged from enlightening me. Fannie turns red with emotions better left unsaid when the topic is broached. There is intrigue here. Guessing the two of you went through something that is difficult to talk about."

Nellie leaned against the post holding up the porch roof. Closed her eyes while she tried to figure out the least damning scenario. Hated to tell him about Lord Abernathy. Understood part of the story. Not all. Never all.

"Mother sold Maggie, our oldest sister, to Nelson Abernathy. You remember the man? At the time the idea was marriage. The two had something planned. We've never found out the exact nature of the sale."

"How could I forget Lord Abernathy? Up at base camp he was tarred and feathered then sent down the mountain to town. You painted some of the tar on his naked body. I enjoyed watching. Was in town under the loving care of a nurse for over a week before he could travel. Why? He wanted Fannie, not you." His gaze searched her for words not said.

"The man wanted both of us, Fannie as well as me. Also wanted our other two sisters. Hopefully, their husbands will keep them safe. He captured Tessa before she married Jason. Tessa, with the help of the Duke of Southcliff, was rescued before anything bad could happen to her."

"I will never allow that man to touch you!" Rory told her undeniable conviction in his words.

"There are other players in this game. Halsey, a pimp in Glasgow as well as Anice. They would stop at nothing to gain their revenge. The distance to Michigan was no barrier for Abernathy. Don't know if it will keep Anice from her plans. We are still in danger."

"Tell me more."

Nellie shook her head. She'd said enough for five lifetimes. Couldn't tell him anything pertaining to her own circumstances. What happened was too mortifying for words. "I'm tired. The sun has gone down. Didn't sleep well last night or the one before. Need to go to bed." She stared at the forest wondering about the walk down the hill.

His eyes blazed as if he was angry. He had no reason for anger. For a man who wanted to learn everything, she told him little. Couldn't say anything more than she already did.

"Don't run away from this, from me. Meet the enemy head on," Rory told her as if he had the right to give directives. "Let me help. I'm not your enemy."

Her fists clenched at her sides. Lips thinned. As if to put emphasis on her words she gritted out, "If the things that happened to me happened to you…" She didn't know how far to go. With those damming words, she opened the door to more questions. Questions she had no intention of answering. Those things never happened to a man. A man couldn't be raped. Forced against his will to have sex. Could he?

"Stay a few more minutes. I won't ask any more questions. Relax. You're right. This day has been trying for you. Since I don't know what happened I've no place to judge. If you tell me I could better understand."

"It's getting cold." She unfolded the blanket before wrapping it around her. Her arms were shaking, not because of the sun setting behind the hills but because of the memories along with the fears shutting her off from creating a new life. Closing her eyes never took away the images.

Rory spread his arm across the back of the swing. "Come sit next to me. I'll keep you warm. Hold you until the chills disperse. Make sure you stay safe." His voice grew husky. Held the sound of desire in the deep timbre. "Can make you heat up all the way to your tiny toes."

Heat up to my toes? She imagined he could. Remembered the kiss as well as how he scorched her. "I better not. Tomorrow will be a long walk home." By the quicksilver scowl on Rory's face, she realized she should not have mentioned the fact she meant to walk home. As long as she had two legs, he could not keep her here. Nellie realized walking would take most of the day. She had no idea the distance.

"I've changed my mind about the sleeping accommodations," Rory was quick to point out.

"You can't…" Rory wouldn't force her to sleep with him. He wouldn't. Would never make her sleep in his bed if she said no. "You can't change your mind." She snapped her fingers. "Just like that. I won't."

"I can and will unless I hear a promise from your sweet lips." He was leaning forward, his forearms on his thighs. Their gazes met then clashed. She didn't want to hear the promise he meant to extract. By the look in his eyes, he would never budge from whatever stance he was taking.

"What?" The question was indignant. "You've no reason to ask a promise of me." Her breathing turned erratic. Rory didn't have the right to keep her here. Didn't have the right to dictate anything to her. "You can't change your mind," she repeated her voice dropping. "I'm going to go home."

"I can unless I get what I want." His eyes blazed. He was angry. She recognized the expression on his face.

"What is this promise?" Hesitant, her body shaking, she asked him. Needed clarification before she could move on with her plans.

"I'm not asking too much. Nothing you can't accomplish with ease. Promise me you won't try to leave until you eat breakfast." He ran the back of his hand along the column of her throat. "It's a long way down the mountain. You will need sustenance."

"This is about eating?" Flummoxed, she felt his dictate was all wrong. She could see him tying her to his bed or locking her in the cabin to keep her from asserting her will…but this? He wanted her to eat? He didn't forbid her to leave. She was confused. Perhaps even a bit disappointed. After he brought her all this way, he meant to let her go with no protest…no arguments.

"Yes. Agnes told me you didn't eat this morning. You ate no dinner except those few nibbles of the biscuit you hold in your hand right now. Can't walk the twenty plus miles to Fox's home on an empty stomach. You will need energy. Fox's home is not an easy walk from here."

"Twenty miles?" she repeated stunned to learn of the distance. Five miles was a long walk. Five miles would take her more than an hour. Could anyone walk twenty miles in one day. If she couldn't, she would spend the night in the forest.

"Will take you most of the day if not all. Expect it will be a scorcher tomorrow. You will need to take water with you. A canteen or two. Yes, two would be the best. Always take water with you if you're going to be gone for the entire day. A body needs water more than food."

Nellie knew him well enough to realize Rory had something up his sleeve. What it was she didn't know. Except for a beat, she did balk when he told her twenty miles. Had second as well as third thoughts about following through with her idea. Didn't seem quite that far when they rode the distance this afternoon. Didn't know what it would hurt to promise to eat. Then he tells me to take water. She would have never thought about water. Weren't there streams along the way?

Nodding her head in answer, she said, "I will eat before I go. Anything else?"

"Need to hear you promise."

"Very well, if a verbal promise is what it takes for you to let me go. I promise to wait to leave here until after I eat. Is that good enough?"

"The words of promise will do for now. In the meantime, just how do you think you are going to walk the distance? Your delicate little shoes will be torn to shreds. Do you have any idea what walking that far will do to your body. You are in no shape…"

With a few blinks, she felt confused. Shreds? Not in shape? Had to admit she'd never walked more than a mile at one time. "I'll follow the road. What else would I do?" Nellie was surprised he wasn't refusing to allow her to go by herself. The man should be objecting. Yelling about how dangerous the walk was. All he wanted was for her to eat as well as bring water.

"You slept the last five miles. There is no road to my home. However, there are many trails. I will not help you leave me. Will never give you directions. You will need to navigate the trails all on your own."

Her chin rose with an inelegant snort following. "I can find my way. As long as I walk down the mountain, I should be fine." She knew she spouted nonsense. Maybe she should reconsider.

"Possibly…" Rory didn't finish, he rose then extended his hand. "If you break your promise to me, you won't enjoy the consequences."

Those words were arrogant male words. Sounded too much like Nelson for her consideration. *Enjoy the consequences.* So far, he'd not taken or forced anything on her. Hoped his actions would stay that way.

Determined, she would navigate the way home by herself.

~ * ~

"Are you positive this was right? Nellie is still so insecure. She's afraid to reach out to Rory for help or to confide in him." Fannie turned her back so Fox could undo the line of little jet buttons traveling down her back. With each button undone, he placed his lips on bared flesh. With each kiss she shivered with the pleasure. Understood this discussion would end before anything could resolve itself.

"The two need private time to hash out all their truths," Fox said while he continued to give his ardent attention to the revealed flesh down the middle of her back. "What we should do is lock them together somewhere."

Fannie squirmed when his sweet caresses reached the base of her spine. He sipped on her flesh. She slipped the gown from her shoulders, revealing more of herself. "Nellie will never disclose what happened during the abduction. There are few people who have learned what occurred. I don't even know the entirety. Doubt if anyone except Nellie along with Lord Abernathy know everything, maybe Anice too."

"Until she speaks all her truths, Rory will be running blind. He needs to understand what motivates his little lady. She should tell him some of what happened to her. How she was intimidated to the point she fears all men."

Fox's shirt hung open. Fannie pushed the fabric down his arms. Ran her hands across his chest paying close attention to the small hard buds so unlike her own. "We should ride to his house tomorrow. Maybe we can help sort this out."

"No." He brought his mouth crashing against hers. She opened for him. Rubbed her against his. Touched deep into the soft darkness. Her shadowy depths always brought him immense pleasure. Needed him to taste her in more intimate places.

"Yes, we need to help. Nellie doesn't know what she wants." Nellie does know what her life could be like with a good man. She is just afraid to reach out then grab happiness.

"The two of them need to hash out their problems in privacy. Our presence will only serve to get in the way. Nellie will hide behind you. Rory won't want to force himself in anyway with the two of us watching."

A little sigh of frustration left her. Fannie comprehended all he said was true. To her way of thinking, she still wanted to be with her sister so she could help her adjust. "I understand. What if they can't find a way to get past her fears?"

"They will…" he told her sweeping her into his arms to carry her to a chair. I have confidence in Rory. He sat holding her in his lap. Running his hands along her arms to her shoulder then back to rest with possessive ease on her hip. He placed gentil kisses along her neck, nudging fabric away with his chin. "Do you wish to make love or argue about what is best for your sister and Rory?"

"Argue."

He dropped his hands, obviously displeased with her answer. Set his hands on her shoulders. His voice was stern when he spoke. "We are not going to intrude. I won't take you there. Since you don't know where he lives, you cannot go by yourself. The conversation is finished."

She moved a lock of hair from his forehead, her mind whirling with endless possibilities. There must be men on his crew who would know how to find Rory. "Does Paul know? I would seek him out."

"Know what?" He was diverting her attention. Pressing light kisses along the column of her neck then lower. His finger tugged on the ribbons to her chemise. With his chin, then his teeth he pushed the fabric aside. Touched his tongue on a hard bud then gave his consideration to the other.

Fannie arched into his mouth, thrusting her breast to get closer. Needed him to pull harder as well as deeper. "How to get to Rory's place. Paul could take me." His hands closed around her breasts.

"Not if he wants to keep his job…his livelihood."

"Are you ready to have another baby?"

Don't Hustle Letty
Good Girls Book One

She's a good girl...

As tempted as Scarlett was, she had too many secrets to let someone enter her world—secrets that would send any reasonable man to the farthest ends of the earth. Bobby was far from reasonable and despite her desperate attempts to hold him at bay, he would not let her past destroy their future. With her escort service, Scarlett used men and their insatiable lust for women to capitalize on the means to survive and prosper. She vowed to never wed, to never put herself in the control of a man.

...nonetheless he has other ideas.

Lord Robert Munroe, with his newly acquired title of marquis goes to Scarlett's for training on how to comport himself. The marquis, better known as Bobby, knows how to pick a pocket as well as get into a bloke's home to steal them blind. What he doesn't know is how to be a gentleman. When he sets his sights on the prim Miss Scarlet, Letty, to his way of thinking, he decides she is the woman he wants to call his wife. He tempts all that she is with sweet words and tender coaxing until she is unable to refuse all he hopes to give her.

Only Caro's Baby
Good Girls Book Two

The Scheme

Genius botanist with theories of inherited traits, Caroline Kenworth desperately wants a baby. Finding a suitable father won't be easy. Caroline's super-intelligence makes her feel pushed aside, unwanted as a woman. As a bluestocking she is determined to spare her child the suffering that plagues her life. Which means she must find someone very special to father her child. A person very...well...ignorant.

The Target.

Duncan Murray, the Earl of Downsberry, well known for his lack of intelligence as well as his rakish ways with women, seems as if he is the flawless man to fulfill the role. His amazing good looks and Scottish brogue are misleading. Caro learns too late that this debonair earl is a lot smarter than she first thought—in addition he's not about to be used then abandoned by any woman who has schemed to steal his sperm.

The Detonation

A dazzling solitary woman whose desires to learn what it would be like to become a mother... A man who is in control of all he does never allowing anyone to usurp his role will settle for nothing less than surrender... Can lust coupled with physical attraction drive two strong-minded yet vulnerable people to a completely unforeseen love?

Honey
Good Girls Book Three

She's a good girl...

Born a bastard, Honey McRae is taunted and bullied by her half-brother most of her life. Branded with a tattoo of the Saber and the Rose by the men's association, she is desperate to be free and escapes the country estate where she was held prisoner. Resigned to a passionless life devoid of men, she fights the nightmares that haunt her. Despite her past fears, she accepts the fact she will never be able to give herself wholly to the man she loves. Until that man, bold and breathtaking, decides he will find a means to woo her into his arms.

Nonetheless...

Stolen at birth and sent to live in the bowels of London, Billy– once a pickpocket and thief–discovers he is actually the Duke of St. Aubries. He is determined to win the woman he fell in love with the first time he saw her, the lady with a tattoo on her breast, a woman who has been cruelly used. He disputes her notion that men are only capable of inflicting pain...instead he binds her to his heart with his gentle and patient loving.

Betsy Be Good
Good Girls Book Four

AN ENGLISH ROSE

Sweet Betsy Darling, the oh-so-prim and innocent tutor for children born of rich aristocrats, is a woman on a mission—she has but a short time to lose her standing as a respectable spinster. Arriving in Glasgow with skirts flying, parasol pointing, and plump mouth issuing demands, she understands only one thing will save her form losing all she holds dear: complete and utter disgrace.

A BRAW HIGHLANDER

Known throughout the city as a bad boy with more money than he needs, Evan Murray has lost his temper one too many times, and now he's suspended from teaching at the university he loves as well as Halstead & Family the financial firm owned by his family. An apology which he refuses to issue is one of two things that will restore his career. The second is his complete and utter respectability! Now he's been coerced into escorting the bossy, parasol toting Miss Betsy Darling, and she's hell-bent on chasing down a tattoo parlor, dressing in skimpy clothing and worse...lots worse.

Gracie
Good Girls Book Five

She's a good girl...

During a tempest, Gracie Seymor flees the hands of an abusive fiancé to find herself tossed from her horse. The blow to her head causes the loss of her memory. In the shelter of a wayside inn, she meets a man who steals her heart. From the moment the handsome man, Gordan Murray, lifts his dark brown eyes to meet hers, they are drawn together, spellbound, into each other's arms then into the night of passion that claims her innocence sending her on a course that will change her life forever.

…Nonetheless he steals her heart

So dependent on the man who claims her virginity, Gracie becomes his mistress even though she understands she should refuse. She's a good girl. Good girls don't become men's playthings. After the night spent with Gracie in his arms, Gordan takes her to a cottage near his home. Here they will confront the specter of her past and discover Gracie's identity. It revolves around a tangled web of secrets coupled with a magical love that cannot be denied.

Dawn
Good Girls Book Six

Dawn Callahan's dream of freedom and a life of independence is shattered. After she realizes she somehow stepped through a portal into a different century all she has left to fight for is her sanity along with a way to return to the time of her birth. To do that she has to give up her autonomy. With no money to her name or a roof over her head, she needs Gordan Murray's help. In return she refuses to give him what he wants the most. Answers to his questions.

On first sight, Gordan means to take her into his home. Intends to give her everything she wants. When she refuses his sincere offers, he withdraws into himself searching for a means to convince her he has only good intentions toward her.

On that sunny day in July when Dawn tumbles from a whorehouse to land on her delectable little butt a woman was the last thing in the world he was looking for. He has a fine life. Finds willing women with a smile coupled with a nod.

Love has a way of changing the rules.

Maggie
Good Girls Book Seven

Sheltered, Maggie MacRae is shocked to learn her mother has agreed to a marriage proposal for her made to a man she detests. All her dreams are ripped away from her when she realizes escape is unlikely. For her, there is no viable way out of the engagement. Choices needed to be made. The man she is to become engaged to is ruthless, a dangerous power. Terrified of her future with this man, Maggie is left with few options.

Feeling as if her world has shattered, Maggie flees the night her engagement is announced. She puts her life in the hands of a man she doesn't know, a man who could be as cold-blooded and treacherous as the one who is now her fiancé…a man who awakens her to a world she never knew existed.

Jasper Kenworthy has spent his life with few cares and he has no intention of changing the patterns of his existence. When he finds that Maggie can offer him something he never thought would be his, it's all the excuse he needs to help her. Yet every breathless night spent tangled together in each other's arms has given Jasper a taste for Maggie. He discovers he would do anything, risk everything to keep Maggie safe and within the shelter of his embrace.

Tessa
Good Girls Book Eight

Never a MacRae…

Beautiful, reserved, and unfortunately naïve the youngest MacRae, Tessa, is caught between her mother's manipulations and the man she has fallen in love with. Now that she finally has everything she has ever wished for, lies rip her life apart. Humiliated by the revelation she is the half-sister to Jason, her husband, she flees knowing a divorce is eminent.

Always a Kenworthy…

Patience being his operative word for the year, Jason finally decides he must put an end to his torment. When Tessa responds to her mother's request to see her, Jason realizes her protection is needed. His firm resolve to safeguard the woman he loves is thwarted when Tessa flees his protection to end up the victim of a man she despises.

www.ingramcontent.com/pod-product-compliance
Lightning Source LLC
Chambersburg PA
CBHW070620260626
47161CB00007B/2515